"I have never read a book in this genre that so quickly and emphatically drew me in and kept me hostage throughout the entire book. I won't say I couldn't put it down because I did (to sleep), but every waking moment found me reading."

— *Readers' Favorite*

"Weaving a tale from the Greek mythology to the Amazonian women is a stroke of genius. It uplifts the story and enhances the excitement many times over. Zenay Bekele Ben-Yochanan is nothing but a great storyteller who can portray women as the greatest species of all... So true!!"

— *Goodreads*

"This has all the hallmarks of making a great series. I would definitely recommend this book and would love to see it adapted for the Silver Screen. I honestly think it would make a fantastic movie. A well-deserved five stars."

— *Emerald Book Reviews*

"Ben-Yochanan had me on the edge of my seat as I waited to see how this stage in Teigra's and Thea's lives would end, and I can't wait to see where they are taken next. Fantasy and myth fans won't want to miss it."

— *The Writer's Scrap Bin*

THE AMAZON LEGACY

PART I

GODS & QUEENS

THE UNTOLD STORY

ZENAY BEKELE BEN-YOCHANAN

Published by Enayé Media Group Inc.

The Amazon Legacy
Part I – Gods & Queens
Zenay Bekele Ben-Yochanan

Published by Enayé Media Group Inc.

First edition November 2017
Library of Congress Control Number: 2017918449
Hardcover ISBN 978-0-9996142-1-1
Paperback ISBN 978-0-9996142-2-8
Paperback ISBN 978-0-9996142-4-2
E-book ISBN 978-0-9996142-5-9

Website: www.theamazonlegacy.com
Email: info@theamazonlegacy.com

Cover Art by Bernard Lee
Printed in the United States of America

In loving memory of my Swedish mother,

Lilian Hammare
1953-2005

With love and laughter, you'd pick me up, dust me off, and cheer me on. You are my inspiration and my personal Amazon warrior. Thank you.

From your one and only daughter, Zenay Bekele
Ben-Yochanan Hammare

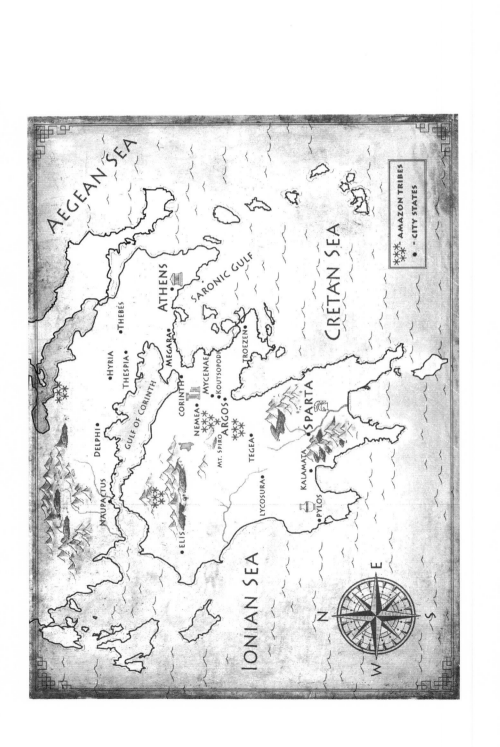

CHAPTER 1
THE WAGER

Zeus and Hera stirred in their palatial bed. With their bodies still entangled from the previous night's lovemaking, Zeus reveled in the way Hera's soft skin pressed warmly against his strong torso.

As the sun rose over the heights of Mt. Olympus, Zeus' desire followed suit, creating a thirst for the pleasure that only his passionate Goddess could provide. Without opening his eyes, he traced the curve of her sensual hips with the tips of his fingers. The arousing sensation of his touch on her skin awoke Hera to her own physical yearning. Their bodies slowly moved in unison, silently teasing and daring each other to touch and caress.

"My beautiful wife," Zeus whispered, as he slipped his knowing fingers in and out of Hera's warmest curves. Feeling his manhood pressed against her stomach, Hera gently caressed her husband, further exciting him.

"My loving husband," Hera whispered.

They both grew more eager with each touch, and soon all that could be heard was their breath and the sound of the rustling sheets. Recognizing his ability to inspire such passion in Hera aroused Zeus. But he was suddenly reminded of the age-old power struggle between them.

Taking Hera's wrists into his grip and moving her hands above her head, Zeus pinned Hera down, rolled his muscular body on top of her, and forcefully thrust himself between her legs, entering her. Although a gasp of surprised pleasure escaped her lips, Hera didn't care for this display of power. As her passion intensified, she decided to satisfy her needs in her own way.

Hera wrapped her strong legs around Zeus' waist and, using the momentum of their rocking bodies, she undulated her hips, rolling herself on top of him. Straddling him with her knees, Hera pushed her hips into his, and pressed her breasts and hard nipples onto his chest, moist with their collective sweat.

Though enjoying the sensation of her resistance, and finding great pleasure in the slippery wetness of her sex, Zeus' need for control was entwined with his arousal. He was unable to lose himself under the command of his wife, and sought to reposition himself back on top of Hera—but she was not willing to succumb. The rollicking quickly turned into a frustrated battle of wills, as neither would relent to the other's desire.

Zeus, using his Godly powers, escaped Hera's grasp by vanishing into thin air—leaving her alone on her knees with nothing under her but the bed.

In the struggle to best each other, their passion had soured, from longing to anger and irritation. Zeus appeared behind Hera, wrapped an arm just under her breasts, lifted, and flipped her again onto her back.

"Aaaah, Zeus!" Hera roared, as she pulled away. "You would rather use our love-making to dominate me than to allow us pleasure!"

"Hera! It is not I but you who will not allow a moment's playfulness in your quest to prove me wrong!" Zeus countered, quickly losing his feelings for romance. The moment had been ruined.

For all of eternity, Zeus and Hera had argued over which sex was stronger. Zeus, proud God of all the Gods—powerful beyond human comprehension—was used to being the most authoritative. He loved the beauty of women, but believed they were too weak to live independently of men. Zeus argued that women needed men's strength, protection, and guidance to survive.

But Hera felt quite the opposite. She'd once held family above all else; but after Zeus' infidelities, her views had changed. She'd become convinced that women were self-sufficient and capable of surviving and thriving without men.

Hera was frequently consumed by jealousy over Zeus' affairs. This usually ended with either zealous and inspired bouts of sex, or a weeklong silence. While their quarrels raged in Olympus, those on Earth would suffer storms of lightning and thunder as Zeus released his frustrations.

"Mortal women are weak and helpless!" Zeus shouted at Hera, still sexually unsatisfied. "Without man, woman would not only be powerless in pleasing herself, but in fending off danger, and would no doubt starve to death. Were it not for their exquisite beauty, women would serve little purpose except for furthering the mortal race through motherhood."

"You are blind and ignorant, Zeus," Hera responded. "Men believe they can dominate womankind and suppress her freedoms, but I tell you that women are strong and independent. Their talents have no limits, and they surpass men in ways beyond measure. Women have little use for men aside from their seed. Men need us to take care of them, while we can survive on our own."

"Ah, Hera, you are the one who's blind!" Zeus declared. "Women are immobilized by their emotions and would be lost without men."

Hera turned away from Zeus, denying him a response. Zeus studied her a moment, then stated, "Heed me, my dear wife. I'll wager that I can demonstrate a woman's willingness to be submissive. By mortal means only, I will approach a woman of your liking and show how weak she is when confronted with the desire for a man."

Hera sat pensively, aware of her own weakness to her husband's sexuality. However, she reasoned that her vulnerability to his irresistible and maddening charms should have nothing to do with the plight of earthly mortals. Hera felt that human women did not need men for anything more than perpetuating the race. As a God, it was Hera's right to gift herself with pleasures of the flesh. When it came to such satisfactions, no one could enrapture her like Zeus, even when they argued.

Hera looked off into the distance, thinking of her feminine counterparts on Earth. There were many women throughout the lands who had forsaken men for their own strength and perseverance.

But the first of these women were the Amazons.

Living in a world of brutal struggle, the warrior tribes of Amazonia grew fierce and sovereign. Aside for the need to procreate, these women were independent of, and far superior to, men in the ways of both battle and governance.

An individual queen ruled each tribe, and the tribes continually bickered with one another, but they all obeyed Amazonian law. They were a source of pride to Hera.

Smiling, Hera conjured a cloudy image out of thin air for Zeus to see. There were five beautiful warrior women riding their powerful horses on a path through a thick and rich forest. A woman with long black hair blowing across her bronzed back led the others. Adorned with a spear in her right hand and leather garments snug against her chiseled physique, she sped along while the others tried to keep pace. She paused for an instant as her eyes, the golden color of honey, surveyed what dangers might lie ahead. The others paused as well, yielding to her leadership as the queen of their tribe, an honor she'd earned through strength and wisdom.

"Ah, Hera," Zeus commented. "I assume one of these women meets your approval? They are without male accompaniment and appear independent. Choose any of them, and I will show you just how willing she is to succumb to a man's bidding."

Hera examined the women, and was pleased with them. "Try your best, Zeus," Hera challenged. "The one with dark hair in the front is the one I pick. You will lose, and you will realize the superiority of a woman through her restraint."

They both watched as the misty vision revealed an encampment where the women had stopped in the woods for the evening. Painted along the skies were pink and orange hues that invited tranquility.

Elektra, the Queen of this particular Amazon tribe, had momentarily escaped the group to drink in the peacefulness of the approaching night. Hera looked where, just a moment ago, Zeus had been standing.

"My dear, no sky could compare to the exquisite beauty that I witness here before my own eyes," the God proclaimed, startling Elektra as he suddenly appeared at her side.

"And your stealth is equal to day's escape into night," Elektra responded, drawing a knife from her waistband.

"Forgive me," Zeus replied. "I mean no harm. I was merely passing by on a long journey and could not help but notice you. Your golden eyes are very beautiful."

"What is your business here?" Elektra demanded.

"Your hair is like velvet coils," Zeus continued. "And it's hung from a body so perfect that its mold must have been carved by the Gods themselves."

"Might I suggest you take your admiration elsewhere?" Elektra replied.

"Pardon me, madam. I simply could not bear to keep to myself the pleasure granted by laying eyes on such exquisite loveliness."

Elektra held firm against his rhetoric, raising her voice a little. "The people of these lands have no interest in you, nor do I."

"Perhaps you've mistaken me and my presence. I do not wish to harm you, nor your lands. I am merely a man tired on his feet from journeying, and long without sight of a woman. You are easily the most beautiful creature I've ever seen."

Elektra was losing patience with this man's persistence. "I suggest you heed my words. These lands belong to the Amazon nation, and as Queen, I demand your immediate departure." Elektra burned her gaze into the man's eyes, making sure that the force behind her message was understood. It was then that she noticed how brightly his crystal clear blue eyes shone.

"I meant no disrespect, Queen," Zeus continued. "I seek only to offer my assistance in helping your group through these treacherous forests. It would be my pleasure to escort you and protect you from any harm."

Elektra laughed. "You presume we need your assistance? I assure you, it is you who likely needs protection at the moment!"

"Beautiful lady, I would like to show my admiration and reverence to you by gifting Your Highness with these bags of gold." Zeus gestured to the ground at his left. Elektra hadn't noticed anything a moment earlier, but now there were two embroidered felt sacks, each overflowing with bounties of shiny gold coins.

"Surely this can be of use to your people," Zeus said with a silken voice.

Elektra was stunned at the sight before her, but managed to restrain herself from visibly reacting. The gold would be immensely helpful to her people; they were always in need of new weapons and farming equipment. But Elektra was aware that nothing was truly free, and this gift was far too generous. The man was offering too much for nothing in return, and her suspicion was aroused.

"Sir, we don't need your services, your compliments, or your gold. I do not invite any man to impose his ways on what we as women need or prefer. It is time you were on your way."

Seeing that his offers had been turned down, Zeus took a long breath and gazed out upon the land as he cunningly changed tactics, this time touching on Elektra's sympathy.

"May I ask you, Queen, for a kind favor? May a weary traveler set to rest here for a short time? I pledge to be on my way as soon as you wish."

Elektra looked at Zeus with great suspicion. "I may grant you a moment of rest, but your time here is measured by the movement of the sun and stars. It will be dark before long. You may rest until the first constellations appear in the night sky. Then you will be expected to make your way onward."

"Bless you, my dear Queen. A compassionate heart to match your unsurpassed beauty."

Zeus took a seat on a large nearby stump. He removed his leather satchel over his shoulder and lay down his arms. Elektra watched him a moment, then slowly returned to the river and filled her water sack. With every movement, she kept an eye on Zeus, ready to pounce should he make an objectionable move. But Zeus seemed to merely take in the comfort of resting. He removed the large cloak that hung from his broad shoulders. He stretched his arms high and wide, and then let his limbs fall limp at his side. Elektra kept her attention on the water, but couldn't help notice the perfect muscles that formed his beautiful, bronzed chest. Suddenly, Elektra realized the striking attractiveness of the strange man.

He stood and moved calmly to the river's edge. Elektra slowly backed up and watched from a distance as Zeus entered the water. He submerged himself, dipping his head beneath the cold current and then, just as suddenly, rose from the depths like a warrior. He slung his long, wet hair back, and Elektra saw the water slide from his chest to his sculpted stomach muscles, past his chiseled pelvic arch, and down into the depths of his loincloth. For a moment Elektra could not remove herself from the thought of pressing her body firmly against his, spreading her legs, and allowing the full beauty of this creature to be thrust inside her.

Sensing her feelings, Zeus knew that his moment of triumph was in reach. He looked back at her with his intoxicating eyes and smiled invitingly.

In a soft whisper, just audible to the Queen, Zeus said, "I seek only to admire the beauty that the Gods have granted you, to lie in your golden shadow, and to partake in pleasure together. Can we not at least enjoy the physical gifts between man and woman bestowed upon us by the Gods?" The irony in his offer did not escape Zeus, and the smirk on his face reflected his self-importance.

Elektra snapped out of her trance, and found herself caught between two thoughts. Being adept in the ways of pleasure, she had many times enjoyed physical intercourse with men. However, she preferred to engage in lovemaking with women, who understood more about what was pleasing to another woman. Zeus, picking up on the turn in her thoughts, quickly tried to make his case more appealing.

"Let us indulge ourselves, and I'm sure you will not be disappointed! I am no stranger to pleasing women!"

Elektra eyed the curious outsider with greater suspicion. The more he spoke, the more the spell of his physical beauty was betrayed by a different intention. It appeared as if his words were a mask hiding the truth. Elektra glanced around the woods. First, she took in his horse, which seemed supremely fit and healthy, far beyond the steeds of most noble men of these parts. She stared at his fine robes, which he had thrown to the side of the river. The untarnished silk of his tunic made her question the validity of his story about being a lone and long-time traveler. There was a peculiarity to the near whiteness of his blonde hair and perfectly curled locks, which she found so sensually appealing a moment ago and had drizzled the fine waters of her imagination. This conjured further suspicion because the Argives in the land for miles outside these forests had hair as black as night. Before she had a chance to further inquire, he spoke again.

"I promise you, sweet Elektra, most enchanting of all the Amazon Queens, the pleasure will be beyond any you have felt on Earth!"

But in his pride, Zeus had blundered. *How does he know my name?* Elektra wondered.

"Ha! Ignorant and arrogant!" she replied. There were few things Elektra disliked more than a condescending and overconfident man; and Zeus' words were not fit for the most skilled of lovers.

"I suggest you be on your way," Elektra said. She reached to blow a horn signaling the others to her position.

Irritated, Zeus considered swaying her through non-mortal means. But he thought better of it, as he remembered Hera was watching with her Godly vision.

"Madam, I meant no offense, and will leave you in peace." Zeus turned on his heel, scowling in his defeat, and vanished into the thickness of the trees. His horse quickly followed; and the golden sacks abruptly vanished from sight.

High above, in the reaches of Mt. Olympus, the echoes of laughter and jubilation fell freely from Hera's lips.

As Elektra lay in bed that evening, pondering the strange events of the day, she was startled by a noise outside her camp. She armed herself and walked toward the sound. A glowing light seeped through the breaks between the trees. Just as she neared the edge of the spectacle, a voice whispered to her, "Come Elektra. You have nothing to fear. I am the Goddess Hera, and I have come to reward you for your strength."

In the midst of a small clearing, Hera stood surrounded by a golden crescent of light. The Queen of the Amazons tossed her spear to the side, dropped to her knees, and whispered into the night air, "Bless you, Goddess."

"Elektra, you have resisted the ways of men and temptations of the flesh, proving to me that you embody the strength of all women," Hera said, soothingly. "As a reward for your actions, I grant you immortality, so that you may aid women for all of time with your determination and superiority. From this moment forth, you will be the true Queen of all Amazonia. As my representative, I will bestow upon you extraordinary power, wisdom, and a keenness of sense with which to lead your people. You will be revered for your intelligence and beauty, even more so than you are now."

Elektra lay prostrate and frozen before the Goddess. "Stand, Elektra," Hera gently commanded. Elektra managed to move, and rose to face the brilliant light before her. The warmth of Hera's glow felt calming to Elektra, who had been in a near state of shock. Hera gazed deeply into Elektra's eyes, and the power of the Queen grew as Hera spoke the words of her blessing.

Liltingly, Hera pronounced, "For all of eternity, you will wear the cloak of immortality, and with it bear the strength and wisdom of the fiercest warrior. In exchange, you will resist man's physical temptations, promising never to surrender your heart or body to any man, at any time. While you may continue to enjoy the pleasures of a woman's touch, the touch of man will take away from you the protections I bestow upon you now!"

In that instant, Elektra was overtaken by a strange, vibrating force. Her skin began to exude an amber aura. Her honey-colored eyes developed a piercing intensity, and the leather girdle beneath her tunic transformed into solid gold.

The girdle was suddenly covered in precious metal, adorned with a medallion embellished with two intertwined serpents. Its weight would have required the full strength of an ordinary man to simply lift it off the ground.

"Elektra, lead well," Hera advised. "Through your example, mortal woman will realize her true power."

"I will, my Goddess," Elektra managed to say. As suddenly as the light had appeared, it vanished, leaving the newly immortalized Queen standing alone in the woods.

* * *

For 300 eons, the eight tribes of Amazon women flourished as one nation: fierce, independent, and self-sufficient. Each tribe continued to have its own Queen as leader, but Elektra led them all as the entire nation's Amazon Queen.

In gratitude to the Goddess who had gifted her with immortality, Elektra taught her people to worship Hera in reverence. Elektra's guidance brought prosperity to all of the tribes, and she was the fairest and most respected Queen to ever rule Amazonia.

Under Elektra's guidance, the tribes realized their true potential. Farming practices were developed to efficiently produce enough food to sustain everyone. All youngsters became well educated in history and the arts.

What had already been a very high level of warrior training reached a new peak. Elektra created an elite band of warriors called the Sondras, whose combat prowess exceeded any group in Amazon history.

As for Elektra, her physical strength in combat was unequaled, and her judgment was almost always on target, leading to quick victories over any opposing forces.

It also didn't hurt that enemies would underestimate Elektra's battle prowess because of her gender and immense beauty. Elektra's beauty had been extraordinary before Hera's gifts, but as an immortal, she was utterly breathtaking.

Under Elektra's wise and steady rule, the lands of Amazonia became peaceful and prosperous. While all of this was pleasing to Hera, who watched over the Amazons from Olympus, Zeus brooded in discontent. He had lost the wager with his wife, and she would often remind him of his defeat. Hera rejoiced in the turn of events, and had hopes that perhaps her husband had finally given up on their eternal dispute.

However, Zeus was far from ready to concede defeat.

CHAPTER 2

TRAGEDY

To reward the loyalty and hard work of her people, Elektra arranged huge festivals for all to enjoy. Male slaves were kept year-round to service Amazonian sexual desires. But during the festivals, the finest male warriors of neighboring regions were invited to pair with Amazon women. The Amazons used these galas to become impregnated with the strongest and most quick-witted of men.

One such festival had been planned to celebrate the coming of a bountiful summer. All were welcome to enjoy the feasting and lovemaking. The women could enjoy one another's company, visit their man slaves, or partake in the variety afforded by their male visitors.

After ensuring the celebration was going smoothly, Queen Elektra retired to a carved wooden settee that she'd set just outside the main festivities. She relaxed into the pillows at her back and enjoyed the feeling of their smooth, woven silk against her skin. She allowed herself to sink comfortably as she closed her eyes and let the summer night wash over her. A cool breeze gave the Queen a brief respite from the stillness of the warm evening air. Sitting on the cushions laid out for her, she sat alone sipping her wine, and watching people dancing and enjoying one another.

"Queen Elektra, may I refill your cup?" The soft voice came from behind her, and the Queen had to turn almost entirely around to see who was speaking. There in the blue night stood a tall and golden-haired woman wearing a thin cotton sheath, barely covering her well-defined and caramel-colored limbs.

"Come forth," the Queen responded, a little harshly, unsure of whom this beautiful and mysterious woman was. The woman moved slowly to the rhythm of the beating drums. She seemed to glide effortlessly and silently, aside from the little bells wrapped around her ankles that chimed with each step.

Once in front of the Queen, the woman bowed with her knees—as was expected —but kept her clear blue eyes locked on the most powerful woman in the land. The Queen, who was accustomed to receiving the utmost respect and obedience from her people, was bewildered by this stranger, whose mystifying gaze never wavered.

The woman finally lowered her head and bent almost entirely down to the packed earth with her strong legs, leaving a ceramic jug of wine on the ground beside her. Queen Elektra could not help but notice the straps of the woman's delicate tunic slipping gently down her tanned arms as she bent. The woman took her time bowing, giving Elektra's eyes a chance to roam, tracing the perfect curvature of her collarbone and the soft shine of her smooth skin. This woman was unique, and Elektra studied her carefully, trying to determine what it was that made her so beautiful. Her long and toned legs were those of a warrior, and her glowing skin looked as though she spent her days bathing in the warmth of the sun.

Just as Elektra realized that she had been holding her breath, the woman spoke to her, in barely a whisper.

"May I be of service to you, Queen?"

Many women offered services of pleasure to the Queen on these nights of delight and festivity. But the Queen had rarely been approached with such directness. As Elektra looked up from the woman's body to meet her eyes, the stranger slowly began to rise from her deep bow. In the heat of the night, the beat of the drums was all that could be heard, and the woman's hips began to move in a methodical, rhythmic pulse. She swayed from side to side, dancing like a leaf hypnotically blowing in the wind, holding the Queen's entranced gaze. Although Elektra would have normally been suspicious of such an unusual outsider, she could not bring herself to question the arrival of this remarkable and lovely being. The softly swaying woman smiled and dropped her head back, letting her wheat-colored hair fall down the length of her back. With her chin pointing to the night sky, she spread her delicate arms out to her sides before bringing them slowly in to her chest. As she lowered her eyes back to the Queen's fixated gaze, her hands moved their way to the straps of her flimsy tunic. Queen Elektra sat mesmerized, watching and holding her breath, thoroughly seduced.

Just as the Queen was about to take a breath and break the enchantment, the woman's hands slipped the straps of her own tunic off her shoulders, exposing her perfectly round breasts. She gave her nipples a gentle twist with her jeweled fingers. Again she dropped her head back, ever so slightly opening her mouth, and allowed her moist tongue to escape her lips. The drums punctuated every one of her movements on this still, warm night. The Queen, finally allowing herself a momentary breath, felt her entire body tingle at the prospect of getting closer to this sensual being.

"Who are you?" she asked, shifting in her seat.

The woman, looking into Queen Elektra's eyes with a penetrating stare, lifted a finger and motioned that the Queen follow her. Captivated by her beauty, as well as curious, the Queen stood and accompanied the seductress.

The stranger smiled but did not speak as she led the Queen into the matriarch's own nearby tent, decorated more elegantly than the rest with gold tassels at the door's entrance. Once inside, the woman backed into the cushions lining the tent wall and parted her long legs. Her tunic, which had been relegated to a type of skirt around her waist, was no longer concealing her lower half, but instead draped along the sides of her hips accentuating her curves. Her swaying golden hair caressed her breasts as she arched her back and pressed her chest forward. With her hands between her legs, she used her fingers to gently part her softest flesh, making clear her invitation to the Queen.

Though Elektra was surrounded by beautiful Amazon women, she was entranced by the exquisite nakedness and sensuality of the stranger. Pangs of desire pulsated with urgency.

Again, the woman motioned for the Queen to come closer. Elektra approached her and stood still, anticipating her own next step. The stranger moved toward her and began to disrobe the Queen. She guided the Queen's tunic off her strong shoulders, and soon her lips were kissing the Queen's breasts. Elektra felt the moistness of the woman's mouth envelop her nipple, and the sensation immediately sent a sharp jolt of desire straight to her womanhood.

Moving her lips slowly over the Queen's taut stomach to her thighs, the woman pulled the sweaty cotton tunic off the Queen's body. She gently pushed the Queen's legs apart and placed her mouth between Elektra's strong limbs. A small gasp escaped Elektra's lips as she felt the electricity of pleasure move through her body. The Queen readily gave in to the stimulation, and when the woman moved her down onto the cushions the Queen did not hesitate. The breathing grew heavier, and each new touch fueled passion that gave way to pleasure.

In the embrace of the golden-haired beauty, with fingers and tongues playing and teasing, the Queen was on the verge of an explosive, euphoric orgasm.

It was then that the stranger began to glow, engulfed in white light. The brightness was so blinding that everything within view seemed to disappear for a moment. Elektra recoiled in shock, but was unable to withdraw her legs as the stranger had a firm grip on them. For an instant Elektra considered grabbing her tunic and running. Then, in the blink of an eye, the stranger transformed from a stunning woman into an equally breathtaking man.

Queen Elektra's surprise gave way to serenity, and she was no longer frightened. Elektra wondered if she was dreaming, noticing that there was something familiar about this man. His unsurpassed beauty could not be overlooked, but where had she seen him before? How had he appeared in the form of a woman?

The stranger looked at Elektra, gazing into her eyes from across the crest of her sex. He stood up between her splayed legs, stepping away but never breaking eye contact, giving her the opportunity to drink in the totality of his beauty. As she tried to focus on his visage, struggling to unravel the mystery of where she had seen him, her eyes could not help but be pulled down below his navel, where his considerable tumescence appeared, almost golden in color, and seemed to rise like a sword ready to charge. She felt herself grow wet again, realizing just how much she wanted him.

"Come back...now..." Elektra pleaded, almost ashamed of how pliable she had become at the hands of this stranger in such little time. *Pride be damned,* she thought.

Surprised at the turn of events, Elektra paused as the golden-haired man brought his face closer to hers. She looked directly into his crystal clear blue eyes. His lips curled in a playful and cunning smirk, just as Elektra remembered where she knew this beautiful face and powerful body. He was the man by the river from three centuries ago. Their eyes and bodies were locked together, neither knowing what the other would do for a speechless moment.

Before Elektra could utter a word, the man put two fingers deep inside her, bringing her attention back to her explosion of pleasure. His touch was irresistible, and Elektra was unable to refrain from her desire, feeling a burning necessity to have him inside of her. She could not help herself, and when the man began kissing her, she succumbed, allowing him to fully enter her.

Forcefully and with urgency, she kissed him hard as he penetrated her, rhythmically filling her with his power and bringing her to within an inch of orgasm. The man's arms were as strong as a herd of wild horses. When he picked her up to place her on her stomach, she felt herself near tears from desire and surprised at her unwillingness to resist. She felt his muscular chest pressing down on her back, his arms wrapped around her front, caressing between her legs. He was teasing the passion that had risen within her and making it clear who was in control.

Her desire was almost too much to bear. Elektra opened her mouth, on the verge of begging him to enter her again. However, this man was no amateur at lovemaking and knew that he had brought the Queen of Amazonia to the limits of her physical longing. He then thrust himself inside her again, using the full power of his hips to reach within her. Elektra had never succumbed to a man in this way, and it had never felt this good. The Queen couldn't remember ever reaching such euphoria. She felt as though her entire body would forever vibrate with the volcanic eruption of ecstasy that she felt in that moment.

But she was wrong, because the pleasure would end. As soon as the last shockwaves of orgasm pulsated through her body, Elektra started to fill with remorse for what she had just allowed to happen.

As night turned to day, a black and cloudy darkness fell upon the Amazon nation as Hera discovered Elektra's weakness and Zeus' scheme. Not only had Zeus gotten the upper hand in their battle of the genders, Hera could now sense the presence of a child within Elektra's womb.

Wrought with anger and jealousy, and hurt by the one woman she'd trusted to uphold a position so dear to her heart, Hera was severely shaken.

Knowing she had to gravely punish Elektra brought the Goddess no joy. Hera had grown to love Elektra over the centuries. But a mortal could not be bestowed with the highest honor from a Goddess and then betray that Goddess without retribution. An example had to be made.

Hera knew the most severe punishment would be to take the child from Elektra's womb. But this was no normal baby; it was the child of the God of Gods. Ending the life of Zeus' offspring would be an affront even more severe than the one Hera had just suffered; and it would carry a punishment too terrible to contemplate.

Hera spent days weighing her options, trying to find a fitting punishment that didn't involve destroying Zeus' unborn child.

The skies were gray and cloudy around Queen Elektra's encampment on the seventh dark day after her passion-filled night with the man she now realized was Zeus. Elektra sat alone in her sorrow, trembling with fear and shame at what she knew was the greatest betrayal she could imagine committing. She shuddered beneath her thin sheath, huddled tightly in the corner of her cold tent. She had not allowed anyone around her for a week. Food had been left for the Queen at the opening of her canvas flaps, but she had barely eaten more than what was needed to survive, and that small amount was only because of the stirring life that was forming slowly in her belly.

Suddenly, the flaps of the tent began to wildly blow.

"You have disgraced me and all women!" Hera's voice boomed within Elektra's tent, although the Goddess was nowhere to be seen. "For this you will be punished!"

"No longer will you be Queen," Hera proclaimed. "Nor shall you enjoy the graces of this green earth. You will be banished from these lands, and as a reminder of your embarrassment, you will be hidden from the living." The blustering winds died down, and Hera's voice seemed to rise from Elektra herself, like a whisper from deep within her.

"A child is in your womb," Hera continued. "While it would bring me great pleasure to destroy this seed of deceit, it will suffice that this child be cursed on Earth to a life of hardship and pain to pay for your weakness. I will bring untold suffering to this baby, Elektra, and you will live the rest of your days knowing it is all because of you.

"Until this child comes forth, you will reside exiled from all your tribes. After it is delivered, you will make your journey to the Underworld—where you will remain for eternity. It pains me greatly, Elektra, that rather than living forever among the luminous women of Amazonia, you will instead be in the dark and fiery pit that is Tartarus. But alas, this is born of your own choices. Take your maid and be gone, you deceiving whore! Live as a recluse, or you will experience the full extent of my anger!"

Shocked and shaking, Elektra bade her maid Elpis to quietly pack a few belongings. Without letting themselves be seen, they slipped out into the night. Elektra and Elpis took to the roads on the outskirts of Amazonia, walking for days with little rest or sleep.

Finally, they arrived at their destination: the mountaintop dwelling of Elektra's wise mystic, Seema. It was the only place Elektra felt safe bringing her child into the world.

When they reached the hidden entrance to Seema's cave and set down their meager belongings, Elektra finally allowed herself to rest. The exhaustion and overwhelming weight of what had transpired came tumbling down onto Elektra's strong shoulders. She carefully lowered herself to the ground. Her cries started with a whimper, and soon openly turned to sobs of great anguish.

"Elpis, what have I done? I have not only condemned this poor child in my womb to a life of pain and punishment, but I have put the fate of all my people at risk."

Elpis moved to Elektra and caressed her tired feet as her tears continued to fall.

"If it were not for my weakness, none of this would have happened."

"My Queen, you are fatigued. You have not eaten or rested properly for days. Let us go inside where I will prepare for you some dinner. Seema will know what to do next." Elpis sat, holding her breath and waiting for a response.

Elektra opened her bloodshot eyes and looked at the loyal maiden who had come with her on the first stage of her banishment. Elpis stared back with deep-set large brown eyes, at the woman she had both feared and loved from the time she was young. Elektra took Elpis' hands in her own, and the two women sat for a moment on the dusty earth, unsure of what their fate would hold.

A woman appeared from the cave. She stood at the height of a child, but wore hardened wrinkles on a weathered body. Her face was framed in long coarse hair as white as snow. "My Queen," Seema said, bowing.

* * *

Back at the Amazon nation, no one knew what had become of Elektra. After two weeks, most doubted she would return. This left the Amazons without leadership. Considering a deadly threat could strike at any time, all of the tribal queens met for a council meeting to determine a course of action.

With an intense air of melancholy hanging over the proceedings, the representatives discussed how to proceed. For once, there was little discord. Elektra had ruled for so long, and was so loved and respected as a leader, it was decided no one could replace her. A unanimous vote declared each Amazon tribe would be ruled exclusively by its own queen again, leaving no central leader for the nation.

Though the tribes of Amazonia would return to functioning as independent groups, they resolved to assist one another whenever the need arose, and to continue to live by the same code that had given them collective strength. To do anything else would be an affront to the legacy of Elektra.

It was the end of a golden era for the nation. But the Amazons would continue living under the principles Queen Elektra had instilled in them.

CHAPTER 3

THE BIRTH

Nine months later, Hera observed the stars and moons aligning in the pattern she'd been anticipating; and she knew it was time for the birth of Zeus' child.

Hera had vowed to curse this child, and she fully intended to fulfill that promise.

Zeus wasn't particularly interested in the baby. However, he relished the fact that the child would serve as a reminder of the bet he'd won with his wife. At the same time, he was aware that when Hera felt strongly about something, she would allow nothing to get in her way.

As Zeus entered Hera's grand marble chambers, he spotted her seated on the balcony overlooking the rose garden, deep in thought. "Hera?" he called out. When she didn't respond, he walked over to her and said her name more softly. "Hera..."

"Yes, Zeus? What is it you need?" Hera absently responded, keeping her eyes on the garden.

"My love, it is you that I need. I came in search of you, as you are endlessly on my mind, and seeing you sitting here like the perfect incarnation of beauty makes me want you even more."

"Nothing would be more pleasing, my love, but I must attend to some mortal tasks first," Hera responded.

"Will you be here when I return?" she asked. Although Zeus' cunning and wily ways had put her in this terrible situation with Elektra and her baby, it was impossible for Hera to remain angry at her husband.

"I will be here when you return, and for eternity after that," Zeus responded. "But your beauty in this moment must not be overlooked. Won't you stay?"

Hera turned her head from the gardens and looked directly at Zeus, her eyes swimming in his golden light. He was seven feet tall, but seemed even taller from the bench where she sat. His blue eyes shone so clearly, like a perfect sky looking down upon her. His broad shoulders and the muscular might of his arms were intoxicating. Hera knew Zeus' seductive power over women when she married him, but thought that her love would be strong enough to harness his sexual thirst. She was secure in the knowledge of her own beauty and strength, and had never wavered in her love for Zeus, even when he spent days away from her.

The event with Elektra, however, triggered a special kind of jealousy. Sharing her husband with nameless women during the throes of his roaming passion was one thing, but sharing him with an immortal whom she had created, and who had come to be with his child, was far worse.

"My dear husband, is it I that you lust for, or are you thinking of another?"

"Now Hera, that was a wager between us," Zeus said. "I was simply demonstrating man's superiority over woman. Can't we let that go, my dear, and focus on some pleasures of our own?"

"Am I to assume your desire for me in this moment has nothing to do with Elektra and the birth of your child? Quite the coincidence, wouldn't you say? Men are so predictable. They presume they are the only ones who can see their devious little schemes when it is obvious to everyone what is on their minds."

"And you, as all women, read too much into every little action! What is simply transparent is assumed to be some elaborate trick!" Zeus retorted.

"So you were not scheming when you slept with Elektra, but were instead simply lusting after the woman?"

"You forget so quickly, Hera. We waged a challenge of the flesh, to which you yourself agreed!"

"I agreed to the challenge lifetimes ago! You failed the challenge and could not bear to let things be. Now I must leave. I have business to attend to that is of the utmost importance."

"Stop, Hera!" Zeus roared. "You are aware that killing another God's child, even one conceived with a mortal, is forbidden! My child shall live, or I will make sure that you regret your decision for eternity." His eyes grew dark, and his brows furrowed.

"If all else fails, then you shout and threaten me, Zeus? Your child of deceit shall live, husband, but its life will not be easy. With all the energy of my will, a curse as dark as night shall be placed on this offspring that it shall never know peace or love. This child of yours will live, but its life will be that of such torment and despair that death would seem a welcome relief!"

Zeus blinked. The curse Hera described was of a cruel nature, no doubt, but then again, he didn't much care about the lives of mere mortals. Whether they lived in peace or in pain was of little consequence to his enormous ego. What he did care about, however, was being bested by Hera.

Hera lifted the hem of her flowing gown and stormed off the terrace. In her agitated state, her impending mission was now more urgent than ever. Zeus felt his own rage rising as his wife disappeared, leaving him standing alone above the gardens of Mt. Olympus. In his frustration and anger at her impudence, he lifted his right leg high and stomped his leather-soled foot onto the stone floor.

"Aaaaaaaaahhhhh!"

As the force of Zeus' heel cracked the marble into pieces of rubble and dust, a shout thundered from deep within him, and gusts of wind from his lips uprooted the flowers in the garden. Lightning cracked in the sky, and the ground shook throughout Earth. Zeus took a step closer to the carved marble edge of the balcony. Knowing that Hera was on her way to curse Elektra's child, he shouted with a violent fury, "Be wary, Hera. Whatever revenge you seek will come back to haunt you!"

Just as Hera departed—the last of her golden light flashing as she made haste to Elektra—she heard her husband's shouts echo and rumble throughout her chambers. She realized that she'd lost precious time arguing with Zeus and had few moments to spare worrying about him.

* * *

Clouds gathered and began to blot out the light of the sun.

In a small cave atop a mountain, Elektra restlessly moved on a bed of straw. Her muscles intermittently tightened and her face expressed pain, yet she didn't utter a sound. Elpis knelt by her side, holding Elektra's clammy hand while wiping her forehead with a cloth between contractions.

Suddenly, a thunderous boom exploded from the sky. It wasn't enough to distract Elektra from the writhing pain in her back and lower belly, but Elpis was startled.

"Don't worry, my Queen," Elpis nervously offered, trying to calm herself more than Elektra. "It sounds like there may be a thunderstorm approaching, but we are safe here. Are we not, Seema?"

Seema, the mystic who had provided refuge and counsel for Elektra for the past nine months, stood in the back of the tent, arms held to the sky, eyes closed. She didn't acknowledge Elpis' question, focused as she was on quietly chanting prayers of protection for Elektra's birth.

CRRRRRAAAAACKKK! Another explosive boom sounded from the darkening sky. Elpis' eyes widened as she jumped from the clap. She bit her lip to stop herself from speaking. Seema began chanting louder, rhythmically intoning sounds foreign to both of the Amazon women. With her eyes closed, she moved to the tempo of the utterances rising from deep within her. It didn't sound like words, but rather a flock of birds singing in one voice.

Seema's arms wildly moved about her. Although she was old and small, her movements were as agile as the acrobats Elpis had seen in the entertainment tents back home. Elpis found herself suddenly relaxing. The sounds were soothing, making her feel like she was being taken on a journey to an unknown, peaceful destination.

Just as Seema's voice reached a crescendo, Elektra had another powerful contraction. She reached out to the side with one hand and grabbed the first thing within her grasp. It was the back of a large chair, carved out of the stump of a massive oak tree. As Elektra clenched her teeth, she felt a portion of the chair snap. Ache washed over her, then subsided, as the sound of Seema's hypnotizing chants filled the room and provided Elektra with a sort of anesthesia. She looked down and realized part of the broken chair was still in her hand. Elpis gently pried the wood free and moved the chair into a corner of the room. Elektra's focus returned to the serene chanting.

Again, thunder rumbled from the sky. Elektra felt a sharp pang deep within her womb, and she loudly moaned. It was time for the baby to come out.

Elpis was a young girl, but had witnessed many births in the camp. She knew she had to move fast. She quickly gathered the clean cloth that had been set aside and positioned herself between Elektra's legs. Elektra took a deep breath, and with the exhalation squeezed her muscles tight and pushed as hard as she could, her entire body tense from her efforts.

"I can see the head!" Elpis bellowed, spurring Elektra on. Seema hopped from one leg to another behind Elektra, chanting furiously.

After another few breaths and pushes, Elektra pushed out her baby's entire body. Elpis jumped to cradle the child as it entered the world.

"What is it? Let me see!" cried Elektra, in a voice much stronger than she expected to hear from herself. Elpis covered the baby in blankets and placed the bundle against Elektra's bosom.

"A girl. She has my honey eyes and black hair!" Elektra exclaimed. "Elpis, hand me the branding mark from the coals...hurry!"

Elpis grabbed a small iron tool that Seema had created to place a special mark on the child, enabling Elektra to identify her in the future. The mark was of two intertwined snakes—precisely the same symbol that was in the center of Elektra's Golden Girdle.

Elpis carefully handed the hot steel tool to Elektra, and gently picked up the small cooing infant from Elektra's chest.

With tears streaming down her face, Elektra gathered her nerve and spoke feverishly. "My dearest child, I will name you Theodora, for you are my princess, my gift whom I will love forever." A tear fell from the mother's chin upon the infant's face and rolled down her plump cheek.

"Turn her, Elpis," Elektra ordered. Red amber glowed on the tip of the marker. When Elektra pressed it to the nape of her daughter's neck, the air hissed with the smoky scent of burning flesh.

Theodora's high-pitched screams filled the tent. Seema placed her small, wrinkled hand on the child's head and continued her soft chanting. They transformed the babe's cries into coos.

Once the child was calmed, Elektra produced a small vial of salve, made of allspice and sandalwood—herbs believed to bring good luck—prepared for her by Seema. Choking back tears, Elektra then took a blade and made a small cut on her own finger, squeezing it until a globule of blood seeped from the wound. She positioned the droplet over the mouth of the vial and allowed it to mingle with the herbal mixture, and then smeared the substance over the seared flesh of Theodora's branding.

"My beautiful daughter, Theodora…my little Thea," Elektra said, raising the infant to the sky, her voice shaking with emotion. "You were born of the Gods, and you are the true Queen of Amazonia! I bless you and leave you the Golden Girdle for your protection. Upon your eighteenth year, you will understand what this means. I bestow its powers and strength upon you to protect the Amazon nation, and to help guide you along your journey."

Seema finally opened her eyes, and with the full force of her power directed all of her accumulated energy onto the newborn baby girl. With her arms and fingers outstretched, Seema whispered the final words of the prayer in an ancient tongue and stepped closer to the baby. She moved with meaningful intention, and brought her face close to Thea. The baby calmly watched the old mystic. With a powerful inhalation, Seema pulled the energy of her prayers in through her mouth and then blew all of the breath from deep within her core directly onto the child's face. Thea's eyes flickered with a flash of light, and her little baby hairs blew around the sides of her round features.

"Elpis, quickly take Thea to one of the tribes," Elektra commanded. "Tell no one where she has come from and offer no information. Remember, the Golden Girdle on the back of the cart must not be seen by anyone. Bury it in the sacred Amazon grounds east of Mount Spiro. One day my daughter may reclaim it and harbor its powers for her own. Hurry! Hera is coming, I am sure of it." Elektra placed a solitary kiss on her daughter's forehead and handed the baby reluctantly to Elpis.

"Yes, my Queen," Elpis replied. She turned to leave, clutching the small child in her arms. A satchel prepared by Seema for the baby's needs was already waiting in the cart.

"Seema, I am entrusting you to keep an eye on the child in my absence. Please see to it that she stays clear of harm." Elektra's eyes welled up once again. Seema responded with a single reassuring nod.

Elektra lay back and felt the pain of a mother's loss. The room filled again with the soft sounds of Seema's voice, offering a peaceful contrast to the torment and unrest within Elektra's soul. Outside the tent the storm raged, reflecting Elektra's anguish. Lightning pierced the sky as Elektra suddenly felt another jolt from within. *What was this? It couldn't be...*

Seema quickly understood what was happening, and her chanting grew louder as Elektra began to writhe in pain with another contraction. Elektra held tightly to her garments and clutched at the surrounding straw as her body trembled with the strain of pushing. Thunder cracked and the ground shook as Elektra's second child now clawed her way into the world. Seema collected the small infant and wrapped the child tightly in a blanket before placing her in Elektra's arms.

"Another girl! Oh, Seema, what will become of her?" Elektra whimpered.

"Her fate is in the hands of the Gods, as always," Seema replied.

"Seema, the branding mark..."

Seema quickly moved to hand the mark to Elektra, knowing their time was running out. Again, screams filled the tent as the mark was placed on the nape of the baby's neck. As Seema soothed her cries with a gentle touch and a prayer-filled song, Elektra placed a loving kiss atop the girl's head, observing that her light blonde hair and green eyes made her look different from her fraternal twin sister. Elektra's heart ached. She wanted to remember her children's delicate features forever.

Before Seema had uttered one complete verse of her protective words, the room began to fill with a brilliant light. It was too late.

Elektra had experienced this grand illumination once before, and she knew the time with her daughter had expired. Seema backed into the corner of the tent, bowing as the illumination expanded. Thunder sounded in the distance. As the light grew in intensity, it slowly contracted in size, ultimately revealing Hera.

The Goddess stood over Elektra with grandeur, garbed in fine robes and jewels. "Just in time, I see," Hera said, as she saw the infant lying in Elektra's arms. "The fruit of your betrayal."

"Hera, Goddess of all things good and pure, I beg you to spare my daughter from a cursed life of toil and pain," Elektra pleaded.

"Ah, but did you think of that when you spit in my face and took pleasure with a man, betraying women everywhere? Did you care when you succumbed to lust after being granted immortality? Why should I spare this child when clearly your defiance demands punishment?" Hera spat these words through clenched teeth.

"Please, Hera, Goddess of women! Offer mercy upon this child! It is I who should be punished. She is innocent!"

"Enough of this, Elektra! You are already weak in my eyes. No need to further my detestation with useless whimpering. Hand me the child!" Hera demanded.

With her last remaining morsels of hope, Elektra fruitlessly continued, "As mother and woman, I beg of you, sweet Hera, to let me suffer on Earth instead of my daughter. Let me be a sacrifice and an example...please!"

"Enough! Your cries fall on infertile soil, Elektra. Your punishment has been decided."

Hera gathered the small child into her hands and held her into the air. Hera's radiance shone bright, illuminating the infant's face as the Goddess spoke her curse aloud.

"From this day forth, the child of Elektra will feel the weight of the mortal world upon her. No road will be easy and no favors will be granted. She will painstakingly earn every day of her survival. This seed of deceit and betrayal will experience the suffering that infidelity brings. Born from the weakness of a woman, she will never know love and will be alone in this world, learning strength and independence only through strife. Cursed be this child!"

Elektra, too weak to stand, began to weep once again. With her eyes and jaw tightly clenched, her sobs shook her body from the depths of her soul. She had never felt such pain and remorse. She knew Hera's curse would be methodically imposed, and there was nothing she could do to stop it from ruining her daughter's life.

"Elektra, prepare yourself to depart," Hera continued. "You too have a journey from which you shall not return. Tartarus awaits your arrival."

Hera drew the child into the folds of her robes. The baby's small body helplessly moved where it was commanded. Her little arms and legs, which had been just a moment ago waving in the air, were suddenly hidden from view.

Elektra felt her body collapse in defeat, fully aware of the disastrous life that awaited her child. Elektra desperately looked back to Hera, hoping to steal just one more glance of the second daughter she was losing. Her hopes proved futile, as the child was tucked into Hera's arm and out of sight. From under the robes, a distressed cry escaped from the baby's mouth, her struggles in the world already beginning. No one would be there to comfort her from this moment forward.

"Mystic! Make sure this wretch of a woman gets to the Gulf of Saronic, where her vessel to Tartarus awaits," Hera directed. "And no trickery, or your own misfortune will await you."

Seema nodded silently and bowed to the Goddess.

"Enjoy your immortal existence within the confines of the Underworld, Elektra. From there you will be able to watch the suffering of your daughter. Perhaps one day you will meet again," Hera said, pounding the final bitter nail into the distraught mother's coffin.

The room again filled with light. The Goddess vanished in a blink, Elektra's child in her arms. The tent was left dark and gloomy.

The storm ended almost instantly. Only a thick, gray mist persisted—one as heavy as Elektra's heart. Although the mother had managed to save Thea, her other daughter had been doomed by Hera's curse. As her soul ached with yearning for her children, her breasts began to painfully fill with the milk that would never reach their pink lips. The pressure began to build in her bosom, and without looking down, Elektra felt the liquid dripping from her swollen breasts onto her empty lap.

This punishment for a moment's indiscretion is too severe for any mother, she thought. But her fate, and that of her daughters, was sealed. As sorrow took hold of Elektra, the sting of her broken heart blotted out her surroundings. Still, she knew she had to obey Hera's cruel demands.

Elektra prayed that despite Hera's curse and the lack of a mother's protection, the world would show both of her girls even a modicum of mercy.

CHAPTER 4

THE MARKETPLACE

The covered wagon pulled into town on the outskirts of Argos in the middle of the night. The area was peaceful and quiet in the hours before daybreak. Statues adorned the entrance, next to a few drowsy Argive guards keeping watch. Stores lined the road. The town was a main outpost for commerce, and this was the day of the weekly marketplace that brought in various merchants and buyers.

As the horses pulling the carriage came to an abrupt stop, the cart jerked, awakening the cargo within. Entangled in a web of chained arms and legs, young girls began to move, trying to free themselves from their companions. Only two dozen remained. Four girls had been sold in the last town, making money for their keepers and slightly lightening the caravan's load. It was impossible for the girls to know whether or not their masters would be kind, and thus whether they should hope to be sold or remain with the caravan as long as possible. Their male keepers were savage brutes, but new owners could be even worse. Many of the girls had been bought and sold several times, and the stories they shared terrified the novices.

The girls ranged in age from five to fifteen. Pinned against the back of the carriage was a girl who was seven. She was tall for her age, and had blonde hair that always seemed to attract attention, despite being tinted with filth. Like the others, she'd been woken by the abrupt halt of the carriage. Her legs were cramped. The circulation had been cut off, and they stung with excruciating pain. She shoved two other girls off her to allow blood to flow back into her legs.

"Out of the carriage!" barked the driver. He was a massive man whose large, round stomach was nearly masked by his height and broad stature.

One by one, each of the girls poured out of the wagon, nearly falling over due to the weighty shackles on their ankles and wrists. The girls' thin frames were covered in a layer of dirt so thick that the color of their skin was difficult to identify.

"The lot of ya' is a mess! Ramos, make sure they're cleaned up before the morning!" yelled the driver, as he turned to his partner who was dismounting a large horse.

"Line up, girls. Rest time is over. Let's move!"

The captives flowed like a stream of cowered figures into a large tent used to conduct out–of-town commerce. The marketplace hosted the sale of everything from grain, spices, woven cloth, and weapons to live animals and slaves. The men of the caravan traveled from town to town, selling their orphaned and kidnapped girls to the highest bidders. Whenever they would come upon a young girl playing unattended outside her home, they would quietly snatch her up for sale in another village down the line. In cities with orphanages, the men would sneak into the dusty yards and grab as many of the girls as they could carry. They moved quickly, making the job of tracking them very difficult.

Little 7-year-old Teigra had been a slave for as long as she could remember. She had no knowledge of family or home. If she were to be sold in the market, it would mark her sixth time.

Most of the girls were sold only once or twice, but Teigra's rebellious attitude often prompted a return to the slave merchants almost immediately after being bought. As a result, she spent more time being whipped and punished than any of the other girls.

One exception was the fifth time she was sold, to an elderly farmer named Nicolaus. Though he worked her hard, he fed her well and had a gentle way with her. She served him with little reluctance for nearly a month—until his heart gave out during an exceptionally hot day in the fields. After realizing what had happened, Teigra escaped, only to be caught stealing fruit in the nearby marketplace three days later. She was returned to Ramos and the caravan.

"Girl, you had better clean up nice," Ramos said, grabbing Teigra's chin in his meaty hand. "Soon you'll be good for only one thing, and I just might keep you myself for that!" he said, laughing.

Without hesitation, Teigra spit squarely in his fat face.

"You little bitch!" shouted Ramos, as he slapped her hard with the back of his hand.

"Ramos! What are you doing, you idiot?" exclaimed the driver. "She's going to be hard enough to sell without being all marked up!"

Despite her stinging cheek, Teigra gave Ramos a smirk as she regained her footing.

Ramos leaned in close, grabbing each side of her face with his hands. "I'd hope for a new master today if I were you, girl. The next journey is a bit long, and I just might fancy some companionship for the ride."

He licked her, moving from lips to cheek to ear. His spiky whiskers and crusty tongue slithered across her face, and his putrid breath left a stench in her nostrils that would linger for hours.

Ramos beckoned to his men. "Boys, get these swine cleaned up." He tossed Teigra aside and added, with a sarcastic chuckle, "I already started cleaning this one."

For once, Teigra looked forward to the crude bath. After removing the only piece of clothing they owned, all the girls stood side-by-side in a line while three men with buckets of water repeatedly drenched them. It didn't matter to Teigra that the water was taken from the horses' trough, as anything was better than Ramos' slimy saliva.

After the girls were soaked, they were given a rag to pass around to wipe themselves. Teigra had seen the men frequently take one of the older girls, still undressed, back to the carriage. After a while, the girl reemerged with red eyes and rope marks around her wrists.

The marketplace was a familiar ordeal to Teigra. She could see the fear in the faces of some of the girls who were experiencing it for the first time. As the morning sun began to light the tent, she knew selling time was near.

"Look alive!" Ramos barked. "Buyers are coming." Soon the bazaar was buzzing with local customers, as well as those from nearby towns and villages. Having been dried and clothed, the girls stood side-by-side, facing forward. Men came by and examined them from head to toe. Some focused on their teeth; others asked them to disrobe. Though many looked, few bought, as slave girls were expensive. The slave traders called out to passersby, trying to bring more business their way.

"Gentleman! Behold, the obedient girl who will tend to your livestock, do your housework, and cook your meals!"

"You'll never have a problem again with a badly behaved or difficult servant! Our girls have been trained to be dutiful!"

"Come one, come all. Test our claims and you shall be pleased!"

It was mid-morning when a man adorned in bright colors usually worn by only the wealthiest of traders entered the tent. Without distraction, he made his way directly to Ramos.

"I'm looking for a strong servant. Is this your lot?" asked the man.

"Indeed, sir!" Ramos replied. "The finest handpicked young ladies west of the Aegean, my lord."

"And your price?" the man asked.

"How can you place a price on such exquisite specimens?" Ramos asked. "But of course we must, for the sake of commerce, sir. These girls have been in our keeping, fed and trained for hard work. Which young lady strikes your pleasure?"

The man strolled past the girls, pausing for several seconds to study each one. He circled them, dissecting them with his gaze, and pinching and poking as he pleased. Most of the girls were meek and looked only at the ground. When he stood in front of Teigra, however, she stood tall, staring directly into his eyes.

"Cast your gaze down, girl!" Ramos ordered.

"That won't be necessary. I will deal with her," the man countered. "Girl, let me see your hands."

Teigra splayed her hands out with palms up for the man to see, keeping her eyes on his.

"And your thighs."

Teigra paused for a moment, then pulled her shift up slowly to reveal her slim but muscular thighs. The man took her jaw in his right hand and lifted her chin, thoroughly studying it. Teigra was tall, and her face was quite distinctive. Her emerald green eyes glowed against her tanned skin, and her chiseled face was beautifully framed by her golden locks. Even at seven, she was one of the tallest girls—and certainly the strongest—but her youth was apparent.

"How much for this one?" the man inquired.

"A fine choice, sir!" Ramos replied. "We were lucky to come by this girl. Strong, young, and beautiful. She will certainly be sold today. Another gentleman was already commenting on her earlier."

"How much?" the man repeated, slightly irritated.

"She goes for thirty-five pieces of gold, but for you...thirty," Ramos replied.

"I will pay twenty-five and no more," the man stated.

"I am sorry, sir, but I could not fathom a price that low!" Ramos responded. "Look at her! She is certainly worth at least twenty-nine pieces."

"Then best of luck to you," the man said, and he turned to leave.

"Okay!" yelled Ramos, before the man could walk away. "Sir, for you, twenty-five gold pieces will suffice," Ramos relented.

Without emotion, the man reached into his purse, counted out twenty-five gold coins, and placed them neatly in a small sack. Meanwhile, Ramos unshackled Teigra at the ankles. Once loosened, she seized the opportunity to repay Ramos for his earlier actions. As he knelt to undo her last ankle shackle, Teigra swiftly thrust her knee into his jaw. Ramos fell backward and Teigra darted for the exit.

Her hands still bound, she ran faster than anyone had expected. However, two of Ramos' henchmen were standing by the opening of the tent, and they corralled her into a corner. With little room to maneuver, Teigra stopped running and motioned surrender. As one man made his way to her, grabbing her from behind, the other stood in front of her, ready to take her by the shoulders.

Teigra butted her head backward, cracking the large skull of the guard behind her, while forcefully kicking the other in the groin.

Teigra tried to flee again—but was halted by the snap of Ramos' thin leather whip against the back of her legs. She fell to the ground in blinding pain. She was returned to an upright position with the forceful yank of Ramos' thick arm.

"My apologies, sir," Ramos said, rubbing his jaw as he turned back to the prospective buyer. "She is a spirited young girl, which can be quite the advantage."

"I am not so sure," the man replied. "I have broken horses and mules, but this girl seems to be more difficult."

"Sir!" Ramos called out. "I assure you she just needs regular discipline. Look at her. She is a beautiful creature—strong and youthful. An unyielding fist will go a long way with her!"

"Hmmm. I will pay twenty pieces for her, and that is my final offer."

Still holding Teigra by her hands, Ramos tightened his grip, twisting her bound wrists behind her back to emphasize his frustration at having lost five gold coins.

"Very well," Ramos reluctantly yielded.

Ramos collected the payment and released Teigra to the man. Beside his decorative tunic he carried a coiled whip made of ornate leather. He was clearly a man of wealth and power, and Teigra held onto a child's hope that this master might be different than the cruel ones before him.

"What's her name?" the man asked Ramos.

"We call her Teigra," Ramos replied. "Indeed, she is like a tiger!"

The man nodded and took hold of Teigra's arm, leading her to his waiting horse. With ease, he lifted the girl, placed her in the front saddle, and secured his items in his saddlebag before mounting the horse behind her. With one arm around Teigra's waist holding her tied hands, and the other arm negotiating the reins, the stranger journeyed home with his newly-purchased slave.

The midday sun was warm, but the shade of the fresh-smelling cedar trees along the dirt road provided them some relief from the heat. Teigra felt her stomach yearn for food and hoped the trip would not be long.

"We do not have far to travel, girl," the man stated, breaking the silence of the woods. "I am called Nestor by others. You shall call me *Master,* and my wife Halos you shall call *Mistress.*"

Teigra remained silent.

"Did you *hear* me, girl?" asked Nestor, slightly raising his voice.

"Yes," Teigra replied.

"I believe you did not!" Nestor responded. "I said you are to call me *Master!*"

"Yes…Master," Teigra replied.

"Neither I nor my wife will tolerate any resistance from you, child," he continued. "You will do your toil or you will suffer the whip. Any stunts like the one at the market, and you will wish you had never been born."

Teigra felt any hope of having gained a kind master rapidly evaporate into the warm, breezy air.

Soon they reached a small knoll, and she could see smoke rising in the distance. Nestor's home came into view, with stone columns and pillars providing support for a clay structure with numerous rooms. The home was partially covered by large swaying trees, opening to a courtyard upon entry of the tall gates. Just beyond the house were several fields of vineyards and olive trees, which Teigra assumed were the source of Nestor's wealth.

"My lady!" Nestor yelled, as their horse pulled into the courtyard. "I have brought a gift for you."

Nestor dismounted and tied his horse before pulling Teigra onto the ground. A short, plump woman came out of the house—unlike anyone Teigra had expected to see, given Nestor's neat and meticulous appearance. The woman's hair was a tangled mess, and it looked as though she'd never bathed in her life. Her breath smelled of wine, and her eyes were glazed.

"What do we have here?" Halos asked, her rough voice full of contempt. "A girl? She looks like trouble to me. Couldn't you do better than this, you oaf? Or is it that yellow hair you like?" She spoke so near that spit spattered Teigra's face. Halos warned, "Any trouble from you, girl, and you'll be sorry."

"Dear, I am sure you will find her quite strong," Nestor replied, almost apologetically. "She nearly took two men to their knees. She will be sufficient for the housework and stables, and perhaps even the fields."

"What? Well, her strength better be put to use with chores and not with causing any trouble for me!"

"No, dear, I have already laid down the rules. Any trouble and she gets the whip."

"Hmph! Any trouble, and I'll see to it that Father hears about this," Halos replied, referring to the magistrate who employed her husband.

Teigra saw Nestor meekly look toward the ground, silent to his wife's threats. He took Teigra by her shackled hands and led her inside, while Halos closely examined the girl as if she were a new horse or milking cow.

Once inside, Nestor took the key that Ramos had given him and unlocked Teigra's hands. She rubbed her sore wrists. It was the first time in weeks she'd been completely free of the shackles, and the feeling was akin to being able to breathe after suffocating underwater.

The home was quite large, with dozens of rooms in addition to the courtyard foyer. Teigra's jaw dropped at the thought of maintaining and cleaning such a massive space. The stone floors went on endlessly, and the walls were at least four times her height. There were large, carved vases and stone sculptures in every corner. Nestor placed the key in his wife's possession, along with the shackles, and excused himself to his duties in the fields. It was then that Teigra realized who her real "master" would be.

"I'll have no trouble with you, girl," barked Halos. "Do as you're told and you'll receive meals and a place to sleep. Don't, and you'll become good friends with the whip."

Teigra's expressionless eyes were fixed on Halos. It seemed that this foul woman came from a wealthy family, and her husband put up with her demeanor for the sake of her money. Looking more closely at her, Teigra could see bits of previously eaten meals lodged in the crevices of her dirty teeth, and stains all over her garments.

"Girl, when I speak, you reply 'Yes Mistress,'" Halos commanded. "Do you understand?"

"Yes, Mistress," Teigra said, finally casting her eyes down, less in obedience and more due to the difficulty of actually looking at the fat, nasty woman.

"Good. Now it's time to get to work. You'll find a scrub brush and soap by the water basin. Start by scrubbing all the floors."

Teigra started walking to the next room to do as she'd been ordered, but the sting of pain across her back crippled her before she made her way more than a few steps. It nearly brought her to her knees; but she took a breath, gathered herself, and rose.

"Girl, you didn't say 'Yes, Mistress,'" Halos observed, with a hint of madness in her small eyes. "Let's try that again."

Teigra stood and turned toward the pudgy woman. "Yes, Mistress," she managed to speak.

"Ahhh, that's better," Halos said. "Now move out of my sight!"

For hours Teigra scrubbed the clay floors. The bath she'd received early that morning had become a distant memory, and she was once again filthy from head to toe. Even worse, she had yet to receive anything to eat. As she watched the sun fade through the window, her muscles ached, her stomach growled, and she was utterly exhausted. Moving around on her hands and knees, she painstakingly scrubbed grime off the hard surface, using the very last of her energy.

Fatigue was setting in, and Teigra's sleepy eyes didn't even see the vase fall from its place. In her exhaustion, she had accidentally sent the massive piece rocking after cleaning the floor around it. She had moved her arm in one wide arc, dragging the wet rag along the floor.

As she turned, the ornately painted vase, standing five feet tall, had been set off its narrow base and came tumbling down behind her, crashing inches from her head with an explosive clatter.

Her surprise was quickly replaced with a searing pain on her back. Halos stood over her with whip in hand, reloading for a second strike.

"I'm sorry, Mistress! Please forgive—" Teigra managed to blurt out before another blow froze more words from escaping.

"You're sorry, all right!" Halos screamed. "The price of that vase is more than the value of your life! Your clumsiness will not go unpunished! Clean up this mess, finish scrubbing the floors, and if you break anything else, you will get the beating you deserve—before being locked away without food!"

The thought of going without food for any longer was even more unbearable than the work ahead. Teigra summoned enough strength to get through her chores, just as night fully conquered the awful day. Her back and legs stung, and her wounds were filled with sweat and grime. Nestor had returned home from the fields, and Teigra could smell fresh roasted fish wafting throughout the house. She returned her brush, rags, and bucket to their place just as Halos came to find her. "It's time for you to go to your room," Halos said, shoving Teigra in the direction of a small dark space.

Tucked away in the back of the house, Teigra's room was only slightly larger than the cupboard where the cleaning supplies were kept. There was a very small window at the top of one of the walls, and half the floor had been laid with straw to fashion a makeshift bed. Two pots sat nearby—one contained water, the other was empty. There was no light or lantern, and the bolt that locked the room was secured on the outside of the door.

"You'll sleep here, girl." Halos briefly disappeared, and then returned holding a modest plate.

"Here is your dinner," Halos said, as she handed Teigra a chunk of bread and a small, moldy piece of cheese. Teigra's stomach grumbled at the sight of the food, meager as the rations were.

"You're lucky to have any food at all after breaking that vase. Get to bed quickly, girl. There will be a lot more work tomorrow." The mistress closed the door and bolted it from the outside. Teigra was left standing inside the tiny, cold, and dark space.

Fortunately, a full moon shone through the tiny aperture, providing her with enough light to see around the shadows. Within seconds, she inhaled the bread and cheese, and drank half of the water in the pot. Before she lay down onto the straw, Teigra took the small cloth left for her and washed her face and hands with the remaining water. It felt soothing on her skin, and despite the sting when the liquid touched her wounds, wiping them clean was a relief.

As Teigra washed her neck, her fingers traced over the raised skin of the branding mark at the nape. She had never been able to see the mark, nor had anyone ever described it to her, but she could feel the raised intertwining lines and somehow sensed they were serpents. She had no idea how the mark got there or what it meant. Long ago, Teigra dreamt it was a mark of royalty, but years of back-breaking labor and cruel treatment had quashed such fantasies.

Teigra settled into the hard bed, covering herself with a thin, worn blanket she found in the corner. She laid her tired head down on a pillow of straw, and in the darkness once again surveyed the dingy room. Alone in her locked cell, with nothing to look forward to but more labor and hardship, she was overcome with sadness at her lot in life. She had barely known a day's kindness or peace. Virtually every moment, as far back as she could remember, had been a fight for survival among cruel and wrathful people. Without making a sound, Teigra closed her eyes and wept.

She had to continually be on guard, but every once in a while, even she needed a release. Lying down at night, whether in a cramped caravan or a small room, she could secretly cry and wish for a better life. There was little relief in her sorrow, but youth has a way of revealing itself on long, lonely nights.

Soon enough, Teigra had cried herself into a deep and restless sleep. In her slumber, she tossed and turned as she dreamed. It was the same dream she always had. Teigra was searching through the forest. She came upon a warrior, and she ferociously battled her. During the battle, the warrior's mask came off, revealing a face that looked exactly like Teigra's. Right before she woke up, her opponent vanished in the mist, leaving her shocked and confused. As it regularly happens, Teigra awoke in a chilled sweat, her heart pounding, wondering what the dream was trying to reveal to her.

While it had put her in a frightful state, her exhaustion was so severe that she soon fell back to sleep. It seemed that even in her dreams she would have to suffer ongoing torment.

A new day would soon be dawning, but Teigra's ability to see hope with each rising sun was painfully diminishing. It had become apparent that the world was a cold and harsh place...and that she could depend only on herself to survive.

CHAPTER 5
QUEEN ALEXA'S TRIBE

In the outskirts of the city of Nemea and east of Mount Spiro, Queen Alexa's tribe was located in a beautiful landscape of greenery. The shades of leaves were immensely varied in their forest dwelling. There were light pale ferns, dangling swampy green vines, and thousands of ancient trees, ranging from the grayish-green of sage to the most vibrant emerald.

Thea noticed them all, loving the way the colors changed with each season. She would often sneak away from her tribe's camp to explore the forest on her own.

At age seven, she was incredibly fast. Running like fire through the woods, the vision in her periphery blurred as she increased her speed. She darted through mazes of trees and bush, jumped over logs, and dodged surprised butterflies in flight.

Her dark brown hair was pulled back and tightly braided in two long tresses flapping against her sun-kissed skin. Her eyes were the color of honey, and she was striking for such a young girl.

At a clearing, Thea stopped to find a large, flat rock. She loved to paint, creating expressive nature scenes and depictions of the Sondra she hoped to join one day. Looking around for a subject, she heard a low-pitched coo coming from above. A massive, yellow-eyed owl had perched on a branch above her—perfect!

The early morning light streamed through the leaves of the treetops, creating illuminated beams. Thea was delighted. She had barely painted an outline of the beautiful winged creature when the owl took flight, seemingly beckoning her to follow—which Thea did, in a sprint.

After its sudden start, the owl paced its speed to match Thea's, and turned in the air to shadow her movements as she darted left and right. Moments like these kept drawing her into the forest for another chance to feel thoroughly alive.

In the back of Thea's mind, she remembered there was an archery contest at camp and she'd have to return soon. Her teachers gave her a hard time when she wandered off on her own, and if she failed to participate in the competition they'd know that she'd again meandered into the forest. Thea had received many scoldings about the dangers of doing this. But she was repeatedly drawn into the thickness of the woodlands where she felt most free.

Figuring she'd have plenty of time to make it home, Thea's attention returned to the owl. She was enchanted by the bird's presence and wanted to remain with it. In a slow sprint, she reached her arm straight up over her head and tried with the tips of her fingers to touch the owl's feathery belly. As if to tease her, the flying bird dipped low while increasing its speed, remaining just out of Thea's reach. Although she sped up to try to catch it, the girl's little legs could carry her only so fast, and she was no match for the bird's swiftness.

Thea felt the urge to communicate with the owl in a manner that approximated its own language, so she formed an "o" shape with her lips and attempted to whistle something resembling a birdcall. The only sound that escaped was rushing air, greatly frustrating her. Why couldn't she whistle when most of the other girls at camp seemed to do it so easily?

With another deep coo, the owl made a final low dip toward the girl before it soared into the heights of the forest and disappeared from sight. Thea squinted into the piercing light of the rising sun between the patches of shadowed treetops. Her eyes moved quickly, searching for the large, wise-looking owl. Then she saw it. It had landed and perched itself into the nook of one of the tallest trees. Thea could just make out the owl's black and yellow eyes staring down at her. Suddenly, it spread its massive wings and took off again. Thea ran to keep up with the beautiful creature, trying hard not to lose sight of it. She was simultaneously running through the thick forest and straining her neck to keep track of the bird. The wind felt wonderful against her face, and imagining what it would feel like to fly fast and high, she wished for wings like the owl.

It was then that her foot caught on something. Concealed underneath the bed of forest leaves was the sharp edge of a jagged boulder, tripping little Thea. She went fumbling forward, her arms flapping helplessly at her sides, reaching for something to slow her fall.

* * *

Unfamiliar voices coming from somewhere nearby intruded on Thea's deep sleep. She fought to ignore them, reluctant to leave the comforting darkness. Then she felt a dull pain on her head and finally opened her eyes.

Thea found herself flat on her back on the forest floor, her head throbbing. She could tell from the position of the sun that it was nearly midday. Fragments of the morning began to filter into her memory. She recalled her chase for the majestic owl, and she remembered tripping. She had no memory of what happened next, but the patch of blood she spotted on a nearby rock completed the story.

Thea heard the voices of several men quickly coming her way. She forced herself to move into a low crouch, narrowing her eyes to the pain in her temples. Hugging the bottom of a tree trunk and hidden by the large fronds of a massive fern, Thea peeked between leaves as the men approached. There were ten soldiers, all armed with spears or swords. The lead soldiers were using the points of their spears to poke and taunt two young, frightened women.

Thea could tell from their coat of arms that they were in the Argive army. Thea had never seen anyone from King Bedros' forces before, but back at her camp the armor, weapons, and other details of neighboring armies were often discussed.

Thea could also tell from the women's style of dress that they were from tribes beyond the southern borders of Amazonia. Their people had been friendly to the Amazon tribes, trading wool, grain, and animals. But these two women had been treated badly. The napes of their dresses were torn and dirty, their hair was tangled into messy knots, and the exposed skin on their arms was red and welted.

"King Bedros couldn't have approved this!" one of the women exclaimed. "When he finds out..."

"And how is King Bedros to know?" one of the lead soldiers, whose name was Draco, asked. "You Barbarians know nothing about how things work. Move, wench!" Draco poked the woman in her ribs with his spear. The woman yelped in pain and her body jolted forward. The soldiers in back began laughing. One of them yelled, more to his comrades than to the women, "We haven't finished with you yet, so don't start getting lazy, you useless outcasts!"

Thea pressed a palm hard to her mouth to hold back any sound, realizing the danger she'd be in if she were found. Then she noticed something moving ever so slowly in the background, just past where the soldiers walked. At first she had thought it might be the branches of trees swaying in the wind. But when she heard the first man fall, she realized the movement was more than just a passing breeze. Thea couldn't gauge their numbers, but she was sure that the nearly invisible figures taking down the Argive soldiers could only be the elite and powerful Sondra warriors of her people.

Frozen stiff with fear and awe, Thea watched as the women neutralized their opponents. She had never seen the Sondras in action and always wondered what they were like in battle.

The men were falling fast and hard, and by the time Draco and the other one in the front knew what was happening, they had been confronted by the lethal Amazon warriors. One of the Sondras leaped forward and seemed to float in the air before almost imperceptibly kicking a leg out and snapping a soldier's neck with the force of her heel. Draco, however, was swift. He got on his horse and sped away; he wasn't about to risk his life for his comrade.

Thea heard gentle whispers behind the rustling leaves of bushes, as the frightened women were calmed by one of the fighters.

Thea caught sight of a black shield with the symbol of the Sondras: the elusive and wise owl. Thea considered emerging from her hiding place, but remembered she'd be in big trouble for wandering so far into the forest by herself. She wondered if it would be best to wait until the Sondras left to find her way back to camp on her own. But then the decision was made for her.

Out of nowhere, an arm draped in black cloth covered her small head with a cloak, blocking her view and plucking her with ease from her leafy hideaway. There were no words spoken; Thea heard only the breathy snorting and pounding gallops of the horse she'd been hoisted onto. With Thea's blindfold still in place, she could not see anything, but she felt the strong hand of a Sondra warrior steadying her as the horse hurtled through the air at an incredible speed.

Bouncing along, all Thea could think about was what she'd just seen in the forest. The Sondras were more swift and powerful than she'd ever imagined. In less than a minute, they'd taken down a group of armed soldiers with ease.

Before long, they arrived at Thea's camp, nestled at the top of a hill in the thickest part of the woodlands. Thea's blindfold was removed, and she was immediately taken to the head instructor at the girls' encampment to face the consequences of having skipped training to run amok in the woods. The commanders and teachers took training very seriously, and Thea knew she would be in significant trouble.

To ensure Amazon survival, each of the eight tribes filled their days with relentless fight training. Everyone was expected to be skilled in the ways of war, with the fiercest moving on to become Sondras. Amazons worked hard to master archery, horsemanship, spear throwing, swordplay, hand-to-hand combat, and all other aspects of battle.

Thea's teacher, who in her youth had been a Sondra and now worked as Queen Alexa's head commander, asked to see the young girl alone.

"Thea, you have disappointed us once again by missing training because of your insolence. This time you put yourself in grave danger. What do you think would have happened to you if the Argive soldiers found you before we did?"

Sitting meekly on a small chair, Thea stared at her feet, keeping quiet so as not to further incriminate herself with her teacher.

The instructor continued, hardening her tone, "Why you continue to waste your time in the forest when you could be training to benefit the whole tribe is a mystery to me, Thea. In addition to bringing danger upon yourself, you've made a mockery of a very important competition that took place today. You leave me no choice but to punish you."

Still looking at the ground, Thea dug her big toe into the dirt, drawing circles as she rotated her small foot. She wished that her scolding would come to an end so she could think more clearly about the events that had taken place in the forest. The instructor sensed that Thea was reflecting on something else.

"Thea! This is not a joke! Enough of this disrespect from you! As your punishment, you will clean out the stables for the rest of the day and will do without supper this evening. In addition, you will spend all day tomorrow practicing your archery. The next time you decide to break camp rules, you will be removed from training and assigned to permanent shoveling of the dung heaps. Do I make myself clear?"

Thea quickly pulled her feet underneath the chair and vigorously nodded her head, letting her commander know that she understood. The instructor huffed a frustrated breath and turned on her heel, leaving Thea on her own.

Maneuvering her way through an array of tents, Thea went to the barns where the horses were groomed and fed. The area was on the opposite end of the camp. As she walked, she thought of the brilliant attack she'd witnessed in the forest. While there were thousands of warriors in the eight Amazon tribes, there were only a few hundred Sondras. Sondras were famed for their ability to infiltrate enemy camps and be almost invisible until they struck. Today, Thea had watched these legends come alive. The Sondras Thea encountered were part of a small band entrusted to protect Amazon borders against invaders.

Thea passed by her group of trainees, lined up after their morning competition. They ranged in age from seven to fourteen, making Thea among the youngest. Most girls sought to become warriors, but many weren't sufficiently skilled. The latter would learn basic fighting skills, but then become farmers, physicians, musicians, carpenters, traders, or even seductresses.

Thea felt the girls' eyes on her and quickened her pace to avoid their scrutiny. At the head of the line stood Queen Alexa's grand-daughter, Laria, who was a few years older than Thea. Laria disliked Thea and drove most of the girls in camp to pick on her. She turned to look as Thea was passing and, with a gloating smile, beckoned her to come closer. A dozen girls stood behind Laria. Thea's best friend, Carina, stood waving like a madwoman. Her arms high above her flaming red hair, she smiled incessantly and gestured as though she was on fire.

Carina was born with a facial discoloration over half of her face that prompted many of the girls to tease and ostracize her. In addition to that, or perhaps because of it, she was helplessly clumsy and managed to fail every exam. Thea couldn't help but smile seeing Carina's exaggerated excitement. Despite the urgency to move on and get herself away from the watchful eyes of her peers, she walked toward Laria.

"So, Thea...how about a friendly competition?" Laria challenged, holding a spear. "Consider this a chance to prove to those of us who think you don't have a warrior's bone in your body that you aren't a complete failure."

"Sure. What do I have to do?" asked Thea.

"Just throw this spear and hit that fencepost," Laria said, pointing to a fence approximately thirty feet from where they stood. "Bonus points if the tip sticks. I'll go first."

Laria raised the spear over her head and threw it with a sharp, fluid motion. The spear found its mark, hitting hard enough to briefly penetrate the wooden post before falling to the ground. Laria's minions clapped and cheered. One of them ran to retrieve the spear, handing it to Thea. "Let's see you beat that!" the girl exclaimed.

The girls surrounded Thea as she focused on the fencepost, the spear high over her shoulder. Carina was wincing, afraid to take a breath.

Thea tossed the spear and it landed impotently, stirring up some dust about halfway to the fencepost. She then turned to Carina and gave her a wink, her way of showing solidarity. Most of the girls laughed. Carina exhaled, shook her head, and smiled.

"Time to start strengthening your hands. You're going to make a great milkmaid!" shouted Laria.

Then, two Sondras appeared on the other side of the group, grabbing everyone's attention by performing combat exercises against each other. The girls all shifted their positions to get a better look. Each of the Sondras was dressed in full battle attire. In addition to their black linen tunics, their faces were veiled with thin black sheaths of raw silk. All Sondras dyed their hair black with the crushed seed of a particular flower, which further helped to distinguish their appearance from other types of Amazon warriors.

The two elite fighters masterfully battled, showcasing the art of Amazon combat. They moved in silence, their lunges and thrusts inaudible to those around them. It was hard not to stop and gaze whenever a Sondra warrior passed by, but even more difficult when they were exhibiting their graceful expertise during practice. Thea watched them as well. Their limbs effortlessly moved through the air. The women were quick and in constant motion, never stopping to rest or reposition themselves. Their leaps and strikes resembled a dance more than a fighting technique. Thea was mesmerized. She could have stood there watching them forever, but decided to steal away while the rest of the girls were distracted.

As the Sondras continued their graceful display of aggression, a short, wizened spectator stood watching across the courtyard beneath the shade of a tree.

It was Seema. True to the promise she made to Elektra, she had kept a surreptitious eye on Thea during the girl's first seven years. Seema could see by the way Thea admiringly observed the Sondras' exercises that the first of Elektra's twin daughters already had lofty aspirations. Seema gave a slight nod of approval that no one would notice.

Despite the hard work awaiting her, arriving at the stables was a relief. Thea loved horses, and being around their calmness left her to her thoughts. It was damp and cool in the large barn, which made her work less grueling. Thea tended to each stall, cleaning out the horses' manure, and adding fresh straw and water. Her mind wandered.

Thea remembered Laria's cruel smile. As the granddaughter of the Queen, Laria was pampered. Her mother, an officer, was killed in battle when Laria was only two years old. So Queen Alexa doted on Laria. She wasn't required to sleep in the huts at night with the other girls. Instead, she stayed with her grandmother in the Queen's quarters, receiving special privileges such as her own horse and the finest weapons.

Like all Amazon tribal leaders since Elektra's rein, Queen Alexa had been a Sondra. Her dream was for Laria to take over her role one day, which was how she justified the advantages she showered on her granddaughter.

Laria knew this, and acted as if she was already royalty. But both Sondras and Queens had to earn their titles through achievement in competition. Queen Alexa couldn't award Laria any warrior position if the girl failed to excel in the tribe's battle contests.

Thea didn't stop for a break during her work in the stables, and was soon covered in sweat and grime. She took a bucket of water from the trough to rinse her face and fingers. Using her small hand to bring a refreshing splash of water to her face, throat, and back of her neck, Thea felt the branded mark at the nape of her sweaty hairline.

Carina had told her what the strange emblem looked like, though she'd never been able to see it herself. The scarred flesh of her neck stood out from the soft skin around it. She could feel the intersecting serpents that had been burned into her, their origin a mystery. What on Earth could they mean, and who had placed them there?

From the corner of Thea's eye, she spotted a small python entering the stables at the far end of the structure. Without hesitation, Thea reached to the side of her leg to grab her knife. The python slithered through the stall's entrance, extending and retracting its forked tongue as if tasting the air before it. In a flash, Thea flicked her wrist and sent the blade spinning toward the serpent seventy paces from where she stood.

With barely a pause, Thea continued to carefully examine the intricate details of the tattoo. For as long as she could remember, the branding mark had been a part of her. She'd been told that a messenger brought her to the tribe and left her in their care when she was just an infant. They'd raised her along with the rest of the Amazon girls but never knew from where she came.

"Finished?" an instructor asked from the door of the stable behind her, shaking Thea from her thoughts.

"Yes," Thea responded, defeated. Thinking about her family and wondering why they'd abandoned her always made her sad.

"Take the lantern and go to your hut, Thea," the instructor said. "Let's not have a repeat performance tomorrow." The instructor disappeared from the doorway.

Thea took a sip from her flask and walked over to collect her knife. The snake's head was completely severed from its body. Her knife stood erect, trapping the python's writhing body in the hard-packed soil. Wiping the blade clean along the side of her garments, Thea made her way to the girl's hut, still contemplating the meaning of her tattoo.

Thea's grumbling stomach reminded her that she'd not eaten supper and was getting hungry. Then she heard rustling in the nearby trees. Exposed by the light of the moon, Carina emerged and hopped into step alongside her friend.

"I had to wait until the rest of the girls were sleeping to bring you this." She handed Thea a portion of that evening's dinner: two chunks of bread, with wild boar and cheese.

"Thanks, Carina," Thea said. "I actually am pretty hungry."

"I thought you might be," Carina said, smiling. "I'd better be going. I don't want my group master to realize I'm not in the sleeping quarters. See you tomorrow, okay?"

"All right. See you tomorrow," Thea replied.

"You know, you might consider holding your tongue now and then," Carina said. "But I guess if you did, you wouldn't be Thea." Carina smiled again, and made her way back to her group.

The other girls were already asleep when Thea entered her hut. She blew out the lantern she'd carried back with her and lay down on the soft bedding, exhausted from the day. When she rolled onto her back, slumber was almost immediate.

But while sleep came easily, it was not without its own battles. In a dream, Thea found herself crouched in the woods, sword drawn. A mist in the air obscured her sight, but instinct told her something dangerous was near. As Thea turned into a small clearing, a veiled warrior approached with sword in hand. The two engaged in battle, with fierce blows powerful enough to cripple a dozen warriors, yet neither one fell. As they fought, Thea escaped a near-fatal strike, then hit back and unveiled her opponent. To Thea's surprise, it was a face that looked exactly like her own. Thea suffered this troublesome dream almost every night. The battle was always vicious, and each time it ended the same way, with her opponent being herself.

CHAPTER 6

A DEFINING MOMENT

At the age of sixteen, Prince Zarek's bloodlust was already well-established. His detractors—who were legion—claimed it began when his mother, Queen Rheia, died during childbirth. Owlish and overweight, Zarek's formative years were not pleasant, despite having all the benefits of a royal upbringing. His father, King Bedros, blamed his sole heir for the death of his wife. Though Bedros tried to give his son the best possible life, he had difficulty dealing with the boy.

Zarek was raised mostly by a series of nursemaids. Some of them he loved. Others requested to be released from their position after falling victim to one too many of their young charge's disturbing and bloody pranks—such as stashing a severed animal head in their quarters.

King Bedros ruled over the city-state of Argos, which was situated on plains northeast of the peninsula, near the Gulf of Argolic. Located north of Sparta and west of Athens, Argos was similar in culture and ideology to Athens, and therefore they were often allies. Like Athens, Argos was known as a haven for artists and art lovers. It produced many notable painters, musicians, and sculptors, and was acclaimed throughout the land for its beautiful vases and life-like statues. As a patron of the arts and a prolific painter himself,

Bedros was very proud of this. He frequently attended plays, gallery openings, and arts festivals.

Another philosophy which ran parallel to Athens—and was notably different from Sparta—was its thinking regarding females. In brief, women were deemed as property in Argos. Their husbands, fathers, brothers, and sons owned them. Sparta, meanwhile, treated women as free individuals. The Spartans were a military people—training their residents for battle from the age of seven. As such, women were expected to contribute to society's military upbringing.

Argos had a large and well-trained army, but Bedros was a peace-loving king and loathed to use it except in response to a direct invasion or defense.

Zarek was usually left to his own devices at one end of the grounds while his father was somewhere else. The labyrinthine castle provided ample hiding places for orchestrating imaginary scenarios. During Zarek's formative years, he would spend hours acting out fantasies in which he was a leader of armies—his favorite part being the violent interrogation, and ultimately torture, of captured enemy soldiers.

At the age of nine, he began using animals, usually stolen pets, as stand-ins for the soldiers. With a crude array of tools—including knives, pins, and eating utensils that he bent and sharpened—these unfortunate creatures were gouged, slit open, burned, and dismembered. When the bones were left intact, he saved them, tying them together and creating bizarre skeletal monstrosities—rabbit skeletons with bird heads, or decomposing rat bodies with attached skeletal wings. When he found an owl's regurgitated pellet in the forest containing the bones of little creatures the bird couldn't digest, he considered it a treasure trove of spare parts. He kept these in a dirty nook in the castle's foundation—a place he was sure no one else would look.

King Bedros tried to encourage his young son to become involved in his love of the arts by providing him with the best painting materials. However, Zarek was unable to translate the visions in his mind onto a canvas. After many frustrated failures, Zarek decided to show his father an artistic endeavor of which he was truly proud—one of his animal bone sculptures. Bedros found it an abomination, and was unable to hide his disgust, hurting Zarek's feelings without even speaking a word.

Zarek's interior life based on violence and ugliness set him apart from his peers. Though he was enrolled in the finest primary school, he was a below-average student, struggling with both schoolwork and the ability to make friends. Being overweight, he was consistently a failure in athletics. Reading was a confusing, frustrating chore for him. Words appeared backward and twisted. He understood less than his classmates and would complete only the bare minimum of his assignments. When called upon in class, he would typically have to make up an answer, or simply cry. This garnered ridicule from his classmates, though they generally kept it to themselves for fear of his family's power.

On Zarek's tenth birthday his father gave him a hunting hound, which he called Alva. Zarek grew somewhat attached to the dog, but King Bedros developed an even stronger bond to the creature, showering it with the affection that Zarek felt should have been directed toward him. Still, Alva would accompany Zarek on his woodland adventures, helping him to capture rabbits.

When he was twelve, Zarek was no longer content killing small animals and birds. He decided to test his emotions to see if he could kill without remorse. To accomplish his mission, he set out into the woods with his dog, and did not stop until they arrived at a favorite spot of Zarek's—a rocky cliff where a stream ran twelve feet below. Zarek sat down on the edge, as he usually did, with Alva beside him. It was a warm day, and Zarek felt the sweat running down his back as he rested in the shade of the trees. After a few contemplative moments, Zarek abruptly placed one hand on the dog's neck and the other on his haunches...and gave a shove.

Though Alva weighed approximately sixteen pounds, he was caught off guard and didn't offer resistance. Giving out a yelp of surprise, he tumbled end over end, hitting the wet rocks below. It was a moment before Alva began whimpering audibly. There was a great deal of blood, and it was clear that at least one of his legs was broken.

Looking down at his suffering pet, Zarek felt a twinge of regret, but he knew he would have to suppress such feelings to accomplish his goals. He would have to come to terms with killing those close to him.

He located a large rock that he could comfortably lift and carried it back to the cliff's edge, just above where Alva lay. He aimed for the dog's head and let the rock fall. The animal's head was instantly crushed, abruptly ending the whimpering. Zarek felt much more at ease with what he had done when he no longer had to listen to Alva's cries.

Later that evening, King Bedros noticed the dog's absence.

"Zarek, have you seen Alva? He never misses his evening meal."

"Father, he ran off into the woods today. He was chasing a rabbit and I lost track of him. I was going to tell you, but I was sure he would come back by now. He always does..."

After several days, King Bedros gave up all hope of Alva returning. But he never doubted the truth of Zarek's story.

As an adolescent, Zarek found a mentor in an old woman named Kthonia who lived in solitude in a forest hut just outside the village. Kthonia was feared by most—even King Bedros—and was viewed with great suspicion by all. Her specialty was the dark arts, dealing in witchcraft and the demons of the underworld. Zarek sought her out and won her friendship behind his father's back. She fostered Zarek's belief in magic, and he frequently solicited her advice about spells and incantations.

While Zarek's skills with torture and darkness progressed, his sexual experience remained limited. This was due to both his antisocial nature and his awkward appearance. During educational retreats with the children of other royals and high-ranking government officials, he'd engaged in mutual masturbation with other boys and, at age fifteen, managed to lose his virginity to an equally unattractive girl he'd known since childhood. Zarek enjoyed the experience and craved more of it. However, as he matured and his desires intensified, his sexual fantasies became violent. He envisioned orgies with dozens of men and women coupled in every imaginable combination, with him at the center of it all. He pictured bodies pumping, throbbing, and writhing...until the moment when he pulled a cord, releasing a hundred daggers from the ceiling, impaling all participants, and drenching him in their blood as he climaxed.

King Bedros required hundreds of slaves to keep his enormous compound running efficiently. Zarek had grown particularly attracted to one slave who worked in his part of the castle. Selene, fifteen and pretty, had been born into servitude, performing mostly domestic duties. Though Zarek knew it would never be socially acceptable for him to enter into a romantic relationship with her, it was common for masters to have their slaves engage in relations, whether consensual or forced. Zarek had no reservations about using his position of power to fulfill his needs.

Over the course of several weeks, Zarek had been gradually attempting to expand the scope of his communication with Selene. Going out of his way to pass her on the grounds of the castle, which usually meant through the kitchen, he would smile at her, and then briefly speak with her in stolen moments away from her duties and fellow slaves.

"Selene, I have a task with which I would like you to help me," Zarek told her one day. "It requires a short walk. Please don't tell anyone, as it involves a surprise for my father and I wouldn't want him to catch word of it."

"Of course, Prince Zarek," Selene replied. "I am honored to serve you in any way I can. Will this task require that I bring anything?"

"Only yourself and your strength," he answered. "Meet me by the stables tomorrow after your chores."

Zarek was restless that night, cementing the plan in his mind. The following afternoon he grew so anxious that his muscles felt as if they were wiggling under his skin. He procured a roast chicken, an assortment of fresh fruit, and a flask of wine, put them in a basket, and went to meet Selene. She was waiting for him when he arrived.

"Ah, Selene," he said. "I've brought refreshments for us, as this may take some time. I'll explain the task at hand when we get there."

They walked through the forest for more than an hour. The heat had made them both perspire, but the sun was beginning to set, offering a respite from its rays. They finally reached the destination Zarek had selected—a grouping of large rocks in a green clearing. They sat down, exhausted.

"We're here!" Zarek exclaimed.

Selene looked around and smiled uncomfortably. "What is it you would like me to do, Prince Zarek?"

Zarek opened the basket and began taking out the provisions.

"Selene, I would like to help you. I could make your life much easier, give you anything you like. I find you very beautiful."

"Master, I don't understand," Selene confessed.

"Here, have some wine. Please, just enjoy yourself." Zarek poured wine into two iron cups.

Selene was confused, but she'd never heard of any of her fellow servants receiving ill treatment in the home of King Bedros, so she drank. Zarek drank with her, and they talked with a decreasing level of awkwardness about events that had been occurring in the castle.

After an hour had elapsed, Selene was considerably drunk. Zarek, determined to control the situation, had been merely sipping his wine. He leaned over, put a hand on her breast, and clumsily put his mouth on hers.

Though she didn't find Zarek attractive, she felt privileged to be with him. The alcohol had prevented her from overthinking the situation. His touch was rough—he squeezed her breast rather tightly—and his kiss was sloppy and showed no restraint, but she acquiesced without protest.

Within moments, he had removed her tunic, and she lay naked on the rock before him. She didn't feel comfortable helping him undress. He lifted his garments over his head, revealing a full and eager erection. The rock was hard on his knees as he knelt, pulled her legs apart, and pushed himself into her. She smiled and cooed at first, but as he began thrusting faster and faster, showing little technique—and even less consideration for her pleasure—she began to grimace in discomfort. Zarek noticed this, and it only encouraged him.

Before she had an opportunity to notice, he reached into the basket he had brought, which he had purposefully kept by his side.

Knowing he couldn't withhold his orgasm for much longer, he gripped a knife, brought it up, and slashed it across the left side of Selene's neck. She jerked back wide-eyed, smashing her head against the rock as she gasped for air, unsure of what had happened. He had opened her jugular vein, spraying the both of them with her blood. She wrenched and kicked, suddenly panicking, but he held tightly to her waist.

Feeling empowered and aroused by what he had done—the culmination of years of dreaming and planning—Zarek climaxed and withdrew as Selene took her final breaths. He sat for a moment and closed his eyes, collecting his thoughts.

"Hades, I do this for you. Fill me with your power. I do not fear the darkness, and embrace you for all that you represent. Help me use the blood of others to gain all that I desire," he recited almost angrily, eyes closed.

It was nearly dark, and Zarek knew he'd have to clean himself up—as well as the rock on which they'd lain—and then find a place to hide her corpse. As his body performed these chores, his mind was already thinking ahead to potential prey.

Zarek also began planning new scenarios, such as involving multiple victims, and bringing along an audience that he'd force to watch his performances.

The possibilities were endless.

CHAPTER 7

SWEET REVENGE

The sun rose over the sea, signaling the new morning. Dawn was a time for the early merchants along the seaside port of Kiato to prepare for another busy day. Vessels sitting just offshore began to pull anchor and dock so the cargo could be unloaded and readied for trade. Others set sail in hopes of a bounty of fish. As Mercury started his race across the sky, the merchants began their pursuit of trade and profit.

A merchant's survival depended on how many people he could coerce to his stall during market hours. Most only did well enough to get by, but their lives were superior to Teigra's in every way. Now fourteen, she'd been a slave to so many masters that she'd lost count. One after another, each would tire of her and sell her back to the traders, or to another master. It was a miracle she'd held onto her will to live, surviving only by her strength and determination to fight through each new day.

Teigra's current master, Acacius, was a tax collector for the Kiato officials, and one of the wealthiest men in town. Teigra had learned long ago that such men often suffered the nastiest wives, and that was especially true of Acacius' spouse, Doris. Teigra couldn't decide whether the most ruthless women sought the richest men, or if these men worked around the clock to avoid their wives and thus became wealthy. Either way, Teigra consistently found herself in the homes of affluent men and brutal women.

Despite her many hardships, she had grown to be tall, strong, and extremely beautiful. Her golden locks, coupled with her emerald green eyes, were captivating. While this made her appealing to the men who shopped in slave markets, it made her life difficult when meeting their wives. Her looks alone were enough to provoke the wrath of an unhappy spouse...such as the one she was currently serving.

"Teigra! Where is our breakfast? You are the slowest dunce!"

"Coming, Mistress," Teigra responded, through clenched teeth.

Negotiating a tray of food, Teigra carefully ascended the stairs into the upper chambers of the house. The tax collector's immaculate home sat on a hillside overlooking the water. Few houses were more than one level, but his was three. From the top room, one could watch the ships on the horizon come and go over the glistening sea. It was a majestic sight that Teigra had noticed while toiling over the massive space.

"Your breakfast, Mistress," Teigra said, as she entered the bedchamber.

"What in the name of Zeus took you so long, child?" scolded Doris. "Now quit wasting time and get to cleaning the stalls. I expect you to be done by midmorning." The woman looked away, acting as if Teigra no longer existed.

"Yes, Mistress."

Teigra gave Doris a hard stare and turned to leave. Acacius hadn't returned home the previous evening, which wasn't unusual, but it always sent his wife into an even more foul mood. Acacius' routine excuse was that the town officials had required him to work late, going over the tax revenues. Acacius was a small man, as round as he was short. Teigra despised him as well, for there was something devious about him. Sometimes she would see him watching her as she scrubbed the floors, his beady little eyes following her as she labored on her hands and knees.

"Girl, did you not hear me?"

"Yes, Mistress," Teigra mumbled. "I heard you."

"You'd better watch that tone, child, or you know the consequences," Doris warned. "Now go!"

Teigra cleaned the stalls outside, shoveling dung, moving straw, and filling the troughs. Acacius had nearly a dozen horses, in addition to hens and goats, but the daily task of tending to the animals was much easier than tending to the couple—at least the animals didn't yell at her or strike whelps on her back.

At age fourteen, Teigra wondered what else the world could possibly have in store for her. She'd seen wealthy children walking through town, smiles on their faces, arm in arm with their mothers. She'd never known such simple peace and contentment. Instead of daydreaming about riding horses, falling in love, and the pleasures of spring, she thought of revenge against Acacius and Doris.

Teigra had been with the tax collector for nearly a year, her longest service to any master. Had she become less defiant? By the scars on her back and legs, it didn't appear so. Doris habitually threatened to trade her for another servant—Teigra had heard her insist on it several times—but Acacius always vetoed her. Teigra had once purposefully spilled a hot bowl of broth on Doris' legs and figured her days at their home were over, but Acacius continued to keep her—after administering a profound beating, of course.

Teigra could see the short little man ride up the hill on horseback. Still dressed in his clothes from the previous day, he slouched on his horse, visibly tired. He trotted over to the stalls and dismounted, tying his horse off for Teigra to lead home.

"Tend to my horse, girl," barked the little man.

"Yes, Master," Teigra replied.

"And when you're done, go fetch some fresh wildflowers for the Mistress," he continued. "Bring them to me immediately."

"Yes, Master."

Teigra led the horse into the stall, and then proceeded up the hilly terrain to collect some of the beautiful wildflowers that recently burst into bloom. The little pig of a man had no doubt been indulging himself all evening and wanted to appease his wife with a pretty bouquet. Teigra could smell the stale stench of wine on his breath.

Doris wouldn't fall for his lies, but at least she'd get what she wanted, a purse of silver coins with which to visit the market for the day. The exchange between this couple always came down to a purse of coins.

Teigra returned to the house with a handful of purple, yellow, and white budding flowers. She could hear the argument as she rounded the curve of the stairs leading to the chambers.

"Dear, I would have been here sooner if it wasn't for the magistrate's demands. He insisted that I produce a full accounting of the town's taxes last evening. It was miserable! I worked tirelessly all night!"

"Surely you could have sent a messenger to your wife! Out of sight, out of mind I am to you."

"Now dear, you know that's not true. The only place I wanted to be was here with you."

Teigra knocked twice and entered their room with the flowers in her hand. Acacius immediately seized the opportunity.

"Look, dear," he said. "I had the girl collect these flowers for you. I saw them on the hillside and instantly thought of your beauty. You share the same innocent tenderness."

"Hmph! This is all I am worth to you—a clump of wildflowers from our own yard?"

"No, dear, not at all. Please, take my purse and go to the market. Buy whatever you'd like. The greatest wealth I have is my affection for you."

Doris gave a slight smile and greedily grabbed the heavy purse of coins. The argument was over. Teigra thought that anything could be had for money or power. Either you bought what you wanted or you took it. There seemed to be no other way.

Teigra spent the rest of the day scrubbing the house floors, cleaning the pots and plates, mending shirts, and tending the livestock. Acacius slept the day away, while Doris readied herself for the market, running back and forth from room to room, in a desperate attempt to make herself more presentable. Her hair was thin and almost entirely gray. She was as heavy as an ox and spilled out of her garments. The robes barely contained her heft. She had rough patches of skin on her arms that were covered with scabs she constantly picked.

Even as she focused on the impossible task of making herself pretty, Doris didn't for one moment let Teigra forget that she was being watched. Teigra looked forward to the Mistress' absence for a few hours. Perhaps she'd be able to take a break and sneak a small snack, for she hadn't eaten since supper.

Teigra's hopes were soon dashed, as Doris gave her numerous dinner duties and chores to perform. There would be no rest for Teigra until all of these tasks were completed. If she failed, her one meager daily meal would be withheld.

Late in the afternoon, Doris finally left. It was only a short walk down the hillside to the center of town, which lay adjacent to a port, so the area enjoyed a tremendous amount of activity that typically went late into the evening.

After strenuous preparation, Teigra completed supper. "Your dinner, Master," she announced, as she delivered his meal upstairs. The smell of the pheasant had tortured her all the way to the bedchambers, where Acacius had insisted on eating.

"Excellent!" he replied. "Teigra, fetch the jug of wine as well." She traveled back to the kitchen to collect the wine, feeling aches in her body every step of the way. The day had been long, and she was exhausted. While Acacius feasted, her dinner of watery stew and a small piece of bread was still hours away.

"Here is the wine, Master," Teigra said upon her return.

"Teigra, stay and keep me company. I do not like to eat alone," he commanded, taking a juicy morsel of the pheasant with his fingers and pushing the meat into his mouth.

"Teigra, you have outdone yourself! This is delicious."

He tore a chunk of bread from his plate and dipped it in the meat drippings. "Oh, how rude of me, would you like a taste?"

"No, Master," Teigra responded, suspicious of his intent. She had roasted the pheasant in wine and herbs, and it smelled delicious.

"You must. I insist. I know you are hungry, girl. My wife has been working you hard, hasn't she?" Acacius asked, in an uncharacteristically caring voice.

Teigra's hunger and fatigue overpowered her suspicion, and she cautiously accepted the meat, eating slowly as he watched.

"How about some wine, Teigra?" he continued. "You must be thirsty as well."

"No, Master," Teigra again replied, puzzled by his kindness.

"Now, Teigra, no need to worry. Here is a cup. Drink."

Teigra accepted the full cup and began to drink, keeping her eyes on her sudden benefactor. Was this some sort of trick? Was he going to beat her for accepting the food and wine? The fowl and wine were like medicine to her body. It'd been a long time since she'd eaten anything other than watery soup and stale bread. Perhaps he was feeling sorry for her, she thought, or had been truthful in his admission that he didn't want to eat alone.

"You are thirsty, my dear," Acacius observed, smiling. "Come here and let me fill your cup again."

Teigra slowly walked to his bed and watched as he poured wine from the jug into her cup. She'd never been served anything by anyone before. The second cup was even sweeter than the first. Her head began to feel light, and she felt a rush of warmth.

"Sit, girl," he said. "Rest your feet a bit. You have been working hard all day, and I am sure a break will do you good."

Teigra did as she was told, feeling less fearful. As she sat next to the Master, she could feel the relief in her legs as the burden of her weight suddenly was transferred onto the soft bed. Acacius gave her another morsel of pheasant, and once again filled her cup with wine. Teigra couldn't remember being treated so well in her life, and had certainly never had so much wine. She gulped it quickly, unsure if she would ever have another chance to taste its sweetness. She was so content that a small smile appeared on her pink lips without her even noticing.

Teigra then realized that Acacius had begun to stroke her golden hair. She immediately tensed up as he extended his touch from her hair down the length of her back and around her waist. She tried to shift her position away from his side, but his meaty hands held her tightly and pulled her closer.

"Now, Teigra, don't you want to please your Master? Come sit a little closer and I will pour you more wine. It would be rude not to accept such generosity."

"Master, thank you, but I must tend to my chores," Teigra said, as she tried to stand.

"Ah, but pleasing your Master is your chore, girl," he said, as he tightened his grip on her waist, his smile turning to a snarl.

Teigra now understood his motives. Unfortunately, her mind felt fuzzy and sluggish.

She tried to stand. Acacius had anticipated this and grabbed her with both arms, pushing her onto the bed.

She tried to kick him, but he straddled her with his thick thighs, trapping her legs onto the bed as he forced her onto her back.

It took only one of his hands to hold both of her arms down. He used the other to pull up the hem of her ragged dress. With a ferocious tug, he pulled hard and tore the old material of the dress all the way up to the neckline. The sight of her young flesh inflamed him, and he bit down hard on her nipple.

Teigra struggled, but the Master's weight was too much for her. When he licked her neck, the wetness of his tongue felt like a large snail oozing across her skin.

Then Acacius reached down to fiddle with the front of his robe. Teigra took advantage of this opening to free one arm and strike him on the side of his head. The blow did little to slow him. However, when he responded by slapping her hard in the face, Teigra was able to regain control of both of her arms.

She could feel his full weight on top of her as he slid down and forced her legs open with one of his knees. "Come, girl," he said. "Don't make this more difficult than it has to be. If you stop struggling, you might even enjoy it."

He lifted his weight for a split second and, as if in a dream, time slowed down. Teigra felt a sharp, searing pain between her legs, and she gasped in horror—it was as if a dagger had struck her soul. The man placed a sweaty hand over her face, covering her nose and mouth, making it hard for her to breathe. She begged death to come and take her. What little innocence was left had now been destroyed.

With each thrust, the sweaty man made a grunting noise and pushed himself harder inside of her. She gave up the struggle and lay quietly, weeping as he finished, feeling pieces of herself drift away into the night air. After all the years of barely holding on, Teigra finally felt herself let go completely.

With a final heave, the man was done. He lay for a moment slumped on her, tired from his exertions and still heavily breathing.

Just then a voice sounded from the doorway. "You two! I knew it!" It was Doris, having just returned from the marketplace.

Teigra found herself uncovered and exposed by the mass of flesh that had just devoured her. Acacius was on his feet, facing his wife with a look in his eyes somewhere between surprise and fear. The room had grown dark, but Doris held a small lantern that shed enough light to expose the scene before her.

"Wha—What are you doing here?" stammered Acacius.

"You filthy beast!" his wife yelled, horrified. "Carrying on with this whore while I was away buying goods for our home!"

"No, no, that's not it at all," he protested. "I...I thought she was you!"

Doris paused, giving him the time to develop his story.

"It was dark and I was in bed, dear," Acacius continued. "The girl came into my room and pretended to be you! I didn't realize!"

"What? You little slut! How dare you steal my bed! You will pay within a breath of your worthless life, you insolent tramp!"

"Smell her breath. She's been stealing wine as well," he said, seeing a chance to strengthen his story.

Unable to speak and still in shock by what had transpired, Teigra could barely move. Rolled up in a ball on the bed, she clutched her legs against her body, trying to repair what had been destroyed.

"Out, whore!" Doris barked, as the whelps of her whip slapped against Teigra's bare flesh. Teigra scurried, fleeing the unending slices of pain as she moved through the door as quickly as possible.

As she ran, her ripped tunic left her partially exposed. She was still wet with her Master's sweat and semen. The Mistress chased after her, lashing as she ran, all the way to Teigra's tiny room at the bottom of the steps.

"You shan't be sleeping in that room tonight, tramp! Get in the chest, now!"

The chest was a wooden crate barely big enough to hold a child. Teigra had spent the night in the chest just once, as punishment for spilling the scalding soup on Doris. She had to squat to fit inside, sitting on her haunches the entire time. After a few hours in the chest, she could hardly move. An outside bolt held the structure shut, preventing escape.

"Get in, I tell you!" Doris screamed, while still doling out lashings against Teigra's back, arms, and legs.

Stinging pain searing her skin, Teigra hurried to do as she was told and squatted inside the chest. Doris slammed the lid shut and secured the bolt while yelling profanities at Teigra, and then stormed off to deal with her husband.

Though the chest protected Teigra from the brutal pain of the whip, her legs were already starting to cramp from the uncomfortable position. The slats of wood were crudely nailed together so there were spaces between them, allowing in small amounts of moonlight from the window. Crunched up against her legs, Teigra could see droplets of blood slowly dripping from her thighs to the rough floor of the chest. She didn't know if the blood was coming from her lashed skin or from where Acacius had torn her on the inside. She was exhausted and beaten, and felt destroyed.

Teigra thought of the animals in the stalls and how they had a better life than hers. She considered the peace of death. But if she were to take her own life, it would mean she'd accepted defeat.

Suddenly, somewhere within the void of her soul, a smoldering rage began to replace the emptiness. A bitterness and hatred that had been longing to unveil itself was on the verge of exploding. It had been given final permission to appear in the absence of anything that could represent hope.

The desire for something more out of life had dimly burned within Teigra for as long as she could remember. Now Teigra could feel all those stifled emotions welling up, ready to be released. What surprised her most was that these emotions were not of sadness or grief for the injustices she'd suffered, but built from a ferocious desire to finally be the master of her own destiny.

A determination rose within Teigra that pulled her into focus. She was not going to allow herself to be beaten and dominated, to be treated worse than an animal, ever again.

Teigra quietly crouched in her locked crate. What had a moment ago been pain in her legs was now just heat fueling the wrath that was burning within her. She knew what needed to be done, and waited with silent resolve for the house to grow quiet.

It was past midnight, but Teigra remained awake. She was replaying the evening's events over and over again in her mind. She thought about how her Master had tricked her, raped her, and then blamed everything on her; and of her Mistress' cruelty toward her every single day since she'd arrived.

The house was dark, but a shimmer of moonlight lit the room in small slivers. Teigra could barely see the door, which was closed. It was time to make her move.

She took a deep breath. With the palm of her right hand, she began pounding upward on the wooden slat of the crate. The wood didn't budge. She methodically repeated the pounding, over and over again, until the pain of slamming her hand against the wood made her wince. She didn't stop to think about the stinging in her hand, but continued to pound repeatedly, with even more vigor.

After what seemed like an eternity, the slat started to loosen. She switched hands and, this time using a full fist, punched upward at the loosening plank of wood.

Feeling the board move motivated Teigra, and suddenly she was full of rage again. Her anger fueled more power within her tired muscles and torn flesh, and before she realized it, she was using the force of her breath to move faster and punch harder. With each exhalation, Teigra propelled her fist upward as hard as she could in the small space, loosening the plank a little bit more.

Finally, she felt it give—one side of the board dropped completely from the nails. She pushed on the plank and felt it lift.

Experiencing such relief that she nearly shouted, Teigra momentarily closed her eyes and smiled to herself.

Reaching her hand outside of the liberated plank, Teigra felt around until she found the latch holding the rest of the lid in place. Her bloodied fingers slipped on the bolt, but then landed on the spot where the bolt held the lid securely in place. There was no lock, only a latch. She wiggled and pushed against the tight latch, finally feeling the rusted metal turn. She clenched her teeth, pressing her body hard against the inside of the chest for leverage. Clink. The lever snapped open...and she was free.

Teigra slowly lifted the lid of the chest. She nearly gasped in pain as she unfolded her legs and carefully stood. Quietly making her way out of the small room where she'd been held prisoner, she walked on the tips of her toes to the kitchen.

Teigra took one of the sharpest knives and placed it in the belt of her shredded tunic. She also took two smaller knives, and used them to methodically create several strips of cloth from pieces of her tunic. She then cautiously made her way up the steps to the main room. Her movements were smooth and deliberate.

Teigra felt no fear and no pain. She wasn't numb, just steadfast and focused on the task at hand. For her entire life, she had been dominated and brutally subjugated. Now that she was old enough—and broken enough—there was nothing left to lose. Teigra silently vowed that she would always fight for herself.

The bedchamber was dark as she made her way through the doorway, moving as silently as a shadow. Teigra's eyes had time to adjust. She surveyed the sleeping bodies of her Master and Mistress. Gazing upon the snoring figures on the bed, she felt only one thing: utter hatred.

Without any need to think, Teigra's body went into swift action, leaping on top of the woman. Before Doris had time to realize what was happening, Teigra looked her in the eyes, smiled, and with a simple twist of her hands on either side of the woman's head snapped the Mistress' neck. Teigra's prey fell limp and lifeless onto the bed.

Acacius awoke at the sound of the cracking bone. Seeing Teigra on top of his wife, he immediately reached for his blade, which he kept on a table by the bedside. He managed to grab the weapon but was unable to use it, for Teigra's own knife pinned his fat hand to the wooden surface of the night table. A crimson spray squirted in every direction. He began to scream in agony—and even more so, in fear. Without hesitation, Teigra grabbed his other wrist and tied it against the bed's iron frame. She then tied both of his legs down using the strips of cloth.

"Help! Someone help!" Acacius screamed. His pleading was futile. No one could hear him.

Teigra took her time lighting a lantern hanging in the doorway. She then walked over to the pathetic, writhing little man on the bed. She would take pleasure in this, although she was aware that her escape was best made under the shelter of what night still remained. Her Master was a well-respected public official, and his absence would be noticed. Someone would be sent to the house looking for him when he didn't arrive at the magistrate's office in the morning. She just had one final order of business to attend to—and it would not take long.

From her belt, Teigra removed the sharpest knife and held it like a hunter going in for the kill. She moved slowly toward the man, seeing the fear in his eyes as the dim light bounced shadows on her face. She then carefully cut the man's tunic from his body in strips, as he whimpered and begged her to set him free.

"Please, please! Whatever it is that you want to do to me, think about it, girl! I can make you rich. I will pay you any amount that you like, just put down the knife!"

"Silence! You dare make me an offer of riches? You putrid, shameful snake. I should cut out your eyes to teach you a lesson! But I have a better plan."

The man was sweating profusely, his contorted face glistening in the candlelight.

"Teigra," he cried, "please, don't do anything you'll regret. I can make you rich! I will say Doris had an accident and you will be spared any repercussions!"

"I have no interest in what you consider 'riches,' you filthy dog! Just as you took from me what was precious, I will take the same from you."

She smiled again, and with fury in her eyes, she took the last piece of cloth and stuffed it in his mouth. Holding his genitals in her left hand and pulling them hard away from his body, she took the knife and held it high. Light from the lantern shimmered off the blade as the fat little man tried to scream through his gag, while his body frantically thrashed about, trying to break free.

In one swift motion, Teigra swung the blade and separated the Master's body from his testicles.

Blood spewed onto the bed and Acacius shook uncontrollably, his eyes rolling up into his head in agony.

Teigra stood back and watched his torment, satisfied. Her revenge was complete.

As Acacius' body slowed its convulsions, his muffled moans grew more labored.

Teigra leaned in close and whispered into his ear. "I think I'll keep these to remember you." She then calmly turned and walked out of the room, taking the lantern, and leaving her former master choking and whimpering as he bled to death in the dark.

Teigra descended the steps, washed, changed into a clean tunic, and packed some food into a burlap sack. She wrapped the bloody, severed testicles tightly into a rag, placed them in her pouch, and tied it.

As Teigra left to make her escape into the darkness of the woods, she broke the lantern open on a large rug in the main entrance hall, setting the house aflame. There would be nothing left but ashes.

Teigra looked into the night and saw a clear sky full of stars. She gazed into the sparkling wilderness and vowed never to fall under anyone's rule again. It was now clear that, to survive, she had to outwit, outmaneuver, and overpower the many cruel people in the world.

She broke into a run and vanished into the woods, with the burning glow from the house at her back. For the first time in her life, Teigra had no master, no mistress, and no one to break her. She was finally free. It was a sensation she would fight to hold onto, no matter the cost.

Deep into the forest, feeling the weight of sleep upon her, Teigra curled up under a fallen tree and slept. She was at peace for the very first time. Her destiny was finally her own.

CHAPTER 8
THE RESCUE

The Amazon woods were alive with the fresh scents of spring, and a mild coolness permeated the air. Wildflowers were blooming, radiant in their colors, and the trees were painted in vibrant shades of green. A sense of freedom blossomed within Thea as she tried to enjoy a day away from training. Nothing was more satisfying than exploring the forest she loved so much. She was now fourteen, and had grown tall and beautiful. She'd kept a spirit of independence and defiance over the years, often managing to sneak away from camp. As she explored the forest alone, she felt perfectly at home, fearing nothing. She usually delighted in these moments, dreaming of explorations she had yet to undertake, but not today.

Thea had traveled to the western edge of her tribe's lands, with a goal to reach the mystic Mount Spiro. The trip was difficult because of the treacherous landscape. It required skill to traverse the jagged rocks, cliffs, and thick underbrush, and she welcomed the challenge. For some strange reason she had been crying. Thea felt sick to her stomach, as though someone or something had attacked her, and she didn't know why. She needed time alone.

After traveling all morning, Thea arrived at the foot of the mountain. On the other side of the rocky descent, she spotted another patch of woods. It included a pond fed by a small stream flowing directly from Mount Spiro. During the rainy season the stream turned into a raging river.

As Thea made her way through these woods, something caught her eye at the pond's edge. Standing brilliantly against the background of freshly sprouting grass stood a beautiful black horse. Thea froze in place and studied the exquisite creature. Never had she seen such a large and grandiose mare.

The creature turned to face her. The horse was incredibly stout, and her coat was so shiny it could be mistaken for black silk. Thea moved closer, pausing in the open so the horse could acknowledge her presence. She expected the mare to run away, but instead she slowly raised her head and looked Thea directly in the face.

Cautiously, Thea approached. At any moment, the mare could have bolted into the woods, never to be seen again; but she remained still and calm.

"Easy, girl," Thea whispered. "Nothing to fear."

When Thea was ten paces away, the horse finally stirred, stepping back from the water's edge, its gaze fixed on Thea. The mare's body stood erect, her head cocked to the side, and Thea could see more clearly how tall and stately this horse was.

She stepped even closer and gently reached out to stroke the bridge of the mare's nose. The horse's nostrils flared and she whinnied, but she stood in place. Thea was mesmerized.

"Good girl. How about a snack?"

While stroking the horse's nose with her left hand, Thea reached into a pouch for a small apple. The horse immediately stiffened her ears when she caught a glimpse of the red fruit. Thea palmed the morsel in front of the mare's mouth, and the apple was devoured without hesitation. With that peace offering, Thea slid her right hand along the side of the horse's neck to stroke her soft, coal-colored mane, finding it difficult to believe that a wild horse would let her get this close. It was rare to come upon an untamed horse, though she'd heard they used to exist in the forest.

"I shall call you Nox," Thea said. "You are as beautiful as the Queen of Darkness!"

Thea placed her left hand onto Nox's neck while reaching over the top of her mane with her right arm. In one graceful move, she slung herself onto the horse's back without Nox flinching. Sitting tall, Thea was in complete disbelief. She had ridden plenty of times and had a natural way with horses, but had never known anyone who could immediately tame a horse in the wild like that.

"Okay, Nox," Thea coaxed, "let's see what you'll let me do."

Crouching over her mane, Thea gave a nudge with her heels into Nox's sides while pulling the horse's mane in one direction. Nox bucked a couple of times at first, but then responded as Thea instructed. From trot to gallop, Thea felt the horse's strength as she rode across the field alongside the pond, leading Nox into the mountains. Nox galloped elegantly along the narrow trail. Riding on her muscular back, Thea sensed the massive amount of power beneath her. This, coupled with the springtime breeze blowing through her hair, made her feel alive.

Thea and Nox slowed to a trot, negotiating the obstacles in the forest, as they made their way back to Thea's tribe. The sun still had plenty of distance to travel in the sky before day's end, but Thea wanted to enjoy the ride home on her newfound treasure as long as she could.

As they moved through a patch of trees closer to camp, Thea could hear some voices in the brush. Slowly dismounting and feeling her feet on the soft earth, Thea led Nox by holding gently onto the long mane. The underbrush was heavy in places, and trying to keep her footsteps quiet was a challenge. Luckily, the conversation ahead was loud enough to drown out any noise Thea and Nox might have made as they crept closer.

"Look what we have here, Theo," said a gruff voice just beyond the trees. "A fine young maiden alone in the woods."

"Indeed, Fedro. What luck the Gods have shed on us today!"

Thea crept behind a tree, leaving Nox a few paces back. The horse stood still and began quietly nibbling on the grass at her feet. As Thea squinted and strained to grasp the scene in front of her, she saw two Argive slave traders dismounting from their horses and walking toward another figure. It appeared to be a young woman lying on the soft grassy floor.

"I suggest you leave!" a meek voice bellowed. "This is Amazon land, and I am not alone!"

Thea knew this voice, but never had it sounded so fearful and weak. It was the voice that continually taunted and sought to embarrass her—the voice of Laria. It grew even more timid as the two men got closer.

"Ha! Where are these others, you silly girl?" demanded Fedro. "You bluff. Make things easy for yourself and be quiet. This won't take very long if you don't put up a fight. First we'll have you, then we'll sell you!"

"Speak for yourself, Fedro. It's been a while, so I'm going to take my time," said Theo. "She's worth a few rounds, at least. To say nothing of the money we'll earn!"

"Get away, you pigs!" Laria feebly demanded, as she inched backward on her buttocks and heels. She was napping, not expecting any danger this far into Amazon land and so close to camp. However, Laria was surrounded by thick trees and large trunks, with her only escape blocked by the slavers. Laria reached for the knife in her belt, but before she could seize it, Theo lurched forward and grabbed her by the arm, placing his own knife at her throat.

"Got her!" Theo exclaimed. "She's a live one! I'll let you wear her out a bit before I take a turn."

"Sounds fine to me," Fedro said, laughing. "I like them feisty!" Fedro was short and heavy, with a large, bald head bulging out from his neck like a ripe fruit about to burst. Thea quietly inched closer behind them as Laria was pushed to the ground.

"No! Please! I will see to it that you are rewarded for your mercy!" Laria said, whimpering.

With a great laugh, Fedro declared, "Now wouldn't that be the height of irony? To be paid by the slave herself!"

The slavers cackled, amused by their wit. Keeping his knife at her throat, Theo took her arms and tightly held them to the ground above her head. Fedro hurriedly dismounted his horse and took his knife out, cut her tunic from the front, and disrobed his lower half.

Hearing the screams from her fellow Amazon, Thea reacted without hesitation or thought, forgetting all of the past discord with Laria.

Thea was about seventy paces away. She moved forward, getting as close as she possibly could without drawing attention to herself. Without making a sound, she reached for her knives, one strapped to each ankle. With a blade in each hand, she sprung into a ferocious sprint, racing through the trees to reach the edge of the clearing where the slavers had pinned Laria.

Thea hastily realized she couldn't risk a direct attack, as Laria might suffer the consequences of the knife that was held tightly against her neck. Thinking on her feet, Thea knew she would have to proceed with precision.

Thea reached back and launched the first knife from her right hand with all her might. Swirling through the air, no sound was heard until a thump on the ground landed behind Laria. Theo, the larger Argive slaver, lay with a knife piercing his neck where it met his spine.

Fedro turned in Thea's direction—but almost instantly met a similar demise. Thea's second knife landed with the same deadly accuracy, this time three feet lower, deep in the slaver's abdomen. Fedro looked down at the dagger piercing his stomach and grabbed the knife's handle, planning to pull it out. Thea bridged the last few steps and, using the full force of her leg, kicked the dull edge of the handle as hard as she could. The man let out a long, agonizing groan and fell backward onto the ground.

Laria, who'd been facing certain assault only seconds earlier, lay safely between the two bleeding corpses.

"Laria, are you okay?" Thea asked, kneeling at her side.

"I think so," Laria stammered, stunned.

"Come, let's get back to camp," Thea said, helping her up.

"Girls!" A woman's voice yelled from behind the clearing.

Thea and Laria watched as two magnificent black horses approached, each carrying riders. Their head-to-toe black outfits and veiled faces identified them as Sondras. Both of the girls felt a sense of relief, having been unsure as to whether or not there were more attackers lurking in the area.

"Are you girls all right?" asked the closer Sondra.

"Yes," replied Laria, her voice still shaky.

"What's your name?" the Sondra asked Thea, recognizing the other girl as the Queen's granddaughter.

"I am Thea."

"Where did you learn to throw a knife so well? Before we could get close enough to help, you had already slain them both."

"I...I just moved quickly to help," Thea stuttered, never having received such a compliment.

"I am Chara and this is Aella," stated the Sondra, motioning to the warrior behind her, who remained silent on her stallion. "Let's get you girls back to camp."

"What are slavers doing on our land?" Laria managed to ask, as she clutched at her torn garments.

"I've never seen slave traders scouting here before," Thea said, fearing her days of solitary exploration were threatened.

"Slave trading is a lucrative business, and wandering Amazon girls are easy prey," Aella said. "They captured Queen Cleo's girls a few days ago. We believe they took dozens."

"Laria, we will be speaking with your grandmother about your decision to travel in these woods alone. I believe you were there when we briefed her this morning on these dangers," Chara stated. "Queen Alexa won't take this well."

Laria looked down at her feet, embarrassed by her weakness. Though she was grateful to Thea, she felt like a failure for being unable to ward off the attackers. She feared her grandmother's disappointment.

"I haven't noticed you in training, Thea," Chara continued. "You may have what it takes to be a Sondra."

Thea felt Laria's eyes burning a hole in her—and for once, Thea felt proud of her skills. She was getting recognition for what had come naturally to her all her life. It was an unfamiliar feeling to be praised, but a welcome one all the same. It occurred to her that perhaps becoming a Sondra was a better way to achieve the freedom she'd always craved. Resisting the rules all these years hadn't helped her.

Thea excused herself to collect Nox, whom she'd almost forgotten. To Thea's delight, Nox stood patiently where she'd left her. Grabbing another small apple out of her pouch, Thea rewarded Nox, and then softly mounted her with ease. When Thea emerged from the thicket on horseback, the Sondras and Laria paused their discussion to gaze at the striking sight of Thea's young frame on the magnificent mare.

"Where did you...?" Laria's voice trailed off in disbelief.

"I found her near Mount Spiro in the wild," Thea replied.

"That doesn't look like a wild horse to me," Laria said, suspiciously.

"She does look pretty tame," Chara agreed. "Let me have a go on her and we'll see just how wild she is!"

Thea hesitated, and then reluctantly dismounted Nox and led her to Chara. The brazen warrior softly stroked Nox's neck. The horse tensed. Snorting a couple of times and stomping her front hooves into the ground, Nox began shaking her head from side to side.

"Easy, girl," Chara coaxed. "It's all right."

Chara mounted Nox with ease—but no sooner had she adjusted herself onto the horse's back then she found herself tossed onto the ground with one strong buck of Nox's rear legs. Slightly embarrassed, Chara stood up and brushed herself off.

"No, that's no wild horse, Chara," Aella said, laughing. "Just a wild rider!"

"She merely caught me off guard."

Chara tried again to mount Nox, but this time the horse made the task more difficult by moving side to side and kicking to keep the agile Sondra off balance. Finally on Nox's back a second time, Chara was more prepared, but the ride was no less difficult. After a few attempts to trot around the clearing, she dismounted in frustration.

"That horse needs to be broken," Chara exclaimed, moving a few loose strands of hair out of her face.

Thea walked over to Nox and began to stroke her mane, demonstrating an immediate calming effect. With a few whispers in her ear, Thea then mounted Nox and trotted to where Aella, Chara, and Laria were watching.

"Well, I guess the horse just needs the right mistress," Chara said. "She is as impressive as you are, child."

Thea offered Laria her hand, which she accepted, and Laria climbed onto Nox's back behind Thea. The three horses then rode back to the camp together as the day faded into dusk. The last streaks of sunlight darted through the trees. The woods appeared just as beautiful as they had earlier that morning, but they no longer felt as peaceful—now holding the threat of real danger to Thea's tribe.

As much as the woods had changed over the course of the day, so had Thea. She had been singled out for something other than her mischief and defiance, and had finally been appreciated for doing things her own way. It made her feel proud and confident for the first time in her life.

It was nearly dark when Thea, Laria, and the Sondras arrived back at camp. The group rode straight to Alexa's hut, not only to bring Laria back to her grandmother, but to inform the Queen of the intrusion onto their land.

As they dismounted, Laria ran ahead to announce the others and begin telling Alexa what had happened. The rest of the returning party patiently waited outside the Queen's hut.

"Grandmother! I'm here," announced Laria.

"Laria, where have you been? It's dark!" The Queen cut an imposing figure in her black cloak and wrinkled complexion. A large golden pendant in the shape of an owl's head hung around her neck from a leather cord.

"I was attacked by two Argive slavers in the woods!" exclaimed Laria, her tears finally escaping down her cheeks, in the safety of her grandmother's leathery, sun-baked arms. "They tried to...to...it was awful!" Unable to finish her sentence, Laria buried her head in her grandmother's lap and cried.

"Laria, are you all right? What happened?" Alexa asked, tightly embracing her grandchild. Her long gray braids hung over the girl's shoulders.

Lifting her head, Laria explained through sniffling sobs, "I was alone by the pond and before I knew it, two attackers came upon me. One held me down with a knife and the other cut my tunic."

"Did they hurt you, Laria?" Alexa demanded. "Tell me now!"

Shaking her head, the girl continued with her story. "Another girl came, grandmother, and then two Sondras arrived. They are outside."

Alexa was a stern leader, but she had a deep love for her only granddaughter. She stroked Laria's hair while absorbing the girl's tears on her chest. She had gained great wisdom in her seventy-three years, and as her thoughts raced, she knew it was only a matter of time before some of Bedros' unruly men would be taking further liberties with her tribe's women. Something had to be done.

Holding Laria by the hand, Alexa exited her hut where the others waited. Both Sondras bowed, as was customary when Alexa emerged from her hut, and Thea bowed following the Sondras' example.

"Rise," Alexa said, with a hint of emotion in her voice. "What can you report about my granddaughter, Sondras?"

"My Queen, Chara and I were patrolling the woods on the western side, and we came upon your Laria being attacked," Aella reported. "She had been forced to the ground and was in great danger. They were preparing to mercilessly have their way with her."

"Were they alone?" asked Alexa.

"As far as we can tell, they were," replied Aella. "They appeared to be a scouting party, Queen."

"I see. Then you rescued my Laria?" Alexa asked.

"No, my Queen, though we were prepared to do so. This brave girl beside us found Laria before we could get close enough. She killed both of the slavers as we were arriving."

Alexa raised her eyes to look at Thea, who had remained quiet, just a few feet to the side of the two Sondras. Alexa looked the girl up and down, taking note of her strong physique and piercing golden eyes.

"You're Thea," Alexa stated. "You have made quite a reputation for yourself in the recruiting camp."

"I'm not surprised," exclaimed Aella. "I have never seen these skills in such a young child."

"Explain what you mean."

"She was at least sixty paces away, and threw killing knives into both men before they even realized what was happening."

"Well, that's certainly not the reputation to which I was referring. Come forward, Thea, I would like to take a closer look at you."

Thea, tall for her age, stepped in front of the Sondras. She was noticeably taller than Laria, who was a few years older. Alexa studied Thea's beautiful dark hair and honey-colored eyes more closely, both of which she felt looked strangely familiar. This was the girl who Alexa's own grandchild had complained about over the years as a troublemaker, and who repeatedly invited consternation from her instructors for her stubbornness and resistance to training. In this moment, however, all the Queen could feel toward Thea was gratitude.

"Young lady," Alexa said, "I commend you for your bravery and skills. You have saved my granddaughter from harm and have made your tribe proud. Wear your badge of achievement with honor, but also in humility. For all Amazons must be both brave and humble to preserve the freedoms we hold precious."

Thea acknowledged Alexa's words with a grateful nod.

"It is my wish that you begin Sondra training immediately," Alexa continued. "If the skills and courage you showed today are any indication of your potential, you may well have what it takes to be one of our elite warriors. You will start on this demanding path in the morning."

Thea bowed and stepped back behind the Sondras. She felt proud; but more surprising, for the first time ever, she felt fully part of the tribe with which she'd spent her entire life. After resisting training and instruction for as long as she could remember, Thea suddenly found herself excited about what the next morning would bring.

She also experienced an unfamiliar desire to help her tribe, and protect it from aggressors scouting their lands. This affected every Amazon, and Thea hoped she may be able to contribute by training to become an elite warrior.

"Did this horse belong to one of the attackers?" Alexa inquired, her attention now on the impressive Nox.

"No, my Queen," Chara replied. "The girl found the wild horse near the mountains. The mare seems to respond only to Thea."

"Thea, as a reward for your efforts, you may keep this horse," Alexa said. "Take good care of her and use her in your Sondra training."

"I will, Queen Alexa," Thea replied.

* * *

The following day, Thea awoke to a new world. As she fell into place among the other girls at the morning training sessions—each one selected from the camp for her superior skill—everyone stared at her. However, instead of staring with smirks and disapproving looks as they'd done in the past, her fellow trainees smiled and gazed in amazement. Girls who'd never acknowledged Thea before were speaking with her and patting her on the back. Thea liked the attention; but more than that, she enjoyed the feeling of being a true member of the group. It was something she'd never experienced.

"Thea, please come to the front," the lead commander instructed.

Thea stepped out of line and made her way to the commander, who held a spear and a Sondra shield bearing the embossed emblem of an owl.

"Thea, I would like to honor you for your acts of bravery in saving your fellow Amazon sister," the commander said. The group of girls applauded.

"Thank you," Thea said.

The rest of the day was comprised of beginner lessons for the Sondra trainees. Thea approached each lesson with a commitment she'd never employed in the camp.

While Laria and the other girls didn't invite her to join them at lunch, they also didn't talk down to her as they had before. Thea knew it wouldn't be long before Laria returned to her old ways, but that didn't bother her anymore. The commanders smiled at her as they passed. Thea was earning their respect. Things were going well.

Thea put all her effort into training. She fully respected the art of becoming a Sondra and was determined to succeed. Her instructors were impressed with Thea's strength and accuracy. It was the training exercises with Nox, however, that Thea loved the most. No one could deny that her new horse rode magnificently.

Days later, Thea took Nox for a solo ride back into the woods, seeking a rock on which to paint. Queen Alexa had limited travel to certain areas, and Sondras were taking turns patrolling the tribal land around the clock for signs of invaders. A curfew was imposed for the first time in Thea's life. Except for the patrols, everyone had to be back within the safe confines of the tribal camp at sundown. After what had happened to local tribes and to her own granddaughter, Queen Alexa was determined to be cautious. It was still early in the day, though, and Thea had several hours to return.

Low clouds floated close to the trees, blanketing the forest in a fine mist. Patches of fog hovered, and Thea let her mind wander into a world of fantasy. Her imagination rambled and her horse followed suit. She let Nox lead the way as she drifted off into thought, picturing herself exploring new, faraway lands, and unraveling the mysteries they held. How she would love to know more about the vastness and beauty of the world.

Nox brought Thea to a stream flowing with fresh water. Nox paused when they arrived and knelt with her front legs, prompting Thea to dismount. Broken from her thoughts, Thea hopped off and walked toward the stream; but as she did, Nox started to whinny, simultaneously nudging something with her nose.

"What is it, girl?" Thea asked.

On the ground next to a moss-covered stone was a small, carved wooden horn. Thea examined it. It was no bigger than her fist. Little of the original covering remained, but she could see that it had once been painted white. Though the wood remained in good condition, it appeared ancient. Some of the decorative symbols etched on its sides were still visible, though significantly faded. Thea decided that if it were offered for sale at market, it wouldn't garner much of a price.

As she examined the wooden horn, the gurgling of the stream made Thea realize how thirsty she'd become after her morning ride. She was still too intrigued by the horn to stop for a drink, though. She placed the horn to her lips and blew. The horn remained silent, which was strange, as the air traveled through the horn exactly like those she'd blown at camp.

In that instant, Nox took off into a gallop.

"Nox, come back!" Thea shouted, but the mare kept galloping at full speed.

Thea wasn't sure what to do. Nox had never run from her before. After a few moments, Thea saw the horse returning. Trotting at a much slower pace, Nox carried in her mouth a pail filled with fresh water from the stream.

"You read my mind, girl!" Thea grabbed the pail and took a long drink of the fresh river water. Nox moved closer, nudging Thea's hand with her nose.

"What is it, girl?" Thea asked.

Thea looked at the horn again, and then at the pail.

"Oh no! Could it be...?" Thea wondered aloud.

Thea sat the pail in front of Nox so the horse could drink the water, then placed the horn against her lips again. This time, as she blew the horn, she thought of one of the vibrant purple flowers they'd passed in the woods along the way. The horn was silent for Thea, but Nox stopped drinking and galloped away into the woods just as she had before. Thea patiently waited, and a few moments later Nox returned with the purple flowers bunched between her lips.

Thea no longer cared that she still couldn't whistle. Using the horn was much better. It was like a secret language shared with her equine friend.

Thea sat on the ground in disbelief as Nox dropped the bouquet onto her lap. She picked up one of the flowers and inhaled its sweet aroma before looking into Nox's large brown eyes and gently caressing the mare's nose. Where had Nox been before Thea had found her? What other powers did she have? Before she could be fully persuaded that Nox could read her thoughts, she wanted to give her one more test.

Thea thought clearly about one additional task and blew the horn. Instantly, Nox knelt onto her front legs and bowed her head at Thea's feet. Thea was astounded.

"Wondrous!" Thea exclaimed. "From where did you come, you amazing creature?"

Thea mounted Nox so they could head back to camp. Thea brought her head down for a moment, rested her chin on the back of Nox's thick neck, and lovingly petted her loyal friend. It occurred to Thea that it would be best to keep Nox's gift, and the horn, a secret. She didn't want to risk anyone stealing her horse or the horn away from her. For whatever reason, Nox had taken to Thea and no one else. She wondered if her horse would be able to read anyone else's thoughts with the help of the horn, but she wasn't going to take the chance of losing Nox by trying to find out.

Thea placed the horn in her pouch and decided it would never leave her side. Since Nox had come into her life, things had drastically changed for the better. Maybe it was coincidence, or maybe a gift from the Gods; either way, Thea was aware of the value of her good fortune and was deeply grateful.

Thea felt happy and proud. She welcomed her new life into her heart and felt, for the first time, that she truly had a purpose. She longed to be a Sondra, and that wish was slowly coming true.

CHAPTER 9

UNCOVERING THE GOLDEN GIRDLE

The moon shone brightly on a clearing just outside the woods. The backdrop of mountains in the distance formed a jagged silhouette. As the moon made its course through the night sky, hovering clouds threatened darkness. Galenos shoveled rapidly, trying to take advantage of what little light remained. With each pitch of earth, the ground became softer, creating a palpable contrast to the rigid corpse beside him. Time was not on his side, and he was sweating profusely as he tried to bury the evidence before anyone could find out what had happened.

Had Galenos known his prey was an Argive officer, he never would have tried to rob him. What bad luck! He was the only traveler on the dreary path that evening, and the man had been dressed in the robes of a layman. It wasn't until after Galenos had struck his head with the ax that he noticed the telltale copper necklace of an officer.

None of that mattered now. All that could be done was to get rid of the body and make a rapid exit. Luckily, Galenos had come across what looked to be an old burial ground. He decided it would be a fitting resting place for an officer.

Because Nemea paid taxes to Argos for protection, there was heavy patrol by Argive soldiers in the city. Galenos was a stranger to the land, and foreigners had few privileges under Argive rule. In Spartan villages, travelers were welcomed and accepted. But Argives considered themselves first class citizens. Everyone else was beneath them. It stood to reason that anyone caught killing an Argive officer was unlikely to get a fair trial. Of course, murder for the sake of robbery wasn't a strong defense. The penalty would be death by torture.

"This is a pitiful excuse for a shovel," Galenos muttered to himself.

Pitch after pitch, he slowly expanded the hole. Grunting with each stab into the earth, the thief looked up at the moon to check its position. Intermittently, he paused to listen for any unexpected noises in the woods, but all he could hear were crickets and the faint cooing of an owl in the distance. If he could just get this oaf buried, he could flee with his bounty and keep enough coins to last for a month.

A clank sounded from the ground as his shovel struck something hard.

"Damn rock!" Galenos said under his breath.

He backed away to let some of the moonlight into the hole. Peeking into the grave without obscuring the light, the thief saw a faint glimmer. Most of it was still covered with dirt, but it was clearly not a rock. He dug around the object, trying to uncover it a bit more, pausing every few minutes to reexamine the shiny mass under the fading moonlight. What could it be? It looked like gold, but appeared to be massive.

Galenos quickly forgot about the danger of keeping the stiff corpse of an Argive officer at his side and became focused on his newfound treasure. As his curiosity intensified, he dug more furiously. There was a possibility that some corpses had been buried with family treasures, perhaps as a tribute to the Gods to gain favor in the afterlife. Whatever the reason, the thief had no qualms about turning them into his own fortune in the here and now.

He made good progress, uncovering a large portion of the mysterious item. When he felt he could get a grip on it, Galenos reached into the large hole and tried to grab hold of the golden mass. His grasp was firm, but he couldn't lift it with just one arm.

After a bit more shoveling, he was able to enlarge the cavity enough to jump inside and attempt to free the treasure with both arms. Eventually, with what seemed like the last of his exhausted will, he unearthed the heavy object.

Using all of his might, Galenos lifted it onto the ground beside the rotting officer. With the moon beginning to crest over the mountains' peaks, enough light was still present to make out the features of his reward. The object appeared to be some type of large harness made of pure gold. It must have weighed two talents, perhaps three—the weight of a large man.

As the thief rolled the harness over, he noticed it was encrusted with emeralds and rubies. Each stone alone was worth several gold coins, but the centerpiece was most impressive. Also encased in gold, it was an emblem of two intertwined snakes facing away from each other. One snake bore a golden amber stone for an eye and the other an emerald. Around the outer portion of the centerpiece were smaller stones beautifully placed within the medallion. He had no idea what this treasure was, but it was without a doubt something that had once belonged to royalty.

As the moon crept past the lip of the mountains, Galenos was reminded of his original task. With great effort, using the shovel for leverage, he hoisted the golden treasure onto his cart, covering it with a blanket to protect it from prying eyes.

The hole was now large enough for the Argive's corpse. With a few tugs and pulls, Galenos rolled the dead man into the moist earth. Grateful for the relative ease he had refilling the grave, the thief leveled the ground flush with the dirt he'd removed. He gathered a pile of leaves from the surrounding trees and attempted to cover the fresh soil. Getting out of the woods and to the next town had been his goal, but he now had a more pressing priority: finding a merchant to pay for this golden treasure. An object of this beauty was not seen every day, and he had to be sure to locate the right buyer.

With his work in the forest complete, Galenos set off on his cart. As he guided his horse along the dirt path, he kept checking the back of his wagon to be sure his treasure was safe in its place. It was unlikely it would slip, considering its massive size and weight. But the more the thief pondered its worth, the more excited he became. The gold and jewels were all he could think about.

After several hours on the road, he saw Koutsopodi ahead, a town he knew well from his travels. He'd never stolen anything within its borders. He preferred to surprise a weary traveler on the road, since guards were few and far between. Koutsopodi was an independent city where Spartans, Argives, and foreigners traded for goods. He could explore a fair trade for his recent discovery with one of its many jewelers. Selecting the right jeweler was critical; he had to find someone who was knowledgeable enough to recognize an uncommon treasure when he saw it and still wealthy enough to pay what it was worth.

Koutsopodi was buzzing with activity. Merchants were trading goods from near and far. Unusual items like exotic spices, fruits, and fabrics came from Egyptian, Scythian, and other international traders.

Galenos made his way through the streets, carefully surveying each of the shops. He passed several jewelers who appeared to handle smaller items and would not be able to provide the sum he anticipated.

Eventually, he arrived at a more established shop, a building just off the center of Koutsopodi. The fact that it was not a tent or table suggested that its owner was a local and reputable jewelry trader; and from the looks of his wares, he would know the worth of the thief's possession.

"Welcome, sir," Philandros said, as Galenos entered his shop.

"Good day," the thief replied, struggling to carry the sack containing his prize.

"Is there something I can interest you in today?"

"I'm hoping I can interest you in something," Galenos responded. He made his way to the front of the shop and lifted his sack with great effort, landing it squarely on the jeweler's table.

"I'm looking to trade this for its value in gold coins."

The jeweler was about to open the sack, but first looked to Galenos for permission. The thief proudly nodded his approval. As Philandros exposed the beautiful array of gold, emeralds, and rubies to the natural light, he struggled to suppress his amazement. He instantly recognized the fabled treasure. It was the Golden Girdle, about which legendary stories had been spun. He had never believed it was real.

The Golden Girdle once belonged to the Amazon Queen Elektra, who wore the ornate Girdle as if it were a crown, encased in pure gold and riddled with precious stones worth a fortune. It had symbolized her strength and immortality—and for good reason, as its weight alone was too much for any ordinary man to bear. When the Amazon Queen vanished, legend had it those who craved the riches of the Golden Girdle caused her disappearance.

"Where did you find this?" Philandros asked.

"That's not your business," stated the thief. "How much can you give me for it?"

The jeweler looked at the magnificent Golden Girdle. Its beauty was enchanting, and his eyes grew wide as he fell under its spell. He schemed how he might possess this invaluable treasure, as he knew he had nothing to offer that could even remotely match its value.

Indeed, its true worth was very difficult to gauge because of the Girdle's rare and precious stones, solid gold composition, and mystical past. Philandros decided that he simply had to have it, and would do whatever was needed to take possession of the mesmerizing piece.

"Hmmm. This gold casing is quite poor, actually," the jeweler began. "There are many blemishes. I question its purity, sir. It looks to be some type of counterfeit."

"Counterfeit?" the thief retorted. "I know gold when I see it, and that's no counterfeit!"

"And these gems are flawed," Philandros continued, as he placed a lens against the stones. "These are poor quality stones, hardly worth a few silver coins."

"You are insane!" barked the thief. "Those are the largest stones I have ever seen!"

"I can give you a dozen gold coins for the item," the jeweler said, putting the lens back into his pouch. "You won't get a better price for it, I'm sure."

"I will take my business elsewhere," the thief responded. "You don't know something extraordinary when you see it, fool!"

When Galenos moved to place the Golden Girdle back into the sack, Philandros began to panic at the idea of losing the treasure. It was the find of a lifetime. The more the jeweler looked at the Girdle, the hungrier he became to have it for himself.

"Name your price then, sir," he offered.

"Ten full bags of gold coins, and nothing less," the thief said.

"That's ridiculous," Philandros replied, trying to show indifference.

"Then we have nothing more to discuss," Galenos said, lifting the sack back onto the ground with all of his strength.

Philandros became overcome with fear that the Girdle would escape his grasp. He quickly looked around the shop and saw no one else. A glance toward the door showed no one nearby. Thinking quickly, the jeweler grabbed a knife that he kept under his counter, cupping it in his hand, under his sleeve.

"Sir, I'm sorry we couldn't work out a deal, but at least let me help you with your sack," Philandros offered.

"I'm fine," Galenos replied. "You've been no help to me thus far, so no need to start now."

As the thief tried to exit the shop, he was stopped by a stinging heat piercing his back to his lungs. The jeweler's knife had found its mark in Galenos' dying body.

Catching the thief as he collapsed, Philandros laid him neatly on the rug that garnished the floor of his shop. He then went to the door and secured it shut, drawing the curtains over the windows. The Golden Girdle was his.

What a fool this stranger was to bring this into my shop! Philandros thought. *This type of treasure can only be properly appraised by royalty.*

Working quickly, Philandros secured the Golden Girdle in a locked chest he kept in the back, and then rolled the thief's body in the blood-saturated rug through the shop and out of the rear door.

As darkness fell, Philandros loaded the corpse onto the thief's cart and left the center of Koutsopodi. The woods were not far away and he could rid himself of the body there, extinguishing any evidence that might suggest the Girdle had not been his all along. Then he'd return to work as usual.

As he traveled, Philandros fantasized about the wealth he would soon enjoy. The legend of the Golden Girdle's existence was true! He could barely believe his good fortune.

CHAPTER 10

A FIGHTER IS BORN

Teigra had been traveling undetected for the better part of two weeks. Her feet and legs wept with blood from the cuts she'd sustained walking through dense brush. She ached with every step. Still, she persevered. She avoided the roads and saw no one.

Teigra was relieved to reach a place where the trees gave way to a meadow. The fading sunlight falling on the tall grass at dusk brought a sense of peace. She looked forward to feeling its softness on her tired soles. As she approached, however, she saw movement ahead and ducked behind a tree. She spotted twenty people in a circle. She couldn't gauge their intent. Goosebumps rose on her arms as she tried her best to stay hidden.

Teigra had no safe place to run. Regardless of the direction she chose, she'd be within the mysterious group's field of vision. She decided to wait a couple of hours until the sun went down and then travel under cover of night.

Taking a deep breath to calm herself, Teigra retracted into a ball and curled against the tree to wait. After a few moments, she couldn't resist the urge to take another look. Peeking around the curve of the thick trunk, she saw a tall figure—moving with an almost angelic air—quickly bridging the distance between the circle and her!

Teigra stood up to run...but a calmness came over her. She somehow sensed there was no danger.

"You!" the figure said. "Please come join us! Do not worry, we mean you no harm."

Teigra turned around to face a beautiful girl with waist-length pale red hair.

"You look hungry. We have food," the girl said. "What is your name?"

"Teigra. Who are you?"

"I am Virgin Photina. My fellow virgin sisters and I are known as Parthenos Girls." The girl's luminousness was breathtaking, even in the fading light. "We have all preserved our purity in honor of the Goddess Hestia. We are blessed to be supported by those who worship Hestia. They call upon us to advise and support them in business dealings, pregnancies, curses, and conflicts."

As she got closer to the camp, Teigra saw steam steadily rising into the sky just behind the group. She realized they were gathered at the edge of a hot spring.

The virgins offered Teigra a seat. With the light of a fire blazing at the campsite, Teigra could see that the girls ranged in age from mid-teens to mid-twenties. They were all breathtakingly beautiful, with dark hair worn long and straight, and porcelain complexions.

Serenely sitting in the center of the circle was a woman dressed like the others, but at least twice as old. She was clearly the leader, and a figure of respect.

"That's Virgin Eudora. She guides us," Photina said. She handed Teigra a cup of broth and a large slice of crusted bread. "To where are you traveling?"

"I was a slave, but I could no longer tolerate the brutality of my master so I escaped. I am looking for a place where I can find work and be treated with kindness," Teigra replied. She looked around, taking note of the soothing calmness that permeated the group. These young women seemed to be leading contented lives.

"I see. Well, once again, you are safe here. We have guards for our protection." She pointed to a trio of large men flanking the entrances to the nearby tents. "We are en route to our next engagement, to give support during a birthing."

Teigra nodded, slurping eagerly at the broth—a delicious concoction topped with a flotilla of herbs. She gazed once again at the older woman in the center of the circle, who seemed to be in some sort of trance. Photina took note.

"Eudora is our leader. We are never to disturb her when she is communing with the Gods. That is what you are seeing now."

Teigra nodded. Minutes passed as Photina disappeared and allowed Teigra to finish eating. Teigra felt at peace with these girls. There seemed to be nothing to worry about, with men present only for their protection.

Photina reappeared with an unexpected question. "Teigra, would you like to join our group?"

She was caught off guard by this sudden invitation, but her response escaped her lips before she even had an opportunity to think.

"Yes! I would love to join!"

"However, there is something I must ask. You probably know what the question is." Photina paused, giving Teigra a chance to anticipate. "Have you retained your virginity?"

Teigra paused, swallowing a rise of unexpected anger. Her face fell.

"No, I have not. I was raped...by my master."

"Oh...I'm very sorry. I'm afraid we cannot accept you. Still, please stay at our camp, where you will be safe until morning."

"I understand. Thank you for your kindness, but I should go on my way," Teigra said.

"Very well, Teigra. But before you leave, I have some things to give you. Wait here."

Photina returned with a cloth sack and pressed it into Teigra's hands.

"Some items I think you could use on your journey," Photina said. Inside was an array of dried fruits, meats, and bread. "And you must take these," she said, handing Teigra a pair of leather sandals. Teigra dropped them to the ground and slipped them on her bare and battered feet.

"Thank you, Photina," Teigra said. "You are very kind."

"I think you will also be needing these."

Photina handed Teigra a knife from her belt and a spear that she'd been holding. Teigra had thought it was a walking stick.

"It was a pleasure to meet you, Teigra. May you safely arrive wherever it is you are intended."

Teigra headed into the approaching night, leaving the Parthenos Girls behind her. Had she not been violated by her master, she would have loved to don a white robe of her own. But she was destined to walk another path. Still, she thought, it signaled good fortune to have such an inviting offer so early in her journey. Perhaps this meant that things were going to be better from this point forward.

Teigra traveled for months, mostly in the forest. She became quite adept at living off the land, hunting, and eating rabbits and other small animals. She preferred to travel at night, which allowed her to traverse open fields and make better time between towns. During the day she avoided clearings, as she felt they left her too exposed. She knew that remaining stationary came with risk. It was better to keep moving.

Teigra's cunning served her well. In addition to her nature skills, she learned how to blend into bustling towns, moving along undetected, and stealing what she needed to survive from markets.

Eventually, the forest ended and she reached Corinth, a city where travelers came in search of goods and entertainment. Knowing she could steal some essential items, Teigra headed straight for the market where a crowd had already amassed. As she surveyed the foods and other items on the vendors' tables, she was abruptly halted in her tracks by an old crone draped in dusty black rags.

"*You! Girl!* You have been cursed, and have been walking this world on your own!" the old woman croaked. Her face was partially obscured by a hood, but Teigra could see her crooked nose and a pair of cloudy eyes that seemed to gaze right through her.

"What? Me?" Teigra asked, startled.

"*Yeeessss.* But there is something that will help you," the old woman continued.

"What?" Teigra asked.

"There is a golden belt, with two golden snakes on it. You must find it."

"And how will that help me?" Teigra asked.

"The curse...it will break the curse that has plagued you since birth," the old woman replied. As soon as these words left her mouth, a crowd seemed to materialize, moving past Teigra. Once they were gone, the old woman was as well.

Startled by this strange meeting, Teigra forced herself to carry on. She had supplies to gather and no time to waste.

Keeping her face partially veiled as she walked among the crowd, Teigra surveyed the merchants' wares, noticing one vendor who had a huge assortment of dried meats in the corner of the marketplace. With a scheming eye, she surveyed the area and began devising a plan. Suddenly, she sobbed loudly.

"Mistress, what's the matter?" asked a tall man in the crowd.

"That man there took what little money I had," Teigra said, pointing to someone standing nearby. "I have nothing with which to buy my food. All I had were two coins, and now they're gone."

She had simply hoped for some coins with which to buy food, but instead the man offered his help, turned toward the one she had chosen to falsely accuse, and grabbed his shoulder.

"Sir, I insist you give this lady her money back," the tall man said.

"What?" the other man asked. "I have no idea what you're talking about!"

"How dare you deny me!" Teigra said, sobbing even louder.

"Just give her the two coins, sir," the taller man urged. "You owe her that, at least!"

"You're both crazy!" the other man exclaimed, sure that the tall man was part of Teigra's scheme.

Infuriated, the taller man shoved Teigra's mark, who fell to the ground. Within seconds, the men were engaged in a full-on brawl. Taking this as her cue, Teigra fell back into the gathering crowd and moved over to the table containing the dried meats. The surrounding vendors were distracted enough to allow Teigra to shove several pieces of meat into her pockets without detection before heading down the road.

"Where's the girl?" asked the taller man, panting and out of breath. "Where did she go?"

"Hey, someone took my meat! Thief! Thief!" cried the vendor, realizing that the fight had merely been a diversion to steal his wares.

Running through the crowd, Teigra no longer tried to veil her face. The vendor was approaching from behind, and the taller man followed. Ahead, she saw two Corinth guards. She ducked into an alley...only to be surprised by the vendor appearing from a connecting pathway.

"Not so fast, girl," the vendor snarled, as he pulled a small knife from his waist.

"Thought you would escape, didn't you, you worthless tramp?"

Arriving soon after were the two Corinthian guards and the taller man. Deciding she was no match for all four men, she dropped her knife, defeated, and was immediately seized by one of the guards.

"She stole my meats!" the vendor shouted.

"Indeed! She took us for fools to steal this man's wares," the taller man said between labored breaths.

The unoccupied guard reached into Teigra's pockets and examined their contents. He saw the fistfuls of dried meats, and she knew that whatever happened now was not going to be good.

"Sir, I have a proposition," the tall man said in a calm, measured tone, taking the second guard aside as he produced a handful of coins. "I will pay the vendor for the stolen goods, along with a bit extra for his trouble, and give you and your comrade a substantial payment for the right to take this girl off your hands."

The guard paused and considered the offer. Letting him have the girl would be a favor, saving them a lot of time and inconvenience. She had made a fool of this fellow, so he was entitled to retribution; and it was clear she had no family.

"What's your name?" the guard asked.

"Lysandros," replied the tall man.

"Well, Lysandros, we don't make a habit of this sort of transaction, but we will let you take this girl, considering the manner in which she inconvenienced you."

The guard accepted the money and pushed Teigra over to Lysandros, who took the dried meat from her hands and gave it back to the vendor, along with the additional coins. The guards and vendor left.

Teigra considered escaping, but the steel of Lysandros' knife pressed firmly into the small of her back changed her mind. One of the guards had given Lysandros a piece of rope, which he used to tie her hands behind her back, and they began walking.

"I've got plans for you, girl," Lysandros told her as they moved forward. "I've needed something fresh, and you're just the thing."

Teigra remained silent, but suspected what this distinguished yet sinister man wanted from her. They were all the same, she thought. Master after master, man after man, they all wanted one of two things: power or pleasure. Most of the time it was both, and Teigra was sure this one was no different. She would just as soon slice him to shreds as lie with him.

Lysandros lived in a wooded area just a short distance from the market. His home, while not palatial, was large and elegant, and he had lambs, goats, hens, and horses. There was a barn where the horses and hens gathered, and a fence surrounded the area. Behind the house was a pair of smaller structures. Lysandros led Teigra there, letting her feel the pinch of his knife between her shoulder blades. As they got closer to these quarters, she saw a handful of guards on the premises, one of whom joined Lysandros.

Inside, there were more than a half dozen girls shackled by the ankles to the wooden supports of the building. Individual stalls held one captive each, all of whom were gaunt. As Teigra passed, some of the girls glanced up at her, while others continued to direct their eyes to the ground. She could tell which ones still had some fight left in them and which had completely succumbed to defeat.

Lysandros and his guard led Teigra to a stall and shackled her ankles. Each shackle was locked with a key, which Lysandros kept on a braided rope necklace tucked inside his shirt. Once Teigra had been secured, Lysandros walked outside without a word. A deathly silence hung in this prison; no one had spoken since she arrived.

"What is this place?" Teigra asked in a loud whisper.

"Quiet! Shhh," came a voice from a distant stall.

Teigra sat in her cell thinking about what had led her to this. The old woman in the marketplace was right—she must be cursed. Even though her life had certainly been a struggle, she always managed to survive using strength and cunning.

What about the Golden belt the woman mentioned? Did it really exist? If so, it could be the answer to all of her problems. But where and how would she find it?

A few hours later, Teigra was startled by the sound of a bowl of food and a cup of water being tossed into the front of her stall. She crawled forward and placed the bowl to her mouth. The meal was much better than she'd expected—bread and some gamey bird meat—and she was very thankful for something decent to eat. The stall had remained quiet, and now all she could hear were slurps and gargles as the other captive women ate their meals.

It was very strange. Teigra had been enslaved many times, but never had she witnessed such a bizarre contradiction: decent food, but prisoners chained up in cells like livestock waiting to be slaughtered. If Lysandros wasn't using them for labor, what were his intentions for them?

The next morning, Teigra woke just before the sun rose. She saw the light in the dawn sky gradually unfold through the cracks in the roof as she lay motionless on the ground. She then heard shackles rattling in one of the other stalls. Lysandros and a guard stood directly in front of her holding one of the other women by her hands.

"Feisty One! Your number is up!" he barked at Teigra. If she didn't know better, she would've believed there was a hint of respect in his voice.

Teigra slowly made her way to her feet—her wrists raw and bruised, her legs aching. She raised her head and glared in contempt at Lysandros, who had a bow and a quiver of arrows strapped to his back.

"Today, we see how tough you really are," he said.

Lysandros unlocked Teigra's ankles from their shackles. Once she was free, he directed her out into the open, along with the other captive. They were both pushed forward toward a large, square pit dug in the earth, approximately ten paces long on each side. After being forced down into it, the women found the ground they were previously walking on at chest level.

The other woman was thin and lean, and muscular in build, her dark hair saturated with dirt. Her eyes still had a distant fire, and Teigra knew she was one who hadn't yet accepted defeat. The other woman noticed the same thing in Teigra.

"You two will fight until I tell you to stop," Lysandros commanded. "There will be no collapsing or quitting. If you fail, your opponent will be justified in killing you. There are no rules. Just fight to win. Fight to live."

Teigra had no idea what was going on. Why would this seemingly dignified man secure her as a slave only to have another slave kill her? He had come to her defense in the marketplace, seemingly out of the goodness of his heart. It made no sense.

As she pondered this, her opponent had already taken a defensive stance in preparation for battle. This clearly was not the first time the woman had been in the pit.

"Let the fight begin," Lysandros shouted.

Unprepared for the battle's abrupt start, Teigra was immediately struck in the jaw by her opponent's fist, sending her to her knees. Before she could get back up, her opponent struck her in the chest with her knee. Teigra scrambled to maneuver away from the suddenly savage woman, but the wall of the pit stopped her in her tracks. Teigra felt repeated kicks to her stomach and back as she tried to curl into a fetal position to protect herself.

She kept waiting for a break in the beating, but the blows came one after the other. Lysandros offered no intervention. It seemed that death was the only thing that could bring an end to the fight.

Suddenly, Teigra felt a fire rise inside her. The resulting pain from each powerful kick was fueling an inner surge of power. Using this newfound strength to her advantage, she grabbed the woman's foot, mid-kick, stopping it just short of striking another blow to her ribs. With a forceful twist, she sent her opponent whirling to the ground, giving Teigra just enough time to get to her feet and regain her balance. As the two of them squared off, ready for the next round, the woman's relentless aggression prevented any emotion from surfacing on her face.

The woman once again swung at Teigra, but this time Teigra dodged the punch and struck her opponent squarely in the face. It was now Teigra's turn to strike back. Like a wild beast, she unleashed a series of blows against her adversary. The other woman, overcome, collapsed on her stomach.

Teigra couldn't help but pause as the woman lay motionless on the ground. Then the woman abruptly rose and started swinging at Teigra. This time Teigra was relentless, unleashing pure physical fury at the woman. Teigra threw punches, even after Lysandros shouted for her to stop. She had lost all control, falling into a trance and allowing her suppressed rage to rise to the surface.

"Stop, girl! Save the killing for another time!" Lysandros shouted. "No point in killing when there's no prize in it!"

When Teigra's fists finally came to a halt, her opponent lay still. Was she dead? As Teigra wondered, a feeling of remorse settled.

Slowly, the woman rolled over onto her back, her face covered in blood. Though Teigra was relieved to see her opponent alive, she was also startled at the realization that she harbored a demon within herself that she'd never fully recognized. She had known anger and revenge, but this unbridled rage was completely new.

"Let's go, you two," Lysandros commanded. "Excellent! Feisty, you may earn your stay after all!" He knew that she was a born fighter. While he had acquired her as mere fodder for blood sport, he now realized that if he groomed her properly, he stood to make a lot of money.

As Teigra crawled out of the pit, the other woman slowly followed. She considered offering the woman a hand, but quickly reconsidered when she remembered the ferocity with which the woman had struck her. Before long, they were both back in their stalls and shackled again.

A few minutes later, Teigra saw another pot of food and water coming through the door into her stall. The doors across from her were staggered just enough so she couldn't see if anyone was being held there. As she reached for her food, she noticed that several extra pieces of dried meat were included. She devoured the entire meal in seconds.

"New girl?" whispered a voice down the row of stalls.

"Yeah," Teigra answered.

"Did you get some extra meat in your food?" the voice asked.

"Yeah, I did," Teigra replied.

"That's because you won the fight. He likes to fatten up the ones he plans to use."

"What do you mean?"

"You'll find out soon enough. My name is Hanna. What's yours?"

"I'm Teigra."

"Hmm. If I were you, I would try to get some rest. You never know when your next fight will happen."

Teigra was perplexed. She tried not to think about it and drifted back to sleep, but the multitude of pains in her body kept jolting her awake. Her joints ached as she tried to find a comfortable position, and her jaw and ribs hurt much worse than before. She hadn't realized how fiercely the other woman had struck her in the pit until feeling the aftereffects.

Three days later, Teigra was stirred by the sound of Lysandros' cart arriving outside. The pink morning sunlight was beginning to cut through her window, and she had no idea how long she'd been asleep. She heard Lysandros walking down the corridor, tossing the morning's rations to his prisoners. When he arrived at Teigra's stall, however, he had nothing in his hand but his key. "Stand up!" he said.

Teigra slowly stood, and Lysandros tied her hands in front of her before unlocking the shackles. She considered grabbing his knife or kicking him backward in an effort to escape, but it was too risky—she would just have to see what was going to unfold. As he led her outside, she could see there was a horse harnessed to a cart. Lysandros placed her in the back, tying her ankles to the cart's frame to prevent her from jumping. She was placed next to a silent, shirtless man who appeared to be from another part of the world. Both his hands and feet were shackled. Then she realized what the structure adjacent to her quarters was used for: male fighters.

"Here, take this bag of meat and eat. I need you to be well-nourished. You're going to need all the strength you can get," Lysandros told her.

Teigra managed to get her tied hands into the bag's opening and put the meat and bread into her mouth. They were delicious—though she was so famished that she would have enjoyed tree bark.

A guard took the reins, and soon they were traveling a dark path lit by a small lantern that Lysandros attached to a pole in front of the cart. Teigra could tell they were headed in the direction of the market. The road was familiar, and she could hear noises of the city in the distance. Just before they reached the market, however, the cart took a turn down another path into a wooded area. In the distance, Teigra could see several lanterns and a group of men crowded around something.

"Now listen to me," Lysandros said, as they approached the dark scene. "You were decent in the pit the other day, girl, but this time things are going to be a little more difficult! I want you to put on a good show for me—"

"Anything I do in there, I do for myself, *not* for you," Teigra spit out.

"Maybe so. But I consider this payment for involving me in your little scheme at the market," Lysandros said.

He pulled the horse over to the side and untied Teigra from the cart. With her hands still bound, he led her to an area where about fifty men were gathered. There was a slightly larger pit than the one at Lysandros' home. Teigra could see a woman fighting, as the crowd cheered and yelled. There was one key difference, though—her opponent was a man! The woman was bleeding profusely from a wound on her arm, which hung limp at her side. The man was tall and wild-eyed. Teigra's heart sunk—this was clearly blood sport, without any honor of competition. While she knew that she had the ability to beat a man in a fight, these spectators—all men—had paid to watch fighters battle to the death, making wagers on the outcome. Her master, a wealthy and supposedly upstanding citizen in the community, was supplying the fighters!

Teigra's mind snapped back to the pit just as the male fighter's knife found its way into the crippled woman's stomach, causing her to collapse to the ground. The fight was over, and the crowd jockeyed for position at the money table to collect winnings and make new wagers.

As the ring cleared, Lysandros was called to draw straws with four other suppliers to see who would be next in the ring. The men made their selections from the clenched hand of the organizer, and Lysandros came up with a long straw before turning to Teigra.

"You're up next, Feisty," he said to her. "Be ready."

Lysandros waited until the last moment to untie Teigra, then shoved her into the pit. She stumbled and fell onto the ground, causing all the men to laugh and jeer. Teigra stood up and felt the stares upon her. Lysandros motioned her to go to one corner of the pit, and she saw her opponent enter. It was a man she estimated at 6½ feet tall. He was dark-skinned and wore only a loincloth. The lamplights created impressive reflections on his muscular, well-defined torso. Teigra could tell this was not going to be easy.

The men placed their wagers, and the circle tightened around the pit as the time for battle was set to begin. Lysandros gave Teigra a knife, which she held in her left hand. She briefly considered fighting her way to freedom, but that clearly would have been suicide.

"The next match is between a girl of Lysandros' and Nicholas' fighter Kunda," announced a man at the side of the pit. He had a booming voice that echoed in Teigra's head. "Fighters, get ready!"

Teigra tightly gripped her knife as she felt the tension begin to rise within her. She noticed her opponent's fingernails were long and filed into points. He focused his intense eyes directly on Teigra. She could feel the man's strength from the other side of the pit, just in his stare.

"Fight!" yelled the announcer.

Kunda lunged at Teigra like a bolt of lightning. She had to twist to avoid immediately catching a knife in her chest. The two circled the pit facing each other, waiting for an opportunity to draw first blood. Kunda lunged again, and Teigra felt a sting as his knife scraped across her right thigh. She stepped back to avoid a second blow, but the large man kept pursuing her, striking her again on the arm. Dark blood oozed from her wound, and the men in the audience screamed in excitement for what looked to them like impending death.

Teigra felt her anger rise once again. Every bit of hatred she'd ever felt unleashed itself in a fury. She hurled her knife at Kunda, landing its blade in his leg. He grunted in pain, but quickly pulled the blade out and tossed it aside before Teigra had the opportunity to drive it in further. He lunged forward, raking his filed nails across her chest. Teigra's tunic was torn, and her left breast was exposed, evoking lusty cheers from the crowd. Four thin cuts seeped crimson lines where her opponent had scratched her.

Despite the pain of her wounds, Teigra kept a clear head. Before she had a chance to overthink, she leaped forward like a panther, catching her opponent off guard. He was knocked backward by the force of her body, hitting his head against the side of the pit. She quickly retreated, grabbing the knife Kunda had tossed aside. Before he was able to regain his wits, she sprinted to the dazed fighter, pushed him forward, and stuck the blade into the back of his neck, severing his spinal cord and quickly putting an end to the match.

As if coming out of hypnosis, she shook off the effects of her rage and slowly rose to exit the pit. Cheers and screams echoed in her head. It was over...and she had won.

Kunda's owner ran over to Lysandros. The man was clearly distraught, and Lysandros tried to contain his excitement as they shared a word. He was convinced that he'd been duped. His prize warrior and meal ticket had been destroyed...by a young woman! This was not supposed to happen. Meanwhile, money changed hands in the crowd.

After tying Teigra to the cart, Lysandros collected his winnings. Soon Teigra was riding back with him, exhausted and drained. She was alive, which was in stark contrast to the condition of the male fighter with whom she had arrived. Lysandros gave her more to eat, along with some water, but she was ready to collapse. The emotional surge had taken every last bit of energy she had. Teigra fell asleep on the ride home and barely managed to stumble into her stall. The straw felt almost comfortable as she made her bed on the ground. Her hand still ached, but not as badly; and nothing was going to keep her from slumber.

She was woken the next morning by Lysandros.

"Good morning," he said. "I must say that I drastically underestimated you. You impressed not only me, but everyone who saw you fight last night."

Teigra was still groggy as he tied her hands. He opened the door and refrained from talking any further until they were outside the building.

"Things will be different for you from now on. You have proven yourself to be a fantastic fighter. I also provide fighters for events of a higher caliber."

They walked down a path past the animals and into a wooded area. There they came upon another building, smaller than the one where Teigra had been held. Lysandros produced a key. Inside were eight more cells, but these appeared to be much more comfortable than Teigra's quarters. They walked down a corridor that ran through the middle of the cells and she could see that all but one was occupied.

When they reached the empty cell, Lysandros used a key to open the door and let her in. There was a bed, with a proper straw mattress—a definite step up from her previous accommodations.

"Your next fight will be in a week's time. I need you to rest up and heal. I'll send someone to look after your wounds," Lysandros said, and he locked the door.

Teigra was still exhausted from the fight. She slept intermittently for two days, after which a physician came by to apply an herbal unguent to her wounds through the bars of her cell.

Of the other seven occupants, five were men and two were women. When Teigra woke after two days of recovery, the male prisoner in the cell across from hers greeted her in a quiet voice.

"Hello. I am Bion."

"And I am Teigra," she replied, still groggy.

"Congratulations on making it here," Bion said. "You are one of the lucky few."

"Thank you. It's good to hear a friendly voice."

"I suppose you are headed for a large fight?" Bion asked.

"I...don't know. Lysandros did say that I was moving up to a 'higher caliber' event. What's it like? Have you been through that?" Teigra asked. She could barely make out the features of his face in the darkness of the cell.

"Yes. You might say I'm a veteran at this point," he replied. "You enter through a door in the floor of the amphitheater and when you look up, you are surrounded by thousands of people who have come to see you die. You must focus very quickly, as the attacks come immediately. And sometimes there are animals."

"Animals?" asked Teigra.

"They loosed a lion during one of my three matches," Bion said. "But the armor of other dead fighters is free for the taking. I recommend grabbing whatever you can."

Teigra knew she had to save her energy. She also realized there was no way out of this cycle. She had proven her mettle, and Lysandros would now milk her for all she was worth...until she lost a fight. And losing a fight meant death.

She passed the hours drawing on the walls of her cell with small stones she found on the floor. Lysandros took notice of her primitive artwork and encouraged her by bringing pieces of charcoal, which she would use to cover the walls with scenes of herself in battle garb or dispatching her opponents in hideously violent ways.

She saw Lysandros only when he brought food—though he had guards and servants, he preferred to serve the food himself. He figured his warriors were always glad to see food, so if there was any way for them to view him in a positive light, this was it.

"You look beautiful...and well rested!" Lysandros told her. "Now come on. Your day has arrived." Guards stood by as he took her to the wagon. "Are you ready? This time, it's going to be a whole other level."

* * *

Over the next year, Lysandros entered Teigra in numerous fights, providing her with ample time to heal and train between events. Each of these fights was on an increasingly larger scale.

Teigra's reputation gradually began to precede her. She fought only in grand amphitheaters, traveling by wagon to many competitions. Though she had days—sometimes weeks—to recuperate from each one, they all eventually melded into one blood-soaked blur.

These large-scale events featured several fighters, with the occasional round of animals. They usually began with Teigra, Lysandros, and the team ushered to the back of the building where the other fighters were being registered, then they were taken down a ramp to an underground holding pen. Guards were everywhere to ensure that none of the fighters tried to gain their freedom. All of this happened as thousands of spectators filed in, hoping to see Teigra kill or be killed.

The air was always filled with tension and uncertainty as the fighters waited for their names to be announced. Finally, a bell would sound, a hatch would open, and they would be prodded to walk up stairs by the guards. As the light got brighter, the sound of the crowd swelled, and they were suddenly being circled by their opponents. Each show would last anywhere from one to two hours, usually with two eight-person teams pitted against each other. During one of these matches, Teigra was able to take a protective metal crotch piece and helmet from a dead female fighter.

The animals that were put into the ring were not meant to leave—they had to be killed. Teigra was sympathetic to these poor beasts, but on one occasion a tiger turned on her and she was forced to take an ax to its head, administering a quick, painful death. This made her a crowd favorite. Lysandros negotiated with the amphitheater workers to get the skin of the tiger, which was fashioned into a wrap that Teigra wore around her legs. She also made a metallic brassiere out of two pieces of mismatched armor. It completed her uniform.

As she got stronger, Teigra began to enjoy the fights. She had developed a recognizable fighting style, striking with a brutal speed that cut her enemies down before they had a chance to react. As her reputation continued to grow, attendees would come specifically to see her and place wagers. The odds were always in her favor. Undefeated, she had become a ruthless killer.

CHAPTER 11

NEW ARRIVAL

A rapidly shifting black shadow signaled to its counterparts to move around the half circle of trees. Without a sound, the three warriors were in position. They were dressed in black armor, and their faces were painted with charcoal. The night was moonless, aiding the stealth warriors in their attempt at invisibility. Handheld torches illuminated the clearing ahead. There, cowering together, were a dozen girls surrounded by menacing Argive soldiers.

"This lot will make a fine prize for Prince Zarek," the leader said, as he surveyed the terrified girls on his horse. "He will be quite pleased."

"Yes, sir," another soldier responded with a chuckle.

"Gather them into a single-file line and chain their ankles and hands," the leader commanded. "Their village is gone, so we can get moving."

As he spoke, the three in the surrounding dark woods silently coordinated the best plan of action. Fifteen Argives stood encamped around the girls, but fortunately most were clustered in a pack.

The time had come to make a move. The lead Sondra motioned with her right arm. In an instant, darts found their way into the necks of the three soldiers at the front. They dropped immediately, possibly due to the precise aim of the darts, but more likely because of the poison that laced their tips.

The remaining Argives tried to run for cover but couldn't tell from where the strikes were coming. Two more soldiers fell, with long darts puncturing their jugular veins.

The woods otherwise were silent. The only sounds were those of panicked soldiers and the thud of bodies falling to the ground.

The leader frantically looked around, trying to locate the assassins. "Use the girls for cover!" he shouted. "On my mark, all of you take a girl as armor." He signaled with a swing of his arm, and each soldier grabbed a girl to hold before him. It was a good strategy; the aerial poison dart attacks suddenly became much riskier.

The soldiers waited, watched, and listened, trying their best to peer into the dark forest. "Extinguish the torches!" shouted the chief officer.

This proved a fatal mistake.

The moment the lights of the torches were gone, enveloping the camp in darkness, the three Sondras attacked. What had been complete silence was now replaced with the sound of necks snapping and last gasps for breath.

By the time the leader relit a torch, only one soldier was still breathing. The girls were huddled together, unharmed.

The attackers were nowhere to be seen.

"Let's move, soldier, quickly! We're outmanned! Grab that horse and—ahhhckkk…" The leader couldn't complete his sentence before feeling the sting of a large dart in his throat. His commands would have fallen on deaf ears anyway—his last remaining soldier lay dead beside him.

With these Argives now corpses, the Sondras emerged from the woods. The girls, who still trembled from the horrors they'd witnessed, did not fear the three warriors dressed in black. Being from an Amazon tribe, they knew very well who had intervened. The Sondras stood tall, and looked as if they hadn't even broken a sweat. In a matter of seconds, and without being seen, they had wiped out an entire platoon of soldiers.

"Are you girls from Queen Kyra's tribe?" asked the lead Sondra.

"Yes, our village was burned by Prince Zarek's men," replied one of the girls, with wet, wide eyes.

"I see." The Sondra shook her head. "Come, let's get you safely to our camp. We are with Queen Alexa."

The Sondras placed as many girls as possible on their three horses and walked through the night to camp. Water was rationed, as were the portions of food they had in their pouches. Queen Kyra's tribe was adjacent to Queen Alexa's, but the journey through the thick forest was still long and arduous. By early morning, the group had finally reached its destination.

The Sondras waited patiently outside of Queen Alexa's hut. It was mid-morning, and Alexa was meeting with her advisors regarding the recent attacks by Prince Zarek's troops. The girls from Kyra's tribe ranged in age from seven to fifteen. All of them were dirty, tired, and scared. The last few days had been unbearable, hiding and running from soldiers. Then they were captured and held prisoner...while the rest of their tribe was annihilated. Had it not been for the Sondras, they would've faced an even worse fate at the hands of Zarek.

After the Queen's advisors departed, Alexa's assistant summoned the three rescuers. A Sondra named Rhea entered first, while another named Aviva motioned for the girls to follow. As they all came into the Queen's hut, they saw Alexa seated alone at the far end. Laria was sharpening a spear in a corner, looked up to see the Sondras and the group of girls, and immediately rose to her feet.

"Queen Alexa, thank you for seeing us," Rhea said, bowing.

"Of course," Alexa responded. "Who is with you?"

"We found these girls in the woods to the south, in the outer limits of our patrol this morning," Rhea said. "They were captured by Argive soldiers after their village had been burned to the ground."

"How many Argives were there?" Alexa asked.

"We encountered fifteen, but there were likely more when the village was scorched," Rhea replied.

"Did any escape during your rescue?" Alexa asked.

"No, my Queen," Rhea said.

Alexa stood and paced around her chair, rubbing her forehead. Queen Kyra's tribe lay just south of her own. If Prince Zarek was attacking there, it would only be a matter of time before his soldiers advanced farther north. Why couldn't his old father or the council stop him? She had no way of retaliating against Zarek without the wrath of King Bedros upon her. This was not a game; the prince was destroying villages, and killing and capturing girls for his sick hobby.

"Rhea, did you survey the village?" Alexa inquired.

"No, my Queen," Rhea replied. "We made the decision to get the girls to safety, and then seek your permission to extend patrol outside our tribe's boundaries."

"Understood. Take a group of Sondras with you and search for any information about what may have transpired. Report back to me as soon as possible."

"Yes, my Queen. What about the girls?"

"Laria can show them to the girls' encampment. They can get cleaned up and have some food. They are now part of our family," Alexa said, forcing a smile in the direction of the girls.

"Yes, my Queen," Rhea replied.

The warriors left Queen Alexa's hut. Laria quickly made her way over to the rescued girls. The tallest one looked to be about Laria's age and was standing at the front of the group. Though the girl was filthy and visibly exhausted, Laria couldn't help but notice how beautiful she was. Laria was eager to demonstrate her usefulness by guiding them to the camp.

"Hello, everyone. My name is Laria," she began. "Let me show you where you can get cleaned up."

One by one, the girls bowed to their new Queen and meekly followed Laria out of the hut. Laria purposefully walked next to the tall girl.

"What is your name?" she asked.

"My name is Melia," the girl answered, without looking up from the dirt path.

"You must be very hungry."

"We have not eaten much for the last few days. Some food and water would be very much appreciated," Melia replied.

Though Melia was filthy and looked as if she'd been crying all night, she was as beautiful as a lark. Her long red hair, although tattered, fell in locks around her face. It was wavy and complemented her milky complexion. She was slender, and her muscular body hugged her threadbare tunic. Laria found herself stealing furtive glances at the other girl, and began to sense a physical desire she had never felt before.

Melia looked at Laria and weakly smiled, but her mind was far away. She couldn't help but think about her friends, her tribe, and her home. Everyone she knew and everything she owned had been lost in a few hours. She'd spent the last two nights fearing for her life, lost in the woods. She hadn't known if she would starve or be found by soldiers, or what her fate would hold if she were discovered. After seeing the remains of her camp, she'd feared the worst.

They reached the opening to the girls' washing area. Laria stopped in front of the large tent and lifted the flap, motioning for the girls to enter. "You can clean up here. I'll be back shortly."

Laria gathered fresh clothes for all the new Amazons and walked back into the tent. She left a clean garment for each girl at the washing basin. As she reached Melia, Laria couldn't escape noticing the beauty of the naked body in front of her. When Melia took a cup from the basin and poured water over herself, it fell like liquid satin over her slender form. Laria found it impossible to shake her gaze as she followed the curves of Melia's body from her breasts to her small navel and hips. Only when Melia looked up to meet her eyes was Laria able to pull herself back into the moment. Laria left the clean tunic on the basin bench and quickly moved on to the next girl.

The camp was less busy than normal. There were no training exercises for a few days, as Queen Alexa had declared a holiday to celebrate the beginning of summer. The Queen had considered canceling the event because of the recent threats to her people, but decided it was more important to provide a bit of normalcy and festivity for the newest members of the tribe.

Laria had taken it upon herself that day to help all the new girls feel as comfortable and relaxed as possible. After she made sure they knew where to find anything they needed in preparation for the evening, she approached Melia.

"I thought perhaps you would you like to go hunting with me this afternoon," Laria proposed, hoping to win a few private hours with the girl.

"I've been pretty exhausted the last few days, to be quite honest," Melia responded.

"Maybe going on an outing will keep your mind off of everything else," Laria suggested. "I can tell you more about our camp while we're away."

"Well, I suppose it could help me sleep well tonight, and that would be nice," Melia conceded.

Laria and Melia spent the entire afternoon in the forest together. Laria showed off her hunting skills, spearing two rabbits, all while continuing to admire Melia's beauty. Melia, on the other hand, had little interest in hunting, but did enjoy passing the time away from her new camp, which inevitably reminded her of her lost village.

As the two made their way back, Laria gently reached out to hold Melia's hand. The sad and devastated girl didn't resist, but Laria was providing most of the grasp. In silence, they walked home after the day's expedition.

Meanwhile, Thea was finishing a grueling day. Sondra training was the most intense physical undertaking, and Thea took it very seriously. Waking each day before dawn, she practiced archery, knife fighting, stealth, and many other skills. Even when aptitude classes within the camp took days of rest, Sondra training would continue. Only during a holiday would the training cease for a few days. Thea found herself looking forward to the first training break in months. After the day's lessons, she could do as she pleased for a while. She planned to put the finishing touches on a painting she'd been working on—a vibrant depiction of herself in full Sondra regalia, astride Nox.

Laria and Melia were making their way back to camp through the thick trees that surrounded the open field where the horses were trained. Thea was trotting on Nox. She immediately noticed Melia, who looked stunning in her new garments, her hair combed and laying gently on exposed shoulders. Thea dismounted Nox and walked toward them, effortlessly leading her horse.

"Laria, who is your friend?" asked Thea.

"This is Melia," Laria said, offering no more than necessary, and looking at Melia as she spoke.

"Hello, I'm Thea," Thea said, reaching out a hand to make Melia's acquaintance. "Are you new to camp?"

"Yes," Melia replied. "I am from Queen Kyra's tribe. It was destroyed by the Argive soldiers."

"I'm so sorry," Thea replied, gently shaking her head with sincere sympathy. "I can't imagine how painful that must be for you."

Melia had instinctively reached her hand out to meet Thea's, but now her drooped head lifted, and her eyes met Thea's for the first time. They were wet with tears, glistening in the setting sunlight. Thea's words had been the first to acknowledge the pain inside her, and the emotions she had been suppressing for days had risen to the surface.

"Here," Thea said, as she handed Melia a small cloth. "I didn't mean to upset you."

"Thea, don't you think you should be running along?" asked Laria. "Melia's had a tough time and she doesn't need to be reminded of it."

"I'm sorry, Melia, really," Thea said, without the slightest recognition of Laria. "If you need anything at all, please seek me out."

"I am sure she will be fine," Laria insisted. "We already went out hunting today to get her mind off things."

"Hunting?" Thea inquired, as if noticing Laria for the first time. "What did you hunt?"

"I caught two rabbits, see?" Laria said, as she held her shoulder bag open for Thea to examine.

"Yes. Well, I suppose that might take your mind off things. Although there are many other ways to do that, which I'd be happy to…" Thea said, trailing off. Her eyes were still locked, unblinking, transcending to a place somewhere inside the portal that Melia's eyes allowed her access to.

"Thank you," Melia replied, unable to resist a small smile. Her cheeks felt flush, and she diverted her gaze to the ground. She took the soft square of cloth Thea had offered and held it flush against her mouth in an attempt to hide her blushing. Thea smiled in return.

Taking offense at Thea's brash advances, Laria quickly devised a counterattack. She had always been aware of Thea's inability to whistle, and decided that this would be a weakness worth exploiting in front of Melia.

"Hey, Thea. Melia and I were whistling on the walk back from our hunt. She's really good! Whistling contest, really quick! Let's see who's the loudest," Laria challenged.

"Ah, I don't know," Thea hesitated, not wanting to admit her lack of ability.

"Come on!" With that, Laria put her lips together and blew, creating a clear, ringing tone. "Your turn, Melia!"

Smiling, Melia took her cue, put two fingers in her mouth and blew abruptly, creating a sharp, shrill, and incredibly loud whistle.

"Wow!" Laria said, as she and Melia giggled. "Excellent, Melia! Your turn, Thea."

Thea could already feel herself begin to sweat, as she expected to embarrass herself in front of this beautiful girl she had only just met. She knew she should refuse, but hoped there was a chance that, just this once, a sound would actually come out when she tried. She put her lips together and blew. The only sound that emerged was a limp rush of air. Laria and Melia laughed.

"Thea, can't you whistle?" Laria asked between giggles. "No second chances! You win, Melia!"

"Oh well, there's always next time!" Thea said, trying to not show her annoyance with Laria. Anyway, seeing Melia laugh was worth it. "Nice to meet you, Melia. I'm *sure* I'll see you again!"

With that, she turned, mounted Nox, and galloped off toward the stables with a small turn of her head to take another look at the beautiful maiden who had made a deep impression on her. Laria started speaking as she took Melia's elbow in her hand; but as the two girls walked to Queen Alexa's hut, Melia didn't hear a word she said.

Although Nox was pounding the soil beneath her, Thea knew the shaking she felt inside her soul had nothing to do with the horse's gallop and everything to do with what she'd just experienced. She went a short distance before slowing Nox to turn and take one last look at Melia. Even from behind, as Melia solemnly walked away, she was intoxicating.

* * *

The skies were crystal clear the following day, and the warmth of summer was already beginning. Thea had been out exploring the forests all morning, even venturing outside the approved safety areas. Fortunately, she avoided any of the patrolling Sondras who might have reported her violation to Alexa. There was something about being in the forbidden land that Thea always found unable to resist.

Her life had drastically changed since she was set on the path to become a Sondra. She finally found the focus she'd always desired, and had thrown herself into the challenging routines and demanding physical exertions of the training. She'd never felt as strong, as clear-headed, or as much a part of something. But deep down, she was the same girl that longed for carefree hours alone in the forest to run and explore.

Thea and Nox came across a magnificent waterfall along the western part of her tribe's region. She had seen it before, but recent rains had more than doubled its size, making it the perfect place to stop for a swim. Thea happily took advantage of this wondrous natural resource.

After her swim, she rode along the stream back to camp. She saw Laria and Melia in the distance, sitting beside a lake fed by the stream. Thea paused for a moment to observe the girls from her safe and unannounced position. She dismounted Nox and stood by a patch of trees, out of sight. Laria and Melia stood at the water's edge, laughing and whistling while Laria skipped stones onto the lake's glassy surface. The day was still, and not a breeze tempered the air. Even from afar, Thea could appreciate Melia's beauty. The tunic she wore exposed her slender arms and legs, and the sun radiated on her auburn hair from the light bouncing across the surface of the motionless lake. As Thea watched, she noticed that Laria was holding Melia's hand. Immediately, Thea's heart began to pound.

Not quite sure how to describe what she was feeling, Thea instantly sensed a returning antipathy for Laria. Neither Laria's history of teasing her nor the natural competition that they always shared in training had created this feeling. Jealousy brewed within Thea for the simple reason that it was not her holding Melia's hand at the lake. She watched as Laria moved to face Melia. She saw Laria lift Melia's chin with a shaky hand. She continued to stare as the Queen's granddaughter gently leaned forward. Thea couldn't endure the display any longer. She reacted without thought or plan.

"Laria! Laria!" Thea called loudly, emerging from her hiding place.

Laria looked up, startled by the sound of her name being shouted from the silence of the trees. She squinted her eyes, looking for the source of the voice. Thea hurriedly mounted Nox and rode toward the girls.

"Laria, I believe your grandmother is looking for you," Thea reported, as she charged into the open field.

"What do you mean? Is she or isn't she?" Laria asked, irritated.

"She is," Thea confirmed, riding around the girls in a wide circle. "Something urgent."

"What is it?" Laria asked.

"I don't know," Thea replied. "No one told me that."

"Fine. Melia, let's go," Laria said, more sternly than she intended.

"Melia, if you would like to remain, I can show you back to camp later," Thea offered.

"I am sure she has no interest in that," Laria said, looking sternly at Thea.

"Actually," Melia said, "I'm not quite ready to go back to camp yet."

Laria looked from one girl to the other, and then back again, trying to dissect their gaze upon each other. "I'll see you soon, Melia," she said, and walked back to where she'd tied her horse along the trail's edge.

Thea's guilt about lying to Laria quickly passed as she saw the chance to spend some time with the girl that so intrigued her. Thea had never been attracted to any of the other girls in camp, but there

was something unique about Melia. It wasn't just her beauty that
Thea found appealing, but also her story. Thea felt she could relate
to her, and welcomed the chance to find out more about her. None
of the other girls in camp had been as isolated as Thea. Even Corina,
who was ostracized for her looks, had a family and somewhere to
feel like she belonged. Thea knew that she and Melia shared many
of the same pains of loneliness.

"What would you like to do?" Thea asked.

"I don't really care. Let's just stay in the forest for a while," Melia
replied, smiling.

"Yeah, I understand. I've lived in the tribe all my life, and I don't
like going back there a lot of the time either."

"Why not?" Melia asked.

"Well, I suppose it's because I never quite felt that I belonged."

"What do you mean?" Melia asked.

Thea slipped off Nox and fell into place beside Melia.

"I always felt like I was different. I don't like to follow rules, and
I used to get into trouble a lot for it. Anyway, I just find it peaceful
in the woods. Nobody's here to tell me what to do or how to be. I
can hear my thoughts better here."

Thea slid her arm down Nox's long neck and stroked her silky
coat. She reached into a pouch at her waist and gave Nox an apple.
Melia studied Thea and her horse for the first time. There was
something strong and determined in Thea that reminded her of the
assertive women in her camp. It made her feel safe.

"That's a beautiful horse," Melia said. "Where did you get her?"

"I found her in the forest one day, believe it or not. Her name is
Nox. Would you like to go for a ride?" Thea asked.

Melia did not answer in words, but flashed a large grin and wide
eyes. Thea gracefully swung onto Nox's back and then held out her
hand to assist Melia. Melia mounted Nox behind Thea, and the two
girls took off in a gallop along the stream, back toward the waterfall.
Thea knew the waterfall would be a nice place of rest for her friend.
She felt Melia's hands around her waist, and her heart began to beat
a little faster. She could sense every stroke of contact between her

body and Melia's—the touch of Melia's thighs against the back of her legs, Melia's breasts against her back, and Melia's hair as it brushed against her arms in the wind. With each gallop, Thea felt a yearning to be even closer to Melia.

The girls rode in silence as Nox took them along the stream's edge in the warm afternoon. Streaks of sunlight made the trees come to life as shadows danced across their path. The peacefulness of the scenery soothed them. For Melia, it seemed to quench a thirst that she had difficulty defining. The tranquility of the stream's song and the breeze across her face temporarily melted her thoughts away.

"The waterfall is incredible," Melia said.

"Nox and I found it like this earlier on our ride," Thea said. "The rains have made it extra special."

They dismounted and walked toward the edge of the waterfall. Without hesitation, Thea waded in far enough to feel the water crash against her arms and hands as she splashed it onto her face. Melia noticed Thea's tall, slender body as her wet tunic conformed to her skin. Water slid down Thea's face and onto her bronze skin before reluctantly going back into the pool at her thighs. Thea had grown into quite a beautiful young woman.

"Melia, would you like to go with me on an adventure?" Thea asked.

"What kind of adventure?" Melia replied.

"Well, it's the season for the Nemean Games. There's a chariot race tomorrow and a nice prize for the winner," Thea said.

"In Nemea? Isn't that outside of Amazon territory?" Melia asked.

"Yes," Thea replied. "I told you I wasn't much for following the rules!"

Melia paused, intrigued by the passion in the eyes of the girl before her.

"Won't we get into trouble?" Melia asked.

"If we sneak out tonight from camp and get to Nemea, we will have a few hours to sleep and then train with the chariot before the race. Once we ready ourselves, we register, enter the race, take the prize, and get back before anyone even realizes we're gone," Thea replied. "Besides, training camp is on break for another three days. How will they know?"

"How much is the prize?"

"I hear it's a full bag of silver coins."

"Do you have a chariot?"

"I know where to find one," Thea said. "I think I can talk my friend Carina into going. She can help us get everything ready for the race."

Melia paused for a moment. She didn't want to upset the Queen of her new camp by disobeying the rules so quickly after arriving. She was grateful to have a new home and was hesitant to test the limits of her new Queen's patience. Sensing her internal struggle, Thea offered, "Whatever you want to do is fine. I'll be going, and you're welcome to come along if you choose. If not, I'll let you count my silver when I return."

The girls laughed and enjoyed the cool and refreshing water. Melia smiled and stepped deeper into the pool, making her way to the waterfall. The water soothed her sun-soaked skin. It had been a few hours since she'd thought about her mother or the tribe; it was nice to have a little vacation from her reflection. Being around Thea somehow provided her the space to be in the moment and out of her past.

Thea and Melia took their time riding back to the camp, as the warm summer temperature faded into the coolness of the early evening. Both sat quietly, feeling as comfortable in the silence as they did with each other. Thea enjoyed the touch of Melia's hands on her hips as they rode, and the warmth of her skin against her back. Her senses were heightened with Melia's touch, causing her mind to venture into thoughts that were new to her. Melia enjoyed the closeness, and smelling the sweet scent of Thea's hair as it brushed against her face. It was like she was absorbing Thea's strength as she laid her body against the vibrant energy of the Sondra-in-training.

Neither wanted the ride to end, but before long they'd arrived in camp. The sun was just setting and dinner was being served. Thea led Nox to the stalls, then accompanied Melia into the dining tent. Laria sat at one end of the tent and glared as she watched them enter. Thea sensed someone watching her, looked in Laria's direction, and was reminded of her lie earlier in the day. For just a quick moment, she felt bad about it again. The girls made their way to the opposite end of the tent where Carina had saved room for Thea, as she always did.

"Carina, this is Melia," Thea said. "Is there room for both of us here?"

"Of course," Carina said, smiling. "Hello Melia, I'm Carina. I've heard about your terrible loss. I hope that we can help."

"Thank you," Melia replied, smiling back.

"So, what did you two do today?" Carina asked.

"We rode Nox out to the western side of the tribe where the small waterfall is," Thea replied. "But the waterfall is now big and breathtaking. How about you?"

"I went to the markets," Carina replied. "It was very busy there. More people than usual."

"Really? I was thinking about heading somewhere similar tomorrow," Thea said in a whisper.

"What do you mean?" Carina asked, taking the bait.

"Well, there's a chariot race in Nemea with a pretty big prize. I was looking for someone who might know where to get a chariot," Thea said, beginning to dig into her food.

"Oh no, Thea!" Carina exclaimed. "I know what you're thinking! You know we're forbidden to leave the area with all that's been going on. Are you crazy?"

Thea looked up at Carina and just smiled.

"Don't answer that," Carina said. "We both know the answer."

All the while, Melia was intently listening, trying to learn more about Thea. Melia was intrigued and fascinated by Thea's lack of fear—she'd never met anyone like her before. There was a passion and fierce confidence in Thea's attitude that she both admired and was drawn to.

"How much does it cost to enter the race?" Carina asked.

"Ten pieces of silver," Thea replied.

"And where do you plan to get ten pieces of silver?" Carina continued.

"I'll figure that out. I just need a chariot," Thea said.

"I am thinking of going," Melia said, drawing both Thea's and Carina's surprised stares.

"You are?" Thea said with an uncontrolled smile.

"Well, yeah. Otherwise, I'll just be sitting around here all day thinking about things I don't want to think about," Melia said.

"Great," Carina said, sarcastically. She then added, as if being forced against her will, "I guess I'm in. I'll get the chariot."

Thea explained that they should all meet outside the sleeping hut soon after the large camp flame at the center of the huts was extinguished for the night. Carina was to get the chariot and a horse from the stalls, while Thea and Melia would ride on Nox. Thea would enter the race with Nox, they would collect their earnings, and then all of them would make it home before sunset. No one would ever know they'd left.

The plan sounded reasonable, and they agreed to meet later that evening. In the meantime, Thea had just one more thing to address.

She pretended to sleep while waiting for all the other girls and commanders to fall into their slumber. Carefully, she escaped her hut without making a sound. The entire camp was quiet and still. Leaping from shadow to shadow, Thea maneuvered between the torch lights that guarded the camp. As she came to the camp commander's area, she crept silently into the head instructor's hut. Her heart beat faster, and she could feel the blood pulsing through her veins. She could hear every sound and feel every drop of sweat on her skin. In the back of the hut sat a small chest.

Thea tiptoed toward the back of the hut. A small bolted clamp held the lid shut, but she'd learned how to get past it with a few coordinated twists and pulls. The sleeping instructor softly snored a few feet away, but Thea moved quickly and without a sound.

She collected twenty-five pieces of silver from inside the chest, tucking them neatly away in her pouch. After reassembling the bolt and clamp, she moved to make her way back out of the hut. But Thea's foot knocked into the edge of the chest, causing the hardware to clank as the chest jolted an inch across the floor.

The instructor stirred and coughed. Thea froze. If her instructor woke, she might pierce Thea with a dagger before even realizing who the intruder was. The moment passed, however, and the instructor returned to her dormant state. With a silent sigh of relief, Thea took the few remaining steps to free herself from the hut.

By the time Thea had arrived back, Carina was walking toward her, leading Nox and another horse, and Melia was making her way to their meeting place through the sleeping camp. Thea smiled at the other two as they left to collect the chariot Carina had parked at the forest's edge. With a little luck, they would avoid Sondras and other surprises along the way. It was time for an adventure.

CHAPTER 12

THE GODS' FAVORITE

While Teigra still resented Lysandros for keeping her a prisoner and forcing her to put her life on the line for his financial gain, on some level she was, for the moment, content. During her year and a half spent training and fighting, her combat power and skill had multiplied, providing her with an unwavering confidence. The training had made her a deadly force of nature. Teigra knew that once she freed herself she would have a much better chance of survival.

Teigra had also become addicted to the adulation of the crowd. She could tell that they loved to see her win. The surge of adrenaline, the smell of sweat and blood, and the energy that poured from an appreciative audience was intoxicating. Ironically, it was in the death of others that Teigra found life.

Teigra very much looked the part of the career warrior. Her costume, constructed piecemeal from the armor of dead opponents, was both impressive and intimidating. A metal V-shape protected her hips and groin, sandals extended up to her knees with formidable spiked shin guards, and her helmet featured an extended piece to protect her nose. Her hair was pulled through a hole in the top, causing her head to resemble a rooster's comb. Her abdomen remained exposed, leaving her vulnerable, but it created considerable sex appeal.

Lysandros was profiting quite nicely from Teigra's skills. His entire attitude had changed toward her. She received even more meat with her meals, and he would bring her small gifts. It was clear that he was developing feelings for her that went beyond a master/slave relationship. Not only had Teigra grown stronger, but she'd also become increasingly attractive. Many men had offered Lysandros significant sums of money to buy Teigra, but each time he declined.

One evening he approached her stall with an update: "You will be participating in a Pankration match in two days in Nemea. We'll be getting up early tomorrow, as we have quite a journey ahead of us. There's going to be twice the crowd because of the annual festival there."

Teigra raised her eyes, but said nothing.

"Here, have some more meat," he offered.

Teigra took the meat and stuffed it into her mouth, staring at him without emotion.

"Perhaps you'd like a special treat," Lysandros said, with a sly smile. "I imagine it's pretty lonely in the stall at night."

"The stall is fine. Men are all pigs," Teigra blurted out as she swallowed the food.

"We'll see. I may be able to change your mind about that. Your life could be a lot easier if you'd cooperate," Lysandros told her. "Or perhaps I might just sell you for a nice profit and be done with you. There's certainly a demand."

"What difference does it make? You'll just keep forcing me to fight until I don't make it out of the arena alive," Teigra snarled.

Teigra didn't show it, but she knew Lysandros was too personally interested in her to sell her. She had managed to fend off his amorous advances time and time again. Though she felt helpless in this fight-heal-fight cycle, she was hopeful there would be an end to it soon...even if she had to create it herself.

As she lay in her cell waiting for sleep to come, Teigra looked across the wall at her charcoal drawings, which were a sort of record of the previous eighteen months, and wondered how she'd managed to survive. Teigra thanked the Gods for allowing her to do so.

She fixated on a scene in which she stood in her armor, trium-phantly holding the severed head of a large male opponent. She tried to visualize a similar outcome for the next day's battle.

*   *   *

Lysandros packed supplies for the trip into his wagon, and with one of his guards they started on their way. Teigra sat in the back, in shackles. Lysandros occasionally tried to make conversation with her, but she kept her answers as monosyllabic as possible.

Throughout the course of their journey, they made several stops to relieve themselves by the roadside. Lysandros reserved privacy for himself, but seemed to take a perverse pleasure in aiding Teigra with her garments and watching her manage her bodily functions while shackled. She knew that only Lysandros could remove her leg irons, and trying to escape across the hot, dry terrain would mean her demise.

Teigra had trouble quieting her thoughts on the way to Nemea. She hated this man who was profiting by putting her life in danger. But was it any better to be a house slave and suffer violence at the hands of a master? She loved the adoration of the crowd, but was it any match for freedom? She felt hopeless, but knew she had to channel her feelings into the kind of anger and ferocity that would help her conquer whomever she'd be fighting in Nemea. She allowed sleep to overtake her.

CHAPTER 13

NEMEA HIPPODROME

The sky began to take on a purplish hue, signaling that dawn was rapidly approaching. Thea and Melia rode Nox at a steady pace, while Carina rode beside them in the chariot. They'd been fortunate to sneak out without the sounds of the chariot waking anyone. By daybreak, everyone in the camp would be starting their routines, and it was unlikely the trio would be missed.

It was mid-morning, and the temperature was starting to rise as they decided to stop and rest. They could tell that it was going to be a large crowd by the increasing number of travelers entering Nemea, a very busy town open to merchants from all over the world. Nemea was patrolled by Argives, but Thea felt no danger. Argive guards weren't there to harass travelers, or anyone else, as that would hurt business by discouraging merchants from visiting; and via local taxes, the Argives received a percentage of all trade conducted. Thea reasoned that Nemea was actually one of the safest places for them.

"Wow, that's quite a crowd!" Carina said. "Are they all here for the chariot race?"

"Probably," Thea said. "We need to find the circus so we can register our horse and chariot."

"My guess is that it's over there," Melia said, pointing to her right.

Indeed, the majority of the audience was headed toward a large round structure, some two hundred paces from where they stood. The closer they got, the denser the mob became. Carina and Thea had been to Nemea with their instructors to witness competitions from time to time, but they'd never been to the main circus and hadn't encountered anything of this magnitude before.

Negotiating a path through the mass of eager spectators, the registration table came into view. Thea checked her pouch and headed over to where a couple of older Nemean men sat, collecting money. They both had white beards and scarred bodies, which Carina, hanging back, found intimidating. Thea thought nothing of it.

"I'd like to enter the chariot race," Thea announced.

"Is that so?" chuckled one of them. "That's not likely to happen, girly. Women aren't allowed to race. Find yourself another town… preferably one not controlled by Argives."

"What do you mean?" Thea demanded. "Women have raced here before. I've seen them myself!"

"Only if their husbands allow it, missy," the man stated. "And you don't look like you have a husband."

"Who says? Don't be so quick to judge," Thea replied.

Thea walked over to Carina and Melia, who were waiting a few paces away from the table.

"I need a husband," Thea announced.

"Boy, when you make decisions, you don't fool around," Carina teased.

"I need a husband to sign me up for the chariot race," Thea said. "It's in the stupid rules."

"Hey, Thea. Look over there!" Melia said.

By the side of the road sat a beggar holding a wine flask. He was leaning against the wheel of a cart that a traveler had conveniently parked. Had it not been there, he would have been lying flat on the ground.

"If we give him some wine, I bet we can get him to be your husband," Melia said.

"Not a bad idea," Thea replied.

Thea walked over to a wine merchant and bought a small flask. The three girls then approached the beggar.

Fortunately, it was early enough in the day for the drunkard to still be somewhat coherent. Had it been evening, additional wine would have made their plan impossible.

"Sir, may we ask a favor of you?" Thea began, showing the beggar the utmost respect. "Would you act as my husband and sponsor me for the chariot race?"

The beggar looked up, astonished that someone was calling him "sir." He immediately snapped to his senses, however, when he heard the opportunity for barter.

"Huh? You need a husband?" the beggar stammered.

"I need you to say you're my husband and sign me up for the chariot race," Thea said.

"A fine girl like yourself should have no trouble getting a husband," the beggar observed.

"Very kind words, sir. But I was just looking for a temporary husband so that I may race. How about it?"

"Hmmm. Seems a bit dishonest to me," the beggar said, leveraging his position.

"I'll tell you what. There's wine in it for you," Thea countered, showing him the flask.

"Now you're speaking my language, girl," the beggar said, getting more animated after seeing what was to be gained.

Thea helped the beggar to his feet and walked him over to the registration table.

"My husband is here to sign me up for the chariot race," Thea announced.

"Ha! *This* is your husband?" asked one of the men. "I'd say you made a poor choice! Come on, girl, you can't expect me to believe he's your spouse!"

"How dare you insult us!" Thea exclaimed, trying to act offended.

"Is this your wife?" the man asked the beggar.

"Yes it is!" the beggar slurred. "She's mighty fine, isn't she?"

"All right, fine. What do I care? A girl getting manhandled out there should be quite a sight. You have the ten pieces of silver?"

"Right here," Thea said, placing the coins on the table.

"What are both of your names?" the man continued.

"I'm Thea, and my husband's name is..." Thea said, then nudged the beggar in his back.

"Drakos!" the beggar blurted out.

The admissions man rolled his eyes, but then looked at her bag of money.

"Which chariot race are you registering for...two or four horses?" he asked.

"Two," she said.

He gestured for the money, which she gave him.

"But," she added, swallowing a little, "one horse is injured. The other can race, though."

The man's face darkened. "You cannot race with just one horse!"

Sighing, Thea said, "Okay, fine. Give me back my money, then."

"Wait." The admissions man thought about it. He reminded himself that the mayor was quite loose when it came to such policies. In the meantime, he thought that perhaps letting her race with just one horse would be good for a laugh.

Shaking his head, the man proceeded to fill out the entry card and give Thea her race number. Thea then walked the beggar back to the cart. Once she handed him the wine flask, their transaction was complete.

Melia and Carina were waiting across the road to see if their journey had been for naught. They were both relieved when Thea showed them her entry number. It would've been heartbreaking to give up after having taken the risk to get this far.

The race began at noon, which left the girls with enough time to prepare Nox and the chariot.

Thea inquired about the prizes when she was at the table. The first place winner received a bag full of silver coins, and second place received fifty silver coins. She had her own ideas about how to make this venture more profitable.

"Carina, I want you to do something," Thea said.

"I already don't like the sound of this," Carina replied.

"Here are fifteen more silver coins," Thea said, handing them over. "Go to the wager's table and place a bet on me. And don't forget your ticket."

"Where did you get all these coins, Thea?" Carina asked.

"Do you really want to know?"

"Uh, no, I don't think I do," Carina admitted.

"Melia and I are going to the stalls to prepare Nox for the race. Meet us over there once you're done," Thea said.

"Okay."

Thea led Nox, and Melia led the other horse with the chariot. The stadium was huge, and the stalls were all located along one side. When they approached a gatekeeper, he attempted to turn them away. But once Thea showed her entry number he reluctantly let them pass.

More than a dozen chariots had entered the race, and each of the riders stared as Thea and Melia walked through the gateway. With all the stalls already occupied by other riders, they settled for a space out in the open. Thea could hear the chuckles and laughs cast in her direction. The crowd was already buying into the "joke" set up by the admissions man. Melia began loosening the chariot harness from Carina's horse while Thea, who was beginning to feel rather nervous, got Nox some water and hay.

"You all right?" Melia asked.

"Huh? Oh yeah, I'm fine!" Thea replied, trying to sound confident.

"Have you ever ridden in a chariot race before?" Melia asked.

"Plenty of times in camp, but not in anything like this," Thea said.

"Aren't you a little scared? I mean, with the Argives and the crowd and all."

Thea paused. Her natural response would be to refuse to admit her fear, but for some reason she didn't want to hide her emotions from Melia.

"Yeah, I'm a little scared," Thea admitted.

Melia appreciated Thea's honesty. Melia didn't know her very well, but she got the impression Thea tended to be fearless most of the time. For Thea to admit fear made Melia feel she'd gained her trust; and it made her feel closer to Thea. Melia pulled the chariot over to Nox and began putting the harness in place.

"Just watch your competition," Melia advised. "My mother used to race chariots a lot, and she said it wasn't the course or the speed that was dangerous, it was the other riders."

"That's good advice. Thanks."

The two girls finished placing the chariot and harness onto Nox, and tied the other horse to a post outside. The other chariots in the race were much more elaborately constructed. Many were lighter, with stronger axles and wheels; some were decorative and ornate.

The riders were also varied. Many were slaves, forced by their chariot owners to participate. But the more experienced riders owned their own chariots, and raced not only for the purse but for side-betting. Nemea was one of the few towns that allowed public gambling, and therefore was popular among the more seasoned riders.

"Hey Thea, your odds are at fifty-to-one," Carina reported as she walked up. "I put all the money on you to win, so you had better not let us down!"

"To win?" Thea asked surprised. "I figured you were going to put the wager on me to place."

"Was I supposed to? I just assumed you wanted me to bet on you to win," Carina replied.

"Uh, it's fine. Just a little more pressure, that's all," Thea said, with a slight smile.

Thea surveyed the other riders one last time, trying to pick out who was likely to be the most trouble. It was difficult to judge by appearance, as they all seemed rough and tough. Thea was just going to have to give the race her best. Fortunately, she had Nox and the little secret that she kept in her pouch. Hopefully, that would give her an edge.

"Hey there, girl," boomed a voice from one of the other riders. "You thinkin' of racin'?"

"I *am* racing," Thea replied.

"This should be a good one!" said the man, whose clothing

proclaimed him a proud Nemean. "Let me know how my dust tastes!" he added, laughing heartily.

"If I'm getting ready to lap you, I will," Thea said.

"You'll be lucky to get through the first lap, girly," the man retorted, his tone taking a turn toward the sinister. "This sport ain't meant for women. You'll just have to find out the hard way."

A horn sounded notifying racers to move to the starting line. Thea stepped into her chariot, attached the reins to her waist, and double-checked to make sure her whip and wooden horn were in place. She felt woozy; but this soon gave way to a feeling of pure determination, mixed only intermittently with flashes of nervousness.

"Thea, don't let that guy get to you," Melia said. "Nobody expects a woman to win, and that goes double for Nemeans. You know what you can do, and that's all that matters."

"Plus, you've got Nox," Carina chimed in. "She won't let you down."

"I know. Thanks," Thea said. "Wish me luck. See you on the other side!"

"May Hera find favor with you," Carina added, as Thea rode toward the track.

Fifteen charioteers made their way to one end of the circus. A massive crowd watched in the stands as each rider took a brief tour of the track before heading back to the starting gates. Tiers of spectators cheered or jeered as anticipation for the race mounted.

Thea could hear hecklers shouting and berating her for being a woman, and she could see the other riders snickering as they glanced her way. The massive attention, while negative, was beginning to empower her. Thea's natural defiance started to kick in, and she became determined to prove them all wrong.

"Okay, Nox," Thea whispered. "It's just you and me, girl. Let's show them what we can do!"

The race consisted of two laps around the oval-shaped circus, which allowed for both long straightaways and sharp turns. Thea knew from racing in camp that the turns were the most dangerous, as all the riders jockeyed for an inside position to reduce the length of

their race. This is where clusters of horses and riders caused crashes...
and where riders could become trampled under the wheels of other
chariots. The finish line was midway down the last straightaway,
located in front of the Governor's seat. The Governor would be the
one to award the victor the palm branch and purse.

Once all the racers were in their stalls with the gates closed, the
audience quieted, waiting for the race to begin. Thea was nearly in the
middle of the fifteen riders, so she knew that she'd need to negotiate
for position, right from the start. Her heart pounded in her chest as
she reminded herself that she was moments away from something
new and dangerous. This was the type of adventure she'd longed
for all her life. Her eyes widened as she saw the gatekeeper prepare
to start the race. When he pulled the lever, the gates opened with
a raucous crash...and Thea suddenly felt that her time had come.

Nox sprung into action as if she'd raced a thousand times before.
Thea remained in the middle of the pack, however, as elbows began
flying between the riders. She caught one in the chin, but rode on,
unaffected.

As the pack raced down the first straightaway, the riders began
to spread out a bit, enabling the faster racers to distance themselves
from the rest. By the end of the first stretch, Thea found herself in
the front four as they entered the turn. She could no longer feel her
heart pounding; her full attention was on her chariot and the race.
Cracking her whip into the air above Nox's head, she moved down
into the turn to gain advantage over the other riders.

As Thea made her move, two of the other charioteers slid together
to block her path. They seemed to be working in tandem, and she
identified one as the man who had insulted her outside the circus.
She found herself behind them and on the inside of the fourth rider.
Her chariot was boxed, leaving her with nowhere to go.

As the four chariots made the turn, the rider on the outside of
Thea began crashing his wheels into her chariot. With each push,
she felt her cart move up onto one wheel before settling back down.
Fortunately, she was able to make it through the curve without
toppling over.

Back in a straightaway, Thea and the smaller pack of riders managed to gain even more of a lead on the rest of the chariots. The man next to her was very tall and appeared to be a native Nemean. She was unable to escape him as he continued to throw elbows to knock her off balance. The crowd cheered when they saw a woman was in the lead pack, and chants for her race number echoed in the stadium.

Approaching the second turn, Thea knew she had to devise a better strategy, or she'd be dodging the chariots that were speeding up from behind her. As Thea and Nox dove into the inside portion of the track, she found herself behind the two lead charioteers, adjacent to the third rider on her outside. The third rider immediately began crashing into her chariot, attempting to tip it over.

After the second collision, the rider bounced outward a bit more. As he attempted to make a third collision, Thea pulled back on the reins, abruptly reducing Nox's speed. Not expecting this, his chariot overshot Thea, landing on the inside portion of the track and almost running off the course. Thea quickly accelerated and moved Nox into what had been the third jockey's position.

As the racers sped down the next straightaway, they had one lap remaining. The pudgy Governor proudly sat in his elevated seat, wearing a pompous grin as they passed. Thea cracked her whip and made an attempt to pull alongside the first two riders. Then the Nemean she'd met before the race raised his whip and snapped it toward her back. The pain seared into her skin and down to her bones. She fell back alongside the other rider as the crowd escalated their cheers at her imminent demise.

"Go back from where you came, girly," barked the large man in front of Thea.

"I will, as soon as I take the prize," Thea spat back.

"The only prize you'll be collecting is a few souvenirs from my whip," he said, sneering.

The lead pack now entered the penultimate turn. Thea was a quick study, and decided to adopt the tactics of her competitors. She pulled her chariot into the rider next to her and banged the hub of her wheel into his. With the second strike, he nearly faltered and fell back several paces while trying to regain his balance. As the group entered the next straightaway, it was clear there were only three chariots that could possibly lay claim to the trophy.

Thea tried to pass the other two on the outside during the long stretch, but she met the sting of a whip once again as she pulled alongside the man who'd ridiculed her. She slightly dropped back, growing infuriated when she saw he was also whipping Nox. Thea quickly pulled back behind the two men and tried to make contact against their backs with her own whip, but the distance was too great. She knew she had to devise a better plan, as the final turn was rapidly approaching.

It seemed to her that the two men in front weren't even competing for the prize. By keeping her out, they were guaranteed the full purse and, she guessed, were satisfied to split their winnings by taking first and second place.

"You try that again, girl, and you won't be around to tell about it!" the man yelled.

"If I can't go around you, then I'll go through you," Thea responded.

Going into the final turn, a small opening appeared between the two men's chariots, inviting Thea to move adjacent to them—but she could sense that it was a trap. If she took the bait, they would crush her between their chariots, destroying her chances of winning. Thea had other plans.

Midway through the turn, Thea partially pulled Nox in between the two men. She caught them glancing at each other and opening the space a bit more. Pretending to take the bait, Thea moved slightly forward without completely occupying the space, and kept her eyes glued on the man to her right. When he went to push his chariot against her, she would make her move.

"Ready to lose?" Thea teased, speaking loud enough so both men could hear.

The man who'd whipped her scowled at her, having had enough of her mouth. He was ready to teach her a lesson. As they came out of the last turn, he attempted to smash Nox between the two chariots, giving Thea the signal for which she'd been waiting. As his reins pulled toward the inside, she pulled back suddenly on Nox and blew the wooden horn she held in her hand. Like a bolt of lightning, Nox darted to the outside as the men bumped their wheels together in the space where they'd expected to find Nox. The bump was enough to slow each of them down, allowing Thea and her horse to pull ahead and along the outside of the track as they all entered the final straightaway. The crowd roared, giving her a surge of adrenaline as Nox sped down the last stretch.

The two men frantically tried to catch Thea, snapping repeated blows of the whip across her back, but she wasn't about to quit. Gritting her teeth, she cracked her whip above Nox's head, pushing the horse on to victory. As the three crossed the finish line, Nox was first by a horse's length, leaving no question as to who was the true winner.

The crowd exploded in a flurry of applause, cheers, and shouts. Some booed the men trailing Thea, while others chanted her chariot number. She was elated at what she'd just accomplished. The circus was in a frenzy.

Meanwhile, a messenger in the employ of the Governor's office sat in the stands, shaking his head in disbelief at what he'd just witnessed. This was clearly an embarrassment, and something that needed to be brought to the attention of the Governor.

CHAPTER 14

NEMEA AMPHITHEATER

When the wagon arrived at the amphitheater, Lysandros and Teigra were ushered into the back entrance. Fighters were escorted down a ramp to a network of chambers below the arena to wait until their matches began.

"This is a big one for you, girl; your biggest yet," Lysandros said. "I don't know who you'll be fighting, but the other warriors here have all survived a lot of matches to be eligible to compete. Like them, you have earned the right to be here. Do yourself, and me, proud." Teigra said nothing in response. She knew this fight would be rough. In the Pankration fights, wagers meant anything was fair game. Apart from gouging out the eyes, there were no restrictions. The fights were dirty, and death was common. Ordinarily, extreme moves were prohibited, but not at the Pankration events.

Lysandros' assessment was correct. She was to fight Theron, an Argive nearly seven feet tall, with bulging muscles covered in bronze skin. Theron had become a crowd favorite in Nemea by savagely disemboweling the bodies of his opponents. At his last match, he severed the head of his opponent and tossed it into the stands.

Teigra and Lysandros waited in their underground pen for over an hour. The heat was oppressive, and the pen stank of piss, livestock, and death. All of the animals and the majority of the people who passed through this area went up the ramp to die, this horrible place providing them their last moments alone. Teigra wondered if she would be any different.

"Lysandros! Your warrior is on!" the guard yelled.

"Be strong, Teigra. Make us proud," Lysandros told her. She shot him a cold stare and made her way up the ramp.

Teigra winced as the sunlight hit her face. Suddenly, the roar of thousands filled her ears. When her eyes adjusted, she saw the spectators. She was simultaneously thrilled by the energy from the masses and sobered by the fact that most of these people had come to see her die.

Her eyes widened. Her opponent, Theron, was before her.

The crowd exploded in cheers at the sight of him. He was all she'd heard and more—a living, breathing statue of a warrior. And he was coming for her.

Mace aloft, he strode across a dusty ground dotted with pools of blood from the mangled corpses of an ape, a large jungle cat, and a few wild dogs. It was a vision straight from Hades. Teigra knew she would have to quickly clear her head if she were to survive.

High above ground, Lysandros stood, mouth agape. Before his eyes, his prize investment was on the verge of ruin. He rushed to the holding pen and scolded the match organizer for putting Teigra with someone who was clearly so much more powerful. It was now obvious Theron was to engage in a much bigger match after he dispatched with Teigra. She was a pawn for the crowd, Theron's warm-up before the main course.

Lysandros was powerless. The contract was signed, so Teigra's fate was in her own hands. Lysandros could only watch the carnage unfold from the stands, like any other spectator.

Theron raised the mace above his head. Its steel sphere was covered with spikes, and it was large enough to block Teigra's view of the sun. She scrambled to think. With only a hand knife, how would she battle such a weapon? Nowhere near the size and strength of Theron, how would she best her opponent?

Theron charged forward. Just as he reached her, Teigra leaped out of the way. His mace hit the dirt, driving up an impressive cloud of dust and sending the crowd to its feet in approval.

Suddenly, Teigra knew her strategy. Her only hope of survival was to take advantage of her nimbleness. While Theron was a monument to strength and size, she was quick and agile.

"You will die, whore!" Theron roared. He unearthed the spikes from the dirt, licked his lips, and flashed a ravenous grin.

Teigra unsheathed her knife from her leg. Despite her obvious placement as fodder for her opponent, she looked impressive from the stands. Her armor made her at once beautiful and sexy, exuding feminine prowess in the most dangerous sense.

The two warriors circled each other for what seemed like an eternity. The noise of the crowd faded. Each fighter tried to gauge the quickest way to bring death to the other.

Theron charged! He swung his mace.

Teigra again leaped out of the way. This time the mace missed by mere inches.

Anger erupted on Theron's face. He then sealed his frustration and grinned with sinister intent. Teigra knew this was mere projected confidence, however. This beast was used to winning quickly by brute force. His veneer was cracking.

He swung again, unleashing a howl from the depths of his gut expressing his desire to make deadly contact and end this battle.

The mace swung with such force that Teigra felt the wind from it brush her face. A deadly spike almost caressed the edge of her cheekbone.

The great Theron had missed—though this time by less than an inch.

Theron's face grew visibly distraught. His matches had never gone on beyond the first swing. He struggled to catch his breath, a match of this length posing an unprecedented challenge to his stamina.

Knowing his strength was starting to decline, Theron did what he'd never done before. He switched tactics.

He stepped beside the mace and used his shoulder to shove Teigra, while quickly placing his foot behind her leg to complete the move and send her to the ground.

Teigra fell back, landing next to the lifeless body of a jungle cat. Her left arm was dampened by the sticky blood of the dead animal. As she gasped at the sight, she was suddenly struck by a crushing blow, just above the elbow, from Theron's mace.

Teigra cried out as the crowd cheered. Theron ghoulishly smiled, finally feeling the comfort of besting an opponent. He quickly abandoned his fears, basking in the glow of another sure victory.

Teigra jumped up and ran, both getting her out of range of the mace and buying her time to survey the damage done. She saw a large wound, the flesh ripped wide open, with vein and bone exposed. The weight of the weapon had clearly caused a fracture. Her mind raced. The pain was nearly blinding. Was Theron's brute force simply too mighty to overcome?

Teigra wanted to put her right hand on her arm, as the pain was like a fire burning a hole in her body. But she needed her free hand to hold her knife. It was her only weapon, and her last chance at survival.

She prayed to the Gods.

Theron trailed her by fifteen feet, pacing the ring, outwardly projecting the confident walk of the victor. Secretly, however, he was buying time to catch his breath. He'd dealt a crushing blow that put him ahead of his opponent, but he was tired and unsteady. He had little energy left, yet knew he still had to deliver a final deadly strike.

The audience expressed its approval with every step Theron took. His face held a plastered grin, promising imminent death.

Teigra had run until she was near the wall of the arena, along the stone barrier separating her from the masses. The crowd was cheering for more blood.

Teigra's hope began to wane. She was losing blood, and her body was using what energy she had left to keep her alive.

She teetered on the verge of death.

Then she heard the sound.

There was a loud collision behind her. Theron was on the ground, grimacing in pain, his mace several feet from where he lay. His exhaustion had caught up to him, and he'd slipped on a pool of gore left from the victim of a previous match.

As the crowd got louder, he struggled to get up, but it was clear he'd injured his leg.

The Gods had answered. Teigra saw her chance.

She ran toward Theron's slowly rising frame, her useless left limb dangling lifelessly at her side. Just before reaching him, Teigra grabbed the displaced mace. She tossed away her knife and lifted the heavy spiked weapon. Teigra then closed her eyes, suffocated the pain in her arm, and strangled her fear of death. She threw her entire body weight into a single swing of the mace. Theron, not yet on his feet, took the spiked sphere in the back of his head.

The rear portion of Theron's skull erupted, and an arc of crimson and chunks of flesh flew through the air. He fell forward, the fresh hole in his cranium creating a red pool to cause problems for some future fighter.

Teigra closed her eyes and quietly thanked the Gods for choosing her. The thousands of spectators jumped to their feet. It was obvious that at least half of them were rooting for Theron, and they were now going to be deprived of their main event. There had not been an upset of this caliber in the arena for some time.

Lysandros watched from the stands, an enormous grin on his face, as guards walked out to usher Teigra out of the arena. Lysandros met her in the holding area, just as the guards were securing her shackles.

"You did great, girl! Really, you could not have been better. Do you know what this means for us?"

"Yes, you get a few more chances to exploit me," she replied.

"No, we're now partners! Don't you worry, we'll get your arm fixed." At that moment, a guard approached Lysandros.

"Sir, we have arranged an escort for you and your fighter out of the city. Some members of the audience are demonstrating great anger over her victory, and we think it is in your best interest."

"Very well. Thank you," Lysandros said.

With that, Lysandros and Teigra were ushered out the back of the stadium where Lysandros' guard waited with the wagon. Before getting in, they collected their winnings, and noticed there were some angry spectators exiting the gates. They had lost their money betting on Theron and wanted revenge. The pair was quick to collect what they were owed and get away.

CHAPTER 15

A WINNER'S FATE

Thea looked around the circus as the uproar escalated. Some spectators were furious that a woman had won. Others berated the riders for losing to a woman. Proud of her victory, she rode around the track, taking in the scene. As she did, one of the men she'd outsmarted rode up alongside her.

"I'd watch your back if I were you, girl," said the charioteer. "Seems to me you may be disqualified for cheating during the race." He then abruptly turned his chariot and rode away.

Thea had a bad feeling. She trotted Nox around the rest of the track, as was customary for the winner, and was planning to enter the central area of the track to receive her victory trophy—but as she rode, she noticed a Spartan officer intently gazing at her.

"Girl, come here," the officer beckoned. "I must speak with you."

He had seen from the stands that she possessed an uncommon beauty. But it was the pluck, strength, and fearlessness that she exuded on the track that told him she was a most unusual girl. By the time she'd won the race, he had become beguiled by her, and knew that if he didn't create an opportunity to speak with her he may never see her again. He also felt it was his duty to warn her of the danger she was facing, which gave him the perfect opportunity to take in her beauty from a closer vantage point while actually doing something to help her.

Thea was only a few paces from the edge of the seats where the officer was leaning. She turned Nox and her chariot toward him. He leaped over the ledge at the bottom of the front row and took several steps until he stood beside her chariot.

Now that she was facing him, he noticed that her honey-colored eyes were unlike any he'd ever seen. Her face was captivating.

"What is it?" Thea asked, turning to face the Spartan as he walked alongside her.

"You should exit now," he began, resisting the urge to smile so she could grasp the severity of the situation. "The Governor has no intention of awarding a woman the prize. There's no doubt you'll be disqualified for one reason or another."

"But I won the race!" Thea exclaimed.

"No matter," he continued. "The Nemeans and Argives won't permit a woman to win. If you stick around, you'll likely end up in prison."

Thea came to a stop; but the spectators jeered even louder, encouraging her to ride onward. While she surveyed the angry crowd, her wooden horn fell down onto the ground.

"You've dropped your horn, mistress," the Spartan officer said, bending to pick it up.

"Oh, thank you, sir," Thea said, smiling as she took the horn from his hand.

"I must say, based on first impressions, you are an incredible young woman. Under better circumstances, I would enjoy the chance to learn more about you. I am Aristo. What do they call you?"

Aristo was handsome, with striking features, dark hair, and dark eyes. But as a future Sondra, there was no way she could tell him her true name.

"Uh...Troublemaker. They call me the Troublemaker."

"You sure live up to your name," Aristo said, smiling with amusement. "Heed my words," he continued. "It is in your best interest to make your exit immediately. I hope we will meet again. Soon."

"Thank you, Aristo. I am grateful for your help."

She smiled and nodded before resuming her lap around the stadium. Aristo watched her ride away. He was filled with a great sense of regret, but realized that things could happen no other way. Still, he was grateful for the opportunity to have gazed into her eyes.

* * *

Needing only to travel a short distance to reach the Governor's office in the building adjacent to the arena, a messenger—alarmed by two surprising victories by women in a single day—arrived at the office, rapped on the door, and was permitted to enter.

"Governor, I have come with some very strange news to share. There have been two upsets in the city's games today. A female warrior slew Theron in the arena, and a young woman has just won the chariot race. Neither woman is believed to be a citizen of Nemea or Argos. Both wins incited some spectators to violence."

"What? This is an *outrage*! What will King Bedros say?" the Governor asked. "These harpies are a complete embarrassment to our city! Bring them to me immediately."

"Yes, my lord. I'll track them down at once."

"Good. I'll dispatch additional guards to quell any unrest," the Governor added.

* * *

As Thea neared the gates, she exited along with several of the other riders. In the mix, she was momentarily obscured. Once outside, she rode over to where Melia and Carina waited.

"You did it!" shouted Carina. "I knew you would!"

"What a race!" Melia added. "You really took a beating out there."

"Yeah, but we have bigger problems now," Thea warned. "A Spartan officer said they were going to strip the victory from me because the Argives won't let a woman triumph. We've got to collect the winnings from our wager before that happens."

Carina grabbed the other horse, and the three moved quickly over to the betting table. Since few had chosen to wager on Thea, the line was quite short. The bookkeeper was none too happy to see the three girls, however. Giving up winnings on fifty-to-one odds would cut substantially into his profits.

"Here's my ticket, sir," Carina said.

"Yeah. It'll be a minute, girl," the bookkeeper replied.

"We're in a bit of a rush, sir. Could you please hurry?"

"Oh, a bit of a rush, eh?" the bookkeeper sarcastically repeated. "By all means then, we'll get you your winnings immediately."

He turned toward his assistant and gave him a wink out of view of the three girls across the table, and the other man began filling a bag with what looked to be silver. Meanwhile, Thea kept checking over her shoulder to see if any trouble was headed their way. She knew that if the victor was changed before they could collect their winnings, they were going to be out of luck.

"What's the delay, sir?" Thea asked.

"Easy, miss! It's coming, it's coming," the bookkeeper responded, irritated.

"Thea, is that the guy you raced against?" Melia asked, pointing toward the stalls.

"Yeah, that's him," Thea said.

The charioteer was clearly looking for someone, and Thea could only assume it was her. The time to get out of Nemea before trouble found her was quickly diminishing. Just as she was about to ask the bookkeeper to hurry again, he presented them with two bags.

"Here you go...750," the bookkeeper stated in a less than enthusiastic tone.

Carina took the two bags and peeked inside to ensure that they did indeed contain silver coins. She gave him a quick "thank you." The three girls then mounted their horses and headed to the road back home. After rounding the far corner of the circus, they were safely out of view from any of the other racers. A few moments later, they could see Nemea in the distance.

"Okay, I think we're safe," Thea said. "That was close. I didn't count on being chased out of town!"

"No kidding," Melia added. "You were incredible, Thea. How's your back?"

"With all the excitement, I had forgotten about it," Thea said. "Your mother was right. The riders were the most dangerous part."

The sun was starting to make its decline in the evening's sky, and they hadn't seen any soldiers in some time, so it seemed safe to take a short break.

"Carina, let's check out the bags," Thea said, breaking the silence of the ride.

"Good idea. I've been thinking about that for a while," Carina replied.

The three girls pulled their horses and the chariot over to the side of the road, and Carina took the bags from her horse's pouches and began to count.

"Ten, eleven, twelve..." Carina counted. "Wait, what's this?"

Carina held up a piece of scrap metal she'd pulled out of the bag, and they all had a sinking feeling. Carina dumped the contents of both bags onto the floor of the chariot stand, and their suspicions were confirmed—aside from the few coins that covered the top, the bags were filled with worthless junk metal. In their haste, the bookkeeper had taken advantage of them.

"There's only eighty-three silver coins total," Carina concluded, after discarding all the scrap.

"Well, it's better than nothing," Melia stated. "At least you got the twenty-five silver coins back that you put in."

"If I could get my hands on that bookkeeper, I'd make him pay," Thea said, angrily. "He'd better hope we never cross paths again."

"Come on, Thea. Let's get going. Stewing about it isn't going to help," Carina said.

Thea nodded. She rose. But a shock of nausea overtook her. She sat back down again, breathing hard, and asked Carina for a cup of water.

CHAPTER 16

FREEDOM

Teigra's mouth was utterly dry. She had lost blood from the wound in her arm. She was very pale, and looked terrible. She was dry-heaving without end, and there was a real risk of infection since she had not received medical attention following the match. This made the journey back to Lysandros' compound near Corinth quite arduous. Knowing that her wound was serious, Lysandros tried to take fewer breaks than they had on the way to Nemea. He also had enough compassion to realize shackles would make her more uncomfortable, and chose to merely bind her with rope.

At one point, Teigra demanded that they slow down the wagon, as she felt the urgent threat of vomit barreling up her throat. Not wanting a mess on his hands, Lysandros had no choice but to heed her wishes. As the wagon slowed, Teigra stuck her head out from its side.

There, on the side of the road, was a woman who was bent over vomiting. Teigra squinted at her... for some reason the woman felt familiar. She wondered if she too had been in a fight. Since the wagon was still moving, Teigra could only catch a glimpse of the stranger before she also began throwing up.

As Teigra rode in the wagon, the pain was nearly unbearable, causing her to see red when she tried to close her eyes. Sleep was not coming to her, but as she tossed and turned, she began shifting the bags in the back of the cart. Suddenly she saw something shiny underneath one of them —a knife, which Lysandros had accidentally placed on the cart during loading.

Lysandros sat in the front, holding the reins alongside his guard, while Teigra was tied to the back. She couldn't reach the knife with her hands, which were tied, but she could manage to touch it with her feet. Without making a sound, she slowly freed the knife from under the sack and dragged it over to where she could reach it with her fingers. With some nimble maneuvering, she finally cut the rope that kept her captive. Suddenly, there was no pain, she felt her strength return, and freedom was only a couple of strikes away.

"A fine night, girl," Lysandros exclaimed, still gazing forward. "A fine night, indeed."

Surveying her surroundings, Teigra surmised that they were in the middle of the woods, probably halfway to Lysandros' home. Her best chance to overtake him and the guard would be while he was still driving the cart. Even with her injury, she felt confident she could dispose of both of them at the same time—her skills were sharp, and her reflexes faster than those of either man.

Teigra was abruptly overtaken by a sort of clarity she'd never experienced before. This man sitting in front of her had turned the tables on her in the marketplace nearly two years ago. She'd been trying to free herself, but her plan had backfired and he bought her for a pittance. He then endangered her life again and again. But in the process, she found strength within herself that she'd never known existed...and had garnered the adulation of thousands along the way. While she wasn't happy that she'd been made to endure her trials under Lysandros, they hadn't really hurt her. They'd made her stronger.

Obscured by the dark, Teigra crept up behind Lysandros, reached around to the front of his throat and scraped her knife across it. He tried to speak, but the only sound was the gurgling of blood in his throat. The guard reached for Teigra's neck, but before he connected, she plunged the bloody blade into his heart.

When the two men had completed their death throes, Teigra pushed their lifeless bodies into the back of the cart, as the horse continued galloping. She took hold of the reins—and kept the horse steady on its path.

After about an hour, she could see Lysandros' home. When she arrived, Teigra tied the horse to a post and broke into the stalls where the other prisoners were kept.

"Wake up!" Teigra exclaimed. "All of you! Get up!"

"What is it?" Hanna whispered.

"Lysandros is dead!" Teigra announced. "I killed him. His bloody body is outside on his cart."

"What?" Hanna asked in disbelief.

"Come on, we have to hurry. We only have the cover of darkness to get out of here," Teigra continued.

One by one, Teigra freed all the girls from their shackles and gave them some of the dried meats that Lysandros kept in his bag. All of them stuffed their clothing and disappeared into the night.

Teigra then moved on to the men's quarters, with Hannah accompanying her. Teigra felt there was an element of danger in freeing some of them but continued anyway, hoping they'd be too grateful to do anything to her. As she released them, one by one, she was reassured. They knew she'd been in the same predicament, and their eyes expressed gratitude.

Finally, she reached her own building and freed her six fellow captives, including Bion.

"Teigra! What has happened?" he asked.

"Lysandros is dead. That's all that matters. Please don't ask how."

"Your arm! You look like you need help."

"Don't worry. I'll be fine. Just go."

"Thank you, Teigra. Good luck to you." With that, Bion fled into the approaching morning.

"Now, what about Lysandros? Should we get rid of the body?" Hanna asked.

"There's no need," Teigra said. "Nobody ever visits here. It will be days before they come looking for him."

"Where are you heading?" Hanna asked.

"Away from here!" said Teigra.

"Do you want me to come along? Your arm looks awful!"

Teigra paused and looked at Hanna. She knew Hanna wanted to accompany her because she was scared, but Teigra was a loner. She didn't want a tagalong.

"I'm going to find a physician to take care of it tomorrow. I'm sorry, Hanna, but no. I need to travel alone. It's just who I am."

"Okay, I understand," Hanna said, with a hint of nervousness.

"Head into the woods and follow the brook to the base of the mountains," Teigra suggested. "It'll take you to a road where you can escape to the next city. Be sure to hide your branding scar and ration your food. You'll be in the next town within a day or so."

"But what if they come looking for us?" Hanna asked.

"Nobody's looking for you, Hanna," Teigra pointed out. "Nobody even knows we're here!"

In fact, the other fighters were unknown to the Corinthian guards...but they knew Teigra. It was the Corinthians who Lysandros paid to buy her; and it was Corinthians who could identify Teigra as the last person to be seen with Lysandros alive. If they came looking for anyone, it would be her; which was another reason she chose to flee alone.

Teigra and Hanna said their goodbyes, and Teigra swiftly raced through the woods. She immediately felt back home in the forest. Her freedom tasted great.

The last thing Teigra wanted was to return to slavery or spend the rest of her life in prison. She raced with a sense of renewed energy as she dodged trees, and erased her tracks in mountain streams and on rocky paths.

Teigra came to the mountains and began to climb the steep terrain. Even if they searched for her, they were unlikely to venture to the other side. Once there, she needed to find a cave—a spot where she could rest for a few days—and tend to her wounds.

Teigra didn't even notice the passing hours as she climbed. She was soothed and energized by the fresh air and bright moon. She intuitively knew her way, even though she'd never been on this mountain slope. When she reached its pinnacle, she felt new life.

Teigra had substantially changed since the last time she lost her freedom. She was now a seasoned warrior, ready for anything.

CHAPTER 17

HOMEBOUND

The girls rode in silence. They realized that their return to camp was going to be a challenge, as they were past curfew. The instructors would have noticed their absence at dinner and would have begun to explore their whereabouts.

Just outside the camp, Thea instructed Melia and Carina to go to the left side of the girls' huts. She then rode the chariot toward the right side to attract attention. She hoped that, at worst, she'd be the only one to get caught.

Once Carina and Melia were past the hut's edge, Thea blew the wooden horn, sending Nox off on her own to find her place in the stable. Thea hoped for a miracle that would allow her to avoid detection. Unfortunately, that was not to be the case.

"Who goes there?" demanded one of the Sondras. "Stop!"

"It's me, Thea," she responded, bringing the chariot to a halt.

"You are well past curfew, and you know the rules," stated the Sondra.

"Yes, I am sorry," Thea said, respectfully. "I just lost track of time."

"Uh-huh. What are you doing in a chariot?" the Sondra asked, becoming more suspicious. "And what are these money bags?"

"I was just taking it out for a ride," Thea answered, ignoring the second question.

"I think Queen Alexa might want to hear about this, girl," the Sondra declared. "Get down and come with me."

Thea tied the horse to a post and followed the Sondra toward Alexa's hut. The Sondra carried the two bags of silver, which made Thea wish she'd hidden them in the woods before entering camp. This was not the first time she'd been in trouble, but it was the first time she'd been taken to Queen Alexa for breaking the rules.

"Sorry to disturb you this late in the evening, Queen Alexa," the Sondra said. "One of the girls was found arriving after curfew with a chariot and two bags of money."

Alexa, clearly irritated that she'd been interrupted, saw that Thea was the one who had broken curfew. She took the two bags from the Sondra and dumped their contents onto the floor of her hut. Silver coins and a few stray pieces of scrap fell onto the ground.

"Thea, I can only surmise you went to Nemea for a chariot race," Alexa said, sternly. "Am I correct?"

Thea considered lying, but was taken aback by the manner in which Alexa had already determined her plot with such little evidence.

"Yes, Queen Alexa," Thea said.

"Are you stupid, girl?" Alexa roared, crouching to look Thea in the face. "Are you not aware that our sisters' villages have been burned to the ground and hundreds have been taken as slaves by Argive soldiers? Do you not remember your sisters in the woods?"

Thea thought it better to remain silent.

"What is this silver?" Alexa demanded.

"My winnings, Queen Alexa," Thea answered.

"You won?" Alexa asked, intrigued. "And how, may I ask, did you get money to enter such a race?"

Thea knew that she was now in real trouble. Being late for curfew for the sake of an adventure was one thing, but stealing from the camp was another. Should she lie or should she reveal the truth? Neither were great options, but Thea erred on the side of courage.

"I took it from the instructor's chest," she said in a very low voice.

Alexa glared at her as Thea hung her head. Alexa then paced across the hut while considering her next course of action. She had to make an example of Thea for the safety of the entire tribe; and on top of that, Thea had to be taught a lesson about stealing. But despite all of this, Alexa couldn't deny her pure amazement that this 16-year-old girl had won a Nemean chariot race. Thea had truly impressed her.

"You will begin labor tonight, cleaning the stalls and stables until all are done, and tomorrow you will work the quarry from sunrise to sunset," Alexa said. "I expect a direct apology to the instructors and to all of your fellow sisters when training camp reconvenes. You are confined to camp for two weeks and may not leave the grounds at all. Am I clear?"

"Yes, Queen Alexa," Thea consented. Of all her punishments, the confinement to camp was the most painful.

"One last thing," Alexa said. "Who went with you?"

"No one, Queen Alexa," Thea replied.

Alexa studied Thea's face for any sign that she might not be telling the truth. "Very well, take her away."

Thea's back stung as sweat filled the wounds left by the charioteer's whip. After hours in the stables, all she could think about was finishing so she could get to bed. As she completed the cleanup of the last few stalls, she heard a familiar voice call her name.

"Thea, how are you doing?" Melia asked. "I brought you some food."

"I've been better," Thea said. "Thanks for the food. I'm starving."

"Thanks for not telling Alexa about Carina and me," Melia continued. "You didn't have to do that, you know."

"Hey, it was my idea to begin with."

"How's your back?" Melia asked. "I've brought an herbal balm to apply to your wounds."

"That sounds really good right now," Thea said, happily. "My back has been stinging all day."

The stalls were dark except for the one corner where Thea had been putting away her tools. A single lantern burned in front of several wooden benches and tables. The night was quiet and still, and the warmth of summer permeated the air. Melia walked over to Thea.

"Here, sit down and let me put some of this on your back," Melia said.

Thea straddled one of the benches and untied the belt around the middle of her tunic. She lifted up her clothing to expose her back, which had been marred by an array of red welts.

Melia removed the bottle from her pouch, straddled the bench behind Thea, and began to softly rub the salve onto Thea's skin. Melia's hands on her back made Thea forget all about her aches and pains. Melia's touch was soft and gentle as she slid her palms over Thea's shoulders and in between her shoulder blades. As Melia's hands moved down the small of her back, Thea could feel Melia's fingers curl ever so slightly around her waist.

Melia was mesmerized by Thea's beautiful figure. She watched her hands glide along Thea's back as she tried to memorize the shape of her body. As Melia's heart began to beat faster, she could feel the summer heat rise within her. She wanted to reach around and cup Thea's breast, pushing her own chest against her back, but restrained herself. What if Thea didn't share the same desire? Melia licked her lips, envisioning what Thea might taste like.

Melia took both her hands, now covered in salve, and began to massage Thea's shoulders, applying slightly more pressure. Melia dropped her hands gradually toward Thea's waist and leaned forward to smell Thea's hair, which fell across her upper back. As Melia moved forward, Thea took both of Melia's hands from her sides and moved them up and over her breasts. Melia didn't resist, continuing to gently massage them as Thea released her grasp. Thea slowly moved her own hands down onto Melia's thighs, which were exposed next to hers along the bench. Their passions continued to rise as their bodies tightly pressed against each other.

Thea's body felt instantly rejuvenated, and she stood to extinguish the light from the lantern. In the darkness, the two girls embraced, exchanging caresses and kisses. Thea discarded her tunic and moved to free Melia from hers. They lay tasting each other's flesh and indulging their passions.

Melia released her painful memories into the night as she fell into the love she had found for Thea. Thea discarded her own pain, which she'd been carrying for what seemed like an eternity. Love had found a way to heal the wounds that had scarred both their lives.

Thea carried the lantern in one hand and softly held Melia's hand in the other. Their silhouettes floated across the camp as they headed toward a hut. Everything seemed new, even to Thea. What had once been a camp of tough-minded duty was now a place where fantasies came true. Suddenly, the dawn held no fear; it was something to cherish and anticipate with excitement. The world had changed in an instant.

CHAPTER 18

DUNGEON OF PEACE AND PLEASURE

The halls were ancient and dusty. Patches of darkness battled patches of light supplied by torches mounted along the walls. With a series of brisk steps, Zarek moved closer to what he'd been anticipating all day. Negotiating several turns, his eyes focused straight ahead as his boots followed the familiar path. He'd grown very fond of the dungeon, where so many delicious memories were born. It was the place that gave him the power and control he felt he richly deserved.

At the end of the last hallway, two guards quickly stepped aside as Zarek approached. He unlatched the door and entered the room. It was dimly lit with small torches. In the middle sat a wooden chair with arms, shackles, and a small tray attached to one side.

Behind the chair stood a harpist, who began playing as soon as Zarek entered.

Next to the harpist was a small audience of slaves tied to their chairs, both male and female, waiting in complete and utter dread for the agony he would soon inflict upon them.

To the right of the chair was a table, on top of which lay an array of tools and instruments unlike any found in a typical marketplace.

There were picks, blades, clamps, spreaders, and probes—none of which had medical or household applications. These were instruments of pain.

The table was also ordained with numerous candles, all aglow and flickering, making the cruel devices dance and shine.

To the left of the chair was Zosimos, Zarek's loyal friend and assistant, whom he'd known since childhood.

Most important was the object of his pleasure, the unnamed woman who sat tied to the chair.

"Welcome, Prince Zarek," greeted Zosimos. "Everything is prepared to your liking."

"Thank you, my dear friend," Zarek replied. "Indeed, I have been looking forward to this all day. Harpist, play a song that is suitable for the cleansing of the soul."

The imprisoned woman was gagged, but her eyes widened with fear as Zarek casually spoke about cleansing. Zarek's reputation preceded him; everyone knew his passionate enjoyment of human torture. She had good reason to fear the worst.

"Ahhh, a fine specimen!" Zarek exclaimed. "Zosimos, repeat the crimes of our guest."

"An Amazon, sir," Zosimos began. "She was taken from a village near Corinth, and has refused to submit to her Argive masters, despite repeated attempts to break her of her barbaric ways."

"I see," Zarek said, as if contemplating the correct course of action. "Secure her head against the back of the chair and re-strap her arms to the tray."

Zosimos did as he was told. The woman struggled, but she was helpless. Sitting erect, with her head flush against the headrest, she couldn't even plead for mercy. With her arms outstretched on the tray, palms facing upward, her moaning increased as she saw Zarek move toward the table.

"Hmmm. What shall we start with?" Zarek asked, wearing a grin as he looked her in the eyes. "A woman must know her place. Seems to me you may have a misperception that you are a man. Therefore, we must change the way you see things."

Zarek calmly took one of the instruments, which resembled a small bow and arrow made of metal. The bow portion was composed of an upper and lower bridge between which a pin could move forward. He placed it directly over the woman's right eye. She tightly clenched her eyes closed and tried to move her head, but it was no use.

Zarek slowly, as if threading a needle, pushed the pin forward, first piercing her eyelid and then her eye, all the way to its core. Then, with one rapid motion, Zarek retracted the pin, watching the woman writhe in agony before repeating the process on her other eye. He felt his power grow as he absorbed her pain.

"Now you have a different 'point of view,'" Zarek said, sadistically grinning as he turned to his most unwilling audience.

The slaves who were tied to their chairs gasped in fear, and one captive woman fainted and slumped over. But with a quick, cutting glance from Zosimos, the nervous group began to wildly applaud Zarek for his performance. None of them knew who might be Zarek's next victim. Meanwhile, the harpist played on, trying his best not to miss a note, for fear a single mistake could usher in his own demise.

"Remove the tray and extend the chair to a flat position," Zarek ordered.

Zosimos did as he was told, and then played spectator while Zarek cut the woman's clothes from her body. She lay blind, exposed, and completely vulnerable, with shock setting in.

"The best way to change a woman from thinking she is a man is castration," Zarek continued. "One must find the presumed testicles and remove them."

Even Zosimos had to close his eyes as Zarek surgically cut the woman's clitoris from her body. Her writhing temporarily increased while he lanced her groin, but then her muscular contractions nearly ceased. Zarek took his prize and smelled it with relish, as if sniffing a vintage wine. The smell of blood always pleased him. It was the source of life, and something he had the power to take.

The harp played on, and the audience nervously applauded.

"Zosimos, I do believe she is dead!" Zarek announced. "I am not surprised, what with her being a woman and all. I find it amazing that so many feel they are as strong as men."

"Indeed, sir," Zosimos said. "One less woman to impede the waves of progress!"

"True!" Zarek responded. "But regardless, I will extract her womb to make sure no seed can come from her poison."

"Yes, your highness," Zosimos replied.

Zarek carefully dissected the dead woman's pelvis, exposing her womb as the onlookers closed their eyes in horror. The harpist struggled to play on, his fingers guided now only by fear. Blood dripped steadily onto the floor as Zarek smiled intently through his endeavor. With a few additional slices, he tossed her womb onto the ground in front of the forced spectators. Despite a slight delay, fear again summoned applause from the group.

"This one is cured," Zarek said. "Have the guards clean up this mess."

Zarek exited the room feeling empowered by the experience. Nothing gave him a rush like the fear of a prisoner approaching the moment of death. He was in control, and he dictated that person's fate.

"Sir, the King requests your presence at dinner," a messenger said, as Zarek exited the dungeon.

"Indeed," Zarek replied, as the messenger continued to bow. "Tell him I am on my way."

King Bedros was aging, and Zarek was eager to fill his shoes. It wasn't only the desire for power that drove Zarek, but his intolerance of his father's weaknesses. He perceived his father as unforgivably softhearted toward his people. King Bedros had not raised taxes for many years, and in Zarek's view he permitted both citizens and slaves far too much freedom. Age had mellowed Bedros, leading him to outlaw torture as a tool of interrogation and punishment.

Zarek believed tolerance of lesser individuals was idiotic. Women and weaker men were meant to serve the most powerful, wealthy, and intellectually advanced citizens. Zarek felt this was where his father had stumbled—being overly kind to those who should be either controlled or conquered.

"Zarek, where have you been this evening?" asked King Bedros.

"Out on an adventure, Father," Zarek replied with a smirk on his face. "Is there a curfew around the kingdom I wasn't aware of?"

"No, but there is a ban on torturing and killing slaves!" Bedros shouted as he stood on his throne. "You are out of control!"

"Maybe if you ruled with a stronger fist, we wouldn't have to tolerate this insubordination, Father," Zarek shouted back.

"Watch your tongue, boy," Bedros warned, standing up from his chair. "You may be the Prince, but you are not beyond a King's reprimand." Bedros returned to a seated position and collected himself before continuing.

Despite the resultant friction that both expected, Bedros insisted that he and Zarek dine together. It was the only time they spent with each other on a regular basis. Though Zarek felt no love for his father, he looked forward to their meals because he took a sick satisfaction in seeing Bedros recoil at his comments. He also reveled in the knowledge that it didn't matter how much Bedros disagreed with him—he could dispatch the old man whenever he wanted. There was no need to hurry, though. Zarek would take his time and devise an appropriately elaborate death for a King.

As it happened, on this night they were not alone. Unbeknownst to Zarek, there was someone behind the curtains facing the back of the throne. Bedros had invited his royal advisor, Leander, to join the dining table that evening; but when Leander came upon father and son bickering he hid, eavesdropping on their increasingly angry words.

"Father, you have lost touch with reality," Zarek said. "Argos needs an iron hand at its helm. If no one takes the reins, our state will become obsolete! How can you not realize this?"

"Son, even if I were to turn the throne over to you, you have no queen! When are you going to settle down and take a bride? The citizens of Argos will not trust you as their King if you are not married. We need to show that you have matured."

"Nonsense!" Zarek exclaimed. "If I took over, I would immediately be acclaimed for saving our kingdom from more years of your crippling indecision!"

"I may be old," Bedros responded, "but I have no desire to see all that I have built crumble under your hands. You have a twisted sense of what is just."

"You must be joking," Zarek said.

"No, my misguided Prince. What you call progress is a license to torture and kill. You will mutilate, destroy, and bury anything in your path to get what you want. I know you have been using our forces to burn down villages in the name of progress. And I know about your abuse of the liquid fire!"

"You weak, old man. I have listened to enough of your mindless prattle. I have suddenly lost my appetite," Zarek replied, savagely stuffing one last large piece of chicken in his mouth and washing it down with a gulp of wine before standing up to leave. "You, King Bedros, are an embarrassment."

Zarek glared at his father and marched through the doorway. Immediately after he was gone, Leander stepped from behind the curtain.

"Ah, Leander, you made it after all."

"Your son is trouble, my King," Leander said.

"I know," Bedros replied. "But he's still my son. How can I deny the throne to my only heir?"

"I understand, my King," Leander said. "But the people come first. The Prince is volatile; his principal hobby is murder. With his temper and lack of respect for life, I guarantee within six months under his rule we will be at war!"

"I need to hear this from you," Bedros quietly responded. "Yet I still hold onto the hope he will change. I thought perhaps his taking a bride would tame his ways, but even that seems unlikely to happen."

"With great respect, Sire, I feel you should pass your power over to a ruling committee. It is essential for the well-being of Argos. To be utterly frank, my King, time is running out. This is the only solution."

Bedros said nothing. He realized the first act of such a committee would be the execution of his son. It was a step he couldn't bring himself to take.

The following morning, Leander called a covert meeting of five of the most wealthy and powerful merchants in Argos. Over the course of a long and difficult day, they decided that they would rule as an oligarchy—but to make this happen, both Bedros and Zarek would have to be killed.

This solution pained no one more than Leander. Although he was Bedros' close friend, his ultimate loyalty was to the state of Argos and its citizens. It was clear that Bedros wasn't going to transfer power to the committee, as that would mean sanctioning the death of his son; so it was necessary for the King to go as well.

With heavy hearts, they set about putting their plan in motion. However, they were temporarily stuck on a key aspect. For a smooth transition, they had to make the dual regicides appear to be accidents.

CHAPTER 19

POTIONS OF FLAME

For nearly three months, Teigra had been a denizen of the forest, living by her wits and off the land. This was a period full of peace and happiness—and one she felt had been earned after freeing herself from Lysandros' clutches.

Then, one afternoon nearing the outskirts of Koutsopodio, while pursuing a rabbit she hoped to have for lunch, she experienced a mishap. In the midst of chasing after the swift creature, Teigra stepped into a snare that tightened around her ankle and hoisted her up, leaving her swinging upside down and ten feet off the ground. Further, as she was pulled upward, her knife became unsheathed and fell to the ground, out of reach.

Whoever set the trap was apparently far away. Teigra remained hanging for well over an hour. She had to occasionally pull herself up and hold onto the rope that gripped her leg to prevent blood from rushing to her head.

Finally, she heard leaves rustling and looked down to find an older man in peasant clothes approaching.

"I think you could use some help! Are you all right?" the man asked.

"Yes, I'm fine. Please, just cut me down."

The man retrieved Teigra's knife from the ground and found the point where the trap's rope originated. He cut the rope carefully, gradually lowering her to the ground to avoid injuring her.

"My name is Vasili," he said. "How did this happen? Was someone pursuing you?"

"No. I was hunting a rabbit and stepped into the snare. I've been stuck here since noon."

"I'm so glad to have found you, then. You must be parched and hungry," Vasili observed. "Please come to my home for something to eat. I live just a short distance from here."

With some caution, Teigra agreed. They soon arrived at Vasili's small, cozy hut. When they entered, there was a much younger man inside who wore peasant clothes like Vasili.

"Teigra, this is Otho. Otho, meet my new friend Teigra—I found her hanging from a tree!" Vasili said, laughing.

"Very nice to meet you, Teigra," Otho said.

Teigra then saw something new to her. Otho embraced Vasili from the back and gently kissed him on his neck. They were lovers. Teigra suddenly felt safer, and the smell of whatever was cooking on their fire made her glad that she took Vasili up on his offer.

"Thank you for inviting me to eat with you," said Teigra.

"My pleasure," Vasili said. "What is your business in these parts? What's a young girl doing in the woods all alone?"

"I have no business here," Teigra replied, trying to seem casual but carefully weighing her words. "I came from the other side of the mountains in search of food. Honestly, these woods are now my home."

"I see. No family, no husband, no master?" Vasili asked.

"None," Teigra said.

Teigra watched as Vasili and Otho busied themselves around their stove, stirring pots and rotating a pheasant. The two caressed each other as they passed, and exchanged endearing looks and smiles as they toiled. Teigra had never witnessed such affection between two people in all the homes in which she'd served. She found herself feeling jealous and curious at the same time.

The three sat down to eat. A tremendous portion of fowl was placed on the table along with apples, pears, bread, squash, and wine. Teigra was so hungry she felt she could have eaten everything by herself.

"Where were you last evening?" asked Vasili. "There's no town close to here."

"I was on the mountain, sir," Teigra replied.

"I see. When did you last sleep in a bed?"

"I don't remember. As I said, the woods are my home," Teigra said. "I have come to not like the civilized world."

Vasili glanced at Otho, who had been quiet most of the morning. Vasili's hair was almost entirely white, and the wrinkles of his face and skin defined his age. Otho, on the other hand, was much younger, with smooth olive skin and curly dark hair. There was a look of innocence in his eyes.

"You are welcome to stay the night, if you wish," Vasili offered. Teigra looked up, surprised at his words. She had not anticipated anything more than the meal.

"That is very kind, sirs. I would appreciate a night's rest under the cover of a roof," Teigra said.

"Very well then, you will stay. Otho and I will prepare a place for you to sleep. Make yourself at home."

Teigra was pleasantly full, and felt comfortable enough to enjoy lounging, but she'd learned to never let down her guard. *Why were these men being so kind?* Kindness hadn't come naturally to anyone she knew, which made her suspicious. Vasili and Otho merely continued with their duties, leaving Teigra to do nothing but relax.

Once night arrived, Vasili and Otho retired to their room. Teigra was given a straw mattress near the stove; its low burning flame kept the chill of night away. Even though she was exhausted, Teigra found she had difficulty nodding off. The home was foreign to her, unusual shadows lined the walls, and she hadn't slept close to men in years. She had been conditioned to fear the worst from them.

While in a light and fitful sleep, Teigra abruptly awoke—without knowing why. All she could discern were the creaks and pops of the night. Then Teigra heard another sound—the crushing of leaves underfoot coming from outside the hut. The noise was irregular, pausing several seconds before resuming its cadence.

Teigra uncovered herself and crawled to the front window. She cautiously raised herself enough to peek outside. The moonlight glared, but otherwise the night appeared quiet and still.

As Teigra continued to gaze, however, a shadow suddenly crossed in front of her! *Someone* is *outside!* she thought. Teigra glanced in the other room and saw her two hosts still sleeping. Slowly, she reached for the knife on her ankle and quietly slid against the wall toward the door. Was there just a single person out there, or were there several? Had the Corinthian guards tracked her all the way here?

Teigra stood erect, with her back to the wall. She could see a knife blade slide through the entryway and begin to pry the lock apart. Her heart pounded and thoughts raced; but her instincts were right at home.

With one swift motion, the lock was freed and the door began to open. Fortunately, Teigra was already behind the door.

By the dim light of the dwindling stove flame, Teigra saw a lone dark figure enter. Teigra did her best to blend in with the wall behind her.

Then, as the door closed, she sprang.

Before the intruder could turn his head, Teigra was upon him, her body crashing into his and her knife pressed to his throat. He instinctively reached for her arm in an attempt to avoid immediate death. Teigra deflected his hand before it could complete its trajectory.

The two flew across the room, slamming into a wall. A stack of pots crashed to the floor. This finally woke Vasili and Otho. Vasili reached for his knife, but stopped when he heard the sound of gurgling. He looked up to see Teigra had severed the intruder's jugular vein.

The dying man was young, with a scar across his eye. He backed up against the wall, his lifeblood spraying all over the hut. "Please, help me! I didn't mean any harm!" he said, wide-eyed with panic.

"What was your business here?" Teigra asked; but it was too late. The invader was a corpse.

"Are you all right?" Vasili asked.

"Yeah, I'm okay. I heard his footsteps outside before he broke the lock."

"Otho, are you all right?" Vasili asked, turning to his lover.

"Yes, I'm fine."

"Teigra, thank you for your help!" Vasili exclaimed. "If you had not been here, we would have surely been robbed; or even worse, killed in our sleep."

"Is he anybody you know?" Teigra asked.

"No. But he's not the first thief to come our way," Vasili said.

"Why? What's there to steal?"

Vasili glanced briefly at Otho, then changed the subject. "Let me get you some wine."

Vasili dragged the dead man outside. Otho began to clean up the crimson mess left behind. "I'll start digging a grave at the first sign of sunrise," he said.

A half hour later, the trio was still too rattled to sleep. Otho rekindled the fire, while Vasili served each of them some wine. Having such companionship was strange to Teigra, but a nice change.

"Teigra, you are welcome to stay as long as you'd like," Vasili said. "We have food and shelter for you. And we would clearly benefit from your help in protecting our humble home."

"Thank you, but I don't know," Teigra said. "I'm not much for sticking in one place."

"You think it over. You'd be doing us a favor," Vasili responded.

The three of them finally went back to bed. With her eyes shut, Teigra thought, *What's the harm in staying for a while? It would be a safe place to hide from the Corinthians, and having a steady meal is never a bad thing. Plus, there's something intriguing about these men.* Indeed, more than anything else, the generosity and natural affection of Vasili and Otho for each other captivated Teigra. *Perhaps I'll try it for a time. What's the worst that could happen?* With the decision made, Teigra was able to drift into a deep sleep.

* * *

Teigra stayed with Vasili and Otho for a couple of weeks without incident. Otho gathered fruits and vegetables from the woods and garden, and did most of the cooking. Teigra hunted for game and gathered firewood. Vasili toiled with potions and liquids, which he created at night. Teigra didn't know what the potions were, but assumed he sold them at the marketplace in exchange for other goods. Then again, she had yet to see Vasili or Otho travel to the market. The hut appeared to be self-sufficient.

"Teigra, would you mind gathering some firewood?" Vasili asked one day. "We're running a bit low."

"Sure," Teigra replied.

She ventured into the forest and made a stack from fallen tree limbs. Vasili had given her a small hatchet to whittle the wood down to manageable sizes. Teigra also kept a bow and arrow strapped to her back in case she should happen across any prey.

The weather was beginning to cool, and the leaves were changing colors—beautiful patterns of oranges, yellows, and reds were now intermixed among the fading greens. Teigra had been thinking about whether or not she would stay through the winter. The idea of shelter and a warm fire against the cold was very appealing.

When Teigra was about to make her way back, she looked down at the hut. From where she stood, she could clearly see through the window of Otho's and Vasili's bedroom. They were being intimate.

Vasili first undressed Otho and caressed his smooth skin. The two men kissed more passionately than any couple Teigra had seen. Vasili gently left a trail of kisses as he descended along Otho's neck and onto his chest. Otho, with his head arched back, savored the sensation. Vasili then sunk out of view, but by Otho's expression, there was little doubt Vasili was still kissing him passionately.

Teigra softly dropped the wood to the ground and moved behind a tree where she could gaze at the two lovers, undetected. She found her own hand reaching between her legs, and started to caress herself. Under her tunic, Teigra imagined that her finger was a lover's tongue, treating her to the delicacies of pleasure. She watched Otho's expressions escalate to euphoria as she tried to follow along with the cadence of her own hand. As Otho climaxed, so did Teigra, feeling an inner thrill that spread through every part of her body.

Unfortunately, unlike Otho, she was left alone in the afterglow with no companion to cuddle. Teigra's joy was soon followed by the bitterness of jealousy as she saw Otho holding Vasili in an embrace, caressing and kissing him in what seemed to be an eternal scene.

Why should they flaunt such affection in front of me? she thought. *And what was the benefit of such love when inevitably it would end in some kind of terrible pain? At any moment one of them could die or deceive the other, and the fragility of their love would turn to poison.* Their naivety was sickening to Teigra. She felt wiser in the ways of men and the world. She concluded her jealous internal monologue by deciding that what her hosts enjoyed was mere fantasy. Teigra stopped watching, made her way down the hill, and threw the tree limbs near the hut's entrance.

"Teigra, thank you for the wood," Vasili said, hurriedly walking out. "Could you stir the fire? I have many potions to make today."

"Okay," Teigra said.

Vasili rolled his large cart of bottles and powders toward the stove as Teigra fed the flames with the wood she'd gathered. His bottles were many different colors, and Teigra was curious about their use. It was the one subject Vasili had always avoided.

Teigra decided to try for the direct approach. "Vasili, what exactly are all these potions for?"

Vasili paused. He eyed her with a discerning look, as if examining her face for any motive other than natural curiosity.

"These are special oils used by kings and queens," he replied.

"Really? Where do you sell them?"

"Sometimes I take them to market, but usually I sell directly to my customers. I have a small but very devoted clientele. They know where to find me. Now please fetch some additional wood, Teigra. I plan on working a bit longer than usual today," Vasili finished, turning his full attention to his work.

Teigra did as she was asked, but she wasn't satisfied with the answer. The oils were colorful, but none of them had a scent that would be attractive to royalty. Vasili and Otho had treated her well, but they were obviously hiding something. Perhaps they were brewing special medicines...or poisons.

While she was sleeping that night, Teigra was woken by the sound of a shutting front door. She got to her feet, tiptoed across the floor, and peered out the window. Vasili had left, and was heading down the path. She looked back toward his room and saw Otho still asleep, undisturbed. She simply had to know where Vasili was going.

Teigra quickly dressed and made a quiet exit. There was no moon and the path was extremely dark, so it took several minutes for her eyes to acclimate. She sped along, hoping to narrow the gap between Vasili and herself. She eventually reached a point where she could see the tiny light of a lantern a few hundred paces ahead. Staying far enough away to remain undetected, Teigra saw Vasili veer off the path down a ravine. Not knowing the terrain, she was especially cautious. There was a chance his change in direction was a trap to catch anyone following him. If she made any noise, Vasili would know he wasn't alone.

At the bottom of the ravine, Teigra could see that Vasili had come to a stop in a clearing and rested his lantern on the ground. As she sat in the brush, she watched him walk to a sizable stone, move it back a few feet, and dig with his hands. After a few minutes, he removed a small wooden chest from the earth and opened it. He lifted a scroll, slowly unraveled it, and held the lantern close while carefully examining its writing.

From the glow, Teigra could see that Vasili also held some small bottles. He poured a few drops in precise amounts from each bottle into a bowl. He then gently returned the scroll to the chest, buried it back in the dirt, and rolled the stone into its original position. Vasili held a bowl of green liquid aloft in the night air. It shone with brilliance, and Teigra found its color mesmerizing.

Vasili walked over to a small puddle of water in the clearing. He threw the contents of the bowl into the puddle. To Teigra's amazement, a huge burst of flame shot as tall as the trees. The flame continued brightly burning, unaffected by water's usual ability to extinguish fire. Finally, after several minutes, the flame faded on its own.

Teigra grasped the meaning of this scene. Vasili wasn't a producer of potions for vain royalty. He was an alchemist—and a weapons maker. His clients were probably the *armies* of kings and queens.

Teigra fled as silently as she could so she could return to the hut before Vasili. She'd heard some of her previous masters speak of a magical fire, but thought the talk was mere legend. What she'd just witnessed was living proof of precisely what her masters had described—a wall of fire so hot that everything, even metal, melted in its path. This was a weapon that could incinerate villages, troops, and even water-borne ships in minutes.

So to whom does Vasili sell his wares? Teigra wondered. *The Argives? The Spartans? Some other kingdom? It's a tool of enormous power for whoever wields it.*

Teigra ran along the edge of the path and close to the trees to avoid being seen from afar. She crept through the door and into the hut, and saw that Otho was still asleep. She crawled back to her straw bed and pretended to be asleep until she heard Vasili return. She could feel his gaze upon her before he quietly entered his bedroom.

Teigra knew Vasili's secret. Better yet, she knew where he kept his secret recipe. She was fascinated by fire, and a fire that burned on water was extraordinary. *This information could certainly prove useful,* she thought before falling asleep.

The next day, the sun shone brightly and a crisp breeze blew through the trees. Nearly half the leaves had fallen, paving the way for winter. Teigra had been out all morning hunting for game—unsuccessfully. Normally, she could at least catch a rabbit or two, but had come up empty-handed. To avoid a complete failure, she gathered some wood and made her way back home. Then the shouting of voices stopped her in her tracks.

"Look, old man, he wants to know where you get the potions—now!" shouted a fierce voice near the hut.

"I have done all he has asked, but I will not share the source of my livelihood!" Vasili declared.

"We'll see about that, you old fool," the man responded. "Grab his plaything!"

Teigra snuck down the slope to see what was happening. Five Argive soldiers stood in front of Vasili, outside the house. The man who was shouting appeared to be a high-ranking officer. She watched two of the soldiers grab Otho and shove him to the ground.

"Stop! We have done nothing to you!" pleaded Vasili. "Have I not always given him potions for his asking?"

"For a mighty high price, you have!" the officer replied. "He's getting weary of your extortion. We're taking over your operation."

"Taking over? You can't do what I do!" Vasili said. "I've spent most of my life learning how to safely create these potions. Be reasonable!"

"Beat him!" the officer ordered.

Teigra watched as two soldiers repeatedly beat Otho with sticks, striking his head and body until he could no longer stand. Meanwhile, two others held Vasili as he screamed and tried to get to Otho. Vasili yelled in pain and begged for mercy, but his pleas fell on uncaring ears.

"Look, I will give you all the potions I have for free!" Vasili shouted. "Please, take them and leave us be."

"Who makes the potions, old man?" the officer demanded.

"If I tell you that, it will be my death," Vasili responded.

"Men, search the house and look for anything that might give us an answer," the officer ordered. "Oh, and beat his plaything to death. If we find the scroll, the old man dies. If not, he's coming with us."

Teigra didn't even consider making a rescue attempt. She liked Vasili and Otho, but she wasn't about to risk her freedom for them. No one had ever tried to save her, and she wasn't about to put her neck on the line. Though Otho and Vasili had a love for each other that she deeply envied, she had to look out for herself.

"Please don't hurt him!" Vasili screamed, as Otho suffered blow after blow at the hands of the Argive soldiers. Otho's body eventually stopped moving, but the thrashings to his body and head continued. Vasili's screams bled into sobs and moans as he realized that his lover was dead. Vasili's will to live vanished, and his body fell limp.

The soldiers exited the house with nothing but a box full of potions in bottles—no scroll, no secret writings. The officer acknowledged their fruitless search and gave a nod, signaling them to bring Vasili along, enchained.

"We'll see if you talk with a little more persuasion," the officer said.

Teigra waited several minutes, and then made her way down the hillside to the hut. The dwelling was in shambles. Cabinets had been emptied and torn apart, beds were dismantled and strewn across the floor, and doors and windows were unhinged. At first, she was surprised the Argives hadn't burned it to the ground. Then she realized they were afraid they might destroy some still-hidden valuable information.

Teigra gathered food and placed it in her pouch. She was anxious to leave since there was a chance the soldiers would return, but decided to first collect Vasili's secret scroll. Clearly, she wasn't the only one who recognized its value.

In daylight, Teigra found the trip to the clearing near the ravine a short and easy one. She also had little difficulty rolling the rock to the side, digging out the chest and retrieving its treasure. Teigra placed the weathered scroll in her bag, and then carefully buried the chest under the stone so no attention would be drawn to the spot.

She then returned to the woods, where she felt safest. Once again, she relished the taste of freedom. But now she also held the promise of real power.

CHAPTER 20

THE COMPETITION

As the annual Sondra competition drew near, the fifty girls whose Sondra training qualified them to participate felt increasing pressure to succeed against their sister warriors. Only fifteen girls from the competition would be chosen, based on top scores and overall performance, to fulfill their dreams and be considered for the position of Sondra.

Thea had spent years training. She'd grown agile and strong, defeating girls larger and more experienced than her in daily combat training. But with the stakes so high, she felt nervous.

One of the contestants, named Latona, towered above the rest. She was as strong as two oxen, making her a formidable opponent.

On the last day before the competition, Thea received the opportunity to test her skills. "Next up in Sondra combat maneuvers, Latona and Thea," announced the lead instructor.

It was mid-afternoon, and all the Sondra trainees stood in a circle outside a small arena. Everyone stopped their quiet chatter as the competitors were announced, realizing that this match would be exciting. Latona and Thea were renowned as the strongest fighters in the camp.

The duo stepped into the circle, standing about five paces from each other. They stared intensely into each other's eyes as they awaited the instructor's signal. They'd never competed head-to-head before, so each girl was uncharacteristically nervous. A spectator wouldn't know it, however, since they both masked their emotions in a strong, confident façade.

"Take your mark, warriors," the instructor called. "Combat!"

Both sprang! They crashed into each other, locking horns. Each defended with equal consideration, engaging in strategic maneuvers intended to cause the other to collapse.

Thea was the first to overcome. She swept Latona's legs. Latona didn't stay on the ground long, though; she regained her footing in a few seconds, visibly irritated.

Thea tried the same maneuver again, shifting a leg behind and grabbing Latona's throat. But Latona jumped back and over Thea's leg, and swung her head to the left, avoiding the attack.

Taking advantage of Thea's forward momentum and outstretched leg, Latona grabbed the leg with both arms. With a twist, Thea's face was in the dirt.

Thea rolled onto her back just as Latona pounced. Thea switched to offense, launching Latona overhead with one foot before Latona could land on her. The ground shook as Latona landed flat on her back.

"Prepare to lose, princess," Latona said, as she sprang to her feet and shook off the dirt.

"I didn't realize you knew how to fly," Thea said.

Latona surged at Thea. The two interlocked, fiercely wrestling for position. Despite Latona's size and strength, Thea lifted the larger girl into the air with both arms and slammed her onto the ground so hard that Latona's brain shook, rattling in her skull.

The girls and their instructors watched in astonishment. Thea handled Latona with ease. Her strength was beyond any warrior they'd seen.

Latona lay gasping for air. In one swift arc, Thea dropped to the ground, wrapped Latona up in rope, and flipped her on her back.

Thea let out a confident breath, gazed out at her audience, and grinned. The look on her face proclaimed her victory.

"Okay, warriors," the instructor said. "Tomorrow is the big day. Get some rest, eat well, and concentrate on what you've learned. Be at the competition fields at dawn to allow yourselves plenty of time to prepare. Good luck."

"Nice move, Thea!" Carina said. "Nobody expected you to handle Latona so easily."

"I was a little surprised," Thea admitted.

The two friends walked over to the stables to start preparing for the competition. Thea had chosen Carina to be her Sondra assistant months ago, and Carina happily accepted. The job made Carina responsible for all preparations, including making sure Nox was ready, and organizing Thea's weaponry and armor. The latter wasn't what Sondras actually wore, because trainees weren't allowed the honor of wearing Sondra garb. But if Thea successfully passed, she'd don the traditional black veiled attire of a full Sondra.

"Where did you get the armor?" Thea asked.

"The same as everyone else, from the instructors," Carina replied. "Everyone except Laria, that is, who got her mother's old armor."

"Yeah, I know," Thea said. "I saw her flaunting it around today."

"She flaunts everything," Carina noted. "Forget about her."

The Gods smiled favorably on the Amazon tribe the next morning, as the sun shone brightly and the sky was clear. All the girls in the competition were busy preparing. The tension in the air was palpable, as each knew the difficulty of the tasks ahead. Doing well at training was one thing, but the pressure and unexpected twists of the competition are what brought out a warrior's true mettle—or her shortcomings.

"What do you think of Nox?" Carina asked. "She looks ready, huh?"

"Definitely," Thea replied. "I have never seen a more stunning horse."

"Good morning, girls," Melia said, walking up at the same time. "Ready to win a competition today?"

"Born ready," Carina said, confidently.

"I think so," Thea added. "You believe my chances are decent?"

"I'd put all the money in the world on you, Thea," Melia said, with a big smile. "I'll be the one yelling the loudest."

Melia helped Thea finish getting dressed, while Carina prepared the weapons and led Nox to where she'd be needed. Thea could feel her nerves become unsettled in anticipation.

The entire tribe had assembled for the competition, so the arena was standing room only. The aspiring Sondras were gathered outside the arena, where they were assigned stations for their horses and equipment.

Thea heard the trumpets blow, signaling the start of the competition, and felt her stomach churn. She collected her spear, bow, and arrows, and headed to the arena along with the others, leaving Carina and Melia behind.

The first of the four events was Weaponry, which consisted of spear throwing and archery. The girls entered in groups of ten and aligned themselves in front of targets located one hundred paces away.

With both weapons, Thea hit the center of her targets, placing her among the top-ranking competitors.

The second event was Horseback Riding. Thea mounted Nox, who looked born to bear a Sondra on her back. The arena was decorated with a series of obstacles, including spiked barriers, rings of fire, and elongated pools. As each was negotiated, the rider had to successfully shoot arrows into targets located a few paces away. Though the target was significantly closer than it was in the previous challenge, this required shooting accurately while in motion. Nonetheless, Thea and Nox flawlessly rode through the course, and Thea again hit all her targets dead center.

"Great job, Thea," Carina said, as Thea rode back with Nox to her designated area. "You guys looked so natural."

"Thanks," Thea replied. "Where's Melia?"

"She went to get a better view in the arena," replied Carina.

"Who's close to us in the point totals?" Thea asked.

"Pola is the closest to you," Carina answered. "She missed the center of just one of the targets while riding. Otherwise, you're well in the lead." Thea didn't know Pola very well, but she liked her. They'd worked together in training and occasionally ate meals together. Pola was warm-hearted and competitive without being vindictive.

Laria had done poorly in the first two events, failing to earn the privilege of advancing. The disappointment was visible on Queen Alexa's face. She'd had high hopes for her granddaughter's future as a Sondra, and then as tribal leader, but those plans now appeared dashed.

The third event was Hand-to-Hand Combat. While the first two events were relatively safe for contestants, the last two were wild cards.

Unlike training camp, combat skills would be tested using fights with the tribe's strongest and most able male slaves, many of whom had extensive experience as gladiators. Each of them was a formidable opponent, but some were stronger and some were fiercer, so it was impossible to predict the nature of any individual battle.

When Thea stepped into the arena, a collective roar rose from the Amazon spectators. They knew she was leading in points and expected a good match. Thea looked across the arena and saw a large man crouched in fighting position. He was weathered and stout, but wasn't much taller than she. Thea closed her eyes and envisioned the men who'd tried to rape Laria. Gradually, she harnessed the same emotions and energy she felt that day.

Thea slowly approached, inviting his first move. The veteran fighter lunged at her. She dodged, leaving him grabbing thin air. Thea took advantage of his off-balance position and swept under his legs, causing him to fall.

The male warrior quickly jumped up and moved toward her again. This time Thea struck first, spinning and hitting him squarely in the jaw with the heel of her foot. He was again knocked to the ground.

The man stood up more slowly this time, but found the energy to continue attacking. He ran at Thea, intending to punch her. She grabbed his outstretched left arm and twisted it with all her strength, contorting his entire body. With his neck exposed, Thea struck it with her right hand. His legs buckled and his body went limp. She quickly straddled the large man, locking him in a flattened position on the ground with her knees and arms. With two blows, Thea had successfully completed the third event in record time.

The final event was the most dangerous: Wild Beast. Each of the competitors would face a panther in direct combat. The tribe captured panthers in the wild throughout the year in anticipation of this moment.

Each girl would be judged for the skills she demonstrated, and would win extra points for injuring the fierce animal. For safety, three expert archers were placed in different positions around the arena. If a panther was on the verge of snuffing a competitor's life, the archers would shoot their arrows.

At this point in the competition, thirty of the fifty girls had been eliminated. Only those scoring in the top twenty would be given the honor to attempt this most deadly of the challenges.

"Okay, Thea," Carina said. "Last event. Are you ready?"

"Yeah, I'm ready. What's to be afraid of? Just a little old panther," Thea replied, trying to mask her nervousness with humor.

Pola had her match before Thea. A black panther paced in a cage at the far end of the arena as the crowd's noise intensified with anticipation. Pola gripped her knife in her right hand and readied herself for the panther's release. Two Sondras opened the cage door, and the panther sprang.

Pola dodged the beast's first swipe of its claws against her body, and she braced for the next attack. The creature slowly stalked Pola, who held her blade in anticipation. When it leaped again, Pola rolled out of the way and threw her knife, lodging it in the panther's hind leg.

Limping, the panther growled at Pola, displaying its impressive teeth. Despite its wound, the beast was not about to forfeit the fight. It slowly encircled her. Pola pulled out her second knife and followed the panther with her eyes and body, moving in a circular motion just as it did.

Suddenly, the panther jumped, and the archers' arrows flew as Pola simultaneously swung her blade. All three arrows lanced the beast, causing it to flaccidly land on top of her. She pushed the carcass off as the crowd roared in applause. She had scored the highest among the competitors so far.

Several of the other women had wounded their panthers, receiving good scores in the final event. Thea thought she'd won enough points to be among the top fifteen girls, but she wasn't sure. If she failed to score a strike on her animal, it might be close. Pola was her primary obstacle to the top spot.

"Final competitor," announced the instructor to the crowd.

Thea entered the arena to see an angry black panther growing restless in its cage. Thea looked fierce herself, holding a knife in each hand as she took her stance. The animal was released, and it ran at her, full speed. Thea patiently waited as the panther approached. When it sprang into the air, she launched one of her knives. The panther came down snarling, the knife lodged in its chest, just under its right foreleg. But the large cat kept moving, almost unaffected.

Thea prepared for a second attack. She could hear a slight wheeze from the animal as a small trickle of blood dripped from its side. The panther, infuriated by the pain, raced at her. This time the beast connected, landing on Thea and pushing her backward. The archers sent their arrows flying, and the panther fell limp.

As Thea stood to the roar of the crowd, she glanced at the dead creature and made her way to the arena's exit. The crowd had already begun to chatter among themselves, some beginning to exit. But as Thea walked across the field, she heard a familiar voice.

"Thea! Watch out!" yelled Melia from the stands.

Thea quickly turned and saw that one of the remaining caged panthers had escaped and was headed directly for her. With Melia's scream, the crowd returned their attention to the arena. Before any of the archers or Sondras could act, the panther was in front of Thea. This was no longer a competition—it was life or death.

Thea grasped her knife and crouched into an attack position, as she felt her heart pounding. She decided she had only one option to avoid the certain impact of the cat's teeth. In one swift move, Thea jumped and landed on the panther's back. Jabbing her knife into the side of the panther's throat, she ripped the blade through the front of its neck. Blood gushed, covering both Thea and the beast, and the panther collapsed.

Thea was covered in crimson as those who watched in disbelief gradually began to applaud. She placed her knife back in its pouch and walked out of the arena to the sound of her Amazon sisters cheering. Carina and Melia were waiting for her.

"Are you okay?" Melia asked. "I was scared to death! How did the panther get loose?"

"I don't know," Thea said. "But I'm happy things turned out the way they did."

Many of the instructors, Sondras, and commanders came by to check on Thea and to congratulate her. She had earned the respect of the entire tribe. No one had ever slaughtered a panther during the competition, much less killed a loose one without the protection of the archers. Thea stood alone in this tremendous feat. Her status as one of the tribe's most elite warriors was irrefutable.

With the completion of the competition, all in the camp proceeded to enjoy themselves. Laria, however, was nowhere in sight. She didn't even extend the courtesy of congratulating Thea on her spectacular showing.

The official ceremony naming the new Sondras would occur in two weeks; but there would be one more challenge, conducted privately.

Meanwhile, pleasure and merriment were in the air. Food was abundant and wine flowed freely. Male slaves were available for everyone to enjoy. Thea, Melia, and Carina amused one another as they laughed and shared stories. The three had become very close and were like family, though Thea and Melia shared a love that Carina had yet to realize. As Thea and Melia escaped to their hut to steal a moment of passion, Carina watched from a distance. She wasn't jealous of them, but was envious for what they shared.

The Gods had not given Carina the gift of beauty. She was physically awkward, and her face was marred by a birthmark. The reddish lesion stained almost half her face, and many people rejected her based on appearance alone. This was the reason the other girls teased her, and why she'd never known romantic love. Thea and Melia had been among the very few who saw beneath the surface.

The festival was Carina's chance for some intimate contact, for which she was starved.

Carina took one of the male slaves by the hand and led him to the hut next to Thea and Melia. The slave tried to look at Carina as she slowly undressed him and began to caress his body. As she outlined the curves of his hips with her hands, he disrobed Carina, exposing her youthful figure. But despite her supple breasts and soft skin, he struggled to become aroused. Her facial scar was a distraction. Even as she softly placed her lips around his struggling phallus, the distraction continued to be a hindrance.

Carina had waited for passion too long to let anything stand in her way. She covered herself in her tunic and momentarily left.

"Thea, Melia," Carina whispered to the two girls who were passionately embraced.

"Carina? Oh...what is it?" Thea replied.

"My slave is having a bit of trouble...you know...getting excited," Carina managed to get out. "I was wondering if both of you could come to our tent to maybe help him get aroused. Possibly watching you might help."

"Oh...um...yeah, sure," Thea answered, looking at Melia for guidance.

"Of course we can," Melia replied.

Carina walked back into her tent followed by Thea and Melia. After a few moments, Thea and Melia resumed their passion as if no one else was around. Carina again threw her tunic to the side and began to caress her slave's manliness with her hands. The slave glanced over at Thea and Melia. They were delicious, and he instantly became aroused.

Carina pulled him on top of her as he entered her ever so softly. As he began to stroke her body with his, his passion soared as he absorbed the adjacent ecstasy. Carina felt a pleasure she'd never experienced before as his body raced against hers. She began to scream in pleasure as the slave gained momentum. The more he looked at Thea and Melia, the more turned on he became, and Carina was the happy recipient.

As the slave watched, Thea turned her body, placing her tongue between Melia's legs while Melia spread Thea's legs open for full sexual satisfaction. Their passions simultaneously climbed as each stroked the other with their mouths. Moans of pleasure mingled with the sound of their lips on each other. All the while, the slave became increasingly aroused, filling Carina even more completely with every push.

Carina's screams escalated, as the slave's desire seemed insatiable. Never had she felt so full from the physical pleasures of a man. Orgasm after orgasm, Carina pleaded for more at the height of pleasure. Her screams had driven Thea and Melia into their own world of erotic fantasy. Before the evening was done, all four had succumbed to the pinnacle of ecstasy. In a shared state of euphoria, each fell asleep, fully satiated and ready for a restful night.

CHAPTER 21

THE RISE OF ZAREK

Leander and the council that decided to take over Argos determined that their plan required the support of the army. At the same time, they needed to operate under a veil of complete secrecy.

Leander requested a meeting with Niko, who was the leader of King Bedros' forces and could summon the necessary might for a coup. The two men convened in Leander's quarters.

"As I am sure you're aware," Leander began, "the King's health is rapidly declining. Even if it was not, his age is a liability." Leander looked into Niko's eyes and observed no dissension.

"And I feel sure you agree," Leander carefully continued, "that it's the duty of any citizen of Argos to prevent Prince Zarek from ascending to the throne."

To Leander's relief, Niko nodded. "Yes. I concur with no reservations. My allegiance is to the King, but any sensible man can see the future of Argos will be compromised in the wholly incapable clutches of his freakish son. But what exactly are you proposing?"

Leander's face became solemn. "Even though the King agrees that Zarek is a disaster, out of fatherly love he has made it clear that under no circumstances will he consent to anyone but his son taking the throne. With the fate of Argos at stake, the only solution is for both father and son to meet their demise. This might seem immoral, especially since King Bedros is a great man; but when you consider the alternative—"

"Now just a minute," Nikos interrupted. "You are the royal advisor to King Bedros, yet you propose his murder? That's preposterous!"

"It would have to appear accidental, of course," Leander continued. "I'm coming to you because we'll need the full support of the King's forces."

"No," Niko answered, growing indignant. "There's not a chance in Hades that I'll lend my support to killing King Bedros. The man has always been good to me, and to this kingdom. I am sworn to his service. I won't go along with any plan that proposes his slaughter!"

"But you must consider the consequences—" Leander began.

"I would gladly turn a blind eye to the death of Prince Zarek. But I cannot have a hand in your plan," Niko said. "Further, I must warn you that there are factions within the King's army that do not hang on my every word. General Draco answers to Zarek, and a sizable faction of the King's soldiers are loyal to Draco. If this were to reach him, there would be bloodshed on an epic scale." Niko's brow furrowed and he took a deep breath, as if the mere thought of Zarek's reaction sucked the air from his lungs.

* * *

At the castle, a day had passed since Prince Zarek stormed off from dinner with his father, and the King had once again summoned him to his throne. Zarek wasn't sure about the old man's intentions, but wanted to be sure he gained something from the meeting. He had put up with King Bedros' excessive tolerance and indecision for far too long.

"My son, please, sit down," the King urged. Zarek complied, sitting across from his father's throne with a barely concealed scowl.

"We both know that my health is failing, and there are those who want to take my place. I feel the time is right for you to assume the throne, even though I am still living."

"What?" Zarek rose, indignant. "You are handing me the throne? You, a complete weakling, trying to protect *me?* How pathetic, Father."

"But…what else could you want? What greater gift could I offer you?" the King asked.

"This is the laughable final act of an impotent old fool! Father, I am *so* disappointed in you," Zarek sneered. "You don't even realize that no one could respect a King who's been handed the throne on a silver platter, which is what you've just tried to do to me. I am not in the habit of being in someone's debt. When I want something, I *take* it!"

With those words, Prince Zarek unsheathed his sword and quickly plunged it into his father's chest. The old man's torso heaved as he gasped. His ill health gave him no strength with which to fight the inevitable. It was only a matter of seconds before the life left his body.

Zarek withdrew the blade from his father's royal corpse. He took the large ruby ring from the dead King's limp hand and placed it on his own finger. He then reached under the dead man's arms and lifted the body from the throne. With a piece of cloth, he wiped away his father's blood and sat down on the throne for the first time as king. Bedros' quick death, lacking in drama or profundity, was seen by Zarek as a final act of weakness.

Zarek soon called for Zosimos. He felt he could waste no time in putting his plan in place. Zosimos arrived in the throne room, trying to hide his surprise at finding the body of Bedros on the floor in a pool of blood.

"Zosimos! You are looking at the new King of Argos!" Zarek exclaimed.

"Yes, Your Highness. How may I serve you?"

"Please bring Draco to me. I have immediate orders for the army," Zarek said. "Would you like me to find someone to take the body away, King Zarek?"

"Not yet, Zosimos. For the time being, I rather like the atmosphere it creates."

Minutes later, Draco came into the throne room. Like Zosimos, he noticed the corpse on the floor but said nothing about it.

"You have called for me, Your Highness."

"Yes, Draco. As you know, leadership of the royal forces of Argos has been under General Niko. That is to change. You will now assume full leadership of my army."

"Thank you, Your Highness," Draco replied.

"I am fully confident of your abilities. You are to tell Niko yourself, and inform all royal guards and soldiers of the change. Those who remain loyal to my father and wish to leave may do so without penalty. However, all who stay will be given an increase in pay."

"Yes, King Zarek. I have no doubt that they will be very grateful. Am I to dispatch with General Niko?"

"No, there is no need to kill him. He will understand that circumstances have changed and will not protest."

"Yes, Sire," Draco said.

"Besides, I have more important business for you. My father's records must be thoroughly combed through. I know he has had relations with a number of women and concubines since my mother's death. I know he has sired many bastards, including that Parthenos girl, Photina. There is a rumor that at least a dozen illegitimate children exist; and a rumor is enough to act on. Any you find must be immediately executed. They are, from this moment on, a threat to my rule."

"It will be done, Your Highness," Draco promised, and exited the throne room.

Draco's loyalty to Zarek was born not of love nor trust for the ruthless young king, but from a mutual respect and an innate tendency toward greed—but while Zarek's first desire was his father's throne, Draco's goal was less clearly defined. Though the two had been allies for nearly a decade, their relationship was a sham. Blinded by Draco's loyalty and servitude, Zarek never realized that his friend and servant had a secret history.

Born the illegitimate son of a Macedonian king and given the name of Bozidar, Draco lived a comfortable life with his mother in the region of Dion. When the king died at the age of forty-four, his true heir, a prince named Sime, ascended to the throne. Immediately, the paranoid young king ordered his forces to seek out and kill any bastard children his father had sired. When word of the new king's manhunt reached the streets, thirteen-year-old Bozidar's mother knew he had to leave or face certain death. She took him to the nearest port and shipped him to Athens, tearfully bidding him goodbye. She consoled herself only with the knowledge that doing so was the only way within her power to save his life.

Bozidar made his way to Athens with nothing but the clothing on his back. Once he arrived, he settled in the nearest marketplace by the port, living a hand-to-mouth existence for weeks, stealing food, and sleeping wherever he could until the day he caught the eye of a military general. The man, named Timaeus, approached him and they immediately became inseparable. Timaeus recruited Draco into his forces, giving him a job and purpose, then set about training the young prince in the Athenian way of battle. Once he had fully earned his trust, the boy told him his story. Timaeus responded by assigning him a new identity; having recently lost a nephew to illness, he allowed Bozidar to take on the dead boy's name for the purpose of public record. From that point forward, Bozidar was known as "Draco."

For the next five years, Timaeus was everything to Draco; father, teacher, commander, and lover. During the day, he treated him as any other soldier, but at night, that was forgotten. General Timaeus was the only person who knew the truth about Draco, and Draco was forever grateful—for Timaeus had not only given him a position in his army; he had given him a life.

One day, it all ended; Timaeus was killed by a gang of thieves while on patrol. Draco was devastated, left Athens, and immediately fled to Argos. Using the knowledge acquired from his former lover, he found work as a guard in the palace of King Bedros. He established a friendship with Prince Zarek. They could sense the greed in each other, which formed the basis of a shared common ground. From that point on, Draco considered himself to be in the service of Zarek, not Bedros. Over half a decade later, the irony of carrying out the same plan that was meant to destroy him several years earlier was not lost on him. Yet he experienced no remorse.

Alone again, Zarek decided that it would be wise to have his father's corpse removed before speaking with his next visitor. What he had to say would be difficult enough for Leander to swallow. There was no need for Bedros' closest ally to be enraged and repulsed upon entering the room. Zarek instructed slaves to take care of the mess.

An hour later, Leander arrived. "Prince Zarek, you have called for me," he said. But as the words left his mouth, he caught a red reflection flash off Zarek's hand. It was King Bedros' ring—and it appeared to have blood on it. Leander suddenly realized he was in danger, bit his tongue, and forced himself to remain calm.

"Yes, Leander. Being that you were so close to my father, I wanted you to be among the first to know that he has passed. I have therefore assumed my rightful position as King of Argos."

"I'm very sorry about your father," Leander said, nearly choking on his anger. "Please let me know if I can be of any assistance, Prince Zarek."

"I do have instructions for you," Zarek replied. "I want you to tell your wealthy friends that Bedros is no more, and I am now ruler of Argos. Any rules made or legislation passed will be done exclusively through me. They may accept this arrangement or leave. My rule begins now—and it will be in blood. You are to call me *King* Zarek. You are dismissed."

"Yes, Your Highness," Leander replied, jaw clenched. He gave an obligatory bow before exiting.

Zarek found the scene amusing. Leander had thought his role as advisor gave him power, but that had evaporated with the life of Bedros. Leander now had nothing and needed to look out for himself, or there was a good chance he'd end up counseling Bedros in the underworld.

Zosimos returned to the throne room to await new instructions. "Life is for the living, not the dead, Zosimos!" Zarek exclaimed. "I will not be observing the customary three-day mourning period. A new dawn has come to the people of Argos, and they should embrace it as soon as possible. I cannot wait to bring them the good news and let them partake in a celebration of our new future. Assemble the citizens so that I can inform them."

News quickly traveled around the kingdom, and thousands of citizens gathered to hear Zarek's announcement. King Bedros had been the most loved king in Argos' history, but like a sword hanging over their heads, the people knew that one day Zarek would take his place. Zarek's ruthlessness and greed for power instilled dread. But all intently listened to discern exactly what the future would hold under Zarek's rule.

"Citizens of Argos, today starts a new era for our great nation!" Zarek began. "King Bedros has left us in the night. But with his passing, new power and a bright future await us all. The measuring stick of a nation is its cultural progress and its influence on its region. Ignorance will not stand in our way. Spartans, Amazons, Persians, Egyptians—all will yield to our will, through cooperation or through force. Rejoice, citizens of Argos! Celebrate! Our future is the future of the world!"

The crowd cheered and applauded, though many did so only out of fear. Their motives didn't matter to Zarek. All he cared about was being king, and they now had to do his bidding.

"Let the festivities begin, citizens!" Zarek continued. "As your new king, I will bring a better life to us all. Our neighbors will fear us, and the entire world will listen.

"New laws will be passed to accomplish our goals. There has previously been a ban on torture in Argos, but this shall be lifted. Those who defy progress—whether thief, slave, or citizen—will not stand in the way of a brighter future! Ignorance must be destroyed by whatever means possible. As a token of my commitment to our great nation's goals, we will launch an attack on neighboring villages to secure what is rightfully ours.

"But first, let us rejoice and celebrate! I declare three days of festive celebration! Your new king and your new future have arrived!"

Again, the crowd cheered. Zarek exited to their shouts and walked back inside the castle, where Zosimos waited.

"Zosimos, keep the wine pouring, my dear friend," Zarek said. "As my new royal advisor, I command you to indulge in this festive debauchery with me!"

"Yes, King Zarek!" Zosimos replied. "Long live the new king!"

"Indeed!" Zarek said. "Now, there are a few matters of business to attend to in the very near future."

"Yes, Your Highness."

"First, Draco has been interrogating our suppliers of liquid fire throughout the land for a couple of years now, with no success. We must find the secret of how to make it for ourselves; we need to determine the ingredients. I don't care if we have to torture the holders to the brink of death. We will find that secret!"

"Understood."

"Next, all the Amazon villages surrounding our region must be burned to the ground. My father disapproved of them and yet allowed them to disgrace us! Women are not our equals, and we cannot allow them to live in our region as such. These Amazons make us look weak. Utilize some of our liquid fire to destroy the villages, and bring all survivors back to me."

"Yes, my King."

"Come to think of it, I would like to make that journey with you. I would enjoy seeing the liquid fire in action."

"Yes, my King."

"Finally," Zarek said, "all residents of Argos exhibiting clear physical or mental abnormalities are to be rounded up and exterminated. From this moment forward, the Argos of King Zarek is to be the very paragon of perfection. I must erase the weaknesses of my father's rule. For too long have we suffered these people.

"But for today, let's enjoy! Fill my glass, Zosimos!"

* * *

The celebration went on for days. Meanwhile, Bedros' body was quietly laid to rest. The ceremony was brief, with no pomp, and just enough formality to recognize the former king's death as official.

Leander and Bedros' other allies were offended by Zarek's disrespect, but they were even more concerned about their own futures.

It was clear the coup they'd planned stood no chance of succeeding against the iron rule of this new monarchy. Their very lives were now in question.

CHAPTER 22

THE SONDRAS

Thea woke in great pain and couldn't tell where she was. Something was holding her upright, and her neck and wrists were locked in place at the same height. Her vision was fuzzy, and something was encrusted in the corners of her mouth. As she opened her eyes, she was blinded by the bright light of the forest. Her tongue was swollen and dry, and her body seemed to be rebelling against her.

While Thea couldn't turn her head, she knew she was in a stockade somewhere in the woods. But who had taken her prisoner? She had been competing in the Sondra competition, and then...

She tried to piece things together, but couldn't connect the dots. All she could do was remain standing, so the weight of her entire body didn't rest on her neck.

Thea focused on staying upright, dazed, for what seemed like hours. In fact, only thirty minutes had passed when she saw a trio of shadowy figures emerging from the trees and into the clearing where she stood. They were Sondras.

"Thea, we are here to inform you that you have passed your torture training," one of them told her. "Congratulations."

They unlocked her from the device, and placed her arms around their shoulders for support. They carried her away as she began losing consciousness. The last thing Thea saw as her eyes closed was a plague of dark bruises marking her thighs.

The official ceremony welcoming the new Sondras to the tribe was to be held in a couple of days, giving those candidates who completed the torture phase time to recuperate. Of the competition's fifteen winners, twelve made it through this final, brutal test. The other three found the pain too much to withstand and would be placed in prestigious positions amidst the tribes less elite forces.

After returning home, Thea slept deeply for seventeen hours. She then took a hot bath and dressed her wounds. She started feeling like herself again.

But Thea was unable to sleep as she lay in bed next to Melia the following night. The induction ceremony for the new Sondras was in the morning. Thea wanted to be a Sondra so badly, and wondered what her new life would be like.

Her thoughts were suddenly interrupted by a shadow at the end of the girls' tent. It made its way to Thea's bedside and knelt down next to her. Always at the ready, Thea placed her hand on the knife she kept on her ankle. Then the shadow spoke.

"I'm Elpis," the figure announced. "I knew your mother. Come with me."

Thea had never heard of Elpis, but she would've gone anywhere for the chance to learn something about her mother. Thea ignored the possibility of danger. Besides, there was something peaceful about Elpis' voice that rang with sincerity.

Thea silently left her bed without waking Melia and followed Elpis to her horse. The two mounted the mare and rode off into the forest. Along the way, they passed a Sondra who stopped them for identification, and then nodded and waved them onward. Thea immediately felt relieved. Who was this person? Why hadn't Thea ever heard of her?

Before long, they reached the top of one of the peaks close to camp, where Thea had been many times. Behind a large rock, Elpis lit a torch to guide Thea through a small crevice entrance to an elongated cave.

As they walked, Thea could see the stars in the sky through breaks in the cave roof above them. She'd explored this area dozens of times but never discovered this particular place.

The walk went on for quite a distance. Eventually, Thea saw a light at the end of the cave. The cave expanded into a larger room in which an old woman sat next to a small fire. The flames made her face glow and reflected her pale blue eyes. Thea would've sworn the face belonged to a child—except the woman's hair was long, coarse, and white. The moon shone brightly through a hole in the roof of the cave. The mixture of firelight and moonlight created a luminescence around her small figure.

As Elpis ushered Thea into the room, the mysterious woman stood. She was barely the size of a child. Thea felt she'd entered a fantasy world as she gazed upon this intriguing character.

"Sit, my dear," the woman said. "I am Seema. I knew your mother and so did Elpis, who brought you here tonight."

Thea was captivated, and had many questions. But instead of speaking, she simply listened, hoping to learn as much as she could.

"For many years we have watched over you from afar," Seema continued. "Those were your mother's instructions. Let me see your marking, child. On your neck..."

Thea was temporarily paralyzed with excitement. This person knew of her secret! She leaned forward and moved her hair to the side, exposing her serpent emblem.

"Elpis and I were there when your mother placed these two intertwined serpents on your neck," Seema said. "It was the symbol by which you could be recognized—the mark of the Golden Girdle. It labels you as the daughter of the true Amazon Queen."

Thea's fascination instantly turned to disappointed skepticism. Was she meant to believe she was the daughter of an Amazon Queen? If that were true, then why had she been abandoned? This old mystic was talking nonsense.

"You grew up alone because your mother was banished from Earth by the Gods, child," Seema said, as if she could read Thea's thoughts. "That is why Elpis and I have watched over you from a distance. Your mother is Elektra, the greatest of all Amazon rulers."

Thea heartily laughed at Seema's words. In school she'd learned much about Elektra, the immortal Amazon Queen who'd united all the tribes and led the Amazons through a golden era. But one day Elektra had vanished without a trace, and no one knew where. "Why should I believe what you say is true?" Thea asked, still chuckling.

"You may choose to believe it or not, child," Seema stated. "But one day the truth will present itself to you.

"You are about to embark on your destiny," Seema continued. "You will begin a journey tomorrow that will take you on the path to become the next Queen of all Queens. Many obstacles stand in your way. These are not for you to know in advance, but they must be conquered before your true destiny can be realized.

"Your mother left behind the Golden Girdle, which holds immortality, strength, and healing powers. It was hidden in the ground but has fallen into unfriendly hands. It will soon be in the possession of an evil king whose goal is to kill all Amazons."

Thea remained quiet for a moment, then spoke again. "Why did you summon me now?"

"Queen Alexa will meet her fate at the hands of this evil king. That is why I have summoned you. You must know—but not tell anyone else—that this is how you will become Queen."

Thea felt overwhelmed. Only a few hours ago she hadn't the faintest idea about her mother's identity. Now she was being told she was the daughter of Elektra, and her destiny was to seek the Golden Girdle and replace Alexa as the next queen! The story seemed too much to believe—but what if it were true?

Then, even more shocking news surfaced. Leaning forward and whispering, as if the Gods could hear, Seema said, "And Theodora, you're not the only one; you have a sister."

Thea felt her blood grow hot with sheer shock. The only thing she could think to ask was, "Where is she?"

"We do not know. Your mission will be to find her."

"Find her? How would I recognize her?"

Seema gently smiled. "From the marking. You both have the same marking. That is how you will know each other."

"Theodora, my dearest, you are about to become a Sondra," Seema said. "This is a great achievement and a significant step toward your destiny, but many challenges await you. Your path won't be easy. You must always have faith in yourself."

Seema paused, then looked Thea directly in the eyes. "You must not tell anyone what was said here. The news of Alexa's fate would cause panic in the tribe, yet nothing can be done to change it. You would be in even greater danger if your identity was prematurely revealed.

"As you embark on this new journey, stay true to your heart. Let honor, and the promises you'll be making as a Sondra, guide you. But never forget from whence you came."

Seema concluded, and then waved her hand as if shooing Thea away. The mystic returned to her seated position in front of the fire and closed her eyes.

Elpis quietly took Thea's hand, leading her out of the cave and back to her horse. Thoughts consumed Thea's mind as Elpis rode without a word. Elpis returned Thea to her camp and, as a fitting end to what felt like a waking dream, vanished into the night.

Thea returned to bed, where Melia remained soundly sleeping. Thea's thoughts were no longer about the morning's ceremony. Everything Seema had told her was turning over and over in her mind. Was Seema truly empowered to see the future, or was she just a demented old fortune teller living in a cave? Thea didn't know what to believe. She decided the only thing she knew for certain was that tomorrow would be the first day of the rest of her life...no matter what awaited her. With that thought, she was overcome with fatigue and fell into a deep sleep.

Morning arrived. The awards ceremony took place in the same arena where the Sondra competition had been held, but was a much more intimate event. Just before sunrise, the twelve chosen girls gathered around a tremendous bonfire, along with all the tribe's active Sondras.

Thea was proud. More than ever, she felt a sense of belonging. Between earning the support of her tribe and what Seema had told her about her mother and her twin sister, Thea felt she was on the right path. She may have grown up as an orphan, but here in the heart of the tribe she had multiple mothers and sisters, each of whom was caring and nurturing. It made her feel very lucky.

In preparation for the ceremony, the girls gathered at a fountain to dye their hair black, which was a required element of the dark "uniform" that allowed Sondras to blend invisibly into the shadows. Surrounding the edge of the circular structure, they all stripped to the waist and dipped their heads forward into the water. Each of them was assigned an assistant who carried a bowl of black dye made from a recipe of herbs and minerals, and who helped to thoroughly massage the color into the hair. As Thea leaned forward, she enjoyed the incidental scalp massage and watching drops of black dye fall from her head and burst into billowy gray clouds when they hit the fountain's surface.

When all the girls were brunettes, they were ready for the awards ceremony.

Queen Alexa proudly entered the middle of the arena, surrounded by her tribal advisors and camp instructors. Encircling the group were all of the Sondras, dressed completely in black attire, with black veils.

"You have displayed impressive skill and determination," Queen Alexa proclaimed. "This was a particularly tough initiation, and we are very proud. Each one of you is a unique and highly valued member of our tribe. We are honored to welcome you to the most elite branch of Amazon warriors, the Sondras."

Alexa announced the names of those selected, and one by one, each of the twelve girls came forward to accept her new title of Sondra. Thea felt like her heart might explode. It suddenly seemed as if her entire life was simply preparation for this moment. She had never wanted anything more than to hear Queen Alexa call her name.

"Thea!" Queen Alexa said, smiling.

Thea tried to show reserve, but she felt her mouth break into a wide and uncontrollable grin. She had done it!

"Each of you has proven yourself to be worthy of the honor and responsibility of being a Sondra," Queen Alexa continued. "It is your duty to uphold the beliefs and values that all Amazons hold dear. We stand for peace and honor. We stand for independence and honesty. We stand for integrity and trust. We believe that each woman should be celebrated for her individuality. When the evil and greedy choose to enforce their will on others, we stand to guard against them. By cover of darkness or by stealth in the daylight, Sondras use their skills to uphold justice."

Alexa paused as those gathered took time to contemplate the solemn pledge of a Sondra. Thea could feel a passion swelling inside.

"Sondras are dedicated to their tribe," Alexa continued. "Among Sondras, there is never an 'I.' It is always 'we.' And *we* are the definition of a sisterhood. These ceremonies honor our newest Sondra warriors."

Alexa then called the twelve girls forward and held up a dozen medallions. Attached to a necklace of black leather, the front of each steel medallion was cast in the shape of an owl, while its back was forged with the identification number the warrior was assigned as a Sondra. As each girl came forward, Alexa placed the necklace over the new Sondra's head, acknowledging her appreciation and respect for what she had accomplished.

Watching the ceremony in a corner by herself, Laria's face couldn't hide her disappointment. She tried to look into her grandmother's eyes, but Alexa purposefully did not make eye contact. Queen Alexa had hoped that her granddaughter would one day follow her as tribal queen, but taking that role required first becoming a Sondra—and Laria had unfortunately proven to be unqualified. As Alexa welcomed the new class of warriors into the tribe, she wished that she were able to call Laria's name, but knew in her heart that Laria was simply destined to walk a different path.

When Alexa watched the Sondra competition, Thea's abilities clearly stood out from her sisters. Since the day Thea had killed the two men in the forest, Alexa had known Thea's skills were extraordinary. She excelled at everything she tried. She'd even won a Nemean chariot race! That was an unprecedented achievement for a girl—as was slaying a panther with nothing but a knife. Alexa was especially proud to have Thea as one of her top warriors.

During the awards ceremony, Alexa noticed for the first time that Thea reminded her of someone. Suddenly it struck her. Thea's hair, now dyed black as a Sondra, made her honey-colored eyes even more radiant...and gave her an uncanny resemblance to the legendary Queen Elektra.

CHAPTER 23

THE ASSASSIN

Teigra had traveled a long distance from Vasili's and Otho's hut, and the food she'd taken was almost gone. Sterna wasn't far, and she figured she could steal some bread and fruit if necessary. But being able to hunt down a nice pheasant in the forest would be much better. Her plan was to continue traveling south, passed Tegea, where it would be safe for her; the Spartan region was more sympathetic and tolerant of women.

Teigra was making her way through trees and down a small hill in search of game when she suddenly heard male voices. *What if they're Argive soldiers?* she thought. Teigra quickly climbed into the upper limbs of a tree. However, one of her arrows slipped out of her pouch, and landed on the ground. *Should I jump down to get it?* she wondered. *No, it's too late. I just have to hope the men overlook it.*

Teigra sat midway up the tree, breathing as silently as possible, as she waited to learn more. Five men made their way toward the hill. As they grew closer, she could tell they weren't Argive soldiers. Their clothes were made mostly of animal skins, and their beards were disheveled, with no markings of allegiance to Argos or Sparta. One carried a large bag, and all of them had knives and bows strapped to their bodies. They seemed to be traveling on foot, as there wasn't a horse in sight.

"I'm hungry. Let's rest and eat," barked one.

"You're always hungry," retorted another.

"You'd be starved too if you'd carried this bag all the way from the mountain."

"Everyone's got to earn their share. Quit griping."

"I don't mind earning my share. I just want to fill my stomach. I say we rest here and eat before moving on."

The bag landed at the base of the tree in which Teigra was hiding. She could smell the men's stench as it rose up into the air. *That odor of sweat and filth would make them easy prey in a hunt*, she thought.

Now that she had a closer look, she could tell they were bandits. Their home was the same as hers—the woods. She couldn't help but wonder what was in the bag.

The men sat around the tree. "Pass me some of that dried meat," demanded the hungry one. Teigra's stomach rumbled, but not loud enough to be heard. She could see the arrow lying just off to the side of one of the men, but he hadn't noticed it.

How long are these men going to stay camped here? she wondered. Teigra hoped she could stay quiet long enough to avoid detection. Sweat began to bead up on her face.

"Hurry up and eat! We don't have all day. Just because you got lazy ain't any excuse to waste the daylight."

"Careful! I'm getting a little tired of your mouth."

"Aw, ain't that a shame! Are you going to tell me to shut up? We all remember what happened the last time you tried that."

The hungry man moved to confront the other. As he did so, his hand struck the arrow that had previously remained undetected.

"What's this?" he said, as he held it up for the others to see.

"How do you suppose that got here, of all places? It looks fresh. The wood ain't rotten or nothing."

Teigra knew what was coming. These men didn't seem too bright, but it didn't take much to figure out that the answer to their question was right over their heads. She froze as best she could and tried to mask herself behind branches, but with very few leaves remaining there was little to hide behind. Then it happened. A man tilted his head up, and their eyes met. And while Teigra's face remained expressionless, his grew a big, greedy smile.

"Hey boys, look what we have here!" the man declared, as he reached for his bow.

"Oh, dessert! I was just getting a sweet tooth," another said.

"All right girl, time for you to come down from that tree. Otherwise, I'll have to place an arrow in you."

Teigra thought about her options. If she resisted now, she was an easy target. There was no way she could get off clean shots at all five of them from a tree branch. Reaching down to grab the small pouch on her waist, she slowly descended the tree.

"Attagirl. A woman with looks *and* brains," the man said.

"She's definitely got the looks," another said.

Teigra reached the ground and turned to face the men. They surrounded her like wolves around a rabbit. They'd forgotten all about their hunger. Teigra could feel a rage beginning to swell within her as her mind was transported back to her Master Acacius' bedroom.

"This arrow yours?" the man asked.

Teigra didn't respond. She simply looked him gravely in the eyes.

"You'd better answer when spoken to, girl! Is this arrow yours?"

Teigra remained silent...but her look spoke volumes.

"I believe this one needs to be taught some respect. Since I found the arrow, I get first crack as teacher. Hold her down!"

Teigra stiffened. Two of the men dropped their food and started walking toward her, while the man speaking began to loosen his garments. If she ran, she'd be caught or lanced with an arrow. But she'd rather die than become an object of pleasure for this dirty band of thieves. Their smell was so strong she could already feel it on her skin.

The forest was normally a quiet place. Teigra had enjoyed it as her home, but today it was just another prison. She tightened the grip on her pouch.

* * *

Without being noticed by the party on the hill, a small group traveled along the path just a few hundred paces away. A small carriage followed two guards on horseback. The noise of the carriage was muted by the shouting and laughter of the men's voices on the small hillside.

"Halt," whispered one of the guards. "I hear voices."

The carriage stopped, and a confident man dressed in royal garments immediately stepped out and approached the guards. It was King Zarek. He was enjoying a routine expedition into the forest in search of victims for his torture chamber. He hoped this interruption meant a morsel for his evening trip to the dungeon.

"What is it?" Zarek asked.

"Voices, Your Highness. Just on that hill," one of the guards replied.

"Zosimos and you, come with me," Zarek instructed. "The rest stay with the horses."

Zarek cautiously made his way behind some evergreens to spy on the others. His guards hurried to follow and ensure their new king's safety.

Zarek immediately focused on Teigra. He measured every curve of her body with his eyes, analyzing her anatomy the way a butcher would a pig. Her blonde hair was dirty but striking as it lay on her shoulders. He was delighted to find something so beautiful to destroy.

"My King, should we intervene?" whispered one of the guards.

"No," Zarek replied. "Just wait for now. Let's see what happens."

Zarek returned his gaze to Teigra, hoping he'd acquired a seat to his own private show. He could hardly wait to see what the bandits did to this breathtaking woman.

"Now, no need to struggle, sweetness," one of the men said to Teigra.

"Unless you want to," another said, laughing. "Can't have you lying there limp and all."

"Let me undo my garments," Teigra said, uttering her first words. "I'm not sure all of you are enough to satisfy me."

Teigra reached down to untie her tunic—but like lightning, each hand grabbed a knife from the sides of her ankles. Before any of the men in the group could react, the two at the front were hunched over with the knives in their stomachs.

Teigra leaped from the base of the tree and ran up the hill as the other three men followed. She felt an arrow fly past her head. Though she wanted to keep running, she knew that escaping these men wasn't likely. They were like her; the woods were their home, and they would search until they found her.

Teigra made it about halfway up the slope when she turned behind a tree. She grabbed the bow from her back and loaded it with an arrow. She let an arrow fly as one of the men appeared right below her. Before he had an opportunity to react, the arrow was lodged in his chest. He futilely grasped at it as he collapsed.

Teigra reloaded and was ready for the next one. As she expected, he appeared right after his comrade; and he made the fatal mistake of looking at his fallen friend and pausing in shock. In a moment, he too lay flat on his back, his chest home to another one of Teigra's well-placed arrows.

Four of the men were dead, leaving only one—the man who'd first noticed her.

Teigra sat quietly, her heart pounding, sweat streaming down her face, struggling to keep her breath silent as she panted. Watching every twig and leaf, she squinted to see the slightest movement. The stillness was soon interrupted when two sweaty hands grabbed her arms, forcing her bow to the ground.

"You're going to pay, wench!" the man shouted. "You've never known pain like what you're about to feel."

The man had a tight hold on Teigra, and forced her off the ground, holding her back against his chest. Suddenly, he swung her around and punched her squarely in the jaw, sending her against a tree before her knees buckled. The sweaty hands lifted her again and threw another punch in her face.

With each blow, Teigra felt her rage growing. The hatred of every ugly moment in her life boiled to a head.

As he was readying his third strike, she leaped out of the way, much to the surprise of both her attacker and the spectators down the hill. She crouched to face her adversary as he regained his footing. He briefly paused to study Teigra. Her wild eyes and determination were imposing and unmistakable, and he thought it best to put his survival before his manhood. He went for his knife, even though she was unarmed.

"The fun stops here, girl," the man stated.

He threw his knife at her, its blade spinning. To his shock, Teigra dodged it, and the blade landed in a tree a few paces behind her. Teigra didn't even bother looking back at the weapon. Without hesitation, she sprang toward the large man, grabbing him by the throat. They fell to the ground, wrestling and rolling down the terrain before being stopped by another tree. Teigra summoned all her strength and threw her opponent against a boulder half buried in the ground. Before he could regain his balance, Teigra pounced once more and snapped his neck, leaving his carcass limp.

Zarek watched with wonder as Teigra massacred the entire band of men. What an amazing feat he'd just witnessed! He was certain he was going to watch a young girl's spirit destroyed by thieves, but instead he'd seen a different kind of devastation.

"Shall I secure the girl, Your Highness?" his guard asked.

"No, not just yet," Zarek said. "Let's see what she does now."

Teigra stood and examined the dead bodies lying around her. Slowly and methodically, she walked down and collected her knives as if carrying out a task she'd done for years. Then, without hesitation, she placed her knife between the legs of each of her assailants and severed their manhood. Zarek was overcome with amazement and joy. A spectacle that had begun by appealing to his sadistic side had turned into an exquisite and unexpected kinship. This woman pleased him not only for her beauty, but because of her own apparent passion for torture! He immediately felt a special bond with this fierce warrior. Perhaps he could find a better use for her.

Teigra, unaware of her audience, sat next to the tree where her troubles had started. She wiped the sweat from her face and cleaned her knife blades before placing them back in their pouches. After taking a moment to regain herself, she noticed the bag left by her victims. *So what's in it?* she wondered. *Gold coins? Silver coins? Jewels? Only one way to find out!* Teigra opened the bag...and was disappointed to see it held the thieves' supplies: pots, jars, skins, and a bit of food. She took a piece of dried meat and began chewing.

"Anything of interest in the bag?" Zarek asked, as he suddenly appeared from the brush. His armed guards immediately stepped behind him, along with Zosimos.

Teigra stood ready for another wave of attacks as she grabbed hold of her knives.

"Please, my fine warrior, I mean you no harm," Zarek said. "We have watched your impressive display. I have no desire to test your talents against my own men. I fear they may not be any match for you."

"What is it you want?" Teigra asked.

"I am Zarek. Have you heard of me?"

"Should I have?"

"Perhaps not. Here, have some bread and wine."

Zarek took some bread and a skin of wine and offered it to Teigra. Cautiously, she took the meal and placed her knives back in their sheaths.

"You have amazing skills," Zarek continued. "Where did you learn to fight like that?"

"I just...learned," Teigra replied.

"Please, eat. You must be famished. Do you live among these trees, or do you call somewhere else your home?"

"These woods are my home."

"I see. And how are they treating you during these colder months?"

"It's not the woods that bother me," Teigra said, glancing toward one of the dead men on the ground.

"What is your name, miss?"

"I am Teigra."

"A fitting name for such a savage warrior. I have a proposition for you."

Teigra looked up from her bread to meet Zarek's gaze. She had already surmised he was a man of wealth and power from his attire and entourage. The bread was delicious, and the wine relaxed her. She hadn't had such a meal since she'd left Vasili's hut. No matter what the proposition was, the food had made her more than attentive.

"I am the King of Argos," Zarek said. "I have much to offer you: food, wine, a warm bed, clean clothes. The best of all things."

He paused to see her response, but Teigra simply kept eating as she listened.

"Let's just say I am in need of an assistant, and you appear to be exactly who I was looking for."

"An assistant for what?" Teigra asked.

"Duties you are well qualified for, Teigra," Zarek responded. "We can discuss the details another time. Suffice it to say you have skills that interest me."

Teigra fully understood what this king was implying. She finished the bread, drank the last of the wine, and handed the flask back to Zarek. Though nothing in her life had ever come easy, it seemed her luck had changed within a matter of minutes.

She held doubts that the King's offer was as good as it sounded. Nonetheless, a steady diet of fine food and comforts would be a nice change from the cold of winter. If things didn't work out...well, it wouldn't be the first time. As before, she would find a way to escape.

Since the King was accompanied by several guards, Teigra wasn't sure she was being given a choice, but she decided to act as if she was. "I'm listening," she said.

"That's an excellent start, then," Zarek said, smiling. "Come down the hill with us. You will ride with the guards back to my kingdom, where we can talk more."

Teigra rode on one of the guard's horses, while two guards escorted the carriage. During the trip, which took the rest of the day, she contemplated Zarek's offer and tried to envision what sort of services he would need from her. She concluded, *What could be worse than what I've already done to survive?*

The sun was setting when they arrived in Argos. Torches lined the kingdom as the group entered the main road. The blazing sun, and the illusion of waves created by the heat, gave the city a surreal appearance, as if it belonged to some other world.

Singing could be heard in some of the homes they passed, and minstrels played on corners. Teigra gathered that some sort of celebration was going on, but she had no idea what the occasion was.

Soon Zarek's palace came into view. It was truly majestic, and Teigra began to understand the power that this man wielded.

Teigra dismounted as Zarek and Zosimos stepped out of the carriage. Zarek made a gesture to the guards and then motioned for her to follow. All the guards bowed as the King and his servants walked through the entrance to the castle. Teigra felt very strange being in such company. Given her past experience with men of power, she suspected Zarek had her in mind for his own pleasure. She might have run, but her curiosity—and the army of guards—persuaded her to see things through.

"Zosimos will show you where you can clean up," Zarek said, as they entered the gates. "Once you've done so and have gotten something to eat, we can talk. I will send for you later."

Teigra nodded.

"Come this way," said Zosimos.

Zosimos was a short and somewhat round man. Teigra towered over him as they walked through the corridors of the castle. After several turns, he showed her to a room equipped with a basin, a small bed, and fresh garments. It wasn't extravagant, but it was luxury she'd never known. She couldn't remember the last time she'd bathed, and she hadn't slept in a bed since she'd lived with Vasili.

"Everything you should need is here, except hot water, which I will have a servant bring you," Zosimos said. "I will come get you once the King is ready."

Before Teigra could answer, Zosimos vanished. She walked over to the window. She was on the second floor and could stare over the main gate of the castle. She could still hear some distant music and song, but the streets were fairly quiet. For all its opulence, there was something eerie about the place. A strange feeling hung in the air that was almost tangible. She couldn't identify it, but it was real, and she was confident she'd figure it out.

The hot bath felt incredible. Teigra's aching muscles and joints were soothed, and it felt wonderful to be free of weeks of grime. The bath and fresh clothes utterly revived her, even though she should have been exhausted from her long day. As she brushed her hair, she caught a glimpse of her neck mark in a handheld mirror. It had been a long time since she'd studied the strange design. The snakes were beautiful, and enmeshed together as if they were a single creature. The detail was so intricate, she knew that whoever branded her had a distinct motivation. When she was a child, she used to think it was a mark of the Gods, and that one day she would rise above her misery to the Heavens. Those fantasies were long gone, but at the moment she was as close to Olympus as she had ever been.

"Miss, the King is ready for you," came a voice from the corridor.

Teigra opened her door to find a servant waiting to escort her to King Zarek. She had to walk across the whole castle, but she eventually entered the King's chambers. There was no comparison to her humble room; his was gargantuan. At the end of a great hallway, he sat upon a throne surrounded by long flowing curtains. Zarek and Zosimos were engaged in conversation, but it immediately ceased when Teigra was ushered in.

"Ah, I trust you enjoy your accommodations?" Zarek inquired.

"Yes, thank you," Teigra replied.

"Now we can have a conversation in private," he continued. "As you have been living in the forest, I assume you know nothing of me. I have recently become the King of Argos at the misfortune of my recently deceased father Bedros. As is often the case with change, there has been some resistance."

Zarek paused to study Teigra's reaction, but she offered nothing.

"Some of my father's allies, wealthy men within the kingdom, have expressed dissatisfaction with my plans to rule, to the point of blatant disrespect. I am sure you understand that disrespect cannot be allowed."

Teigra was beginning to grasp the ego of the man.

"As I watched you from afar today, I thought you could understand the need to properly dispose of such attitudes. With both your abilities and stunning beauty, you could be the perfect assassin."

"But I'm no assassin, King," Teigra said.

"Correction. You haven't yet worked as an assassin. But a professional mercenary couldn't have handled those men any better, my dear. And don't think I didn't watch as you castrated each of them. I knew then that we have much in common."

Teigra blankly stared back, giving away nothing.

"I will pay you well, without question," Zarek went on. "But this will be between you, me, Draco, and Zosimos. No one else will know."

"And if I refuse?" Teigra asked.

"Oh, but you won't. Here." Zarek knew he had the power to get her to do whatever he wanted without rewarding her, but he wanted to give her something. He was already fond of Teigra—beautiful, resourceful, and not at all afraid to get blood on her hands. He hoped that paying her would result in her trust…and maybe even her friendship.

Zarek tossed a bag at Teigra's feet. Some of the many silver coins spilled over when it struck the ground. It was more money than Teigra had seen in her entire life. Her eyes couldn't focus on anything but the treasure. She could already tell Zarek was foul and rotten. But with rare exceptions, she hadn't liked any men she'd met. Why not pad her own pocket by disposing of them?

"Understood, girl?" Zarek asked.

"Understood," Teigra replied.

"Very well! Tomorrow we will discuss your first assignment. Until then, enjoy yourself. We are still engaging in our celebration feast."

"Celebration?"

"Of course. Our country has a new king!"

"Of course," Teigra said, straining to avoid sounding ironic.

Teigra was escorted out by Zosimos, who pointed her in the direction of her room. Before going in, she asked if he could recommend a tutor for her. After all, now that she had money, it was a good time for her to learn how to read and write. When she returned, she sat back and ate until she was full, and then curled up on her bed with the bag of silver coins clenched to her side.

Yesterday, she was a refugee in the forest. But now she'd become a king's assassin! She wasn't sure whether her life had improved, but it was certainly more comfortable. As the moon slipped past the window, Teigra drifted off to sleep.

* * *

Following the Kings's orders was neither Draco's top priority nor in his primary interest. With a far-off throne that he could potentially usurp, he realized that he had both the strength and knowledge to take what was rightfully his. He and his men had spent the weeks since Zarek took the throne disposing of the rumored bastard sons of Bedros—many of them mere children.

A force of ten men following him through the trees, Draco realized what he would do; being an official heir himself, he must father a child to continue his royal bloodline. He had been away from his birthplace for so long, he no longer knew the status of the kingdom or who ruled it. There would always be a remote chance that he could return and somehow take his rightful place by proving his birthright—and he must also pass that right on to an offspring. The mother of the child would be inconsequential, a mere vessel.

The one missing piece of the puzzle was Photina, Zarek's half-sister. Her mother, Zenobia, had been the favored concubine of Bedros for many years. Zarek had described Photina as having the most luminous red hair he had ever seen, though the last time he laid eyes on her was some years ago, when he was in his teens. The word he had received was that she was a member of the Parthenos Girls, which meant that he didn't have to worry about her siring any heirs. Still, Zarek wished her dead just to put his mind at ease.

En route to find a village, Draco rode across the outskirts of Argos, dusk quickly falling across the sky. Who would receive his seed? Would she resist? Merciless creature that he was, the mere notion of his intentions excited him. His men still followed close behind, the hooves of their mounts beating out conflicting rhythms.

He passed a beggar woman, walking through a clearing. She was young enough, but still not suitable. He rode onward. Many minutes later, he saw firelight in the distance. Curious, Draco and his men advanced. As they approached, they could see it was some sort of camp, with people dressed in white robes.

"Halt, men!" He ordered his troops to dismount, leaving their horses. Still undetected by the women at the camp, they traveled the remaining distance on foot. Approaching, they saw that all of the robed figures were beautiful young women with long hair, standing in a circle around a raging campfire. He realized that he had found the Parthenos Girls...and Photina! He immediately began searching for the brilliant red hair Zarek had described.

"Men, don't lay a hand—or anything else—on these girls. They are sponsored by some very prominent and wealthy citizens, some of whom have ties to King Zarek. Letting your desires get the best of you could mean your neck...or your balls at the very least," Draco whispered to his soldiers, who nodded in disappointment as they neared the circle.

Five large guards stood in front of the women as Draco and his men approached.

"Who are you and what is your purpose here?" one of the guards asked Draco.

"I am Draco, royal commander under King Zarek," he answered. "And I am here to do whatever I please," he sneered. With that, he gave a forward gesture to his men, who descended on the sentries standing between them and the girls. White robes began frantically dancing in the twilight as the girls fled the melee. While Draco's men rapidly dispatched with the Parthenos Girls' guards, he took off through the trees, following the fluttering swaths of white cloth, which resembled ghosts in the fading light.

As the others fled, he caught up to one of the women trailing the group. He smiled to himself as he noted her brilliant red mane blowing behind her. Reaching out, he was able to grasp her garment from behind, tightening it in his fist. She gasped, collapsing to her knees. He responded by lifting the garment above her head, gazing with anticipation at the pristine whiteness of her naked flesh. He knew that he had found what he was looking for.

Draco had already decided that he would disobey the King's orders. He was far enough from the city limits that he felt he could have some fun without anyone noticing. Besides—he had already killed those bastards of Bedros. This one posed no threat.

"Don't....please don't..." she begged.

He pulled a length of rope from his belt, securing it around her delicate wrists, and lowered her to the ground.

"Tell me, oh beautiful ginger one...what is your name?" he asked.

She snarled and spit into his face, saying nothing. In return, Draco unsheathed the blade dangling from his belt and pressed it against the milky flesh of her neck. She squealed in shock.

"Photina!" she gasped. "It's Photina..."

"Just as I thought....and hoped," he told her, removing the knife. A razor-thin streak of blood remained where it had touched her skin.

Already hard, he knelt down, unfastened his tights and took out his manhood. He felt her about to buck—she was preparing to bring her knee upward to meet his dangling testicles—but she was thin and easily overpowered. He blocked her leg and worked his hand between her thighs, finding her sex. Steadying himself with his other hand flat on the ground, he pushed himself toward her as she sobbed.

She screamed, trying once again to rock to and fro, queering his aim, but his strength was too much for her. "You'll never get away with this! I don't care whose command you are under! I will see to it that you burn in the fires of Hades!" she groaned, before spitting in his face.

Her sneer, at odds with her otherwise perfect features, and the string of spittle connecting her lip to her chin, only acted as fuel for his lust. She started sobbing as he forced himself inside her. She turned her head and stared off with glazed eyes. He quickly ejaculated after only a few strokes, and sloppily withdrew.

"But you don't get it, woman…King Zarek sent me here for your head!" Draco told her, smiling. "All I took was your purity! You're getting off very easily…"

Extremely pleased with himself, he stood up and got dressed. Photina remained on the ground, naked, crying, and smeared with earth. A trickle of blood traversed her thigh.

"Stop crying and consider yourself fortunate, woman, for you may now be carrying a future king.

"You're a monster," Photina screamed, pulling her garment over her nakedness as her tears continued to flow. "Any kingdom ruled by the fruit of your loins would be *rotten* with injustice. Your subjects would be better off *dead*."

"I realize that you may feel like you have lost your purpose now that you may no longer call yourself a virgin. But believe me, one day you will come to appreciate what I have given you. For now, my dear, I must leave you." Draco unsheathed his dagger, smiling as he cut the rope from her wrists. "I am doing you a favor by telling you that you should be neither seen nor heard anywhere near the kingdom of your half-brother, Zarek…and any time you mourn the loss of your maidenhead, just remember…if I had followed his orders, you would no longer be breathing! Now go catch up with your friends. If they reject you, what kind of friends were they to begin with?"

Photina stood up, slightly crouching from pain, and slowly walked into the forest. She looked back over her shoulder at Draco.

"You *will* suffer for this. I would've preferred death" she told him in a whisper.

Draco joined his men. They remounted and returned to the kingdom.

Later that night, Draco convened with Zarek, who was eager to hear of his exploits.

"We traveled for miles through the villages on the outskirts of the city, and I found her…Photina. She is dead, along with the Parthenos Girls' guards. But you I took great care to guarantee that none of my men sullied any of the others."

"You killed Photina?" Zarek asked, laughing. "Good work, Draco! I think that means the slate has been wiped clean!"

Draco concurred, knowing that he would sleep soundly that night in the knowledge that he had taken the first step toward securing his future.

CHAPTER 24

THE FESTIVAL

A month had passed since the induction of the new Sondras, and Thea and the eleven other upstart warriors had begun their patrolling duties. Their hard work would soon be rewarded by the annual Summer Festival—thirteen wonderful days of fun, frolic, and indulgence celebrating the new season. All were encouraged to partake in a sumptuous feast of food, drink, and flesh. Summer was a time for love and rebirth, for freedom and pleasure, and for exploration and independence.

The Festival grounds were set up half a mile from camp, by a large clearing on the edge of a lake. Covered by a blanket of lush grass, it was the perfect spot for a celebration. On the morning of the festivities, horses, chariots, and hundreds of people arrived, minstrels and musicians played among the tents, and feasts were prepared for everyone to enjoy. A makeshift town had been erected for the sole purpose of providing pleasure.

The large number of attendees from distant lands was confirmation of the Summer Festival's reputation. Colorful uniforms showcased the diverse origins of the guests, as did their gifts of rare spices, beautiful fabrics, and elegant trinkets. The excitement was intoxicating.

Many Spartan military officers regularly attended for the erotic pleasures. Egyptians and Scythians were also welcomed. Only Argives were shunned, due to their policy of aggression toward the Amazon nation.

On the first morning of the Festival, Thea woke with the same confusion and anxiety that had been plaguing her since Seema's revelations. Could she truly be the daughter of Queen Elektra? Would her tribe really lose its beloved Queen Alexa? The thought of Alexa's premature death was as terrifying as the lofty destiny that was supposedly Thea's responsibility to fulfill. Both predictions had been dominating her every thought, to the point where she was increasingly exhausted from the lack of sleep.

Carrying the weight of Seema's revelations had made Thea feel terribly lonely. She'd shared the encounter exclusively with Melia, but only mentioned Seema's prediction that she'd become Queen. She hadn't discussed her twin sister because she didn't believe it, and was having trouble adjusting to the thought of it. In any case, they had a long, hearty laugh about the Queen prophecy, as Melia thought it was ridiculous. This didn't rile Thea. In her mind, it was also absurd.

But the idea that Thea would assume the throne because of Alexa's death was so dreadful she couldn't even say it out loud. So while Thea had shared almost everything with Melia, she was still holding onto a secret that was digging away at her heart.

Melia began to stir, and took her time to roll over and face Thea. Melia's eyes were still not fully open as she leaned in to kiss Thea, who turned her head away.

"What's on your mind? You've been so distant lately. Even when you're in the room, I feel like I might as well be talking to the wall," Melia said.

"I'm sorry. It's got nothing to do with you. I'm just processing a lot. The last thing I want to do is hurt your feelings." Thea paused. "I've just been feeling that I need some time to myself."

"How am I supposed to take that? You need time alone? You mean you need time where *I'm* not around. Is that how it is?"

"Melia, no, it's not like that..." Thea tried to sound reassuring, but she completely understood how Melia felt. "It's just...between the patrols, and the weird meeting in the cave last month..."

"Really? I thought I was here to listen and support you when you were feeling sad or confused," Melia said, clearly wounded. "But I guess not."

"Melia, it's not about—"

"Maybe you should leave."

"I *do* feel I have your support. There are just some things—"

"*No.* I mean it. Get out. *Now,*" Melia barked.

This confrontation, though shorter in duration than she'd envisioned, was probably overdue. Thea didn't feel like she had the strength or tranquility of mind to figure out how to fix things. Heeding Melia's warning, Thea jumped up and began putting on her clothes before trying one last time to calm her down.

"Really, Melia, I—"

"*Go!*"

Thea left the room and didn't look back. She quickly washed up, and then went to the Festival...alone.

Thea tried to put herself in Melia's shoes. She knew she'd been preoccupied since she learned about her destiny. Daughter of Queen Elektra...Golden Girdle...heir to the Amazon throne...the death of Queen Alexa...it really was too much to absorb. Thea hoped the Festival would take her mind off her troubles.

Halfway there, Thea already heard flutes playing. She also smelled the mixed aroma of meat, smoke, and spice filling the air. The fire pit was active, preparing an array of well-seasoned pheasant, rabbit, and other game. Though she was too stressed to maintain much of an appetite, the scent was doing a good job of making her hungry.

Thea decided that the Festival came but once a year. The best thing would be to push everything out of her head and try to enjoy herself.

After arriving on the grounds, Thea put on a veil. All revelers were encouraged to wear costumes or masks, but some sort of facial covering was *mandatory* for Amazons. Anonymity was vital in their dealings and dalliances with visiting men. It also fostered a surreal, dreamlike element of excitement that promoted more indiscriminate coupling.

In addition to being a celebration and a time for giving thanks, the Summer Festival was about facilitating fertility. While pure sex was the main attraction for many of the celebrants, including warriors of other countries, for the Amazons this was an opportunity to become pregnant with the girls who'd be the future of their nation. Trading, food, and performers dominated the daylight hours, while orgies prevailed in the evenings.

Thea was one of the exceptions. She could have sex with men as much as she liked. But warriors—and especially Sondras—were barred from having children until age 30, to avoid anything interfering with their duties during their prime years. A bitter infertility potion was made available every morning of the Festival to Amazon warriors who enjoyed dalliances the previous night.

Conversely, Amazons with impressive fighting skills who were past their prime were singled out for child bearing to ensure their tribe was continually infused with strong new blood. It was the duty of such women to try to become pregnant, and this was especially important during the Festival.

When an Amazon gave birth to a girl, that child was raised as an Amazon.

If a boy was born, he was traded to another country—usually Sparta—in exchange for a girl, or put up for adoption so reputable families in need of male children could raise him.

Outside the Festival tent, Thea could see throngs of delighted Amazons and travelers in the pathways. Jugglers were tossing objects through the air, jolly gamblers were gathering around games of chance, and some revelers had already begun dancing.

Before long, Thea came upon Carina, who was enjoying a large plate of food. She flashed Thea a wide, beaming smile.

"You look happy this morning!" Thea offered. "Can't imagine why..."

"I bet your imagination could provide you with an answer if it tried hard enough," Carina responded, still smiling.

"I suppose it might have a guess."

"Yes, I like the Summer Festival," Carina said. "The slave was great, but an exotic foreign officer would be even better. Who knows what the night will bring?"

Carina greatly benefited from the disguises the Festival required. Covering her unsightly facial birthmark instantly made her as attractive as just about any other woman at the celebration. When Thea encountered her, Carina was wearing a cat mask.

"Where's Melia?" Carina asked.

"She stayed home. She wasn't feeling up to this today," Thea said.

"Sorry to hear that. I was looking forward to seeing both of you."

As the girls strolled the grounds, Thea saw several Spartans. All were on horseback and fully decorated in their uniforms. When she caught a glimpse of the one who led them, something sparked in her memory. She realized he was Aristo, the man who'd warned her to flee Nemea after she'd won the chariot race. At the time, she appreciated his tall stature and handsome face; but what made him most attractive was his kindness.

Carina and Thea spent the entire day taking in the sights and sounds. Wine had never tasted so sweet; and they gorged themselves on meat, fruit, and a variety of foreign delicacies from remote locales.

Time quickly disappeared. What few clouds remained framed the setting sun. Bonfires decorated the grounds, casting an eerily beautiful flickering light on the acrobats, dancers, drums, and spectators. As day turned to night, the mood of the festival transformed from merriment to passion.

Carina and Thea strolled into one of the festival tents, wine in hand. Pillows and animal skins lined the floor as men and women caressed each other in rhythm to the music softly playing in the background. Quiet laughter mingled with gentle moans of ecstasy, as both girls began to succumb to the intoxicating sway of the room. Some of the participants were costumed as tigers or panthers. Others were decorated with jewels and plumage. With a glance and smile at Thea, Carina excused herself to join the pulsating sea of flesh and desire.

Thea looked around the tent. With wine coursing through her veins and the eroticism in the air, she was soon longing for sensual pleasure. Walking across the large tent, she saw Aristo, who was not yet mingling with a woman. This time he spotted her as well. Though the lower half of her face was covered, he recognized her eyes, and he could hardly believe his good fortune.

Thea's figure was even more captivating than before, and her dark mane lying across her shapely breasts was a tantalizing sight. Her newly blackened hair had thrown him at first, but he was quickly transported to the moment when he first saw those spellbinding eyes. If there was such a thing as love at first sight, he had experienced it. He'd thought of her frequently since the chariot race, and dreamed that this moment would come.

"We meet again," Aristo said, his rugged handsomeness giving way to boyish excitement as he intercepted Thea.

"Indeed," Thea replied, smiling beneath her veil.

"I'm glad to see you made it out of Nemea safely," Aristo told her.

"Thank you, but we managed to get swindled in the process."

"Not surprising for a Nemean chariot race. By the way, my name is Aristo...in case you don't remember."

"Ah, yes...Aristo. And I'm..." She paused to remember the alias she'd given him. "The Troublemaker," he interjected. "You see, I did not forget. In fact, I have something for my beautiful Troublemaker. I think you might appreciate it."

Aristo reached into the leather satchel draped across his shoulder and withdrew a beautifully decorated wooden horn, which he handed to Thea. Unlike the horn that beckoned Nox, this one was free of any blemishes, painted ivory, and ornately carved with elaborate designs and symbols.

"I'm sure you didn't have this in mind for me, Aristo," Thea said. "There are many at this Festival who would enjoy such a beautiful gift."

"Not true!" Aristo replied. "I have carried this with me since I first saw you drop your old wooden horn in Nemea! I bought it just for you. I thought if our paths ever crossed again, it would be yours."

"Isn't there a special woman in your life who might appreciate it?" Thea asked.

"No, not at the moment. My wife died two years ago. There have been a few since then. But this was bought especially for you—the only woman I've ever seen win a chariot race! How could I forget?"

"Thank you," she said, flattered by his response. He had no idea what power her battered wooden horn carried, but his gift was thoughtful and exquisite.

"Wait right here, Aristo. I must retrieve something from my tent. *Please,* don't go anywhere!" Thea smiled coyly. She had left her bag back in her tent, and it contained a few things she thought would be useful. Within a few minutes, she'd reached the tent, threw the bag over her shoulder and walked back to Aristo, her brain buzzing with the kind of anticipation she hadn't felt since her induction into the Sondras.

Aristo, grinning, looked as if he hadn't moved an inch.

"I see you're still here!" Thea said, grabbing Aristo's hand and slowly pulling him from his position. I think...you should join me for a walk."

Aristo nodded and smiled.

The moon hung low in the evening sky, large and bright. Thea led Aristo out of the large tent and down a narrow path leading into the woods. She took him to a small clearing on the opposite side of the lake, where they could see celebrants in costume passing in front of the Festival flames. Between the moonlight and the bonfires, a surreal glow permeated the dark veil of night. Thea's body began to tingle with anticipation for what she was about to do.

She wasn't nervous. She was aware of the power she had over him, and it made her feel wonderful. This was to be a new experience—her first physical intimacy with a man. She was hungry to find out what it would be like.

"I knew I would see you again. I've been...waiting for this for some time..." Aristo said. His voice wavered like an awkward adolescent until it came to a halt, overcome by what he was gazing upon.

Stepping back several feet so he could see the entirety of her body, Thea used one finger to flick her garment off her shoulder, letting it fall to the ground. The moonlight was bright enough to outline her soft young bosom and bronze skin, making her look like a Goddess among mortals. Aristo's senses heightened as Thea revealed herself to him. Now standing before him wearing only her veil, she gave him a moment to take in her nakedness before slowly walking into the lake until the water reached her hips. She waded out several feet and swam in small circles as Aristo remained on the shore, watching her with a smile.

"Hey, Spartan! Are you just going to stand there?" Thea asked. "Undress for me! You don't need that sword where we're going!"

Taking her cue, Aristo dropped his bag to the ground, abandoned his sword and belt, bent down to unstrap his sandals, and discarded his tunic gently to the side without uttering a word. He stood tall and still at the water's edge as Thea methodically examined him, in awe of the way the moonlight shone on his muscular figure. His wavy black hair was like a lion's mane. His beauty was stunning, and she was becoming aroused just looking at him.

He stepped into the water, taking slow steps until he was deep enough to swim out to her. He could not believe his luck. There was nowhere else he wanted to be. Once he was close enough to reach her, Aristo grabbed Thea and pulled her to him.

"You sure are some Troublemaker," Aristo told her as they held each other, their hands slowly caressing each other in the cool, dark water.

Thea removed her veil, revealing an impish smile. She ran a finger along his neck, up behind his ear, and down again.

"No, I don't think I am..." Thea replied with a laugh.

He pulled her close once again, and she felt hardness between his legs. She caressed his thigh as he leaned in and hungrily kissed her. Their lips parted, making way for moistened tongues to touch. The kiss lasted several minutes. She could feel his need to have her growing stronger, until he gripped her buttocks with a powerful right hand and began forcing her toward him.

"Wait, Aristo. Wait..." she requested. "Let us go ashore." She wanted to prolong the moment, playing with him a bit longer before she succumbed.

They emerged from the water holding hands, arriving at the spot where they'd left their belongings. The night was warm, and they felt comfortable and refreshed as the water dripped from their bodies. Thea had brought a thin blanket in her bag. She spread it on the ground and lay down on it. As Aristo knelt to join her, she produced a bottle of aromatic oil and gave it to him.

"Rub this on my back," she sweetly ordered him.

He was enjoying allowing her to command him. As giving orders was a large part of his daily life, he found that taking them from a beautiful woman gave him an unfamiliar erotic charge. He uncorked the bottle, poured a few drops on his hands, and began massaging the oil into the soft flesh of Thea's back. She expressed her gratitude with a few moans of pleasure and a thankful smile. Aristo continued for several minutes, working his hands down over the curve of her back, onto her muscular thighs, and up again. As Thea relaxed, he slid a hand down into the area between her legs, applying the slightest pressure to her womanhood as he continued to massage her. She didn't protest.

"Now do my front," she told him, as she propped herself up on one elbow and rolled over.

Though he was beginning to feel the longing ache between his legs, he complied. Seeing her nude figure in the moonlight felt like a gift to him. He poured oil onto the smooth flatness of her belly, then massaged it in with his hands slowly and assuredly, taking in every inch of her flesh with his eyes. After a few moments, his hands moved up to her breasts, their softness providing little resistance under his slick hands. Her nipples were erect before he'd even reached them.

He wasn't able to hold out long enough to get to her lower half before he straddled her and began kissing her again. They continued like this for several minutes before he repositioned himself so that his right leg worked its way between hers. She responded willingly, spreading her legs and sighing.

He gently placed his hands on her breasts, cupping and caressing them. He proceeded to stroke her soft skin and tenderly kiss her neck. His mouth traveled deliberately down to her breasts, savoring every sweet step along its path. He wrapped his arms around her waist and knelt down to allow his tongue to move onto her stomach. Thea's hands found their way to his silken hair. Her heart pounded as her hands passionately tugged at his head.

"I just wanted to tell you...you're the first." She nervously smiled, revealing the first cracks in her confidence.

"You mean you're..."

"I've not been with a man before. Be gentle..." she urged him, reaching for the oil. "And use some of this."

Aristo crouched before her, his considerable manhood at full attention. He took some of the oil and rubbed it on himself to minimize any of Thea's discomfort. After a moment, he leaned forward, positioned himself between her legs, found her wetness with his free hand, and guided himself in.

Thea groaned—the initial sensation was pain. She momentarily felt like she was being split in two. Aristo noticed the look on her face, withdrew himself, and applied more of the oil. He entered her again, and this time she found herself experiencing a mixture of pleasure and pain that she was able to withstand.

He was delicate at first, allowing her to grow accustomed to the sensation and preserving her body's yearning for more. Then he unleashed his full passion, thrusting inside her as she felt wholly consumed with pleasure.

She caressed his chest and body, intermittently tasting his flesh with her tongue. She could feel her passion swelling. Her body was overcome by waves of euphoric bliss. Aristo's warm breath on her skin gave her chills of ecstasy as his hands slowly slid from the small of her back onto her waist, and then along her thighs. His touch was gentle, but strong enough to keep her body pressed firmly against his, with motions that were purposefully teasing, creating an ebb and flow that took her spirits up and down as if taking a journey without any possible end—yet somehow she knew she would eventually reach the destination. Every part of the trip was worth the experience and the time it took to arrive there.

Though she was near delirious with the pleasure and newness that her body was feeling, she experienced momentary flashes when she was taken out of the moment and made to ponder just how strange—and long overdue—it was to lie with a man. Though she loved women, the male anatomy certainly had its merits! Her sex was mingling with the flesh of another in such a new and thrilling way and she felt like she'd been missing something. Still, this was not the beginning of a romance—that would be impossible. It was exploration, pure and simple. But that didn't make it any less satisfying or sweet.

Thea broke the grasp of his hands, wrapping her arms around Aristo's shoulders and curling her legs around his waist. He could feel her nails scraping skin from his back as he forced small screams to escape from her mouth. Together they moved their hips, faster and faster, until their bodies beat together in unison, racing to taste what seemed an unobtainable delight. Finally, they arrived.

The sweat of their bodies glistened in the moonlight, and their embrace lingered for a long while as they enjoyed the afterglow of their pleasure.

Eventually, they went back to the water's edge, waded in, and bathed each other. Returning to shore, they walked back to the blanket, took another slow look at each other, and embraced.

Thea released herself from him, turning to retrieve her tunic from the ground. As she put it on, Aristo grabbed her wrist and pulled her close to him once more, kissing her again before she gently pushed herself away. With a seductive smile, she dressed. Now that she'd fulfilled her desires, she thought of Melia, and pangs of guilt surfaced. She glanced down to see a small spot of blood on the blanket, and realized the significance of what she'd just been through. She looked again at Aristo but chose to deal with the consequences later.

"I'm hungry!" she told him, as she finished putting on her clothes. "Let's go back to the Festival for more food."

Thea remained with Aristo for the next five blissful days, donning her veil as she strolled the Festival with him, sampling the delicious food during the daylight hours, and returning to their quiet spot by the lake as darkness fell to enjoy each other's bodies before collapsing to sleep.

Thea was as happy as she'd ever been, but she knew the relationship was temporary. She was an Amazon, and a Sondra, and Aristo could have no permanent place in her life.

As for Aristo, he understood she had reasons for revealing little about herself. He decided not to press the matter and simply enjoyed their time together.

After five days, Aristo was called to duty. His men were to assemble a few miles away. The following morning, he prepared to leave.

"So, beautiful," he said, "this has truly been a dream. Not only did my wish of seeing you come true, but I could not have asked for a more glorious five days. You are a truly incredible woman."

"And you will always be my first," she said. "I wish it didn't have to end. But I think both of us knew we would only have this short time together. That's what made it even more special."

"So...we should certainly not wait until next year's Festival to meet again..." he said.

"Oh, we'll see about that..." she replied.

"Listen, I must tell you something. I didn't want to spoil our time with anything grave, but you should inform everyone in your tribe that since King Zarek took over from his father, kidnapping, torture, and murder have increased in all surrounding states. I've seen horrible things on my travels in recent weeks."

"We are well aware," Thea told him, looking serious. "We've already lost several good women in the past year due to his sick appetite. Since we learned of Bedros' death, we have increased patrols around our camp. Everyone is more cautious since Zarek came to power."

They embraced each other, kissed one last time, and then parted ways.

When Thea returned to the Festival, she felt intoxicated. It was as if all her senses had been heightened. She smelled the spiced meats and took in the colored costumes with an intensity she'd never enjoyed before. She felt an inexplicable sense of peace.

She thought of Melia, realizing just how important her lover was to her. Feelings of guilt rose again, though she couldn't help making a sexual comparison in her mind between Aristo and Melia. It was hard to say who was better. But she knew she wanted to have more experiences with Aristo. Certainly there would be a next time... wouldn't there?

Still on a high from being with Aristo—but worried she was covered in the musky scent of a man—Thea tried to think of what to say to her partner. She stopped to wash Aristo from her body. Then she returned to her tent, where she found Melia in bed, just as she'd left her. Melia turned.

"I want to say that I'm sorry, " Melia began. "I decided to give you your space. I have no reason to smother you."

"No, Melia. I owe you an apology. You mean everything to me. I'll work on my moods. I just ask you to keep in mind that I have a lot to deal with right now."

"Honestly, Thea—is there anything I should know?" Melia asked. "Anything that you haven't told me?"

"Well...there *is* something," Thea admitted. "One other prophecy from Seema. It was just too upsetting for me to share with anyone... even you."

"What is it?" Melia asked.

"Seema told me that Queen Alexa is going to die. She said that will be how I become the next Queen."

"Really? That's all it is?" Melia exclaimed. "Thea, I promise to keep it a solemn secret. But I have to say again, that old woman sounds crazy. I can accept you as my Queen, for whatever reason, if that means anything to you!"

"That's sweet," Thea said with a smile, putting her arm around Melia. "I was at the Festival. It's really great this year. I think we should go back there together."

They crawled into bed and engaged in a reconciling embrace for several minutes before Thea nodded off.

Before long, however, Thea suffered a familiar nightmare. Her new role as a Sondra hadn't put an end to her worst dream, in which she battled against a faceless foe. In all of Thea's real-life fights in training and competition, she'd never encountered anyone as fierce as the warrior in her dream. Did this person truly exist, waiting to face her in the future?

As always, Thea woke from the nightmare with a start. She tried to go back to sleep, but her thoughts couldn't be calmed. As she lay awake, she heard a commotion outside and went to peek past her tent's door. A patrolling group of Sondras ran past her on the way to Alexa's tent. Something had happened.

CHAPTER 25

IN SEARCH OF DESTINY

I t was midday when Philandros, the jeweler, arrived in Argos. The guards at the city gates verified his papers and allowed him to pass. Now he simply had to gain an audience with the King. Philandros knew nothing of King Zarek, other than his reputation for dealing harshly with prisoners...and his penchant for collecting art and historical treasures.

The jeweler had reached Argos, traveling cautiously along the way. He'd made sure to avoid the mistake of the fool who'd entered his shop, knowing that only royalty could pay the true value of what he was carrying. The gems and gold alone were worth a fortune, but the legend surrounding the object made it almost priceless. With this one sale, he would secure his wealth for the remainder of his days.

Philandros urged on his horses. A few hours later, his carriage arrived at the gates of the castle. "I come to request an appointment with His Majesty, King Zarek," he told a royal guard.

"Not a chance, beggar," the guard responded. "The King has no time for your nonsense. Be off with you."

"But sir, I can assure you I am no beggar!" Philandros replied, offended. "I have come here with the prospect of conducting some very legitimate and respectable business with the King. In fact, I have in my possession a valuable treasure that I can assure you will greatly interest him."

"And what might that be?"

"It lies within this chest."

"Open it, then," the guard commanded.

The jeweler climbed down from his horse and walked to the back of his cart. He unlocked the chest and opened it for the guard to see, before quickly slamming it shut again, locking it tight. The momentary glance that the guard caught was enough to make him want the Girdle for himself. But the glimpse hadn't been long enough for any feelings of avarice to override his sense of duty.

"Now, may I please have an appointment with the King?" Philandros asked.

"I think not. Give the chest to me and wait here. I will know if he wants to see you after he has examined the treasure," the guard replied.

"Ha! As if you won't steal my treasure! Do you take me for a fool?" the jeweler asked.

"Then you won't see the King!"

"Well then, be sure to tell King Zarek that you've cost him the chance to own one of the world's most prized artifacts. I will just have to take it to Sparta, where I am sure it will receive the appropriate attention."

Philandros turned to leave, but the guard suddenly feared what could happen if King Zarek learned such a prize had been on his doorstep without him being notified. He knew that torture was a distinct possibility.

"Wait!" the guard shouted. "Remain here while I go to see if I can get you an appointment."

Philandros waited as the guard disappeared inside the castle for several minutes. The guard then returned, opened the gate, and escorted Philandros inside. The guard guided the carriage as far as it was permitted. He and the jeweler then unloaded the chest and carried it through a maze of hallways, finally arriving at a large banquet room. The ornate entryway was trimmed in gold, and the large arching doors were gold-plated. The guard prompted Philandros to set the chest down. "Wait here," he added, and entered the King's chambers.

Through the doorway, Philandros could see King Zarek seated on a throne at the far end of the room, accompanied by several attendants. After some discussion, the guard beckoned to the jeweler.

"Speak, peasant," Zarek commanded.

"I can assure you, King Zarek, that I am no peasant. I am a jeweler, Your Majesty. I trade with many of the wealthiest people in the region. I have traveled from Koutsopodi to present to you a treasure that I believe will interest you."

"And what treasure would that be?" Zarek asked.

"The Golden Girdle, Your Majesty."

"Golden Girdle? I have not heard of such a thing."

"Oh, it is the subject of great legend, Your Highness! It is a beautiful belt bearing a wealth of exquisite jewels, and it is cast in pure gold!"

"Let me see this Girdle," Zarek ordered.

Philandros took out his key and unlocked the chest, which had been placed at Zarek's feet. As he lifted the lid, the Girdle reflected the sunlight entering the room's cathedral windows, and shone brilliantly in a myriad of colors. Its exterior was almost blinding, and the jewels sparkled with a similar intensity. Zarek was instantly drawn to it.

"Hmm. It is quite fascinating," Zarek said, as he rose from his chair to inspect the Girdle more closely. "Where did you find it?"

"I bartered for it, Your Majesty," the jeweler replied. "I hoped to receive just compensation for bringing it to you, my dear King."

"Just compensation? And what might that be?"

"The Girdle is one of the greatest treasures on Earth, Your Highness. How could one name a price for something so precious?"

"And yet you speak of compensation. Surely you have a price in mind, peasant."

"If I may, Your Majesty, I have lost my store and have traveled many days to get here," Philandros said. "There is no question of its tremendous value. I thought thirty talents would be reasonable compensation for the effort required to bring it to you."

"Thirty talents! Did you really expect to gain thirty talents?"

"But Your Majesty, the jewels alone are worth that! I am an authority on the value of such things!"

The longer Zarek stared at the Girdle, the more entranced he became. It was as if it had some sort of magnetic power. He knew he had to possess it, but negotiation was not in his nature.

"Let me ask you a simple question," Zarek said. "Why should I pay anything for something I can simply take?"

Philandros paused, and instantly realized he should've taken the time to learn more about the reputation of this king.

"I mean, did you really expect to collect anything for bringing this to me?" Zarek continued. "I believe our discussion is over. You may leave now, peasant."

"But Your Majesty, I brought you this treasure out of loyal service, and in hopes of being treated fairly! With all due respect, I am *not* a peasant! I am a respectable merchant!"

"Your service is appreciated, and you *are* being treated fairly," Zarek declared. "Now go."

Suddenly, Philandros was seized by an irrational desire to keep the Golden Girdle. He wasn't only upset about being cheated. He didn't want to be parted from his prize. "You are an evil and treacherous king," he exclaimed, spittle flying from his mouth as unbridled anger caused his eyes to widen. He drew a small knife and moved to lunge at the King, but quickly found himself subdued by guards who pressed a blade to his throat.

"Poor choice, my good man," Zarek said, staring him in the eyes. "You have forfeited your fair treatment and will now pay the penalty. Guards, take him to the dungeon and prepare him for my personal entertainment. I think we've found the next performer in my show!"

As the knife was removed from his hand and the guards escorted him away, Philandros began flailing about in a last-ditch attempt to free himself.

"Oh! We have a fighter! How bold this one is!" Zarek exclaimed.

The guards tightened their grip, subduing Philandros by painfully pulling one of his arms behind his back.

"Did you really think you could get away? Did you? Answer me!" Zarek shouted.

"Uh, this is all a misunderstanding," Philandros said, sweat pouring down his forehead. "Please, if you let me go, you may take the Girdle as my gift—"

"Oh, I was going to take the belt anyway," said Zarek. "And you didn't answer my question! Apparently some part of you thought you *could* get away! Now I'm going to ask you another question. What do you think we do with people who try to escape before I am finished dealing with them?"

Philandros trembled, unable to answer.

"Guards! What do we do with people who try to get away from us?" Zarek asked, his anger rising.

With that, one of the guards further restrained Philandros from behind, locking his arms under both of the jeweler's arms. The other guard then pulled a wooden baton from his belt and quickly struck each of the prisoner's knees. Both times, there was the unmistakable sound of breaking bone. Philandros' cries of pain echoed throughout Zarek's chamber. The guards each took an arm and escorted him out of the room. Whimpers filled the air as his broken legs dragged limply across the floor.

"Don't worry, we'll be seeing each other again. There's more in store for you!" Zarek shouted across the room.

When there was no one else in the chambers but Zosimos, Zarek crouched down to examine the Girdle in more detail. It was truly mesmerizing. He tried to lift it out of the chest, but struggled to raise even one end before letting it fall back down. There was no question it was made of solid gold. Resplendent rubies and emeralds encircled its centerpiece. Etched within the gold were two intertwined serpents, each possessing intricate details emphasizing their strength and treacherousness. The more Zarek studied it, the more enraptured he was.

"Zosimos, do you know anything about this Girdle? It is truly one of the greatest treasures on Earth!"

"Your Majesty, all I know is that it figures very prominently in the legends of the Amazon nation."

"That's a start. Send for Kthonia," Zarek commanded.

"Yes, Your Highness."

The witch Kthonia's dark knowledge and advice had been highly valued by Zarek since he was an adolescent. Already an old woman when he met her, she was now ancient and unable to walk. Nonetheless, she was among the very few people Zarek considered worthy of respect. When he ascended to the throne, he installed her in private quarters on the royal grounds so he could call on her whenever needed. He felt sure she'd know a great deal about the treasure that lay before him, and whether it possessed any mystical power that he could leverage.

Four guards fetched Kthonia, bringing her to Zarek's quarters on a chair supported on two rods. As usual, she arrived looking hunched and wild-haired. She was clad in layer upon layer of black burlap, her skin leathery and weathered. Her left eyelid opened only halfway, partially shading an orb covered in a thin, milky film. Her mouth was absent of teeth, and she clutched a small cloth sack in her left hand. When she entered the room, the air filled with a strong but cleansing scent of herbs and incense.

To most, Kthonia appeared crazy. But Zarek was able to look past her appearance and appreciate her wisdom. He'd sought her counsel many times, and she'd never misled him. The guards placed her chair on the floor so she could face him.

"My dear Kthonia. It is a pleasure to see you."

"And it is my pleasure to serve you, King Zarek. How may I be of help this day?" Kthonia responded, in a reptilian rasp.

It was at this moment that Teigra approached the throne room from the connecting hallway. She'd had a strange dream during the night about an incident she hadn't thought about for years—an old woman in the marketplace who'd told her she'd been cursed. It had gnawed at Teigra all morning; and for some reason she couldn't explain, she felt Zarek was involved. Even though she didn't have an appointment, she decided to walk to his throne room, hoping to catch him when he wasn't busy. As she neared the doorway, however, she could hear that he was in a meeting. She paused to listen outside the door for a short while, if only to better understand the sort of man for whom she'd agreed to work.

"What do you know of the Golden Girdle of the Amazons?" Zarek asked.

"The Golden Girdle! A unique object," Kthonia began. "It's been worn by only one woman, the immortal Queen Elektra, who reigned over all the Amazon tribes for 300 eons. Her Girdle became a symbol of Amazon independence and national pride. But no one knows what became of Elektra, or of her Girdle, since she disappeared two decades ago."

"Well, Kthonia, feast your eyes on this," Zarek said, opening the chest.

"*Ahhhhh!* It is exquisite!" Kthonia exclaimed, gazing more closely. "By the Gods! It appears to be the very Girdle of legend!"

"Kthonia, does this belt possess any power?" Zarek asked.

"According to legend, the Girdle grants immortality and strength to its bearer. But the legend also says that only the rightful Queen is able to wear it."

"Wear it?" Zarek asked in amazement. "How could anyone *wear* this thing? Its weight is tremendous! I can't even *lift* it!"

Zarek closed the chest, leaving it unlocked. He wasn't sure what to do with the Girdle, but he was happy to have it in his possession. He felt powerful just from owning it.

"Give me a moment, Your Majesty, and I'll tell you more," Kthonia said. She opened her sack and removed a small iron bowl atop a three-legged stand. She motioned for a servant to place a table before her, then set the object on it. Kthonia pulled out several small cloth bags, each tied with a piece of string. She opened each bag, pinched a small amount of its contents between her thumb and forefinger, and dropped the ingredients into a bowl. While she performed this ritual, Zarek looked on in silent reverence.

Kthonia motioned a servant to bring over a torch and a small piece of kindling. She set the wood alight and dropped it into the bowl. Instantly, clouds of smoke and an earthy odor rose from the concoction.

Kthonia closed her eyes, inhaled deeply, and waved her right hand through the smoke as if trying to find something within it. The room was deathly silent for several minutes as Kthonia fell into a trance. Her breathing slowed, her ancient head lolled slowly around her neck, and a single line of spittle trickled out of the corner of her mouth and down her chin. Finally, she spoke.

"Oh...I can see nowwww..." Kthonia intoned. "First, I must warn you. If you take this Girdle as your own, you are in grave danger of your blood being spilled by a warrior woman."

"A woman?" Zarek asked. "It's hard to imagine any female being a threat to me. On the contrary, this belt may be the key to destroying the Amazons. But since you've never been wrong: What can I do to prevent this from happening?"

"I see this tooo..." Kthonia replied. "The power of the Girdle can be unleashed by only one person. She is the daughter of an Amazon Queen. You must capture and kill her before she attains the Girdle to harness its power. You must exercise extreme caution, for this woman has the ability and determination to destroy you."

"Is this the same woman you said might spill my blood?" Zarek asked.

"Yessss," Kthonia answered, still staring into the rising smoke and inhaling its fumes. "I see a beautiful young warrior. If she gains possession of the Golden Girdle, the Amazon nation will regain the immense power it once had. *This* is the woman you must beware!" Kthonia snuffed out the smoldering mound before her, shook her head, and regained her senses. "I apologize, Your Majesty," she added in her normal raspy voice. "It gives me no pleasure to bring you this news. But it is my duty to be accurate."

"Of course, Kthonia," Zarek said. "I would expect nothing less than the truth from you, no matter how unpleasant, and I thank you for it. You are a great and much appreciated resource."

Kthonia took a few moments to recover from her trance, poured the embers from her bowl onto the table, and slowly and methodically packed up her tools. The same four guards then hoisted her in her chair and carried her out of the throne room.

"Zosimos, are any of the female warriors we captured still alive?" Zarek asked.

"No, Your Highness. All the Amazons we've caught have been killed."

"Very well. Please send for Draco. He will need to destroy more villages. I do not want him to stop until he has rounded up all the Amazons he can find!"

"Yes, my Lord," Zosimos replied.

"Guards, place this chest in my bedchambers," Zarek ordered. "Zosimos, follow them to ensure the chest arrives safely. I must prepare for the evening's festivities."

When Teigra heard the guards exit the throne room, she quietly backed up a few steps, then walked as if she had just been passing by at that moment. The guards paid no attention to her. The weight of the chest was so great, however, that one of them let it slip from his hands, accidentally dropping it to the floor and popping it open. The Golden Girdle shone in the hallway like a small sun. Teigra felt an immediate and powerful attraction to it.

Then she noticed the two intertwined snakes encased in gold. The old woman in the Corinth marketplace mentioned a golden belt with two snakes—a belt that would end the misfortune that had plagued her entire life! Teigra kept moving to avoid notice. But she decided at that moment that she must take possession of this magnificent Girdle.

CHAPTER 26

MISSION AND MERCY

She had caught only a quick glimpse, but images of the Golden Girdle were haunting Teigra's thoughts. The possibility that it could be what was needed to fix her cursed life made Teigra almost unbearably eager to see it again.

Teigra had spent an hour walking the grounds of the castle to clear her head and plan a strategy. It was late morning, and Zarek typically met with his council, so his bedchamber would be vacant—and that's where the chest had been temporarily placed. This was a chance for Teigra to examine the Girdle more closely and privately, and she decided not to squander it. She reentered the castle and made her way through its corridors, taking care not to be noticed.

Teigra knew there was a sentry standing watch outside Zarek's bedchambers at all times. So she opted for a different entry point. She walked to an adjacent banquet hall with no guards, and used its stairs to get to the castle's roof. She then crept across the roof to the spot above Zarek's room. Securing a rope around a chimney, Teigra climbed down the side of the building—which faced a vacant courtyard—and in through the window. She tucked the rope into the window after her.

Teigra was delighted to see the chest waiting for her. She cautiously lifted the lid, its hinges making only the slightest squeak.

She was nearly blinded by the Girdle's resplendence. Teigra ran her hand across it, feeling the various textures, until she came to the emblem depicting the intertwined serpents. It looked majestic, beautiful, and dangerous all at the same time.

Then she had a realization that shook her to the core: *It's the same symbol as the marking on the back of my neck!*

Teigra now understood her obsession with the Girdle. It was hers by destiny's design. She was meant to have it.

Teigra had trouble tearing herself away from the Girdle, but knew that the longer she stayed, the more at risk she was of being discovered. She reluctantly closed the chest, climbed the rope to the roof, and made her way back to the castle's hallways. However, she kept a clear image of the Girdle in her mind's eye.

That afternoon, Teigra was summoned to Zarek's chambers. She arrived to find him waiting for her.

"Hello, Teigra. I have some instructions for you. They are rather straightforward."

"Yes, King Zarek," she said. "I am prepared to carry out your orders."

"A former colleague of mine, Leander, has become poisonous to my reign. I would like him disposed of."

"Consider it done, Your Highness."

"I have learned that he will be having a dinner meeting with some of his associates tomorrow evening. Make sure none of them leave Leander's home alive. Please see Zosimos for all the necessary details."

"As you command," Teigra said.

After obtaining the location and names of her targets, Teigra had no responsibilities for the rest of the day. She decided to leave the castle grounds and stroll around the nearby shops, taking far more money in her purse than she intended to spend. She relished having legitimate status within a major city, and the feeling of freedom after being enslaved for most of her life. She'd obtained a certain degree of authority—she was a genuine king's assassin, and tasked with killing high-ranking officials! *How quickly one's life can turn around,* she thought.

After happily exploring what the market had to offer, Teigra made her way back. The sun was setting, and the cool evening air felt good on her face. As she walked the sprawling grounds of the palace, she heard the faint sound of music in the distance. Setting course toward the melody, she came to a stone entryway that appeared to lead to a series of passages. Unable to fight her curiosity, she entered, still following the music.

The passageway led her underground, before leveling off and zigzagging to the left and right. Lit torches hung on the walls, providing just enough light to see any given path. As Teigra crept along, the music grew louder. She could hear the ethereal tones of a harp, intermittently punctuated by applause. As she got closer, she also heard a familiar voice—King Zarek.

Peeking around the edge of the passageway, she saw Zarek standing amidst a room of seated guards. He was sharpening a tool of some sort, brushing it against a stone. Every so often he would speak, which would be followed by a round of clapping. The soothing harp continuously played.

"Zosimos, repeat the crimes of our guest," Zarek said.

"They include witchcraft, thievery, treason, and a refusal to share the secret of the fire," Zosimos said.

"I see," Zarek said. "Guest, what do you say regarding your crimes?"

There was silence.

"Hmm..." Zarek began, looking over the prisoner. "I presume you acknowledge your crimes and sins. However, we must learn the extent of your treason. Should you receive the maximum penalty, the punishment is death by fire! May I have two members of the jury collect the pyramid chair for tonight's investigation?"

Teigra could see a pair of guards depart the scene, then return with an oddly shaped chair that they placed before Zarek. The chair looked like a throne, with a high arched back and exaggerated armrests. But the armrests had shackles; and there were restraints on the legs. The cruelest thing about the chair was located on its seat: in the middle sat a pointed piece of wood, vertically placed and shaped like a small pyramid. Teigra gauged it was about the length of her hand.

"Members of the jury, please sit our guest in the chair," Zarek said.

The two men collected the prisoner, who'd been stripped naked, and placed him directly on the seat, positioning the pyramid-shaped piece of wood directly under his anus. He tried to prevent his body from dropping onto the pointed edge by propping himself up with his hands; but as his hands and feet were shackled, the chair's device impaled him. He screamed as his weight forced him downward.

"Perhaps you would like to share your account of treason *now?*" Zarek suggested.

No one made a sound as the harp continued providing a beautiful backdrop to the cruel scene taking place.

"I see. Members of the jury, shall we increase the weight of the situation?"

Applause broke out again. Zarek took hold of a large, flat piece of iron. Even using both hands, it was a considerable effort to lift. He then placed it on the lap of the man in the chair. The weight of the object forced the man further onto the pointed piece of wood. A piercing expression of sheer suffering painted the man's previously stoic face. At this moment, Teigra recognized the man. It was Vasili.

Tendrils of deep red blood trickled down the sides of the chair as Vasili writhed in agony against the shackles. Teigra's heart ached. Vasili was the first person she had felt true affection for in her life. She considered running in to rescue him, but realized that was impractical. Not only would she be unsuccessful, but she would forfeit her own life in the process.

Teigra tried to quiet her mind and think of a way she could prevent her new employer from killing her old friend. Vasili had been there for her when she was injured and in need. People who'd shown her any kindness were very rare. She had to do *something*. Then it hit her...the torches!

Walking quickly but quietly down the hall, she grabbed one of the torches she'd passed on her way. A small wooden table sat against the wall. She pulled it into the middle of the hallway, and used the torch to set it ablaze. Within moments, smoke filled the area. She waited thirty seconds, then snuck back down the hallway to an adjoining corridor, where she found a signal bell hanging from a hook on one of the dirt walls. Knowing the smoke would just now be reaching the room where Vasili was being held, she rang the bell as loudly as she could. She heard shouts of "Fire!" followed by mad scuffles to escape.

Teigra had no idea what would become of Vasili, but at least this would delay any infliction of further pain. A few guards passed her in the hallway, but paid no attention to anything but escaping the fire. When Teigra sensed that everyone had cleared out, she made her way into the smoky room. All the spectators had fled—even the harp player was gone—but Vasili remained strapped to the chair, naked, bleeding, and coughing.

"Vasili, it's me...Teigra."

"Teigra, my dear..." was all he could manage.

"We have to get you out of here," she said, as she held her breath and tenderly put her arm around him. "This is going to hurt," she said, slowly helping him off the spike. He'd lost a good deal of blood, as evidenced by the wet and filthy chair. His stained tunic had been tossed onto the ground. She retrieved it and helped him put it on. He could barely stand, but she supported him as they moved through the corridor. Fortunately, Zarek and his minions were gone. They'd left Vasili behind to burn like garbage.

As they made their way through the tunnel, Teigra exercised great caution. Her goal was to get Vasili off the castle grounds and to someone who could care for his wounds.

"Teigra, why are you here?" Vasili asked.

"Please, Vasili, don't ask questions. I'm going to get you to a doctor. Once you are well enough, I advise you to run away from here without ever looking back."

"I will, my dear. I hope you are not in trouble. I owe you my life."

"You're more worthy of saving than any man I've met, Vasili. Now please, heed my advice."

They continued walking, Vasili on his own feet, and Teigra bearing the brunt of his weight. She could sense the pain he experienced with every step.

As they were crossing a small passageway, Teigra spotted a tall figure to her left. The man, who was walking unhurriedly, turned around. It was General Niko.

Teigra stopped, hand poised to draw a weapon. To her shock, Niko put his hands up, showing no intent of violence, and gave her a half-smile with an accompanying nod of consent. Niko found Zarek's proclivity for torturing repellent, and actually admired a captivating young woman helping one of the victims. Making it clear he had no intention of stopping her, Niko continued on his way.

Teigra encountered no one else as she and Vasili made their way out of the tunnel. It had grown dark, and Teigra was able to use vacant areas and shadows to smuggle Vasili off the castle grounds. She then took him to a nearby physician. She paid half of his fee to nurse Vasili back to health—and keep his presence a secret—and promised to return with the rest of the payment once Vasili was healed. The physician told her that it would likely be a week before Vasili would be able to walk on his own. She again urged Vasili to leave as soon as possible, as Zarek's guards might come looking for him once they failed to find the burned remains of a body strapped to the chair.

Seeing Vasili tortured had touched something deep within Teigra. She was not one to feel pity, but she hated evil men. Vasili was the only man who'd shown her true kindness, and he was nearly destroyed by the same kind of evil scum who sucked the possibility of joy from her life—from her slave masters, to Acacius, to Lysandros...and now Zarek, who Teigra had realized was rotten to the core.

She was overcome with profound guilt, not only for being unable to prevent what had happened, but for her association with the man responsible. Teigra felt a moral struggle rising within her. She despised King Zarek for the disgusting acts she'd witnessed him performing, but she also loved the freedom and elevated role he'd awarded her.

She said a tearful goodbye to Vasili and stepped outside into the darkness. She walked briskly back to the castle grounds, and then to her bedroom. Teigra pulled out the bag of silver coins Zarek had given her and thought once more about her mission. She wondered if any of the men she'd been ordered to kill were also kind. Eventually, she drifted off to sleep, deciding success was critical to her personal survival.

In the morning, Teigra woke with confidence and determination, feeling her first mission for Zarek would be easy. To remain relaxed and clear-headed, she chose to pamper herself, as if she were preparing to attend an important banquet. She drew for a while with supplies she'd purchased the previous day, creating scenes of herself carrying out her upcoming assassinations in heroic fashion. She then had a hot bath, soaking for the better part of an hour, before rubbing herself down with aromatic oils and pulling a new tunic over her glistening skin. Lastly, she napped, and woke feeling reinvigorated as the sun was setting. Zosimos had provided her with directions to Leander's home. She studied them and left her room, three daggers concealed in sheaths inside her garments.

She arrived in time to watch Leander welcoming the last of his three scheduled visitors. Through a window, she could see everyone enjoying vast quantities of food and drink. It was the eve of the full moon, and these four high officials made a habit of meeting at this time each month to discuss the affairs of the day. Teigra prepared herself.

A few minutes later, a loud knocking interrupted the conversation. Everyone Leander had expected was already at his table, so he had no idea who'd be knocking so late in the evening. He reluctantly released his grip on his wine glass and made his way to the entrance.

Leander opened the door to find an exquisitely dressed woman with a veiled face. Her blonde hair lay softly across her shoulder and back, and the pristine blue eyes peeking over her veil were mesmerizing. She was a beautiful creature, and Leander paused to take in her beauty before speaking. She was attended by Leander's private guard, who'd knocked on the door to announce her arrival.

"And to whom do I owe the pleasure of this spectacle of beauty?" Leander asked.

"The lady states she was sent as a gift," the guard announced.

"I was sent by King Zarek as a peace offering, sir," Teigra replied. "I am here for you and your guests' pleasure. Do with me as you will."

"King Zarek, eh?" Leander said. "Perhaps he is softening, and realizing the benefits of working with those who have influence. But then again, perhaps he is only mocking me."

"I know of no mockery, sir," Teigra said, respectfully. "I am here to be enjoyed."

"Well, by all means, come in. It would be a shame to deprive you of your duty!"

After sending the guard back outside, Leander led Teigra into his home, caressing her body as he closed the door behind her. She felt disgusted as his big hands groped at her. *He's no different from any of my masters,* she thought. *It will be a joy to dispose of him.*

As she looked around the room, three other men were reclining on plush pillows on the floor, sipping goblets of wine, and tasting fruits and figs at their leisure. Teigra assessed how she could most efficiently accomplish her task.

"Good evening, fine gentlemen," Teigra said, as she smiled beneath her veil. "I come with King Zarek's blessings. He asked that I provide entertainment for all of you this fine evening."

"Funny, we were just speaking of the King," said one of the men.

"Indeed! Perhaps he is already feeling the pressures of the monarchy upon him," said another. "We know he's not suited to the throne like his father!"

"Let's not insult someone who's given to us so generously," Leander said. "Have you ever seen such an exquisite specimen of a woman? Venus herself would be jealous."

"We know what it takes to appease you, Leander," the fourth man said, chuckling.

Teigra started dancing to music she conjured in her head, encircling each of the four men, one by one. As she moved, she caressed each with her hands and whispered seductively in his ears. Her gyrations were enticing, beckoning more than just their attention.

"Here, let me help you relax," Teigra offered, as she gently helped Leander to the pillowed floor. "I am proficient in the art of satisfaction."

"Oh, I have little doubt," Leander said. "Your hands were made for pleasure, my dear!"

Teigra positioned herself behind Leander, and massaged his temples and neck. He loosened his tunic and let it fall to his waist as he enjoyed her touch. She gently pressed her breasts against his back, and moved up and down so he could feel her hardened nipples through her garments against his skin. The other three men sat across from him and longingly gazed at Teigra as she catered to Leander's wants. Everyone was comfortably relaxed, suspecting nothing.

Teigra let her hands fall along the sides of Leander's back and drift downward. She whispered ever so softly in his ear: "Ready for the climax, Leander?"

Before he could process why this seductress would disrespect him by calling him by his first name, Leander felt the sting and twist of a dagger pierce his heart. He immediately started to choke on his own blood. The three men saw his distress, but two collapsed before they could rise. One had a knife lodged squarely between his eyes, while the other found a blade centered neatly in his throat. Within seconds, the three men lay dead. The fourth found himself alone with a highly skilled assassin.

"Guard! Guard! Help!" the man screamed.

Teigra smiled and shook her head. In one smooth motion, she pulled the blade from Leander's back and leaped over his body to tower over the sole survivor. With one perfect thrust, she disposed of him as quickly as she had the others. All the gladiator fights she'd won had taught her to be efficient. Killing came as naturally as breathing.

The door swung open, this time without a knock. A lone guard entered and stood paralyzed with shock at the massacre before him. That one moment of indecision was all Teigra needed. Shutting the door behind him, she cut his throat from ear to ear.

Teigra retrieved her knives from the bodies, then eyed the feast on the table. Realizing she hadn't yet had dinner, she sat down and proceeded to eat her fill. Resting her feet on the floor decorated by five corpses, she also sipped and appreciated the excellent wine. When she was sated, she rose, dipped each of her crimson-covered daggers in Leander's wine goblet, wiped them clean before placing them neatly in their pouches, and left.

The next morning, Teigra reported to King Zarek. He commended her for the efficiency of her first assignment and gave her additional payment as a bonus. With Leander gone, his whims would be met with even less resistance.

* * *

Four days later, Vasili felt his health returning. Although he still had considerable discomfort where he'd been violated, he was able to walk, and even occasionally smiled at the birds in the trees.

It was a bright, sunlit day when he was finally able to leave. For his physician, it was a time of great relief. Caring for someone Zarek was actively hunting made him jump at every little noise, and continually look through his window to see if any soldiers were approaching.

"Take good care on your journey, my friend," the physician said, patting Vasili on the back. "I've no doubt your fortunes can only improve."

Nodding, Vasili forced himself to push away thoughts of both his fallen lover and the torture he'd endured under Zarek. For him, the music of the harp had been forever tainted.

Just as Vasili was readying to leave, Teigra appeared. Her head was hooded so she wouldn't be identified, but Vasili knew her body movements and immediately smiled.

"Right on time," Vasili said. "I'm leaving."

Casting off her hood, Teigra looked at the doctor. "He is?"

The physician gave a solemn nod. "Considering the circumstances, he's in impressive shape. It's as though the Gods themselves helped him to heal."

Wordlessly, Teigra pressed even more coins than she'd promised into the physician's hand. Teigra considered complimenting his work, but since he'd just credited the Gods, she decided to leave things at that. After all, there was no point in giving a man too much pride.

Stepping toward Teigra, Vasili stretched out his arms, offering a hug. She awkwardly stirred, pretending not to understand his gesture. Laughing a bit, Vasili tightly wrapped his arms around her.

"Thank you, my dear," he whispered in her ear. "Now I shall go retrieve the key tools of my trade."

Though Vasili was attempting to be oblique, Teigra knew he was referring to the liquid fire scroll, which he still believed was hidden where he'd left it. A pang of guilt shot through her, but she hadn't the heart to tell him that she'd taken it. She silently vowed to make it up to him someday.

Vasili kissed Teigra on the cheek.

In a rare and jolting moment, Teigra felt her heart grow warm. Before anything else strange happened, she broke free of the hug and gave her friend a nod. Her chest quickly returned to its normal, stony state.

On the inside, though, she found herself feeling something very strong toward Vasili. It was a sweet, simple, and rather innocent feeling. Could it have been...*love*?

She shuddered at the thought.

CHAPTER 27

THE COUNCIL MEETING

Once Zarek's deadly new policy toward their people became clear, the eight Amazon Queens put aside their differences and assembled for a war summit. They wouldn't leave the room until they'd established a plan to defend themselves.

Their task was a difficult one. All their armies combined were only a fraction of Zarek's in number, so they couldn't beat him with sheer force of arms. They'd have to employ cunning and a superior strategy.

The Queens discussed the matter around a long, grand table. Each of them wore jewelry, much of it brand new, as it was a custom of Queens to give one another presents when meeting.

On one side of the table sat Eudokia, Sybil, Antonia, and Marcia.

On the other side sat Sostrate, Anaxilia, Cassandra, and Alexa.

All of the Queens were beautiful. Some were blessed with extraordinary faces and figures—one-in-a-million looks seldom encountered outside of folklore. Others were captivating because of their confidence, power, and charisma.

There was always an air of competition among them, with no Queen feeling comfortable when bested by another. But the lethal mutual threat posed by Zarek created a newfound sense of unity.

"So we are all in agreement," Alexa began, "that we cannot destroy Zarek's army. I suggest that instead of focusing on his henchmen, we attack the source of the problem by killing *him*."

"We'll never get to him," said Cassandra. "He's prepared for such attempts and has guards around him at all times."

Anaxilia chimed in, "I agree with Cassandra. Even if we end Zarek's life, who's to say one of his chieftains won't continue his grisly work?"

"But Zarek is unique," Sostrate observed. "His level of aggression is monstrous. I'm guessing many of his men are as concerned about him as we are. Besides, what have we to lose by attempting an assassination? It will be perceived as a show of strength; and if we're successful, those who succeed him are more likely to cease hostilities."

Alexa nodded. "Otherwise, we're left with half-measures. Killing some of his generals will only make him angrier. Going into head-to-head combat with his vastly larger forces will whittle away our troops to nothing, wasting thousands of Amazon lives. Killing Zarek is the only way to end this. Since my Sondras are schooled in carrying out covert missions, I do not consider it an impossible task."

Shouting and arguing ensued. Even though Alexa's logic was sound, there were egos with which to contend.

Finally, Sybil made herself heard above the chatter. "Enough! We cannot be divided! Fine. Let's attempt to slay him. How exactly do we do it?"

Ten seconds of awkward silence. Then Eudokia said, "There is a great deal of liquid fire in his castle. If an Amazon team can find where it's stored, they can probably burn the entire place down."

All the Queens' eyes grew thoughtful. Picturing Zarek's palace erupting into mystic flames, as he raced around trapped, was a satisfying image.

"A fine suggestion, Eudokia," Sybil said. "But I have yet to hear anyone explain how a team gets inside the castle or learns how to navigate it."

"I suppose we can get information from the ladies," Sostrate said.

"Ladies" was a polite way of saying "whores." There were plenty of concubines in the castle, and some of them served as Amazon spies.

"The ladies are an asset, no doubt," Marcia said, "but their value is in gathering generalized information. I've tried having them draw maps before, and they simply aren't proficient." The other Queens who'd dealt with the ladies nodded in agreement.

Alexa then stated, "We *can* get a map of the castle."

"How?" Anaxilia asked.

"We go to Tegea."

"Tegea?" Marcia asked. "They are allies of Zarek!"

"Precisely," Alexa said. "Zarek's most prized architect dwells there."

"I find that hard to believe," said Eudokia. "Wouldn't Zarek's most prized *anything* live with *Zarek*?"

"Normally, yes," Alexa replied. "But this man, Esopo, began his service decades ago for Zarek's father, and now he's too old to travel, so he's been allowed to spend his last years at home with his family. Zarek communicates with him using messengers."

"But if he has such valuable maps," Cassandra said, "then surely his residence is surrounded by guards."

"It is; but not too many for us to handle," Alexa replied. "And once we get a map of the castle, we'll be a step closer to launching the mission."

"It's ambitious, and it's dangerous," said Sybil. "But it's starting to sound feasible."

"Hold on now," Antonia said. "Are we certain the Spartans won't help? Their army is comparable in size to that of Argos. If they allied with us—"

Some of the Queens interrupted with agitated sighs. "Zarek is no threat to the Spartans—at least for now," Sostrate stated. "Spartans don't wage war if there's nothing in it for them. The Amazon nation must live or die alone. To expect men to save us is living in a dream world."

Antonia started to get angry at the dig. Alexa cut in, "It's a fine thought, Antonia, and one well worth bearing in mind, should circumstances change." Antonia calmed and sat back down. "But for the present, Sostrate is right. We are on our own."

Queen Alexa then asked if anyone had anything more to add. In unison, they shook their heads. She stood up, waited for the others to follow, and said, "In Gods & Queens we trust."

They repeated after her, "In Gods & Queens we trust."

With those words, the Queens adjourned.

* * *

After the meeting, in the hallway of Alexa's grand dwelling, Eudokia and Sybil happened to walk by Thea. It was all they could do to prevent themselves from gasping.

Placing a hand against her chest, Eudokia whispered to Sybil, "Is that a ghost? She looks exactly like Elektra. Same eyes, same hair..."

Trying to suppress her own feelings, Sybil nodded and shushed her fellow Queen.

Averting their eyes, the two Queens joined arms and continued down the hallway.

Thea had not heard a single word.

* * *

An hour later, Xene, a Sondra officer, entered Thea's tent and ordered her to get ready for a trip to Tegea.

"Tegea?" Thea asked, feeling both excited and apprehensive. "What's there?"

"A mission," Xene said, smiling with anticipation. "We are to seize maps of Zarek's castle."

"*King* Zarek?" Thea asked.

"Yes," Xene said, laughing. "Do you know another Zarek?"

Smiling shyly, Thea replied, "It sounds important. We would need those maps only if we intended on paying the King a visit."

Xene nodded and walked toward the door. "One step at a time. For now, simply rest. This will be your first major mission, and we will need your energy come sundown."

Thea did her best to take an afternoon nap, but it wasn't easy. Her mind was flooded with thoughts of adventure, while her body kept making subtle practice kicks and punches beneath her sheets.

* * *

When sundown arrived, Thea and five other Sondras galloped toward Tegea, with Xene at the lead.

Riding hard, they arrived near the city several hours later, in the thick of night. They headed straight to the architect to carry out their mission, traveling through the woods to avoid detection. While this might have been an insane strategy for most soldiers, Sondras were well accustomed to long, arduous travel directly followed by demanding combat. Because this was Thea's first mission, it was her job to retrieve the maps while the others did the fighting.

The sky was black when they reached the forest at the perimeter of Esopo's home. It was the perfect time to launch an abrupt attack.

They found twelve guards stationed around the house. Xene whispered, "We'll split up now. Aello, Iris, and Jocaste, take positions in the other three quadrants. When you hear my owl call, each of you take out three guards as quickly as possible, while I do the same. Thea, stay here by the entrance. When you hear my second call, race to the front door and storm inside for the maps. You understand?"

"Yes," Thea said, her heart beating.

The other four Sondras vanished. It happened so quickly that Thea briefly thought she was dreaming.

But it was very real. Sondras prided themselves on their speed and precision.

Similarly, the assault on the twelve guards was swift and brutal. Xene placed her horn to her lips and blew, making a sound like an exotic owl. The next instant, all four Sondras attacked with animal-like fury, delivering long swords, swift kicks, and lacerating punches into the throats, chests, and bellies of their targets. None of them saw death coming. Only one guard, in the eastern quadrant, even managed to reach for his blade; but just as his hand connected with the handle, his Adam's apple received a Sondra's sword.

The Sondras dragged the corpses into deep, shadowy crevices around the property. All their violent work was concealed until sunrise.

After Xene removed her weapon from her final victim's bleeding neck, she sheathed it and set her eyes on the forest. She then blew her horn a second time. Any moment now, Thea would come running.

Thankfully, there had been no noise throughout the assault—aside from quiet bursts of choking and gargling—so chances were good that old Esopo was upstairs sound asleep.

Xene saw Thea bolt out of the trees. Her muscular legs were fast and unstoppable.

Thea briefly thought of Nox, hoping the mare would be okay by herself. She then brushed the thought away, for it wasn't fitting for a warrior to worry about an animal, even one so deeply loved.

When Thea reached the wooden door, she knocked it down with one hard kick. Xene wasn't far behind. It occurred to Thea that this was a bit like a training session—only the stakes were very real.

Xene stepped into the open doorway and watched Thea rush up the stairs. Unless Esopo's age had eroded his hearing, he was probably aware of their presence. It didn't matter, though, as his protection was dead.

Upon entering Esopo's bedroom, Thea saw him standing at the room's dim center. He was a small man, and his face bore a look of sheer terror.

"I do not intend to harm you," Thea said, her eyes scanning the space for a desk, cabinet, or basket that might bear maps. "But I need you to hold out your wrists."

Suddenly, two guards appeared! Growling, with teeth bared, they charged at Thea. For a split second, she was caught by surprise. They tackled her to the floor and pummeled her with their steel-gloved hands.

Within moments, those hands became fists.

Thea was surprised to feel the cracks on her cheeks. *This old man was good for more than designing buildings*, she thought. *He's designed a solid system of protection.*

Thinking of how embarrassing it would be if the others came upstairs and saw her on the floor, Thea sprang into lethal action. She reached up and grabbed the first guard's head, with one hand on his jaw and the other at the rear of his skull, and twisted. The sound of the snap was unmistakable. His eyes rolled up and his tongue fell out.

Without missing a beat, Thea stuck two fingers into the other guard's eyes, gouging them out. His hot blood rushed against her palm. She reached into his skull with as tight a grip as possible, twisted her hand, and caved in his head.

Covered in blood, Thea sped out from under the two dead guards to handle Esopo.

But he was gone!

Then Thea heard a loud *crash* in the hallway. Xene entered the bedroom holding her bloody sword.

"Any others?" Xene asked, viewing the guards' bodies.

Shaking her head, Thea said, "Just the old man."

"I got him," said Xene, sheathing her sword. "Which is fine, for it sends a message."

"What's that?" Thea asked, her hands hurrying through the drawers.

"That we are not to be trifled with."

Then Thea found exactly what they'd come for: a drawer filled with maps, all of them rolled up and bound by string.

Written along the surface of one map were the most pleasurable words Thea would see that day: "King's Castle Grounds."

Thea grabbed it and tossed it to Xene. They traded nods.

But the mission was not yet complete. The three other Sondras were all around the house, stealing gold, diamonds, and fine silverware. Meanwhile, Thea and Xene made a point of stealing every single map—every single planning tool—in the architect's home. The best way to avoid anyone guessing who they were or what their goals were was to make their mission look like a robbery.

The Sondras stole everything worth taking, and left the house a near-empty mess.

* * *

The next day, when the team of Sondras rode back home, the pride of their victory swelled within their hearts.

That pride quickly vanished, however, when they entered their camp and were greeted by an overwhelming sense of quietness.

Something was wrong.

Usually, there was a wave of attention when they returned. Children would greet them and ask questions about their adventures so they could act them out the next time they played. Even Thea knew this, for she'd been one of those excited children.

But now a thickness hung in the air. Not a single human being was in sight. Thea turned to Xene, their horses side by side. "Zarek?" she asked.

Xene shook her head. "If there'd been an attack, we'd see smoke in the sky and blood on the ground."

They rode on, pressing deeper. When they saw an overflowing gathering outside of Queen Alexa's tent, they increased their pace and sharpened their eyes.

Thea was the first to dismount. Xene was just a step behind.

Running up to one of the locals—an aging woman with a talent for knitting winter cloth—Thea asked, breathlessly, "What is it? Is Queen Alexa sick?"

The knitter shook her head.

"Dead," she said.

Thea's body was struck with a lightning bolt of shock. She turned to Xene, who was still right behind her. Xene's eyes sparkled with a flash of emotion.

She looked again at the knitter and asked, "How?"

"Zarek," she explained. "She went on a brief journey to gather weaponry for future missions, but her guards were destroyed by his army. And so was she."

Shaking her head, the knitter ducked away.

Thea just stood there, staring at the tent. The Queen's corpse had been brought back from the field. It was Amazon law that if the Queen ever went missing, she had to be sought within four hours and returned home—dead or alive.

Thea tried not to fall prey to dizziness. She had lost the only Queen she'd ever known…and she now had much greater reason to trust Seema.

"The prophecy," Thea whispered to herself.

"What?" Xene asked.

Thea shook her head. "Nothing."

The two of them moved toward the tent.

CHAPTER 28

THE ENCOUNTER

Upon returning to the castle, Teigra was glad to hear Zarek had gone out for an afternoon hunt. No doubt his absence came as a relief to the entire castle staff. His increasing paranoia was beginning to weigh heavily on everyone. Zarek seemed to fear enemies from every corner, from Amazons to rebellious citizens to officials in his own government. Teigra thought there was no end to Zarek's list of enemies. She briefly envisioned a bloody, brutal existence in which she was killing thousands of people, all for the sake of making Zarek feel safer.

To take a break from such heavy thoughts, Teigra made her way to her new favorite spot in the castle. It wasn't as private as her quarters, nor as peaceful as the sparrow garden in the back, but it ignited her passions.

Teigra climbed through a window, walked along the castle wall, and arrived at another window looking into the treasure room.

Among the plates of gold, goblets of silver, strings of rubies, bevy of emeralds, fine vases, grand sculptures, and the staggering paintings was a piece she'd come to value above all others. The room had become the new home of the Golden Girdle.

Teigra longingly gazed at it. Just being near it filled her with renewed energy and hope for a better future.

Teigra promised herself that when the time came to move on from Zarek, the Golden Girdle would leave with her.

* * *

Also thinking about the Golden Girdle was Thea. As she and eleven of her fellow Sondras moved like panthers through the forest toward King Zarek's castle, they whispered among themselves about their mission: to slay Zarek, free any Amazon prisoners, and burn the castle to the ground.

Thea had an additional agenda she kept secret from her comrades. It was based on the last piece of intelligence they received before leaving—a report that Zarek's treasure room held the Golden Girdle. Thea decided that beyond accomplishing their main goals, she would take on the private mission of locating and obtaining the Girdle for herself.

Thea felt a twinge of guilt for pursuing her own interests instead of focusing exclusively on those of her tribe. But according to Seema, the interests of Thea and the tribe were inexorably bound. If the Girdle could give Thea power, she'd use it to fight for the Amazon nation.

Thea reflected upon Queen Alexa's burial. It had been both a grand and sad affair. The other Queens, who traveled home a day prior to Alexa's death, returned to bid her a proper farewell. They all had immense respect for Alexa. Her exemplary job of overseeing the council meeting ensured she left strong, positive memories with her peers. When the Queens gave their heartfelt eulogies, many shed tears.

Thea knew she'd always miss Queen Alexa. She couldn't wrap her head around Seema's claim that she was fated to *replace* her. By tribal law, a top-ranking Sondra would be granted the throne. In Thea's mind, that put many other, more experienced Sondras ahead of her. At any rate, the matter wouldn't be resolved until a proper mourning period had taken place—and, with luck, the well-earned death of King Zarek.

The band of Sondras reached the forest's edge, where Zarek's castle stood in clear view. The sky was beginning to darken, allowing the black-garbed and black-haired Sondras to become almost invisible to anyone viewing the woods.

Klotho, the mission's leader, reminded the Sondras of their instructions in a string of tight whispers: "We are to divide into three groups of four. The first group heads to Zarek's bedchamber and kills him on sight. The second group attains the liquid fire and burns down the palace.

"The third group guards the first two. Like water, you shall move fluently and gracefully. Wrap your eyes around every corner. Kill Zarek on sight. Slay any interfering guards. Do not doubt the menace of Zarek and his men!"

These final words caused some tension. The implication was that if any of them were captured, death would be preceded by rape and/or torture. Thea briefly thought of Aristo and what a perfect gentleman he was. She'd recently learned that he'd been promoted to General. She felt bad that ruthless thugs made women suspicious of even men as good-natured as Aristo.

Thea snapped out of her reverie. As she'd been trained, she was in a fast run before even thinking about it.

The Sondras penetrated the castle through a little-known and unguarded opening on its western side revealed by Esopo's maps and confirmed by Amazon spies. Thea and the other three in her group split up in four directions: north, south, east, and west. Their quietness, dark clothing, and ability to blend into shadows made them inaudible and nearly invisible. They were poised to operate like tornadoes, ready to pull any of Zarek's minions into their deadly vortex.

Once Thea was well into her eastern perimeter, she set about securing her section of the castle.

Meanwhile, Klotho's Sondras worked their way over to Zarek's bedroom. After opening his door, however, they encountered the first major setback of their mission: it was empty! Klotho assumed that Zarek's massive paranoia—which was well-founded—caused him to periodically order the relocation of his bed.

She hoped that didn't mean the liquid fire had been moved as well.

Klotho took a deep breath. To her left, a short-haired Sondra named Pola whispered, "What now?"

Klotho's eyes moved as she considered strategies. After a few moments, she said, "We seek the fire. We double Team Two's efforts. Now!"

Without another word, Team One started dashing to the room holding the liquid fire. Klotho hoped they'd find it, because the longer they stayed in the castle, the more vulnerable they became.

Barely a minute later, Thea spotted Team One and got updated before they sped on. *Well, there's no use in preserving an obsolete plan,* she thought. *I might as well head to the treasure room.*

Getting around the castle was easier than she'd feared. Though it was quite large and sophisticated, it was essentially a grid, giving its curves and corners a certain cold logic. Within minutes, Thea was six turns away from the treasure room, and eager with anticipation. But she almost ran head-on into a stout, mustached soldier.

Thea noticed the soldier before he noticed her. As fast as he could, he reached for his sword, but his speed was no match for Thea's. Using a palm-length triangular blade, she opened up his throat. A rainstorm of blood poured onto the floor. The reddened ground caught his body when he fell.

Thea dragged the body into one of the darker corners, but there was nothing she could do about the blood. She sped on, knowing time was not on her side.

Reaching the treasure room was more challenging than she'd anticipated. Its doors were locked with heavy steel. Going in through the front wasn't an option.

Thea spotted a window. She dreaded this strategy because she wasn't a fan of heights, but could think of no other solution.

Within moments, Thea had climbed out the window and was tiptoeing alongside its walls. She dared not gaze down, and her lungs grew tighter with every step.

As Thea made her way toward a window within the treasure room, she spotted a rich golden glow in her peripheral vision. She felt in her bones that it was the light glinting off the Girdle.

Within seconds, Thea was directly in front of the window—and her jaw dropped. She saw a room crammed not only with riches, but with rows upon rows of stunning works of art: paintings, sculptures, wall hangings, and figurines, each more beautiful than the one before it. But the greatest sight of all was the belt covered with gold and precious jewels.

Thea was so taken with these sights that she could do nothing but stare in wonder. Then a reddish blaze stole her attention. Fire! *The other Sondras must have found what they were seeking,* she thought. The flames were consuming a distant part of the castle, and were a harsh reminder that she had to get moving.

Reaching into her bag, Thea took hold of a long strand of rope. She planned on flinging the rope around a ceiling beam, then sliding her way down to a safe landing.

When Thea opened the window, however, she was shocked to see another rope already hanging from a nearby beam. On the one hand, it was very convenient. On the other, it could mean a rival was already inside. Thea had no time to ponder. In a swift, smooth, and elegant leap, Thea grabbed the hanging rope, wrapped her mighty hands around it, and slid her way down into the golden, shimmering brightness of the treasure room. She landed perfectly.

Once in the room, Thea found it even more awe-inspiring. So much beauty was on display that she felt her heart risked being shattered. The designs of the vases defied her wildest imagination. There were virtually *rivers* of jewelry that caught light from every direction. She didn't dare gaze at the magnificent paintings for fear of losing herself in them. The room bested all but the finest museums. To think that all these precious treasures belonged to a monster was heartbreaking.

All these thoughts came to a fast stop when Thea located the reason she was there. Set casually on a table was the Golden Girdle.

Thea felt her throat catch as she looked upon it. Here, at last, was the supreme symbol of Amazon power. The feeling of destiny hit her like a thunderbolt when she saw the intertwining golden snakes, echoing the mark on the back of her neck.

If the legends are true, she thought, *I need only touch it and my life will be transformed. Maybe I really will become Queen.*

Thea hurried toward the Girdle, mesmerized—and therefore oblivious to the subtle stirring in the dark corner behind her, and the pair of eyes that were cloaked in the darkness, watching.

* * *

Teigra had been enjoying her private time in the treasure room when she heard the startling sound of the window opening. When she saw a female roughly her own age enter, Teigra's heart started hammering and she sprinted for the shadows. She wasn't frightened, but felt shy about being caught with her obsession.

Teigra watched from her hiding spot with fascination. The last thing she'd ever expected was for someone else to enter as she had. She was even more surprised when the young woman began gazing upon her prized Girdle with an intensity similar to her own.

When she saw the girl moving for the Girdle, however, rage filled Teigra's veins.

Just as Thea was about to touch the Girdle, Teigra bolted forward to crash into Thea from behind.

But Thea was trained to have eyes in the back of her head. She spun around and swung her fist at Teigra.

Teigra, in turn, was so fast and agile that she caught Thea's fist mid-flight.

Their eyes met. The two sisters finally stood face to face, though neither could fathom the true identity of the other.

"Do not touch that," Teigra growled. Thea snapped into action, swinging her foot toward Teigra's face. An inch from contact, Teigra caught the foot with her free hand and lifted her own foot, striking Thea hard in the groin. Thea felt substantial pain; and that made her mad. The fight had become personal.

Thea swallowed her pain, dropped her elbow, and crushed Teigra's knee, forcing it to bend against the joint.

Writhing, Teigra rested her outstretched head on Thea's abdomen as she windmilled her opposing leg into the air and crashed it into the side of Thea's face.

The two dusted off their wounds, having both suffered blows from the kind of fighter neither had encountered.

They briefly locked bodies like two elk, striking and blocking with animal ferocity. The two warriors moved in perfect rhythm, harmoniously spinning to a symphony of violence.

While far more punches were intercepted or dodged than delivered, the ones that landed opened ghastly wounds. Blood splattered some treasures, while others were completely destroyed by the deadly dance.

As Teigra swung her legs and fists, she found herself alternating between two extreme feelings. The power of this mysterious intruder created a fear in her she'd seldom experienced. At the same time, the heightened level of skill the stranger brought out in Teigra gave her immense joy. Fighting an opponent so challenging and evenly matched was one of the greatest thrills of her life.

Thea, in contrast, felt only fear, as she was juggling multiple responsibilities in her mind. She needed to get the Girdle, rejoin her fellow Sondras, and bring down this castle for the sake of the Amazon nation…all while prevailing in the fight of her life.

Her teeth pressed hard as Teigra swung a forearm at Thea. She connected with a crushing blow to Thea's nose. Reeling with dizziness, Thea swung her entire head at Teigra's, smashing their skulls together with blinding force.

Both fighters were severely staggered, seeing stars. But Teigra was used to being battered and recovered a second faster.

Spotting an opportunity for a finishing blow, Teigra spun around to knock her opponent out for the count. But something caught her eye. A cluster of armed guards, having overheard the brawl, entered the room.

Teigra stopped her leg, mid-air. The warriors were pulled out of the fight with each other and into a different reality. They were now both intruders who Zarek might horribly torture to death. Strewn about were smashed paintings, cracked vases, and other priceless items broken beyond repair.

Slightly smiling, Teigra lowered her foot, and Thea lowered her defensive hands. Their fight was over.

The two warriors turned from each other to face the guards. "I heard her rummaging around in here," Teigra said, "and entered just as she was about to seize the treasure."

Thea stole a glance at the rope. Teigra's eyes followed. It was wildly swinging from the energy of their battle.

To both women, it brought to mind a noose.

CHAPTER 29
CAUGHT RED-HANDED

While Thea and Teigra fought, larger battles raged throughout the castle. Over time, Zarek's men were inevitably victorious, through sheer force of numbers. The Sondras whose throats weren't sliced and who avoided arrows in their hearts were rounded up and dragged to Zarek's throne room.

Zarek smiled as he wiped his mouth with a silk burgundy rag, his eyes aglow and his skin charged with blood. The throne room was filled with guards and prisoners. Thea had overheard that the castle staff was finally getting the fire under control. Zarek was completely calm.

Thea wouldn't have wanted to meet Zarek under ordinary circumstances, much less after he'd just undergone an attack. Even though the shrewd step of mixing up his castle's holdings had thrown the Sondras into disarray, Zarek was not a man who relaxed in victory. On the contrary, victory tended to make him more restless.

After sucking in a great deal of air, Zarek rose from his throne and watched his guards brutally position Thea onto her knees before him on the marble floor.

Zarek said, "We live in a land of prophecies, woman. Those with second sight can tell what is to come. And before you visited my home, I was informed you'd arrive. Who was it that sent you?"

During the course of her training, Thea had undergone torturous inquiries such as this one. It was a meaningless line of questioning, designed only to break her will and give control to her opponent. Instead of responding, she remained stoically silent. Thea felt that engaging this man for even a single moment would be to give up far more power than any Sondra ever should.

Feigning a smile, Zarek let his eyes study Thea from different angles, the way one might examine a visitor from another world. Thea knew this was theater, and this horrid man was simply getting ready to change his approach.

Thea's heart thundered inside her chest. She looked around, observing her fellow warriors soundly imprisoned, and an assortment of grim-faced guards offering no apparent escape.

Suddenly, Zarek positioned his face right in front of hers, filling her entire field of vision. His breath smelled of wine and fish. He hissed, "Not interested in being helpful, are you?"

Her training still solid, Thea remained close-mouthed.

"Very well," Zarek spat, his reddened face tightening in the process. "I imagine you see no gain from identifying who sent you. But what if..."

Zarek sprung to his right, where one of Thea's fellow Sondras was now kneeling. The other Sondra instantly tightened up her body.

Just then, Teigra, freshly cleaned up from her fight, entered the throne room through a velvet curtain to Zarek's rear. She crossed her arms over her chest to observe the spectacle.

The Sondra's tension grew more severe when Zarek held a sharp knife in front of her. Thea felt adrenaline coursing through her body, but she dared not show her fear.

"What if your silence costs you your friend?" Zarek concluded.

Unable to help herself, Thea began to shake her head.

"What's that? I don't hear you!" Zarek roared.

Her training abandoning her, Thea's throat took over and she cried "*No!*"

All of the Sondras were now grappling with fear. None were visibly displaying their emotions, but Zarek had gained complete control.

He spun his gaze at Thea. "No? Why not? If you like silence so much, why should your friend not be silent?"

Thea's head shook back and forth in impotent, meaningless protest.

Before she could voice a single word, Zarek thrust his blade into the Sondra's eye. Blood sprayed so far that it nearly hit the opposite wall. Not interested in shortening the woman's agony, Zarek took his time twisting his knife around in the girl's eye socket.

Some of the Sondras, including Thea, unflinchingly watched. Others could not help but avert their gaze. To look away from a fellow warrior, according to Sondra philosophy, was to abandon that warrior. Although the sight was horrific, Thea forced herself to watch.

It was something she'd never forget.

"Are you ready to converse with me yet?" Zarek asked, plucking his knife straight from the gushing eye socket and letting the woman's limp body tilt to the floor.

"Yes," Thea wheezed, not yet knowing how much she would reveal, and feeling nauseous over the idea of revealing anything.

"Are you sure?" Zarek asked, promptly returning to his toying mode.

Thea's head was all nods. One came after another, in the exacting yet sluggish rhythm of ocean waves.

"Are you the one who has come to slay me? The girl with a taste for my Golden Girdle?"

Before Thea could answer, Teigra uncrossed her arms and stepped forward. "No," Teigra said, trying not to sound urgent. "After I overheard her from the hall, I walked in and found her trying to haul away a sack of coins."

Thea was taken aback by her treasure room opponent's interjection. What motive did *she* have to draw attention away from the Girdle? Was she somehow aware of its power?

Again, Zarek leaned over Thea, filling her sight. He didn't seem placated by Teigra's words. Studying his face, Thea noted that he was not an ugly man, but merely an overwhelmingly mediocre one. Bland of appearance, bland of soul. Perhaps if he'd been a freak of nature on the outside, it would have made him humble and he wouldn't have grown into a monster.

Thea was terrified to see this man, with a savage jungle where his mind should reside, moving in the direction of Klotho. This Sondra was extraordinarily brave, maintaining her center and treating every moment as though it might be her last.

As Zarek paced toward Klotho—his blade dripping red—his face began to change. Her visible bravery struck him as offensive. Surely no person could be brave when he was near!

Looking back at Thea, Zarek asked, "Do you find your friend strong?"

"Yes!" Thea yelled loudly—too loudly.

Zarek's eyebrows notched upward. "Oh? Do you now? Do you find her brave?"

"Yes, I do!" Thea shouted, hating herself for conversing with this man, yet feeling that every second before Klotho's demise was a precious one.

Then, in a moment of charged surrealism, Klotho reached out, grabbed Zarek's blade clean from his hand, and swung it toward his neck!

Although it lasted only a second, Thea witnessed a dash of fear on the King's face.

The attempt to wound Zarek had no chance of success. Klotho suffered an attack, and was instantly perforated by a spear from one of the nearest guards. She was struck in the chest—right between her lungs, beneath her heart, and above her belly. Blood poured from her like a fountain. Even as the life escaped from Klotho's body, bravery never left her face.

Zarek acknowledged the guard with a nod. "Good work," he said.

The guard returned the nod. Then Zarek said, "But far too slow," and stuck his knife into the guard's Adam's apple. Gurgling on his own blood, the guard collapsed.

This display made everyone perspire.

Returning his gaze to Thea, Zarek grinned. The guard who'd just saved his life was dying on the floor behind him. "See how it works around here? No one can ever quite grasp my logic. Isn't it exciting?"

For the first time in a very long while, Thea felt that she might cry. She thought she could prevent it, but couldn't be certain.

"I'll show you my theater room. Nothing is ever expected. No prophecy could anticipate what unfolds in *there*."

Thea didn't know what Zarek was referring to, but she was sure it wasn't good.

CHAPTER 30

THE THEATER ROOM

The theater room turned out to be the most unpleasant place Thea had ever encountered.

Rumors about Zarek's "torture performances" had floated far and wide, but Thea had imagined them as small, intimate affairs conducted in a cramped space. This was an auditorium that could accommodate a massive amount of people.

There were at least two hundred spectators in the audience. Thirty or so were onstage, but that granted them no special status. Everyone in the room except for Zarek and his men—and Teigra—was a slave or prisoner.

Everyone—including Zarek's men and Teigra—was vulnerable to the deadly whims of the King.

Zarek was using a blade to tickle the abdomen of an Amazon Thea had never seen before, but who was rumored to be a thief. She appeared to be a civilian, as her gaze and body language lacked the discipline of a warrior. This made Thea more sympathetic for her when Zarek thrust his blade into her belly.

Zarek had not stuck the blade in very deep, however—enough to draw blood, but not enough to be fatal. Clearly Zarek had worse things in store.

Thea's instincts were proven dreadfully accurate when Zarek proceeded to slice a large patch of the woman's skin, ripping her flesh upward like a loose, limp door. The woman transitioned from shrieking to panting, as her pain rose to the point where she could produce no sound.

Thea saw a short, hooded castle worker approaching Zarek with something in his hands. After a moment, she identified it as a steaming pot of water. Although she couldn't see the water, she could hear the sound of it boiling.

"Very good!" Zarek said, as he examined his victim's innards. "Who says one must be a hunter to eat?"

Thea made note of the King's lack of cleverness. Clearly, he was a hunter of sorts, and clearly he and his men had hunted down this woman to serve as his prey.

Zarek intended for this woman to eat herself.

Thea struggled with the urge to look away. But she knew that she had a duty to be a strong Sondra, and she had to take in all types of experiences if she were ever to become Queen.

So Thea—and many of the others—watched as Zarek sliced out a large chunk of the woman's intestine and dropped the dripping gob into the pot of boiling water. As he did so, he laughed. Most of the audience screamed, fainted, or vomited. The rest sat stoically, staring at the spectacle as if they were watching their own fates unfold.

Once the intestinal meat was thoroughly boiled, Zarek scooped it from the pot with a sparkling silver ladle and—proving Thea's guess entirely correct—popped it into the woman's mouth.

Her first instinct, as that of any person, was to spit it out. But Zarek was fast to cup his crusty palm over her mouth, and then nod his head as he made her chew her own organ. To help the chewing along, Zarek massaged the woman's cheeks, creating the motion on the outside that he wished her to perform on the inside.

After this action was completed, Zarek turned to the audience and threw his arms into the air, gesturing for them—*forcing* them—to applaud.

Amid their sickness and panic, the enslaved audience did as instructed.

Every cell in Thea's body was on the verge of collapse. This crazy man's actions were shocking her system; and worse, risked disrupting her will.

But that was the point of his theatrics. He was gaining deep pleasure from being cruel, but also from warping his prisoners' realities so deeply as to put them entirely in his control.

It was madness, but with a method.

Even though Thea's mind was flattening, she sought to combat the process. Looking around, she sensed she might be the only one capable of doing so. The eyes of her fellow Sondras, though strong, were beginning to lose a bit of their luster. As for the other captives, they were already lost causes, mentally shrunken and far away.

Meanwhile, Zarek had gone wild, slicing and chopping and stabbing the woman's exposed abdominal organs, and placing more chunks and pieces into his pot. In no time at all, Zarek's whole face was red. Thea noted with some nausea that his face looked better with some color. Nodding to his hooded helper and tossing in two great pinches of spice, Zarek gave the crowd a wide smile, announcing, "Not to worry, my friends! Your King is one to share!"

With that, several guards infiltrated the crowd, plucking pieces of intestine from the boiling water and shoving it into the mouths of random onlookers. Sometimes they shoved so hard that the poor objector choked and perished. For the most part, though, audience members ate to stay alive a little longer.

Thea questioned the wisdom of the latter, thinking death might be preferable.

She then watched a teenage girl getting up from her spot on the stage and running. Thea shook her head and mouthed the word, "No."

Inevitably, the red-faced Zarek noticed the escape attempt. He nodded to one of his guards, who restrained the woman and forced her onto her knees in front of Zarek.

Thea thought Zarek would force his manhood upon this young creature, given her position before him on the ground.

However, Zarek had an even more grave punishment in mind. With his wide eyes brighter than ever, he said to the runner, "Trying to stretch your legs?"

The runner screamed and wept, struggling against the guard's grip.

"Such beautiful, muscular legs you have," Zarek commented, studying the young girl's form. "Perhaps I could see them better if you took a seat."

No sooner had these words left Zarek's mouth than one of his helpers placed a stool behind the girl. Then the guard who was restraining her yanked her upward and slammed her down in the seat.

It occurred to Thea that the helpers moved so seamlessly, it was as if they were reading Zarek's thoughts. She didn't think he was signaling his intentions, as he appeared to be a man without a grasp of subtlety.

Interrupting Thea's contemplation, Zarek produced a clean, long nail...that rapidly became unclean when he hammered it with a mallet into the runner's bare thigh.

Although the action was horrible, the room did not seem shocked, given the forced cannibalism that had preceded it.

However, when a lanky, smiling helper appeared beside Zarek holding a fiery torch, the stakes skyrocketed.

"Now, I'm no expert," Zarek said, grinning, "but it seems to me that it would be most difficult for even a young girl like yourself to run with nothing but shards of bone inside your leg."

Thea instantly knew what would happen next. The lengthy nail, which was still lodged inside the girl's thigh, was heated to an absurd degree by the helper's flaming torch. The metal grew so hot that it melted the girl's skin and the muscles beneath it. Then the concentrated heat shattered the bones within the screaming girl's leg.

Thea couldn't hear the shattering, but she could *feel* it. Sharp waves of sympathy ripped through her body. The runner's leg contorted in a variety of odd directions, losing all of its shapeliness.

At last, Thea determined what was happening. The helpers were quick with the props not because they read Zarek's mind, but because *the punishment always fit the crime.*

It occurred to Thea that the poor soul who'd had her intestines mutilated must have been accused of stealing from the kingdom's kitchen.

A method to his madness, indeed.

Zarek turned his gleaming face to the audience, forcing another wave of inauthentic applause.

Even though the King was insane, identifying his process made Thea realize that on some level, however distorted, this was a fellow who could be reasoned with. There was enough logic within his damaged mind to engage in a battle of rationality.

Thea hoped her deduction was correct, because the moment she submitted to his insanity she'd be allowing herself to die.

Thea spotted Teigra sitting in the front row, her face hard and her eyes expressionless as she observed the horror show. It seemed to Thea that this woman had no intention of helping Zarek perform. Why was she excused from such duties? What special status did she hold?

More importantly, why in the world had she covered for Thea in the throne room? What secrets dwelt within the hardness of those eyes?

"Sir!" Thea screamed, in Zarek's direction.

The mere thought, let alone action, of summoning this man's attention was more terrifying to Thea than anything she'd experienced. However, if she were to survive his insanity—let alone someday sit on a throne of her own—she had no choice but to take her chances.

Wide-eyed and exhilarated, Zarek looked at Thea. He nodded to the lanky helper beside him, indicating that he should monitor the burning nail, which was continuing to wreak havoc inside the teenager's leg. The helper nodded back; and Zarek, flanked by a pair of guards, headed over to Thea.

"Yes, my dear?" Zarek asked, his voice filled with sarcasm. "Is there something that I may assist you with?"

Everything within Thea wanted to rise up and snap this man's neck. But she would do herself, her fellow Sondras, and the other prisoners no good by a failed attack attempt that courted certain death. After forcing a swallow, Thea said, "No. But I wish to assist you, Master."

Zarek punched Thea in the nose. Thea reeled backward, just shy of a true fall. Zarek cracked his fist against her face again, this time in her left cheek.

Then again.

And again.

Thea felt her skin growing tender, and her hot blood escaping through little slits left behind by Zarek's rings.

"You do not use my words against me!" Zarek roared, his fists continuing to come down on Thea in a storm of violence. "If you wish to 'assist me,' then just assist me!"

"Please allow me to," Thea whispered.

After slapping her hard across the mouth, Zarek said, "Who's stopping you?"

"No one."

Zarek chopped her in the eye socket. "Who?"

"No one!"

"Then *speak,* you wench!"

"I..."

Zarek kicked her in the chest. But still, she did not fall.

Finally, Thea cried out, "I am the least of your concerns! I know of no prophecy, Master! It's the Spartans you must be concerned about! They work with us! They wish *to kill you*!"

"The Amazons?" Zarek asked, his fists now mercifully at his side.

"The *Spartans!*" Thea screamed, fearing another blow, yet not receiving one. Free to go on, she said, "Our mission was to steal the secrets of the liquid fire."

"Why would you think," Zarek asked, now out of breath, "I have such secrets?"

Thea shook her head. "It was a reasoned guess. You have the fire, after all. And the Spartans have a great interest in your fire."

Thea could see from Zarek's expression that he was processing her words. And the fact that his violence had paused was a good sign that he believed her.

"Why," he asked, his voice having grown somewhat quiet, "did you visit my treasures?"

Thea shot a glance at Teigra, who sat stoically, hiding every trace of feeling. She then answered, "To steal gold, Master. I was seized by greed."

Silence overtook the stage. No doubt the other Sondras were either confused or impressed by her improvisation.

But regardless of their opinions, this much was certain: Thea had just started another war.

Given his paranoia, Zarek would most certainly make targeting the Spartans a top priority. Once Zarek began striking at them, the Spartans would have no choice but to fight back—fulfilling Alexa's final wish.

Teigra continued to watch the show. Thea studied her face as closely as she could. Was there a trace of curiosity within that cold gaze?

What could we teach each other? Thea wondered.

Thea decided her question could wait. Zarek was making his way toward the room's exit, apparently having elicited enough blood, vomit, agony, and death for a single evening.

Despite her physical and emotional pain, Thea experienced a small measure of pride. She was able to put an end to the dreadful show.

Moreover, she'd managed to execute a strategy fit for a Queen.

* * *

Draco waited until Zarek finished bathing before approaching the King in his quarters. Draco bowed a little, then handed Zarek a clean, dry cloth. Half-nodding, Zarek took it and wiped droplets of water from his skin.

"Is she telling the truth?" Draco asked.

Zarek gave Draco a hard look. "If I were a prophet, I would know."

"A tricky situation."

"Indeed."

"And a vulnerable one for us," Draco said.

There was a dreadful pause.

"Not if we act first," said Zarek.

Draco did his best to avoid showing any reaction. "I understand you can't know. But do you *feel* she's telling the truth?" Draco asked.

"It doesn't matter," Zarek said, tossing his towel aside. "That's not the question."

Draco briefly studied the ground. "Then, Your Majesty, what is the question?"

"It's 'How soon do we commit to war with the Spartans?'" Zarek said. "Whether the girl is truthful or not, we can bear no risks. We must destroy those savages, as we are doing with the Amazons.

"And we shall start planning for it with the rise of the sun."

* * *

Teigra lay awake in her room, as sleep was a stranger. Too many questions ran through her mind.

Why had that girl said those things about the Spartans? Was she being sincere, or was it some kind of a trick?

What was her mission in the treasure room? Why had she ignored all the priceless artifacts to focus on the Girdle?

Meanwhile, Teigra realized the value of the mystic scroll she held, a value she could not appreciate before she knew how to read and write. If countries might be willing to go to war over it, then she should be able to fetch a life-altering price. She would have to seriously consider where to sell it after she fled from Zarek's kingdom.

Then again, she was in no rush to leave the castle until the Golden Girdle was in her possession.

Teigra tossed and turned, knowing she needed answers—and soon.

For the sake of stilling her unquiet mind, she poked over the rim of her bed, stretched downward, and studied a carving she'd made on the floor just beside her bed's left leg, where she liked to rest her head.

It was a flawless rendering of the Golden Girdle, carved into the floor's brownish wood.

* * *

Thea took it as a symbol of some special—albeit dubious—status that she was placed in a cell by herself. All the other prisoners were piled together, virtually on top of one another. This might not prove to be a good thing in the long-term, as Zarek could choose to pay her grotesque private visits. But for the moment, she was pleased to be alone, with some peace to analyze and plan.

Prior to settling down upon her bare wooden mattress, Thea glanced out of her cell's tiny window. It was smaller than the size of her hand. She was nonetheless grateful for the air it brought, as well as the sight of the forest.

The thought of Nox galloped through her mind.

Shaking her head, Thea put two fingers in her mouth...and tried to whistle.

As usual, the effort failed. She produced a silent, pathetic nothing.

How her childhood adversaries would have loved to see that.

Her spirits low, Thea turned from the window and made her way to bed.

* * *

She had no way of knowing it, but Nox was in a small barn just two hundred yards away, held with dozens of other captured horses. When Thea had whistled, Nox began to neigh and jump, beating her back legs against the stable's heavy wooden door. In between strikes against the barrier, she jumped high into the air.

Fearing for their lives, the rest of the horses scattered to other parts of the stable. Nox ignored them and continued battering the door.

CHAPTER 31

THE SLASHING

Thea's eyes focused on the floor just beside the left leg of her bed. Carved into the cheap, faded wood of her cell was a perfect rendering of the Golden Girdle. She'd crafted the image with a small piece of steel she'd accidentally stepped on while pacing her confines. The steel had nearly injured her foot, but she saw its potential and made it into a tool for artistic expression.

Thea found the image of the Girdle calming, and also carved a grand mural onto her cell's western wall. It depicted landscapes and suns and moons, men and women and children, great battles and small romances. It was a busy, overflowing scene, and it made no logical sense, but that didn't matter to Thea. The mural contained everything she dreamed about, and everything her cell prevented her from seeing.

She purposely left one thing out of the larger mural—the precious Golden Girdle. The menacing guards who stopped by twice a day to toss her scraps of food—and sometimes fists and kicks—would notice if the Girdle appeared on her wall. So she only carved it into the floor, a place no one was likely to look.

No one would think to search that spot except her sister, who'd carved the exact same thing in the exact same place, relative to her own bed.

"You have a head full of dreams!" shouted a guard near Thea's cell door.

She had been lost in thought, busily adding a row of small ducks to a green (in her mind) pasture she'd carved the day before. Thea turned her attention to the guard, whom she mentally called Flat Face because his nose looked like two nostrils set on a level plane. At first, Thea had thought he was deformed, but realized he was merely ugly.

He walked toward her, sneering, studying the wall and her barely-clothed body with a series of rapid, jerky glances.

"The others pay no mind to your activities, but I see it as a defiance of Zarek!" His loud voice filled her small cell. Thea held the puny piece of steel in her hand and briefly considered using it to open the man's neck, but thought better of it. Many other guards would quickly rush in and slice her to shreds with their swords.

"Give it over." Flat Face held out his upturned palm.

Thea hesitated for a moment, then placed the piece of steel into Flat Face's hand. As soon as he closed his hand around it, making a convenient fist, he punched Thea hard in the stomach, sending her to the ground.

She struggled to catch her breath, which had been efficiently knocked out of her.

* * *

On a rare day away from his grounds, Zarek balled his hands on his hips, studying the skeletal structure before him with wide and beaming eyes.

It wasn't much to look at in its current form. But anyone with vision could see it held the promise of an impressive building.

More specifically, the place was to be a temple.

A temple erected to honor Zarek.

It was planned, of course, by the man himself.

Zarek was busy with the task of conquering neighboring towns and villages and adding them to his expanding kingdom. But this project remained among his favorites. The temple was being constructed next to a tall, thick wall that marked the border between two territories—a border that had become meaningless because Zarek now controlled the land on both sides.

"We need more artists, Draco!" Zarek shouted, making sure to draw the ears of the many locals, all of whom were frightened to have the King so close.

Draco stepped beside Zarek and looked at the bare beginnings of the structure. "Indeed. It is going slowly."

"*Painfully* slowly!" Zarek screamed, in a mix of impatience and black rage. "It's a temple in my honor. Have the workers forgotten this?"

"No, Your Highness," Draco said, "but I am in agreement that they need to improve their speed."

Zarek turned to Draco, fixing his hard, blank eyes upon the man, briefly wondering whether to split his skull in half with a mallet. But Draco was one of the few people alive he considered a peer.

Instead, Zarek simply continued the conversation. "Have you seen my treasure room?"

"Indeed I have."

"And do you know how long that room took to build?"

Draco shook his head.

"It took mere *weeks,*" Zarek declared. "And I accepted nothing but the finest of pieces."

Zarek paced around the perimeter of his embryonic temple. "Scour the slaves," he said. "Find the ones with speed in their hands. They will paint this structure. It must be done *now.*"

Draco's head tilted downward as he nodded.

Stirring, Zarek asked, "Do they not respect me? They've been moving like snails."

"Well, after all, they are mere slaves."

Zarek's darkest rage showed on his face. "Slaves can be swift," he told his friend.

"Yes, certainly. They can." Draco gave his king a smile.

"So we just get faster ones…and more talented ones."

With his plan expressed, Zarek continued pacing. Following, Draco said, "Well, as it happens, I've learned that one of the prisoners possesses considerable talent…"

Zarek listened intently as the men walked.

* * *

Thea's heart thundered inside her chest. The sight of Zarek, flanked by two guards, entering her cell was like something out of a dream. What business did a king, even an insane one, have in such a place? His presence seemed much too large for this tiny, pathetic room.

"We meet again," Zarek said, as he lacerated Thea with his charged, empty eyes.

Thea's blood was moving through her body with such speed and aggression that she wondered how long she could remain conscious.

"I hear you're an artist," Zarek said.

"I am," Thea said, recalling how important it was to the King to be answered.

"And now I see it!" Zarek all but cried, setting his sights on her wall mural. It was incomplete due to Flat Face's rude visit the day before, but it was still quite impressive.

As Zarek studied Thea's art, moments stretched into eternities. Even the guards were tense. As the madman's eyes swept over the landscapes, and the scenes of love and war, Thea had to keep reminding herself that she'd reserved the Girdle drawing for the floor by her bed. There was nothing on the wall to give her away...she hoped.

After several lifetimes of silence, Zarek spoke. "We're building a temple in my honor!"

Thea nodded. "Sounds very nice."

"It will be. And we need artists. Good ones. And fast ones! So you will work on it. Plus, you'll get some sunlight onto that awful, white skin."

Again, Thea nodded.

Zarek turned back to the mural. "Lots of people in here. Do you like people?"

"Yes," Thea said, doing her best to sound enthusiastic.

Zarek found it a puzzling answer. His eyebrows drew close together, and he took a small—yet, in her mind, enormous—step toward Thea. "What is it that you like about them? I'd think it a pleasure to be alone down here without people bothering me all day."

Thea scanned her entire mind and body for the right answer, but her fear was too great and her blood flow too fierce to think clearly. All she could do was shake her head.

Just like that, something in Zarek *snapped.*

"You lie!" he screamed. "You're like me! You've no need for people."

A wave of terror ripped through her brain. "No, I love people. I miss them. I miss the people I care about."

To her own ears, the answer sounded tiny and sad. Apparently, Zarek heard it the same way.

"No, you don't! You hesitated! You're like me! I'm a king. You, in your mind, are a queen!"

The guards behind Zarek seemed to hold their breath.

"We're taking you back to the theater room," Zarek said. Then, extremely quickly, he turned to walk away. Under his breath, he said to the guards, "Get it ready for tomorrow. First thing in the morning."

When Zarek left, Thea was more terrified than ever.

* * *

Thea was led across the castle grounds, past the widening stares of all who dared to view her. Her eyes were covered and her mouth was stuffed with a gag. She could think of only two things.

First, she was most certainly about to die.

Second, the prophecy had been a bunch of nonsense.

Thea couldn't see who was in the theater room, but judging from the heat, thickness, and noise, she guessed there were hundreds in attendance.

Zarek's voice rose. "We slay this woman for the crimes of deception, attempted thievery, and rebellious artwork!"

Were Thea not in such an awful position, she would have found the last charge quite hilarious. To be killed for creating art was akin to being hated for making love.

"As well," Zarek went on, "this girl's presence has been foreseen. She seeks to destroy and overthrow me! This I have learned from an oracle!"

Thea found nothing ironic or humorous in this accusation. She truly was a player in a prophecy. If she'd had even a remote chance, she would've destroyed this man and taken his undeserved kingdom away from him.

Just as Zarek's footsteps stomped toward Thea, a familiar voice called from the crowd: "You fool! This woman is not the one of whom the prophets speak! *I am!*"

A massive collective gasp shot around the great room. It was as much from surprise as it was from the fear of a slave calling Zarek a fool.

His voice somewhat weak, Zarek shouted back, "Who declares this? Who challenges me?"

Thea, for one, could not wait to find out.

"I am Laria!" the voice cried. "Granddaughter of the mighty Queen Alexa of the Northern Amazon tribe!"

Another gasp shot around the room, this one filled with genuine surprise—along with Thea's breathless, gagged gasp.

Thea's mind went wild. It wasn't possible Laria knew of the prophecy. Could it be that Laria, having failed to become a Sondra, was choosing to become a hero? This was an old and proud custom among the Amazons. Those without natural gifts were able to achieve greatness by giving their lives to save others. Laria, who'd always been so cruel, was demonstrating a staggering maturity and bravery.

If Thea could speak, she would object. In that moment, the Sondra tradition meant nothing to her: She didn't want anyone dying to keep her alive.

However, Thea remained tightly gagged.

She heard the sounds of Laria being dragged onstage by a group of guards.

Zarek spat out words to one of his soldiers: "Is-she-who-she -says-she-is?"

"Yes, Your Highness," the guard replied.

No! Thea shrieked in her mind. *She is not!*

But the fact that Laria was Alexa's granddaughter was enough for Zarek to believe she was destined to take Alexa's place as Queen.

His face shaking, Zarek started to shriek. He had so little control over himself that he sounded more fearful than angry: "You murderer! You destroyer of fate! *The prophecy saw you!*"

Thea shook her head, wishing more than ever that she could speak.

But Zarek's focus was entirely on Laria. "I will see you *dead*!" He unsheathed a sword from his side and lifted it high above his head. Taken by surprise, Zarek considered this task too urgent for theatrics. Without hesitation, he swung his sword and smashed it sideways across Laria's innocent neck.

Laria's head landed on the stage with a thud.

The audience, having been conditioned to do so, applauded.

Far from content, Zarek proceeded to chop up Laria's body, cutting her arms from her shoulders, her calves from her knees, and her breasts from her chest.

Laria's still-warm blood splashed Thea in the face. Thea even tasted a little, and could not help but think she was tasting her savior. The blood mixed with Thea's tears.

By the time his slaughter had concluded, Zarek was grinning from ear to ear. Thea felt some guilty relief when she heard his sword clatter to the stage.

Then Zarek directed a few simple words toward her:

"You'll be sent off to work at the temple."

Thea felt that the Gods themselves had intervened.

For both she and the prophecy lived.

CHAPTER 32

THE TEMPLE

A t some point during her second week painting the temple, Thea felt a rush of life returning.

Being appointed to painting duties was a fortunate thing. Not only had it saved her life, but it put her in a privileged class of prisoners.

Those working on more mundane aspects of the temple, such as constructing walls and roofs, were forced to wear chains on their ankles all day. But the artists, who needed to climb into tight corners and work on tall ladders—and whose imaginations were encouraged to roam—were allowed to be physically free as they worked. No one worried about it, as the artists were unthreatening and, by nature, typically gentle souls. The guards didn't suspect that leaving Thea unchained risked everything.

In contrast, *all* of the prisoners were shackled at night—both ankles and wrists—before being permitted to sleep. If a careless guard locked Thea's chains too tightly, she'd suffer from the hard, aggressive bite of the steel until morning.

Still, the days were becoming a welcome treat for Thea. She didn't want to appreciate them too much, as that would give Zarek control over her. But it was undeniably enjoyable for her to paint every day.

She didn't dwell on the fact that her art was being created in tribute to a mass murderer.

One thing that especially puzzled Thea was the giant stone statue being crafted by the sculptors in her group. It was a statue of *Zarek*.

What was the point of that? Thea wondered. *Was this temple being built for the sole purpose of worshiping Zarek as a God?*

As she worked, Thea also found her thoughts wandering to Melia. Where was her lover these days? Was she well? Was she even still alive? Thea believed she was; that she would somehow sense if any serious harm had come to her beloved.

Thea's thighs stirred at the mere thought of Melia. She found that picturing Melia's wondrous face and full, ripe lips caused her blood to rush. This helped her paint faster.

As Thea's mind raced, seeking out more cherished memories and sensations, her thoughts also traveled to Aristo. She had the same questions about him: Was he well? Was he still alive?

Whom would she prefer to see? Melia and Aristo both offered such divine pleasures, it was hard for Thea to decide. Melia was gentle and sensitive, while Aristo was powerful and fierce.

As she swung between memories of her two lovers, Thea found a most unexpected third face entering her mind. It was someone for whom she had no romantic interest, but had come to play a major role in her life.

Seema.

Thea had no doubt Seema was alive and well. She simply wondered if the old woman was right. Was Seema's prophecy truly a gift from the Gods, or the result of a senile imagination?

On one hand, Thea had managed to survive Zarek. Considering how dangerous he was and how fixated he'd been on her, that was something of a miracle.

On the other hand, Thea was enslaved, and her future seemed bleak. How could she change her status from helpless prisoner to conquering Amazon Queen?

Thea could think of only one solution: Escape.

If she'd never met Seema, Thea might've considered escape much too risky.

But Thea reasoned that if the prophecy was true, then she had a responsibility beyond ensuring her own life—it was her duty to serve the Amazon nation.

Further, if the prophecy was real, then how could she be killed trying to fulfill it?

Then again, if Seema was wrong, then at least Thea would lose her life attempting to save herself and her fellow Amazons—which would make it a noble death.

Thea began planning.

She took careful notice of the temple's daily routines. She was pleased to observe that, day in and day out, the guards did the same things.

In the morning, they woke the prisoners, counted them, and fed them bread and water. Then they unchained those assigned to paint.

For the rest of the day, the guards ensured everyone worked hard. By the time the sun slipped below the horizon, the prisoners' muscles would ache. The guards then ushered them into a giant hall for dinner...which mostly consisted of more bread and water.

After dinner, the guards counted the prisoners again, directed them to a vast room to sleep, and placed any who were unchained back in irons.

It was at night, while mixed in with several hundred others, that Thea quietly talked of escape with three of her fellow Amazons: Chloe and Reah, who were also painters, and Mila, who was working construction.

"Only one period of the day is ideal," Thea said. "It's between the conclusion of the day's work—when Chloe, Reah, and I are unchained—and the final head count. Mila, at some point before dinner, you must cause a great commotion. While the guards are distracted, the rest of us will hide. Then, as everyone shuffles off, Chloe, Reah, and I will slip away into the night."

"What sort of commotion?" Mila asked.

"I trust you to think of something effective," Thea replied. While Mila was the youngest among them, Thea knew she was brave and willing to risk her life for her fellow Amazons.

"But where will we go after we get out?" Chloe asked, her voice coming out in a thin, near-silent whisper, so low in volume as to be easily mistaken for meaningless gibberish spoken during sleep.

"Thea and I will go to Genet, she's the nearest concubine in the Amazon protection allowance," whispered Aviva. "We're deaf and blind in here, so we'll need up-to-date information on our sisters, Zarek's progress, and the Spartans."

"But where will *I* go?" Chloe whispered back.

"You must run off in a different direction, across the woods," said Aviva. "That will distract the guards and keep them off our trail."

Chloe was clearly frightened; but she simply replied, "Understood."

"A dangerous mission," Thea whispered to her friends.

The others could only nod in agreement.

******

Teigra's horse charged through the dark forest.

Its breath was labored. Its gallops were increasingly choppy. But the animal had no choice but to continue. If Teigra wasn't at the castle by dawn, someone was bound to notice, and she feared suspicion would grow like devilish flames.

It was actually flames that had inspired Teigra's nighttime journey. She'd relocated her priceless scroll, hiding it under an exotic tree with thick gray bark in an entirely inconvenient location. One had to cross over two rivers and a frightful ditch to access it.

Teigra was confident about the security of her hiding place, but was losing faith in her horse. On her way back, it'd been terrified by a snake that had bitten its leg, and it took Thea two hours to calm the animal. If she had to proceed on foot, her odds of making it back to the castle in time were slim. She feared this could place her life in jeopardy, as she had no good reason to be away at night. She wasn't even working as an assassin anymore—with a war that needed continual funding, she'd been reassigned to collecting taxes from wealthy citizens—and it didn't take much to rouse Zarek's suspicions.

Teigra once again explored her feelings about living in the castle. On a purely physical level, it was the most comfortable home she'd experienced. But the King she worked for was the most evil of all her masters, and she'd grown to hate him. *He's worse than a beast*, she thought.

In fact, such a comparison was an insult to beasts. Perhaps in reaction, her horse gave up its last bit of spirit. It went into a wild roll, its head crunching down and its back plowing into the ground. Teigra was slammed down along with it.

The animal's tongue hung out, big and meaty. Its eyes were open and blank, sending a spooky feeling through Teigra. But that feeling was no match for her pain. Her ankle felt like it'd been split from within.

Unable to believe her bad luck, Teigra cried out into the emptiness of the night.

* * *

Teigra walked for an hour after her horse died. She had no plan other than to keep moving.

Then she unexpectedly heard galloping. Turning around, she saw a familiar figure. It was General Niko, the man who'd let her escape from the tunnels with Vasili. By coincidence, he was riding in the area.

When Niko's eyes fell upon Teigra, they widened, then gleamed. Despite the pain she was in, Teigra knew the man was attracted to her. She had seen such looks on the faces of men in the past; the kind that said they'd love to have her for supper.

Teigra's body now felt another sensation in addition to the pain shooting up from her leg: disgust. This was someone who used to work for Zarek's father. Although he abandoned that position and opted for independence following Zarek's ascent to the throne, he'd been associated with that menace. For Teigra, that was enough to make him worthy of hatred.

As Niko climbed off his horse and walked toward Teigra, she reached for the knife sheathed in her boot. The leg that wore the boot was badly bent, however, and to even touch it with her fingertips filled her with agony.

Teigra let out a girlish scream that made her feel embarrassed.

Niko strolled right up to her. Teigra swung at him with her right fist. Catching her hand, Niko shook his head. "Come on, I'll help you," he said. Closer, his eyes seemed filled with attraction, and perhaps something greater...something like caring.

"No," she said, spitting out breath, determined to avoid the helpful advance of this man.

But it was too late. Niko scooped her off the ground and carried her over to his horse.

Teigra—hurt and disgusted—felt something that she had not felt in a long time travel through her system: affection.

This man who had helped Vasili was now demonstrating humanity like Vasili. *Maybe*, she thought, as the two of them galloped into the night, *he is actually worthy of trust.*

Just as the thought crossed her mind, she fell into a deep, exhausted sleep.

* * *

As it happened, Teigra's fears were groundless. Zarek wouldn't have noticed or cared if she'd been late.

His feverish mind was occupied with orchestrating his troops—10,000 and growing—to overtake more territory, and to prepare for an invasion of Sparta.

Zarek had decided to strike Sparta in eight weeks, on the night of the famed Carneian festival. An event charged with celebration and free spirits seemed like the perfect cover for surprising an enemy.

Meanwhile, Zarek focused on the burning village spread out before him. Its inhabitants had caused him great disappointment. Rather than consent to the aggressions of his troops, and allow him to take over and install a severe taxation operation, they'd attempted to fight back.

A poor move on their part, thought Zarek. *Very poor.*

He'd turned the whole area to charred rubble in fifteen hours. Almost all of the villagers had been murdered or placed into slavery. Only several dozen strong young men were spared those fates—in return for their pledge to join Zarek's growing army.

Zarek found one of these recruits sitting on a black heap of rubble, his eyes pouring tears. The home where he'd been born had been reduced to a flaming mass.

"Cheer up, my lad," Zarek said, patting the boy on the shoulder. "Your next home will be in Sparta."

* * *

At sunset, when all the exhausted workers were being led into the dining hall, Mila launched into her first *real* work of the day.

She tore off all her clothes, screamed, and twirled about the temple's main corridor.

Naturally, every guard's eyes turned her way.

So did the tired eyes of her fellow prisoners, the lids of which had been half-closed just a moment before. Although the sun had dropped, their attention had risen.

What had gotten into this girl?

The guards, both bemused and aroused, marched in Mila's direction, their attention so focused that none of them noticed Aviva slipping down the rear staircase, Chloe sliding out a tiny side window, and Thea tucking herself into a dark alcove near a doorway to the roof.

When Mila started to scream even louder, shouting obscenities about the Gods, a rush of commotion emerged from the great corridor—with hundreds of prisoners and dozens of guards all shouting.

This, Thea knew, was her moment.

With her heart beating like mad thunder inside her chest, she went through the door and rushed up the stairs to the roof. During her painting work, she'd noticed that this roof was conveniently located very close to a thick assortment of trees.

All she had to do was jump to the nearest treetop, then leap across the roofs of neighboring structures until she was out of reach of the guards. She'd then race to the home of Genet, a loyal ally from the Aksumite Kingdom who lived in a garden community several miles to the east.

Meanwhile, her friend Aviva would escape into the dark forest and separately head for Genet.

As for Chloe, she'd have to improvise a path that would attract and distract the guards.

That is, of course, if she managed to survive.

Thea's breath left her body in thin, constricted spurts. She opened a second door, this one leading to the high and humid rooftop of the temple. If even a single guard was up there, she'd probably be dead in seconds. However, to the best of her knowledge, the guards all descended to eat supper at this time. It was a risk she considered worth taking.

The thickness of the night wrapped its warmth around Thea's body.

She ran over to the rooftop's ledge, the bricks of which were young and uneven, a result of the temple's unfinished condition.

She reminded herself to be careful with every step. She half-smiled at how ridiculous it would be, after all she'd been through, to die from stepping on a faulty brick.

Keeping an eye on her bare feet, Thea skipped onto the roof's ledge, then readied herself to spring to the nearest treetop. It was only nine feet away. The strength of her legs would be more than enough to carry her that distance.

Taking three breaths, she thought of Seema.

Thea hoped with every fiber of her being that Seema was correct.

With her heart smashing against her lungs, Thea wondered if her friends Chloe and Aviva were okay. Hopefully they were free, and she'd see both of their grinning faces in the future.

But to get there, Thea had to jump.

Her courage seemed to falter. Thea was overflowing with nerve months earlier—which felt like a lifetime ago—when she braved the heights of the castle to enter Zarek's treasure room.

Since then, Zarek had hollowed her body and spirit.

But she was determined not to let him win.

Wrenching every bit of strength, Thea jumped off the ledge—and managed to grab hold of the nearest tree.

She realized that there was no time to spare. From below, she heard the sound of a horn.

While it wasn't yet counting time, a guard had taken notice of the escape. The chase was on!

Her lungs worked so hard that she thought they might produce smoke. Thea leaped from rooftop to rooftop, astonished every time her feet managed a safe landing. Beneath her were hundreds of people from the nearby town shopping and going about their business, despite the blaring horns emitting from the temple.

Zarek's men were also going about their business...which was trying to find and slay the escapees.

Thea felt immense relief when she arrived at the town's outer edges, looking down from the roof of a pottery shop at a forest pathway that led directly to Genet's home. She saw various people on the ground leading their donkeys or traveling on horseback. But to her right she saw nothing but nature: beautiful, blissfully unpopulated nature.

She was close.

For the first time in weeks, she felt a surge of freedom. She also felt herself believing in Seema.

Despite her tired eyes and her throbbing, frightened brain, Thea soon found herself on the walkway to the home of Genet.

Thea carefully listened as she moved forward. She knew that one of Zarek's soldiers could pounce from the forest and slash her throat. But all she could detect from the nearby grasslands were crickets chirping and lightning bugs brightening the night.

It occurred to Thea that the danger could come from within Genet's house, where guards were hiding. Even Genet herself might wield a treacherous blade.

Thea dismissed such notions as soon as she saw Genet greet her at the door. Genet's eyes—wide, brown, and mystifying—instantly made Thea feel safe.

Thea passed out in Genet's arms.

Genet let out a laugh. But very quickly, the concubine transitioned from seeing the humor in Thea's fainting to appreciating the gravity of her situation. Moving rapidly, Genet dragged Thea inside her home.

CHAPTER 33
WAR PREPARATIONS

When she finally woke up, Thea still felt safe. She wondered if this was because her mind was so weak with exhaustion. At this point, there'd be dangerous men all over the kingdom on the hunt for her neck.

"Do you know of Melia?" Thea asked. She said this before offering any form of greeting or gratitude. This made her feel a bit ashamed, but she needed to know.

Smiling, Genet said, "Indeed I do."

Now Thea was entirely alert. Her eyes fluttered.

"Go slow," said Genet, touching Thea's shoulder. "Melia has been staying here, the haven for Amazons closest to Zarek's temple, hoping that you would escape."

Thea was overjoyed. She was even more pleased when Melia suddenly appeared before her in the flesh, wearing a sheer silk dress. With a burst of new energy, Thea stood to greet her. The pair shared a long hug. Thea let her palms sink into Melia's back. Melia's tears splashed onto Thea's bare shoulder.

"I missed you so much," Thea cried.

Melia was too overwhelmed to speak a word.

* * *

Handing Thea a generous slice of cheese and an almost-over-flowing clay cup of ale, Genet offered her guest a smile. Thea was too forgetful in the ways of free people to smile back. She felt grateful, but her face failed to follow. Genet's smile persisted, regardless. She was tall of body and dark of skin, with beautiful, almond-shaped eyes and long, curly black hair.

There were beautiful women all around her, some with very little clothing, and a couple with no clothing at all. These were Goddesses on Earth, mystics of the flesh. With a sweetness rising in her chest, Thea found herself remembering what it felt like to love.

Looking at Genet, she wished to touch her—not for romance, but in a simple spirit of friendship.

Thea placed her palm on Genet's forearm. She then refocused on her mission, saying, "Tell me about Zarek's plans."

"Oh," said Genet. Her expression darkened, providing every indication that she was dismayed by the mere thought of the man. "Where to begin...?"

"How's his war progressing?"

Genet nodded. "You use the right words," she said. "This is 'his war.' He's slashing through the peninsula like a blade through cream."

Thea took a breath. This wasn't really a surprise. She'd never encountered a man so intimately acquainted with the utility of violence.

"Nearly every week he claims another town. Did news of this not reach you in your imprisonment?"

Thea shook her head. "Sometimes a word of truth leaked through, but it was virtually buried among all the other rumors. We lacked your...proximity to what's real."

This was a polite way for Thea to say that the concubines, by sleeping with the enemy's men, were as close as possible to valuable information. They received it while their backs rested on soft silk mattresses. They got vital news whispered directly into their ears.

Genet wrapped a thin but elegant cloak around Thea's shoulders. It wasn't meant to warm her as much as to restore her native attractiveness. Grateful for the gesture, Thea held the cloak against herself.

"What of the Golden Girdle?" she asked, the words coming out fast, betraying how vital she considered the matter.

Genet paused.

"Do you know it?" Thea asked.

"Not until recently," Genet said, "when a castle intruder was suspected of trying to steal it."

Thea smiled inwardly, realizing she was the "suspect." She then pressed on: "Does it remain among the treasures?"

Genet took a moment to think. Thea found her spirits sinking as she wondered whether Genet had the information she needed.

"It's underground," Genet said at last, "in a tiny city constructed beneath the castle. But there's no way to get to it."

Thea's jaw dropped.

"It's in a different room of treasures, behind thick metal doors, with two guards standing outside."

Genet looked Thea in the eyes. Her steady gaze made Thea's skin feel smooth. "Were you the one who sought it?" Genet asked.

"Yes," said Thea, impressed by the concubine's intuition. It made her trust Genet's information.

"Is Zarek planning to rain terror on Sparta?" Thea asked.

Genet gave a firm, sure nod. "Yes…and soon; the night of the Carneian festival; My girls know his plan of attack."

Thea found her mouth curling into a sneer. It was so like Zarek to plan an assault on a night intended for wine and pleasure. Her sneer only deepened when she remembered that *she* was responsible for Zarek's targeting of Sparta.

However, now was her chance to restore balance.

"We must get a message to the Spartans," Thea said.

Genet shook her head. "No, my dear. It cannot be done. The risk of being caught on the way to Sparta is too great."

"It's a mission of great importance!" Thea snapped, clearly showing that she had zero patience for even the slightest disagreement. "We must tell General Aristo of the Eastern League. I have a friend on her way here who can do so."

"A friend? Why not *you?*"

"Because I will soon be following through on another objective."
Genet nodded.

Thea continued, "Aviva will go. She should be arriving any moment now."

"Very well," Genet said, her faraway eyes indicating that she very much doubted this "Aviva" would ever appear.

Thea went on, "I will write down the warning about the Carneian festival. The message must be passed on with an object."

"An object?" Genet's eyes briefly narrowed, concealing their brownness

"A *horn*," Thea stated, letting the word land hard so as to be remembered later. "This will ensure General Aristo trusts the source. We must tell him Zarek is going to attack Sparta, and precisely when and where. Aristo will take the necessary actions. I trust him."

Nodding as she took in the plan, Genet gave Thea a little smile. It was a subtle way of showing she could tell Thea had a special interest in this Spartan general.

A bit embarrassed, Thea rose to her feet. At long last, she felt her energy replenished. "Before Aviva arrives, I need Zarek's attack plans. Can you manage that?"

With a casual shrug, Genet nodded.

* * *

Zarek was in the map room, which was tucked in a dark corner of the southern wing of his castle. He was studying complex maps of the region illustrated by master artisans, the hands of whom would have trembled had they known how much brutal violence their work had enabled.

Zarek was finalizing his plans for conquering Sparta. His strategy was to have his fleet of ships wrap themselves around the curving body of the peninsula, and then hook upward, coming at Sparta from the south.

In the meantime, to create maximum terror, he would have another legion on horseback crush the Spartans from the north. Even if Sparta saw one offensive rolling in, it would be blindsided by the other.

He expected the sea fleet to be the stronger assault, though. It would have the advantage that had served Zarek so well for so long—the deadly liquid fire.

"Your Highness," said an aide near the room's open door.

Zarek turned.

"We've secured Mycenae."

It was all that Zarek could do to conceal his smile.

Another day, another city. Soon all of the peninsula would be his.

* * *

Teigra was digging a tunnel to the underground city by way of a well near the stables. The well was rumored to be out of use; and fortunately for Teigra, that was accurate. Otherwise, she would have drowned.

Teigra would've taken any risk in pursuit of the Golden Girdle. She had no official reason to enter the underground city, so her only option was to sneak in.

She was making exemplary progress with her tunnel, carving it deeper and deeper with a series of swift and lethal blade strokes.

Then, from above, she heard a blaring horn—the one that meant a slave or prisoner had escaped.

The last time this happened, Teigra had been the one to capture the fugitive. Her blood grew hot at another opportunity to hunt.

Teigra stealthily left her tunnel and approached a guard for news. "Three women have escaped," he replied. "One has stolen a horse."

Could they be Sondras? Teigra wondered. *What if one of them is the warrior who was after the Girdle?*

As Teigra got on a horse, she thought, *Nonsense. Chances are I'll never see her again.*

She charged ahead, doing her best to rapidly narrow the distance between herself and the high clay gate in the distance.

As she grew closer, Teigra saw what at first appeared to be a fellow soldier and skillful horseback rider. She admired the person's technique.

Then she realized that it was no soldier. The slave rags gave her away...

Letting out a giant shriek, Teigra commanded her horse to race toward Chloe. As she did so, Teigra threw a long, tight line of rope.

The rope nearly hooked itself around Chloe's torso, but missed by just an inch. Chloe's stolen horse carried her into a nearby patch of woods.

Teigra followed.

* * *

Aviva kept her body extremely still as she sat on the stool and let Genet cut her hair. As Genet snipped, she whispered, "Such lovely hair. I doubt the Gods wish for it to be wasted."

"It's for a good cause," said Thea, who was pacing nearby. "If she looks like a girl, she'll never get her message anywhere near Aristo."

Genet and Aviva both nodded, as Aviva's brown locks formed a sizable pile near the tub's drain.

* * *

Zarek relished the sensation of the hot steam entering his lungs, as well as the feeling of his pores opening up and shedding sweat. The poisons of the battlefield were at last seeping out of him.

Zarek was at a bathhouse an afternoon's ride from his castle. Surrounding him were his generals—and an assortment of beautiful women wearing nothing but the occasional cloth thrown over a shoulder. Many of the generals were chasing after the women, but Zarek was far more interested in talking about battle. The touch of a gorgeous woman couldn't get his blood pumping as much as the thought of conquering another village.

"To Corinth!" Zarek roared, raising a goblet of wine above his head.

Quick to catch on, his generals raised their own goblets. Those who didn't have goblets raised their fists.

"To Corinth!" all of them yelled in unison, their minds on fire with visions of their conquest.

"And to Mycenae!" Draco yelled, holding his goblet up as high as he could.

The men again toasted their cups, crying out the word "Mycenae!"

"Tripolis!" another man cried. Instantly, all of the other men echoed him in force: *"Tripolis!"*

Some of the generals were bored by this sudden celebration, preferring instead to receive the touches of the women—or, in some cases, the men or teenaged boys.

However, they were all shrewd enough to play along, toasting as loudly and merrily as they could manage.

Then, in a moment of pure predictability, Zarek raised his goblet above his head—this time standing—to toast the most important prize of all. "To *Sparta!*" he screamed, his shrill voice filling up the whole space, and turning the heads of the bathers in attendance.

Valuing their lives, the generals also erupted, over and over again: "*Sparta! Sparta! Sparta!*"

Invading Sparta would be a highly impressive military feat. From Zarek's perspective, it would also send a message to the rest of the world that he was a king to be reckoned with. To conquer the renowned city of Sparta would be to bring down a giant, the final battle before the peninsula would be his.

It would be something that could be done only by an even bigger giant.

Perhaps only by a God.

Zarek smiled at the thought. He enjoyed thinking of himself as a God. He loved the notion that others would think of him that way as well.

His pulse was soaring…until the messenger tapped his shoulder.

Looking at the boy's face, Zarek saw that something wasn't right.

"Your Highness…" The boy was so frightened that he barely had a voice.

"Speak, young man! I'm celebrating and relaxing!" Zarek shrieked.

"Um…" There was more dreadful hesitation from the messenger. The generals and concubines looked on with curiosity. "Three prisoners have escaped, Your Highness. Females, all of them. Your men have captured one, but two remain missing."

Zarek's eyes sharpened. He wasn't sure if this news truly troubled him, as he was preoccupied with grander matters. But he knew the escape indicated a weakness in his security, and that a forceful reaction was needed to maintain respect for his power.

"Who are they?" he asked, staring a hole through the trembling boy.

"I know the name of only one. They call her Thea. She is said to have entered your treasure room, and to have a talent for art—"

"I know!" Zarek shouted.

The boy's skin reddened, an indication of his rapidly beating heart.

"Be gone," Zarek hissed, slapping the boy's backside. The gesture drew laughter around the bath, but many of the generals coldly stared. They'd noticed that Zarek showed little interest in sensuality, and wondered what ill fantasies occupied his mind.

"I think," said Zarek, his voice low enough to sound introspective, yet loud enough to be widely heard, "that I have neglected my hobby. The theater room has no doubt grown cold by now. I wish to warm it up."

Draco gave Zarek a nod as he moved from the pool, ready and eager to carry out his leader's orders.

"I wish," Zarek continued, "to make an example of this wench slave."

Draco hurried over to his silk robe, got dressed, and made his way out of the bathhouse.

* * *

General Aristo was about to receive his own message.

While traveling on horseback through a great field amidst several hundred of his fellow Spartans, Aristo saw two small hooded figures riding in from the western woods. They were clearly civilians, but moved with an urgency.

As their hoods dropped, the riders were revealed to be boys— although Aristo's observant eye identified one to actually be female, and quite attractive. Aristo watched the short-haired girl trade fast words with one of his guards. He then saw the boy move closer to her side, no doubt to better serve as her protector.

After a minute, the guard turned to Aristo, made stark eye contact with him, and pointed.

What business could these strangers have with him?

The thinly-veiled female and her boy companion rode his way. For the sake of keeping his authority intact, Aristo had to remain aloof.

"General Aristo of the Eastern League?" Aviva asked.

"Yes," he answered, keeping a clear view of her in his peripheral vision.

She produced a tiny cloth scroll. His eyebrows lowered, and Aristo reached for it.

The words he read nearly halted his pulse.

Aristo's head began to swim. The note claimed it was from his Troublemaker, and stated in clear terms that Zarek was headed for Sparta!

He pocketed the note and gave the messenger a grave look.

"From whom did you get this message?"

Reaching into her pocket again, Aviva produced another object—hard, compact, and shiny.

A little horn.

Aristo felt his heart melt. He had to regain his concentration. These were not useful emotions for a warrior.

No doubt the scroll had been authentic. How would anyone else know of his relationship with her?

He took the horn from the messenger.

"We have to go back to our King!" he shouted, his voice deep and commanding.

At once, the hundreds of horses changed their course.

CHAPTER 34

WAR

Lightning struck the sky like a mad white whip. The sound of thunder was like the heavens crashing to earth.

But in spite of the weather, the theater room was reopened.

Chloe's pulse was also thundering. The sudden heat generated by the hundreds of slaves and prisoners in the audience made her feel like she would throw up. But she'd received so little bread and water since arriving three days earlier that she wouldn't have been able to vomit if she'd tried.

After being dropped on the hard wooden stage, Chloe saw two other prisoners. One was the guard who'd been on duty during her escape. The young man had clearly never seen the horrors of this room before—the blood-stained curtains, the shackled audience members—and was shaking like a fish scooped out of the ocean. The other prisoner also appeared to be a former guard. Chloe had no idea what his "crime" was.

The younger guard looked at Chloe. But when Zarek entered wearing a thick velvety gown and a glistening ruby-and-emerald crown, all eyes turned to him.

"Who's this?" he asked a torturer, aiming a chubby, crusty finger at Chloe.

Chloe's throat was closing. Apparently, there'd be no preambles to this show.

"One of the wenches who escaped!" the torturer proclaimed.

Chloe observed that the man had been brainwashed.

Nodding, Zarek said, "I'll get to her in a moment."

His eyes scanned the room's assortment of brutal weapons until they settled on a large, round cage with a pacing lion. The lion kept sticking its tongue out and licking its nose.

Zarek pointed at the young guard. "Throw him in there!" Zarek shouted at the torturer.

The King then gave the audience a glance.

All of them pretended to cheer, fervently.

It happened so quickly that Chloe had no chance to look away. The smiling torturer lifted the guard off the ground and tossed him, screaming, into the lion's cage. Within moments, the bars of the cage were drenched in blood.

Chloe hoped to die that quickly.

But when Zarek commanded Zosimos and the torturers to lay her out on a metal table, she knew that wouldn't be her fate.

Zarek leaned so close that Chloe could smell his breath. She briefly thought of biting his neck.

"Where are your two companions?" he asked. "And what did you have planned when you escaped?"

She looked away from him, her mouth tightly closed.

Nodding, he held up a long nail in one hand and a mallet in the other. "All right, then," he said. "I'll make sure your pain is equal to your silence."

Through a window high behind the audience was an explosion of lightning. A moment later, the entire theater room shook with thunder.

Chloe noticed that one of the torturers, who was now holding her legs down, was the same female who had flung a rope around her torso.

* * *

To her great surprise, there was a strange softness that Teigra was feeling for Chloe. She took care to keep her expression hard, knowing that Zarek might decide to torture her next.

Why am I feeling a single thing for this girl who'd almost outrun me? Teigra wondered.

Teigra lacked the experience to understand these emotions. Rather than try to deal with them, she let go of Chloe's legs and walked away.

* * *

"Yes, indeed!" Zarek yelled from behind Teigra, glorying in the spectacle of the young guard who'd been eaten and the soon-to-be-dead Chloe. "Play with *him!* There's plenty to go around!"

Zarek was referring to the third "star" of the show—the other former guard, who was tightly tied to a stiff wooden post. Teigra knew his crime was failing to capture any of the escapees. Zarek assumed she'd inflict violence on him.

With a harsh glare in her eye, Teigra walked over to the guard and punched him brutally in the midsection. While everyone's attention was focused on his pained coughing, Teigra stealthily withdrew a knife from her boot...and slipped it into the hands tied behind his back.

No one noticed.

"Good luck," she whispered, coldly.

Teigra then left the theater room. She no longer had the stomach to be part of it.

* * *

Niko was on his way to the castle. He was coming from a meeting in the marketplace with a woman in her fifties who had long white hair woven with a lovely dash of red. A former concubine and now a successful merchant, she quietly spoke to Niko while molding a clay pot. Niko thanked her, patted her arm, and made his exit.

As he did so, a pair of eyes watched him from the trees near the woman's shop and wondered about his dealings with Photina's mother.

* * *

Only when she reached the vacant castle garden did Teigra allow her feelings to resurface.

She unleashed a few tiny sobs. Not since she was an infant had Teigra experienced such unguarded emotion.

She had no clue what it meant, and she had no chance to analyze the situation; for while her head was hanging low, she walked right into Niko.

"Teigra!" he said, unable to mask his sheer delight. "How wonderful to run into you. But shouldn't you be working?"

"They're well equipped," she muttered. Although her exterior was flat and cold, she felt a ripple of heat. Pleasurable heat.

She was happy to have bumped into him.

What's going on with me? she asked herself. *First the ankle knife slipped to a prisoner, and now affection for this man?*

"You seem troubled," Niko said. "Care to speak about it?"

Looking down again, she shook her head. Then, surprising both Niko and herself, she said, "Meet me at my quarters. Midnight."

Teigra walked away without another word.

As Niko watched her go, he sensed something was off. It wasn't only Teigra's unusual behavior, but something else that he couldn't quite put his finger on.

Niko's radar was highly sensitive. There was a little slave boy hiding in the bushes who was listening to every word the pair exchanged.

* * *

When midnight came, Niko was right on time. From the look in his eyes, he was impressed by the elegance of Teigra's quarters. To lessen the tension, he spoke about work: "How long are you planning to stay with Zarek?" he asked.

She shrugged. "Until the time is right."

"Right for what?"

"To leave."

They traded glances. He rushed to her. He kissed her.

They kissed for a long while.

Eventually she pulled away, but smiled a little as she did so. "Enough for now," she said, her breath quickly leaving her body.

"But you invited me..." Niko said, clearly eager.

"Thank you for coming," Teigra replied, glancing at the door, indicating that it was time for him to go. "I wish to take it slow."

Nodding, Niko proceeded to exit. He thought to tell her about his afternoon meeting at the marketplace, and the strange feeling he had when they made their midnight plan, but he decided not to.

As Niko exited, the little slave boy watched him from the corridor.

* * *

The slave boy hurried to Zosimos' home. Zosimos knew who it was from the light-knuckled knock on the door. Zosimos didn't even have to say a word. He simply knelt down before the child to receive the inevitable message.

Eagerly, the boy whispered words into the older man's ear.

Zosimos nodded.

He then said, "So, she must be alive..."

* * *

Aristo dramatically cleared his throat.

"Listen now!" he roared to over one thousand of his men, the sound of his words echoing off the walls of the great hall in which they were gathered. "We have important information. We intend to use it two short days from now—to crush the Argives before they have another *thought* about crushing us!"

The men who didn't cheer nodded their heads.

"Between the message I received and the added facts we've gathered," Aristo continued, "we have firm knowledge of three pursuits from Zarek. Two are by land and one by sea."

The men were focused, and none of them dared risk missing a single detail.

Aristo went on, "We shall handle these weaklings in a way that is noble. This means that we slay none of their children. We harm none of their wives. We do not set fires in their cities. Rather..."

Every ear was listening, the crowd swelling with tension.

"...we attack their plan!"

More cheers. More nods. Some stomping of feet.

Unrolling a great map on the wall, Aristo said, "Moreover, we shall do so after they enter our terrain..."

* * *

Thea's sleep had been ruled by nightmares about Aviva failing to successfully deliver the message to Aristo. What if someone along her path saw through her disguise and slew her? She also had nightmares about Chloe in the theater room. News of Chloe's capture had quickly traveled to Genet's home.

Thea's mind had become a sea of sadness. She had to get to the Girdle—and fast.

Genet stood before Thea's bed. She was stunning.

Her outfit was somehow loose-fitting and tight at the same time. No doubt she'd just finished resting—or perhaps she was preparing to.

In any case, Genet's beauty sent a shot of envy through Thea's body. It was kind of her to serve as Thea's host, but being exposed to such beauty at a time like this was overwhelming.

Regardless, Thea was glad for Genet's visit, for she had a plan to discuss.

"How are you today?" Genet asked, smiling just a touch, in light of the recent news about Chloe.

Thea couldn't work up an answer. Instead, knowing how quickly she had to act, she sat up and said four terse, loaded words:

"I need your help."

"I'm afraid," Genet said, "my help has reached its limit. Zarek's making a play for Sparta. He'll soon control all the lands of our people. Unless your Spartans help us, he's not an enemy we can challenge."

Genet was eloquent for a concubine, Thea thought. She had a good mind for argument, and a strong ability to sense the general nature of Thea's inquiry.

Regardless, Thea said, "You have to, Genet."

"Thea, we're friends. I enjoy our friendship. But it cannot be based on risk."

"Just one last thing—"

"No."

"Can I at least explain?"

Resting her hands on her waist, Genet said, "I'll listen, but that doesn't mean I'm agreeing to anything."

Quietly, not wanting to seem a burden, Melia slipped her way out of the room.

"You need to help me get to the castle," said Thea, "so I can seize the Golden Girdle and slay Zarek."

"Now I *know* I'm not agreeing," Genet said, her voice tight with gravity.

"Look," said Thea. Then she moved her hand to the back of her hair and swept it up, revealing her unique branding—a precise match of the symbol on the Golden Girdle.

Genet's brown eyes locked themselves on its singular beauty.

"When did you get that?" Genet asked.

Thea let her hair drop back. "When I was an infant," she said. "According to the one they call Seema, I am destined for greatness."

Genet looked into Thea's tired eyes, clearly failing to see how that was possible.

"If I put on the Girdle," Thea continued, "I can seize my destiny and become a lethal opponent to the King. But first I have to *get* to it."

Still firm, Genet said, "Thea, whatever it is you are asking, I advise you to take it up with Melia. I simply cannot tolerate any more risk for my girls or myself. Do you understand?"

Thea nodded. Melia made her way into the room as Genet left. "Melia, my dearest, I will tell you my plan and what I need you to do." Melia nodded. "Once you have done your part, you shall immediately leave for Mount Spiro and the safety of Seema's cave."

* * *

With Zosimos at his side, Zarek studied his temple, which was near completion.

"A masterpiece," Zarek declared. "These artisans have outdone their savage natures."

"It is indeed worthy of you, King Zarek," Zosimos replied.

Zarek nodded, his eyes soaking up the splendor. He was impressed with the color, the balance, and the intelligence that shone in the design elements.

"Everything is coming together," Zarek said. "My men shall soon descend upon Sparta like a rain of fire."

Zosimos grinned in agreement. He considered telling Zarek of his recent discovery, but decided not to spoil his mood.

"Another day and a half," Zarek went on, "and I'll command the Spartans." Smiling, Zarek turned to walk away.

"Where shall I send these artists when they're done?" Zosimos asked, his thumb aimed at the temple workers.

Without turning, Zarek responded, "To their deaths, of course."

* * *

Teigra was in a shop near the temple when she saw Zarek on his way back home. She could glimpse him for only a moment, for her attention was on the short man she was repeatedly slapping with her palms.

He kept muttering words of protest, but they made little sense coming out of his aching, pathetic mouth.

Teigra continued to whack him, clean and hard.

She hated doing it, but told herself the job was almost over. In another day, there'd be no more tax collecting. Zarek would have control of Sparta, and would soon be finding new inspiration for his madness.

She wanted nothing more to do with it. She had to leave. She wished not only to be rid of Zarek, but to flee Niko and the strange feelings he was eliciting.

She'd miss her comfortable quarters, but would welcome the familiarity of a wandering life. While she'd live in fear, at least she wouldn't disapprove of herself.

Teigra slapped the debtor in the jaw again. He fell. Her fellow Argive tax collector kicked the poor man's ribs, making Teigra wince.

The Golden Girdle flashed within Teigra's thoughts. That would be her final errand.

Once she finished tunneling her way beneath the castle grounds, it would be hers.

* * *

That night, the Argives fell.

By sea, several thousand of them charged the Southern coast, their grand ships packed tight with liquid fire. While the Spartans had a formidable reputation as land soldiers, their naval fleet was laughable, mostly consisting of modest ships and rowboats.

The Argives expected to smash through it quickly and easily.

As their mighty vessels drew closer to the coast, shrieks of orange exploded in the thick of the night.

Throats were opened. Hearts were jabbed. Eyeballs were turned into liquid.

Many died upon the grand ships before they figured out what was happening.

The Spartans hammered them with arrows, and the tips of those arrows were ignited with fire.

It wasn't liquid fire, but was just as dangerous. Once enough fire reached an Argive ship, the stored liquid fire would ignite, and the ship would erupt in cataclysmic blasts of flames.

The Argive sailors panicked and tried to reverse their course.

However, as more arrows fell, their fiery fate was sealed.

* * *

Meanwhile, by land, two thousand Spartan soldiers charged the six thousand approaching Argives.

The Argives were bold in their response. They hit the Spartans with swords, arrows, whips, and chains.

They took off Spartan heads and left cracks in Spartan spines.

Aristo was among these Spartans. With a voice unable to prevent itself from cracking, he yelled for his men to retreat.

Their horses' hooves charged like a hurricane across the ground, and the Spartans made their way toward a vast, rocky enclave in the forest's eastern corner.

There were two walls of parallel rock. The Spartans poured into this passageway like wine into a goblet...and ran out the other side just as swiftly.

The Argives were hot on the Spartans' heels. But when they entered the enclave, they found that its exit had been suddenly sealed off with boulders.

More boulders soon fell from above, smashing open the heads of the men and destroying the bodies of their horses.

It was as though heaven had opened and unleashed a storm. The Argives who tried to turn around were met with death by boulder. Others perished by slung arrows and thrown blades, but it was the stones that drew most of the blood.

On the other side of the now-sealed corridor, Aristo heartily laughed. He'd orchestrated false retreats before, but never had one provided him with so much joy.

* * *

Further to the north, half a day's travel from Sparta, seven thousand Argive soldiers were asleep in thin, pitched tents.

They remained asleep as their horses wandered away.

The animals had been released by the hands of tiptoeing Spartans, the smiles of whom brightly shone in the dark night as they unlatched the fence that was intended to keep the animals in place.

Without horses, there would be no escaping.

As the men slept, the Spartans descended with great force. Crackling torches were thrown at their tents. Eight-foot lances were thrust into sleeping lungs.

The men woke confused, terrified, and scrambling.

Hundreds of them tried to run off on foot, only to find spears in their backs or knives in their chests.

To attack men as they slept was an uncommon form of brutality. But these were *Zarek's* men…and no women or children were hurt.

CHAPTER 35

THE CASTLE

Melia and a well-built slave named Baako worked swiftly just outside of Genet's home, enclosing Thea's body within the bottom half of a stout, square cart.

Less than an hour later, Melia and Baako made their way down a hallway on the castle's ground floor.

Baako pushed Melia's cart, as she occasionally glanced up at him. His height could shame many shacks in the nearby villages. He'd been told to push without saying a word, using his sharp, mean eyes for intimidation.

They were to wheel Thea to the castle's underground, and tell the men guarding the valuables room that they had to drop off a vase.

They actually had a vase—a beautiful item stolen from a private living room within the castle mere hours earlier. It looked quite fine and rare, and caught a good amount of light as it sat, still and noble, atop the racing cart.

Melia was heavily breathing and sweating from nervousness over the incredibly risky plan. She had to still herself. It wasn't sexy to perspire, and she'd need her feminine appeal to get past these guards.

As she and Baako made their way into the underground section, Melia did her best to look like someone who knew exactly what she was doing. Not only would the guards pose a challenge, but many other pairs of eyes—official and civilian—would land on them throughout their walk.

Silently, she cursed Thea for putting her up to this. On the other hand, if Seema's prophecy were true, then Melia would be doing the most important work of her life.

She could only pray for a good result.

The eyes of the two guards went hard as Melia's servant wheeled the cart to the grand metal door. The door's burgundy color suggested that regal items were stored behind it.

"What is this?" asked the first guard, staring a hole through Melia.

"A vase," she smiled, touching her hair. She was pleased to find that it was only slightly moist. "You know what that is, don't you?"

The question was meant to be flirtatious, but the two guards weren't taking the bait.

The second guard sneered, "We got no word of a vase. Who sent you?"

"Zarek?" said Melia, forming the word as a question—as though *she* were the one who was surprised. "It was very important to him that it arrive tonight."

After trading irritated looks, the guards both shook their heads.

"We have to run this by our superior," the first one said, beginning to step away.

Baako did his best to stare the guard down, but it wasn't stopping him from moving.

"Um," Melia said, preserving a tone that was as light as possible, "I don't think Zarek wishes to be woken."

These words stopped the guard from moving.

"Quite a cranky sleeper," Melia winked. "I've seen it firsthand."

Now the guards were pausing—and stuck.

Sounding chirpy, Melia went on, "Look, I'm not here to take. I'm here to give. If I made an error, you can smash the silly thing in the morning."

She could see by the men's expressions that they were calming.

After a miniature eternity passed, the first one opened the door and said, "Okay, bring it in. But be fast."

As Baako and Melia entered the long hallway leading to the treasures, they left the cart in the center of the room, and made their way out to the impatient guards.

* * *

Once Thea heard the door close, she moved. Her fingers started prying open the door to the cart, while she took care not to lose her grip on the small ax in her right hand. There'd been no time for rehearsal, so it took her a while to figure out how to wrench the damned thing open.

Once she managed it, she remained in blackness. The valuables room was a deep, thick murk.

Thea rubbed her eyes, trying to adjust to the dark as quickly as possible, then crawled out of the cart. The vase started wobbling.

Thea's heart almost exploded; but the vase settled. Her sight was improving, and the room looked grayish instead of utterly black.

Where was the Golden Girdle? she wondered.

Thea crawled, figuring that staying in contact with the ground would prevent her from accidentally walking into a wall. She began to make out the shapes of things. According to the map she'd studied, she had to dig out through the room's northern wall. She now had to use her internal compass to—

The vase shattered against the sandy floor!

Thea heard a steel key go into the slot. The guards were opening the door.

She considered what was in her left pocket—a last request that Genet had granted her. It was a small ceramic tube carrying a lethal dose of poison. She planned to swallow it if the Golden Girdle didn't do what Seema had promised.

But now the guards were a moment from entering. Thea agonized to think that she'd never even get to try it out.

At that moment, she saw the Girdle! It was just ten feet away.

The door swept open, bringing in a harsh burst of light.

There was the Girdle, golden and regal. She kept on crawling.

The guards started running.

Thea stood up and ran to the Girdle.

* * *

Aristo was so charged up that he could barely contain himself. It was mere days earlier when he'd learned of Zarek's plans for invasion. Not only had his men warded off the attacks, but they'd sliced through Zarek's army like a blade through butter.

Sparta could now overtake Zarek's kingdom!

Aristo had to conceal his excitement. After all, he was a general, and he couldn't appear too eager. However, his words came out fast when he ordered his troops to press on to the north.

There would be no sleep for them.

They would arrive at Zarek's castle with the sun's rays.

Although he shared his thoughts with no one, Aristo was intent on tracking down and rescuing his Troublemaker.

* * *

It was near dawn when Zarek received the news about his army's swift and total demise. The word came from a wounded, bloody soldier who'd successfully fled from one of the Spartans' land attacks. The soldier had scrapes on his face and chest, the work of arrows that had grazed him.

Zarek was examining his nearly-completed temple. When the awful news reached his ears, he was overtaken by shock. Even though he could still see and hear, he felt blind and deaf.

For his entire life he'd been accustomed to the comforts and joys of power. All of that was about to end. He still had numerous guards, and a beautiful kingdom with great halls to roam. But it wouldn't be long before the Spartan fighters descended upon his home.

The soldier shook in Zarek's presence, awaiting his own death.

Somehow, Zarek felt no need to inflict harm upon the young man. He touched his arm and said two words that had never left his lips before: "Thank you."

That was it. The young soldier, having been spared, walked away.

Then a sharp knife entered the rear of his right lung.

It had been thrown by Zarek, its trajectory targeted and clean.

Zarek looked at his temple. *Meaningless*, he thought. *A structure erected in honor of a falling king.* He hated his life. He hated himself.

More than anything else, he hated whatever traitor had warned the Spartans.

"Sire?"

The voice belonged to Zosimos. Zarek looked up at his old ally, sneering. "Yes?" he asked.

"What is our plan now?"

Zarek stared hard at Zosimos. "Do you deem me a magician?" he spat.

"No, Sire. Just a wise and capable leader."

Zarek calmed a bit and nodded. "I will tell you when I know," he replied.

Zosimos nodded. He wondered if he should share with the King what the slave boy had told him—that Photina was indeed alive. He also wondered if it was important to let the King know that Niko and Teigra were privately seeing each other.

Zosimos considered, and then sealed his lips, realizing a pair of overwhelming realities.

First, Zarek seemed incapable of absorbing any information in a meaningful way.

Second, as a result of losing his army, Zarek could no longer be thought of as a true king.

"Thank you, Sire." Zosimos bowed his head and hurried on his way.

* * *

In a vast field not far from the castle, Draco and one hundred or so of his surviving soldiers walked—heads hanging low in shame—back to the castle and their king. A few of them rode horses, but Draco was not one of them. His horse had been slain in battle, along with many others. He knew that he could justify taking a horse from a lower-ranked man, but he did not care to exercise that power.

He preferred to travel slowly.

The closer he got to his destination, the more clearly he realized something: Reporting back to Zarek would be deadly.

Zarek wouldn't tolerate the sight of Draco and his defeated men. It was almost certain he'd make a ghastly display of killing them all. He might even accuse them of being the ones who tipped off the Spartans.

"Stop," Draco said.

His men did not hesitate. They all ceased to move.

"We will not report back to our king," Draco declared, causing many of the men to exhale with relief.

"We will instead," Draco went on, "rob the castle of treasure, food, and other supplies for survival. We shall do so swiftly, before the rise of another sun. We shall then disappear from Zarek's world for good."

Draco found himself greeted by nods and smiles. One young man spoke up as they all took in the order: "But Draco," he asked, "where exactly shall we go?"

"I think that it is time to pay a visit to my brother."

* * *

The two guards were seconds away from entering the treasure room. Despite their presence, Thea was too close to the Girdle to resist it. She had to *somehow* put it on.

So she lifted it. It was, to her shock, far lighter than it looked.

Footsteps fell close behind her.

As Thea donned the Girdle, the beam of light through the door grew larger, allowing Thea to see herself. No longer were there any cuts or scars on her flesh.

It was a miracle. All her wounds, small and large, had been healed in seconds.

Thinking fast, Thea silently rolled into a dark corner. She held her breath and waited for the guards to leave.

After several agonizing moments, one said to the other, "Must have been a rodent." The two walked out.

Only once the door was closed and locked did Thea breathe.

She was now clear to begin the second part of her plan: the digging.

Holding the ax, she began to feel around the still-dark northern wall. It was made of very thick dirt, and it could easily take two days to dig herself out.

No matter, she thought. *I have enough food in my pockets to last that long.*

Thea's hand landed on a spot that was somewhat weaker than the rest of the dirt wall. It wasn't much of an opening, but enough to start digging.

She struck the wall with the ax. A little dirt fell away.

She struck it again—and the wall began to crumble...

* * *

Six hours later, Teigra put down the torch in her tunnel and took a break from her furious digging.

Suddenly, her whole body tensed. There seemed to be *motion* on the other side of her tunnel's wall. Was someone there?

It seemed impossible. What person could reside within the dirt? She decided it was probably a ferret or some other underground creature.

Nonetheless, she took a step away from the wall, watched, and waited.

* * *

Thea continued digging. Her tunnel, unlike Teigra's, was extremely narrow, and allowed her no room to stand. Over and over again, she struck the dirt with her ax.

In time, it fell away as though it were made of water.

Before her stood a familiar-looking girl holding a torch. Hard face. Strong eyes.

It was that lethal woman from the treasure room.

She was staring directly at Thea's Girdle.

* * *

Zosimos did his best to keep up as Zarek strode to the temple wearing his most jewel-encrusted crown. Several guards surrounded them.

"Your Majesty," Zosimos said, trying to find the right words, "is it truly wise for you to be out and about right now?"

Zarek didn't look at Zosimos, and yet Zosimos detected the rage in the King's eyes. "Are you calling me *unwise*, Zosimos?"

Gulping, Zosimos said, "Well, the Spartans are on the way, Your Majesty..."

"The Spartans cannot touch me!" Zarek shrieked, sending a jolt of shock through Zosimos' body.

"You're correct, Your Highness. Most correct."

They walked to the nearly-finished temple. The statue of Zarek was almost fully erected, and hung at an angle from two strong ropes tied to a pair of beams.

Suddenly, Zosimos had an epiphany. The King was intent on raising his statue before the Spartans struck.

Realizing the madness of Zarek's plan, Zosimos slowed his step. He allowed the guards surrounding them to grow closer to Zarek.

He then stopped walking altogether, turned around, and ran back to the castle.

Zosimos' departure didn't even register to Zarek. All he could think about was his statue.

* * *

Thea's ax clanked against Teigra's sword.

Teigra stuck her sword at Thea's ribs.

Thea skipped backward, then swept her calf against Teigra's leg, knocking Teigra over.

The moment Teigra fell, she snapped back onto her feet, swinging her sword at Thea's face.

Thea quickly ducked. She felt the sword tickle her hair. Rather than stand back up, Thea swiped her ax at Teigra's belly, slicing open its flesh.

The wound wasn't deep, and Teigra didn't even react. She chopped her sword downward. Thea blocked it with her ax.

Teigra swiped her sword from the right. Again, she met the steel of Thea's ax.

Thea quickly circled to Teigra's rear, then smashed the ax at her back. Teigra turned around at the last second and blocked the blow with her sword, then swiped upward, diagonally, toward Thea's face.

Spinning in circles, Thea gained a little distance from Teigra. She took a silent breath, then rushed at Teigra with her ax above her head.

Teigra moved out of the way and tried to trip Thea. But when Thea felt the touch of Teigra's leg, she bent her own leg and brought them both to the dirt-covered ground.

The two girls jumped back up, facing each other.

Again, they charged, but by now it was clear that landing a clean blow was nearly impossible. They were so evenly matched that it seemed the conclusion of the battle would depend on which of them ran out of energy first.

As the duo fought, each was shocked by the quickness and agility of the other. Except for the belly strike, every time Thea thought her ax was about to connect with Teigra's flesh, Teigra would move out of the way and Thea would find herself connecting with only air.

Who are you? Thea wondered, looking at this familiar stranger. *Why do I feel so odd in the presence of this woman?*

Thea stepped quickly to the right, circling Teigra's body so she could put her in a headlock and snap her neck. Achieving the headlock wasn't difficult. But before she could follow through with the snap, Thea noticed something: her own tattoo.

It was located on the back of Teigra's neck.

Impossible! Thea thought. In shock, she loosened her hold.

Teigra seized the opportunity, spinning hard toward Thea and slicing her shoulder with her sword.

Thea winced as she bled. But hardly any blood flowed...for her wound closed just a moment after it appeared.

Not only was the Girdle giving Thea more stamina, it was making her impervious to wounds!

Wholly shocked, Teigra took a large step backward. Thea ran toward Teigra, swinging the ax.

Teigra lifted her foot and kicked Thea in the stomach. Thea coughed and bent at the waist, giving Teigra a chance to swing her sword down into her wrist.

Remembering Seema's prophecy, Thea dropped her ax.

Teigra lifted her sword above her head, intent upon stabbing Thea...but Thea clapped her hands together around the blade, prior to impact. Thea then swung to the left, removing the sword from Teigra's grasp, and turned it back on her.

But Thea couldn't stab this woman. She couldn't end the life of her twin sister, the woman who shared her mark, and who presented so many mysterious questions.

"Who *are* you? What's your name?" Thea asked.

Before Thea got the last word out, Teigra ran. She fled not out of fear, but sheer strategy. She reasoned there was no way she could defeat her opponent, much less seize the Girdle, under these conditions.

So Teigra decided to retreat and give herself time to make a new plan.

Alone, and with sword in hand, Thea decided it was time for the next phase of her mission—which was to cause a great commotion.

Looking up, she saw a circle of light. It was the opening of a well.

Thea slid Teigra's sword between the Girdle and her flesh. She then dug her fingers into the rocky wall and began to climb.

* * *

After reaching the temple, Zarek finally noticed the absence of Zosimos. He had been far too focused on carrying out an impromptu "ceremony." The King looked out over a crowd of hundreds of villagers he'd forced to follow him into the temple. They were all in a state of utter confusion.

"You shall forget any notion of *Gods!*" he screamed. "You shall wipe from your mind thoughts of worshiping any entity whatsoever... who is not *me!*"

Zarek's guards traded subtle glances. They silently acknowledged that the King had finally lost what was left of his mind.

* * *

In the process of gathering his belongings, Zosimos came to realize what most desperate people do: very few material things in life are of true importance. He pocketed a ring that his dear mother had given him as a boy, several bags of gold and silver coins, and a few items of clothing.

Then he made his way into the forest.

While racing through the foliage, Zosimos knew that a Spartan warrior or a Zarek loyalist could appear and snap his head from his neck. But he reasoned that risk was preferable to staying with Zarek.

Sunlight flickered through the trees. If he could clear the forest, he had a chance.

He just had to be fast and smart.

* * *

Thea crawled out of the well. Throwing her torch on a marketplace hut, she created a great blaze.

Scores of people came running to contain the spreading fire. Thea used the distraction to slip back into the castle. She found a prison guard who proved quite easy to slay, and took his keys. With them, she began opening the door to every cage she could find.

Thieves, murderers, and innocent people poured out of their cells. So did Sondras and other Amazons.

One dark-skinned man with a missing eye placed a crusty hand on Thea's shoulder. "You are a Goddess," he said.

She shook her head. "Just a warrior," she replied.

Continuing to open cells, Thea yelled, "Get out! Everyone move! *You're free!*

* * *

Zarek's grand speech was interrupted by the sound of horns.

Could that be what it sounded like? he thought. *Were prisoners escaping?*

"What is that?" Zarek asked the guard nearest him. Before the soldier could even open his mouth, a local shopkeeper ran in, overweight and out of breath. "Your Majesty," he exclaimed, "there is havoc at the castle!"

"What kind?" Zarek sneered. "Spartans?"

The shopkeeper shook his head. "The prison cell doors are opening!"

"Well, they do not open by themselves, you fool! *What is going on?*"

Zarek dispatched his palace security to the castle but kept his personal guards.

These men were the best trained and best paid in the kingdom. Zarek reserved their use for emergencies; and his current predicament fit the bill.

Sixty of his top personal guards now surrounded their king. None of them looked at him, as they were all too busy watching for signs of danger.

Meanwhile, the hundreds of people brought to the temple remained glued to their seats. Zarek informed them that this was a mere interruption, and the holy ceremony would commence in minutes.

In other words, Zarek lied.

* * *

Outside of the castle, as fire and smoke rose to the sky, Thea's eyes fell on Bethany, an Amazonian concubine. "Have you any news of Zarek?" Thea asked.

"He's still alive," Bethany replied.

"I know. But where? In his chambers?"

Bethany shook her head. "The temple," she said. "Some kind of ceremony."

"Thank you," Thea answered. Thinking fast, she ran for a horse.

But before Thea left, she threw the prison cell keys into the nearby flames. The act of lighting fires went a long way toward amplifying the chaos, and this gave Thea no small amount of pleasure.

At the stables, Thea unsheathed her sword and looked around. Nox was nearby; she could *feel* it. It was a shame that she lacked her horn, but she made do with what she had.

Thea stuck her fingers in her mouth...and tried to whistle.

As always, nothing close to a whistle came out, just a near-silent, impotent sound. Thea's shoulders dropped. She tried again. Same thing: a hiss of breath where a whistle belonged.

Yet, from the stables, a startling sound emerged—a horse's hooves beating against the wall!

Over and over again, they *pounded.* Thea's heart leaped. The pounding grew more and more intense, until a stable wall split open and dozens of horses poured out.

Leading the escape was Nox.

A smile lit Thea's face. Nox jumped over the fence and raced to greet her.

* * *

As Zarek stayed huddled amidst his personal guards, one of them finally turned to him and asked, "Your Majesty, are we not vulnerable in this position?"

"*I'm* not," Zarek said. "I have *you!*"

"Yes, but—"

"But nothing!" the King yelled. "You speak when spoken to! Do you understand?"

The guard automatically nodded, but realized he was obeying out of sheer habit. The truth was that this king was clinging to the final remnants of his power.

The harsh reality was that no one would object to Zarek's death.

* * *

Teigra, like Zosimos, was in her quarters getting ready to flee the castle grounds. She sheathed another sword along her right leg. Losing her first sword made her blood boil. But with a long journey ahead, any weapon was better than none.

As Teigra packed, she heard a strange sound. It stood apart from the general commotion of people.

Curious, she looked out the window...and saw Niko. He was surrounded by four of Zarek's guards. Two were holding him, and the other two were brutalizing him with punches.

He'd already been badly beaten.

Without a second thought, Teigra leaped out of the window and ran.

She landed in front of the men. As they turned, she swung her fist. She caught the first one in the jaw, sending him to the ground.

Another lunged at her. She spun and kicked him in the stomach. Bending over, he puked on Teigra's shoes. Knee springing upward, Teigra struck him in the jaw and knocked him out.

The other two men let Niko go. Spitting teeth, the former general fell.

One man swung a blade at Teigra. She clapped her hands together, catching the steel, and twisted left, then right.

The first man she hit got back up. He and the other guard who'd held Niko charged her.

Teigra twirled in circles. Her left leg swept the first one's calf, knocking him over again. Still spinning, her right leg crunched the second man's waist. The sword between her palms drew blood.

The one with the cracked waist-bone screamed and swung a fist at her. She ducked, and he punched air.

Teigra sprang back up and head-butted him. Hot blood ran down his face.

Niko abruptly rose and locked the bleeding man in a stranglehold.

The guard whose sword Teigra was holding pushed forward. She let out a groan and pushed him backward, letting his blade further cut her palms. She backed him up toward a thorn bush. He looked behind him, saw what was coming, and tried to push back.

Teigra let out a roar and dug her feet hard into the dirt. She then sprang her body forward, as though taking flight. The guard lost his balance and fell into the thorn bush. He let out a cry as the thorns punctured his skin. Teigra took the opportunity to snatch the sword from his grip.

Just as she turned, the other man lunged. Teigra slit his throat.

Releasing his stranglehold, Niko sawed the eyes of the man he'd been holding with his own sword. Then Teigra lanced the man's heart.

The remaining man in the thorn bush cried. Heartless about his pain, Teigra turned and took aim. She glanced at Niko, and he nodded.

Teigra stuck the sword in the man's right lung.

He cried no more.

As Teigra finally exhaled, Niko came up beside her. "Good timing," he said.

She gave him a grim smile.

"It's not safe for us here anymore," Niko said. "We must leave."

He held out a hand. She took it and squeezed. "I still have business. But go. I will see you another day."

Niko stared into her eyes. He saw that she would not be swayed. "Be safe," he said. He leaned out and kissed her.

She kissed him back before vanishing into the crowd.

* * *

Teigra tore through the masses. People ran in all directions, some carrying weapons to defend themselves, others grabbing sacks of food stolen from shops.

Zarek's kingdom was crumbling. Chaos spread like hungry fire.

Teigra ran into an alleyway, sought a ladder, and climbed to the roof of a ceramic shop. She knew that few others would dare travel by rooftop; and by leaping from one structure to another, she'd soon have a view of the whole area.

Teigra's strategy paid off. In minutes, something caught her attention. It was a horse of impressive muscle and speed racing toward the temple. Most important was its rider: *Her!*

Teigra had found her target: the one with the Girdle around her waist.

Without a thought, Teigra *dove.*

She flew through the air—and landed on top of Thea.

Thea was smashed off Nox and into the dirt. Teigra struck her with both fists, her teeth bare, letting out growls.

Thea rolled her over and got on top. Teigra spiked her sword's tip into Thea's side.

Hissing, Thea stood up.

Then, with great restraint, she backed away.

"How'd you get that mark?" Thea wheezed.

Teigra sat up and managed a better grip on her sword. She struggled to stand, then ran at Thea.

As she neared her opponent, Teigra saw something strange: There was no blood! It was as if she hadn't stabbed her.

Teigra swung her sword. Thea ducked and sprang right. Teigra stalked her, swinging harder. Thea unsheathed her own sword and swiped it at Teigra.

Metal hit metal.

"You're my sister," Thea breathed. "We both have that mark!"

Teigra coughed out disbelief. "I have no sister, no family. *Don't think you can trick me!*"

Thea swung. Teigra swung back. Thea ducked. Teigra leaped. Thea swung again.

Teigra growled. Thea hissed.

Spinning, Thea grazed Teigra with her sword.

Scowling, Teigra charged Thea, but Thea leaped to one side. She then stepped forward, jumping behind Teigra. She had to keep fighting.

Thea tried to cut Teigra's back.

Teigra whipped around and slashed her sword at Thea. She struck only metal.

Thea danced to her right and swung at Teigra's neck.

Teigra bent backward, ducked low, and charged with her blade out.

Thea ran backward...and crashed into a homeless beggar. The beggar yelled, "Watch it!"

Thea turned to look at him, and Teigra took advantage of the opening by sprinting at Thea...and laying her hands on the Girdle.

The slashes in Teigra's palms closed.

Thea saw what happened and looked up at Teigra. They both *froze.* Teigra's eyes grew wide and she backed away.

Thea reached out and slashed Teigra's forearm.

Again, Teigra rushed Thea and touched the Girdle. Her forearm healed.

The sisters stared at each other, wide-eyed.

Screaming, Teigra swished her blade and slit Thea's throat.

Thea let out a gurgling "Aaaarrckkk..."

She couldn't breathe. Her eyes watered. She dropped her sword and reached for her gushing throat.

But within a moment, the wound closed.

Teigra stared, mouth agape. She bent down for Thea's sword. Thea reached for it as well—but too late.

Teigra came at Thea, swinging both swords.

Ducking down, Thea locked her arms around Teigra's waist. She dug her toes into the dirt, then pushed her forward so they both tumbled over.

Nox neighed at her master. Dust covered the sisters. The masses hurried past them.

They wrestled, leaving sweat in the dirt. Teigra still held both swords, but Thea made sure she couldn't move.

Showing her teeth, Teigra growled.

Teigra bent down, mouth open, and sunk half her teeth into Thea's throat.

Crying out hard, Thea strained to move. She felt tendons in her neck break, and saw bright blood rushing out. Teigra tasted the blood and grinned.

But, like before, Thea's neck healed. The only blood left was on Teigra's tongue.

Teigra glanced at the Girdle.

With an animal cry, Teigra twisted her body, pinning Thea onto her back. When Thea landed, Teigra raised a sword.

Thea rolled, and the sword struck dirt.

Finally, Teigra saw Thea's neck.

The *mark*.

Teigra froze.

They locked eyes. Teigra screeched, "*You* have the mark!"

"Yes," gasped Thea. "That's why I asked about yours. We're the same."

Teigra stared in shock.

"Why do you seek the Golden Girdle?" Thea asked.

Loosening her grip on the swords, Teigra muttered, "I was told it would save me. It's meant to ward off my curse."

They continued staring.

Teigra asked, "What about you?"

Looking down at the Girdle, Thea said, "It's my mother's. She left it for me."

"*There!*" cried a man's voice.

It was a castle soldier. He pointed and said, "She wears the King's jewels."

He moved toward Thea. Teigra stood up to make way. Then she looked at Thea, and Thea looked back. The man's shadow fell over them. Six other guards joined him.

Without warning, Teigra spun wildly and cut through three of the seven men like lightning through clouds. She sliced one's throat, another's belly, and the third one's groin.

Teigra tossed her sword back to Thea. Catching it, Thea sprang up and charged the man who'd spoken, cleanly thrusting the blade through his neck.

Thea plucked out the red steel. She turned her sword on the other three guards. Almost instantly, she took off one's head, then obliterated another's skull.

The sisters eyed the last man standing.

They went after him together, vigorously swinging their blades. Teigra chopped his arm from his shoulder. Thea jabbed her blade through his heart.

As he fell, the sisters again traded looks.

"Where now?" asked Teigra.

"To a prophet I know," said Thea. "She can tell us how we're connected."

Teigra nodded.

Thea looked east toward the temple. "But first," she said, "we must confront Zarek."

Nodding again, Teigra stood beside Thea. Together, they walked east.

Nox ambled behind them.

CHAPTER 36

THE STATUE

Hundreds of people were still gathered in the temple. Zarek held court, babbling his way through a mad and devilish sermon, the content of which no one could quite comprehend. His audience, though still subservient, knew full well that his mind had slipped. His skin looked almost as pale as his giant stone statue.

"I impress upon you all," he screamed, spittle gathering at the corners of his lips, "that sometimes Gods appear in the flesh! Such a God appears before you now! As *lightning!*"

Just as these strange words left his lips, Thea and Teigra entered through the temple door. Some eyes traveled to them, while others stayed fixed on the madman.

All of his personal guards were protecting Zarek. Some were near the doors, others in the hallways, and a couple stayed close to the King. These were men of astonishing training and lethal skill. Their eyes went to Thea, Teigra, and their blood-soaked swords.

As for Zarek's eyes, they went straight to the Golden Girdle.

"Wench," he shrieked. "How did you seize my treasure?"

"It's not yours," Thea said, drawing gasps from the audience.

Zarek didn't seem to hear her. His gaze switched to Teigra, and his finger pointed at her. "*Traitor!*" he screamed as loudly as his lungs would allow.

Zarek eyed his guards and, without saying a word, commanded them to kill.

The guards charged at the sisters in a mad swirl.

Teigra slashed her sword into one's stomach, then spun right and sliced another's neck.

Thea spun around, striking her blade against throats, arms, and eyeballs.

A fat guard charged Teigra and jumped on top of her. Falling back, Teigra rolled to the side. The floor clapped against her, and dust rose. The guard tried to grab her neck...and found a sword jutting out of his own. Thea had lanced the blade straight through him.

Thea pulled out her sword and continued to spin. She jammed her weapon through one man's wrist, then kicked another's kneecap, snapping his leg backward.

Two guards jabbed Thea's lungs from behind. She whirled toward them, sawed the first one's throat, and plunged her blade into the second's one heart.

As they died, her wounds closed.

Teigra stayed on the ground, slithering among Zarek's men like a snake. She smacked her sword into calves and ankles. Blood rained down on her. The guards screamed, their red flesh hanging and then peeling free from their bodies.

Another man jumped down at Teigra. She rolled, and twisted his sword so it crunched into his belly.

Another guard stabbed at Teigra, pinning her hair into the dirt. Teigra rolled again, letting the hair get torn. She jumped and kicked the guard so hard his face caved in.

Teigra felt blood flowing from her eye. She realized the sword had damaged more than her hair. She sped toward Thea and touched the Girdle.

Her wound healed almost instantly.

Seeing this, a wounded guard crawled toward Thea. Thea swung her sword down at him. He ducked and managed to touch the Girdle. He then stared at the bloody gash in his stomach.

But he did not heal. He gurgled blood and fell dead.

An arrow struck Thea's neck. She plucked it out and twirled it back at her attacker, sending it through his eyeball and knocking him from his second-story perch.

More arrows flew.

Thea ducked and spun.

Teigra sought the ground again.

Zarek looked on, shocked by the growing pool of blood on the ground.

Some of the audience members were struck by stray arrows. They died quiet deaths amidst the savage battle.

Roaring, Teigra ran up a staircase at six guards holding bows. They fired at her. Snorting bear-like breaths, she ducked, bent, and leaned, avoiding injury. When she reached the first man, she pierced her blade through his stomach.

Downstairs, Thea continued to twirl like a dancer of death, stabbing through the armor of three more guards.

Teigra reached the second bowman and slashed her sword across his face. As he yelled, she sheathed her weapon, grabbed him, and threw him over the railing. He landed headfirst, his neck snapping against the ground.

A tall bearded man grabbed Thea's sword. He was so strong that he almost broke its steel. Thea let her feet sweep forward, slid between his legs, and rose up on his other side. As he still held her blade, she withdrew an ankle dagger and plunged it into his crotch. Blood ran down his legs.

An arrow hit Thea's back. She plucked it out. Teigra turned to the man who'd fired, broke his neck, and hurled him over the railing.

Downstairs, his body crashed into Zarek!

Everyone—Thea included—gasped. When Zarek stood, his face was crimson with rage. *"Kill these wenches now!"*

The guards who'd stayed near Zarek looked at Teigra. Sword in hand, she jumped from the railing to ground level. She split one guard's skull open. When two more neared, one lost an arm and the other got stabbed in the teeth.

Fast as wildfire, Thea ran to Teigra. As guards came at her, she swung. Blood sprayed. Hands and arms rained down. Eyeballs rolled. Intestines poured out of men like jellyfish.

Thea locked her back against Teigra's. Teigra liked that. It felt safe; and something she'd not felt before…*united*.

"You okay?" Thea asked.

"I think so," said Teigra. "Just a little tired."

Teigra noticed her right palm was split open. She reached around Thea and touched the Girdle. Her palm closed.

Clearing her throat, Thea shouted to the remaining guards, "You don't want to do this! Why should you lose your lives for a fallen king?"

"*You blasphemer!*" Zarek shouted.

Ignoring him, Thea went on, "His war is over. His reign is over."

Some of the guards relaxed their stances. Whispers and murmurs surfaced. Seeing this, Zarek lifted his arms and declared, "I will give you riches! Greater than you've ever dreamed! Will you allow yourselves to be scared off by a couple of women? *Kill them now!*"

That was all his personal guards needed to hear.

Teigra blinked. Thea shut her eyes for one long moment, then opened them, steeling herself for more carnage.

Sneering, the guards closed in from all sides.

Roaring, Teigra impaled one's lung. Spinning, Thea slit open another's neck.

Flesh and steel filled their sight.

Suddenly, a great horn sounded. A commoner appeared at the temple's doorway and announced, "*The Spartans have arrived!*"

The fighting stopped. There were whispers from the guards.

Zarek's face was drenched in a sheet of sweat.

Some audience members began exiting.

After some hesitation, so did his personal guards. It was now clear the riches Zarek had promised would never materialize, and the only reward for being loyal was death.

Freed from battle, the sisters directed their attention to Zarek. "What are we going to do with you?" Thea asked.

Zarek's flesh was boiling, so intensely he was shivering. As his lips bubbled spit, he said, "I *do* have riches. Underground. I can share them with you. We'll escape together!"

Shaking her head, Thea told him, "I don't need you for that. I can take your riches."

Zarek's breath quickened. He eyed Thea's sword. He wore the certainty of a man who knew he was standing at death's door. Sensing this, Thea said to him, "Not to worry. I will not kill you."

Eyebrows bending, Zarek studied her.

"I will let the people decide your fate," she declared, looking at what remained of the audience.

Some moments passed. Zarek's breath was uneven. At last, a woman rose from her seat and yelled out, "*Slay him!*"

That was all it took. Dozens of audience members got on their feet. They waved their fists in the air and repeated the woman's words: "Slay him! Slay him! *Slay him!*"

Zarek shrank before their eyes. Thea looked at the crowd with a gentle smile.

His hands trembling, Zarek leaped toward a dead guard, snatched a sword, and drove it into Thea's upper back.

She felt her left lung bend from the rear. Warm blood rose in her throat. Gasping for air, she turned toward the former king, her flesh taking leave of the blade as she did so.

Thea healed.

Zarek's eyes grew wide and moist. Thea marched over to him and slammed her fist into his face. His nose shattered, and blood sprayed.

Zarek raised his hands.

Thea smashed her fist into his face again.

And again.

Thea's teeth were bare, and her eyes filled with fury.

Zarek's own teeth fell on the ground. He reeled.

"Put him in chains. He will have his time in court," Thea wheezed to the remaining guards.

As she walked away, the crowd fell silent.

An eerie calm filled the temple.

Then Teigra screamed, "Nooooo."

Teigra sped toward Zarek. She grabbed his hair with one hand and stabbed two fingers from the other hand right in his eye sockets.

As the audience gasped, Teigra ripped Zarek's eyeballs from his skull. Hot blood rushed down his face as he shrieked, then vomited. Thea stood shocked.

But Teigra wasn't done. She threw Zarek directly in the shadow of his giant statue. As Zarek blindly stumbled, she cut the supports.

The massive stone structure toppled Zarek, crushing him...and shattering into a thousand pieces.

Zarek was dying, but still had a few breaths left in his lungs. She cut into his chest with her sword and pulled out his still-beating heart. Teigra held it before the spellbound audience as blood oozed down her arms.

The audience was frozen.

Teigra cried, "As this cruel monster always said, 'The punishment shall fit the crime!' He lived a heartless existence. Now he shall be heartless for eternity!"

A great cacophony erupted from the audience. Most cheered. Some cried. Many turned their attention upward and thanked the Gods.

Thea approached Teigra. "Are you all right?" she asked.

Teigra nodded. "The people have spoken."

* * *

Outside, all was chaos.

Hundreds of people were running or riding in all directions.

The castle soldiers who resisted the Spartans did so only out of confusion, as there was no cause left to fight.

What remained of Zarek's forces lacked both numbers and a leader. The Spartans easily dispatched them, and took command.

Thea and Teigra, both covered in blood, sought Nox and another mare. They planned to ride to Seema in search of answers.

Then a man on horseback caught Thea's attention. The sun was at his back so she couldn't see his face. Still, she somehow knew exactly who he was.

Aristo.

He rode toward her, wearing a grin. It was not only a grin of victory, but of love. He was ecstatic to see her.

Thea went to Aristo, touched his face with both hands, and kissed him. The thought of Melia briefly crossed her mind, but she brushed it aside and concentrated on him.

Teigra looked on, feeling a slight touch of envy. But that was overrun by deep admiration for her fellow fighter. An image of Niko fired through her mind.

"How are you?" Aristo asked.

Thea was so overcome that all she could manage was a little nod.

Aristo touched her chin and asked, "Where can I find you? Are you staying close?"

She shook her head. "I'm truly sorry. I must leave."

He wasn't smiling anymore. "When will I see you?"

Thea gently stepped away and said, "When the time is right."

Thea gave Teigra a nod and said, "Let's go."

Teigra held up a finger. "I now realize that I have something to take care of first."

Thea looked into her eyes. "When you are done, come to Mount Spiro. I shall meet you there."

CHAPTER 37

MOUNT SPIRO

Teigra rushed to her castle quarters for the last time and grabbed her personal belongings. She searched her heart for a feeling of sadness, a trace of longing over leaving this life behind; but there was none.

However, she did have a stop to make before leaving.

Teigra rode deep into the forest, her senses on high alert for wandering soldiers.

No one bothered her. The world had already become a more peaceful place.

Before the sky grew completely dark, Teigra found the scroll for the liquid fire stashed in the wilderness, right where she'd left it. Working quickly and with great concentration, Teigra sat on a rock and scratched a fresh copy of the ingredients onto a piece of paper.

Once she was done, she took a breath.

It was time to pay a visit to Vasili.

* * *

When Thea arrived at Mount Spiro, her heart swelled with sadness.

Her former home had been obliterated. It was a wounded society, with burned houses and forlorn residents. She even saw some injured

Sondras—women who'd once walked tall and proud—lurking along roadsides with bent backs.

As she rode to Seema's cave, Thea thought about all the work ahead of her. There was much to be done to repair her tribe. The first thing that needed rejuvenating was her people's faith.

As that thought crossed Thea's mind, she felt her own faith restored.

Suddenly, A beautiful woman ran toward her. It was Melia, as fresh-faced and gorgeous as ever.

Thea brought Nox to a stop, leaned over, and kissed Melia on the lips.

While enjoying the sweetness, she couldn't help but think of Aristo.

She wondered if one person could possibly be in love with two.

Thea blinked the thought away. She smiled at Melia to hide her inner stirrings.

She tried to focus on more important matters, such as the fact that she urgently wished to speak with Seema—as soon as Teigra joined them.

* * *

Vasili smiled at the sight of Teigra. Though she represented a period of great challenges and sadness, he responded to her visit with warmth.

"I'm living on a cattle farm now," he explained. "A young man is helping with the business side." *And,* Teigra guessed, *with personal pleasures as well.*

Teigra glanced at the sky. The sun was dropping. Meeting with Thea at Mount Spiro was of great importance. So without wasting any words, she simply handed Vasili a piece of paper.

It wasn't the copy of the liquid fire ingredients, for she'd deemed it only fair for him to receive the original.

The copy was for her, should she ever decide to make use of it. Knowing she wasn't a perfect scribbler, she didn't want to risk providing Vasili with a possibly inferior version. He deserved the best she could give him, and handing it over to him allowed some warmth to enter her heart.

As he studied the scroll, Vasili's eyes began to water. Teigra noticed for the first time that age had seized him. His forehead was lined with wrinkles and his hair was almost entirely white. His neck, which had once been tight and firm, was beginning to sag. His recent hardships had taken their toll.

As tears ran down his face, he thanked her, touching her wrists and shoulders.

He then looked upward, thanking the heavens and the Gods.

Liquid fire would be his again. His business would transform and surge.

"Perhaps you'll pay me another visit sometime?" Vasili suggested.

Teigra didn't see how or why this would occur. But life was nothing if not surprising.

Giving the old man a little smile, Teigra remounted her horse and took off for the mountains.

* * *

Although Thea and Teigra had eagerly anticipated their meeting with Seema, once the three of them gathered in Seema's cave, the mood grew dark and their spirits sunk.

Thea guessed this was because they were learning too much at once. It was a lot for anyone to process.

Both Thea and Teigra had to get accustomed to having a sister.

Further, each had to absorb the story of their origins—Zeus and Hera's wager, their mother's failure and banishment, Thea being born first and getting blessed, and Teigra being born second and getting cursed—but all this could not compare to the revelation that Zeus was their father. Both sat motionless, awed by what they'd learned. He was to blame for tricking their mother and causing the ripple effect. They were deep in thought as Thea became increasingly sensitive that it was their mother's situation and Teigra's curse that prevented a mood of relief and celebration. Both predicaments caused an ache within Thea's heart.

She could only imagine how Teigra felt.

As they listened to Seema, Teigra said very little, remaining deep in thought. A detectable sadness danced in her eyes. What use was it having Zeus as her father? Not only was she cursed for life, but she now had to live with the knowledge that her sister was heir to the throne...*and* the Girdle!

Even Thea, who benefited from these blessings, recognized the cruelty of depriving Teigra.

When Seema explained that the markings on their necks were brandings that their mother made to ensure they could be identified, Thea wondered whether that had been a good idea. For as much as Thea loved having a sister, knowing what the Gods had set in motion for her was excruciatingly painful. She wondered whether she might have preferred remaining ignorant that her victory was, in a way, at the cost of her sister's pain.

When Teigra opened her mouth, it was almost too much for Thea to bear. Teigra's words would make the mythic tale told by Seema terribly real.

"*Why* was I cursed?" Teigra asked, even though it had just been fully explained.

Averting her eyes, Seema said, "Your mother loved you both, Teigra. She was put in an impossible position."

Teigra wiped a tear from her eye.

Seema continued, "She would have given her life for you, but Hera didn't offer her that choice. The wisest course is for you to count your blessings. You have a sister now. A family! And you have a tribe to which you belong."

Thea felt her own tears building.

Seema continued, "You are not lost in this world, Teigra. The closer you remain to the Girdle, the less potent your curse will be."

Showing sheer fury in her expression, Teigra got up and exited the cave.

Seema sighed. "Give her time. It's a lot to take in. She has suffered immensely in her life. To learn that you are cursed by a God is far from comforting."

"But we can communicate with the Gods," Thea said. "And we can rescue my mother. We can undo—"

"Perhaps," Seema said, with meticulous patience. "But child, there are other, more pressing matters before us. You are Queen now. That means engaging your people, and helping them rebuild what was destroyed."

"Yes," Thea said, feeling bad for forgetting how much was at stake. Getting up, she said to Seema, "In the morning we shall start to rebuild."

Smiling, Seema replied, "Then a truly lovely morning it shall be."

* * *

Seema was alone at night, fetching water from her well, when Teigra appeared in the darkness with grave, unblinking eyes.

"I want the Golden Girdle," Teigra stated. "It wards off my curse. She does *not* deserve it the way I do."

Feeling vulnerable to Teigra's fury, Seema smiled and said, "It belongs to Theodora. Just stay close to her."

"It's not fair!" Teigra bellowed, her words piercing her heart.

Breathless, Seema looked at Teigra.

Lowering her voice, Teigra said, "She can still be the Queen. But the Girdle is *mine!"*

Teigra then vanished into the darkness, just as quickly and quietly as she'd appeared.

Once she was alone, Seema let out a breath. She scooped a bucket of water from the well, thinking that this tale was far from over.

Indeed, it was just beginning...

CHAPTER 38

THE PETS

"Zeus! *Zeus!*" Hera's voice rang out. She was walking through every hallway, but her partner was nowhere to be seen.

In Hera's right hand was a large, swelling watermelon. In her left hand was a small, soft peach. Balancing these items on her palms, she made her way toward the master bedroom.

In truth, Zeus was entangled with a female mortal, enjoying the pleasures of her ripe body on his and Hera's bed. When he heard his jealous wife approaching, however, he quickly turned his mistress into a plant. His manhood was restless. He desperately wanted to finish making love to the woman, but that would have to wait until Hera departed.

"What's going on here?" Hera asked, as she entered their bedchambers. "Did you not hear me calling?"

"Yes!" Zeus declared, his volume ear shattering. "I was just about to call back to you."

After giving him a suspicious look, Hera said, "Did you see the fight on Earth? What the girls did to the King? It was most entertaining."

"I did." He nodded, his mind far away.

"It occurs to me," said Hera, "that those sisters have suffered a great deal. Perhaps their fate can be altered so they can see their mother."

Bored with the whole conversation, Zeus merely raised his eyebrows and gave a vague little grunt.

"Come with me," said Hera, circling the bed and making her way to the balcony overlooking their breathtaking rose garden.

Sighing, Zeus did as he was told. He stood to Hera's right, looking over the railing to view thousands of perfect red roses in bloom.

"Do you see these two pieces of fruit?" Hera asked.

"Hera, seriously. What is this all about?"

Hera replied, "You do recall our wager, don't you? About which sex is the strongest?"

Nodding impatiently, he said to her, "Yes, I do. *And...?*"

"Your two daughters have met. They wish to speak with us, and to save their poor mother."

The couple eyed each other for a moment. Zeus asked, "Will you help them?"

"I don't know yet," she answered. "But I am fond of them. They are both strong women."

Zeus said, "Let me know what you decide. It's all very exciting."

Ignoring his sarcasm, Hera responded, "Which of these two would you declare to be more masculine? The grand, strong watermelon? Or the small, soft peach?"

Zeus was nearly shaking where he stood, so eager to end the conversation. "I don't know, Hera. If I must choose, then the watermelon. With all that size and presence, it's surely more like a man than the weak, pathetic peach."

With a glow of satisfaction, Hera tossed the watermelon over the railing.

Some thirty feet below, it splattered on the ground. Zeus' eyebrows rose.

"Was I wrong?" he asked, his boredom thundering through his voice.

"No!" she declared. "You were most correct. For the watermelon, like a man, is hard and grand on the outside, but soft and weak on the inside. But the peach..." She dropped the other fruit to the ground far below. It landed with a dent and a slight crack, but otherwise remained intact. "The peach is soft and, as you say, 'weak' on the outside. But hidden within it is quite an impressive core."

Hera stared at Zeus. "Do you take my point?"

He said nothing.

She went on, "Do you not see how this strong core is what allows mortal women to bear children, and to endure the hardships of life with more grace than men?"

Exhausted from Hera's theatrical example, Zeus pivoted on his heels and walked back toward their bedroom. "Why was this demonstration so urgent?" he asked.

Hera followed him in, and then noticed a new object by the bed. Slightly raising her voice, she said, "I see we have a new plant."

"*Oh!*" Zeus shouted, unable to achieve any subtlety. "Indeed. It is...a gift! For you, my love. I thought it would brighten up the room." He hoped she would decline it and leave the plant alone.

"For me?" Hera asked. "How wonderful. But you do know, Zeus..."

Zeus looked at her.

"...that I much prefer pets to plants."

With that, Hera changed the plant into a small white rabbit.

Zeus let out a great sigh, shaking his head with visible disappointment.

Hera bent over and scooped the bunny into her hands.

"What a generous husband I have!" she declared, giving her husband a wink. "I think I shall go spend time with my new gift."

"Very well," Zeus replied, his words thick with disappointment.

Hera walked back down the hallway with the rabbit in her hands. She knew full well it had a previous life, but chose to let that pass. After all, Zeus had done his best to avoid hurting her. That showed he cared...in his way.

Hera thought about their little wager, and how atrociously her husband had behaved. She then thought about the two sisters on Earth, and how their lives should unfold.

But more than anything, she thought about men, and how smug they were to believe that women couldn't get along without them. Men would never survive without women.

As Hera made her way down the hall, she plopped the rabbit in a cage that was filled with other creatures—parrots, dogs, cats, and so on—all of whom once were lovers of Zeus.

"Welcome home," Hera said to the rabbit. She walked onward, down the long hall, toward whatever new schemes and bets and plots awaited her.

ACKNOWLEDGMENTS

To my two pillars, Sophie Chagrin Cohen and Alex Ruti Alpert, who always stood firmly planted in their reassurance whenever I questioned myself. Their unwavering support pushed me, and kept me moving forward. Thank you for believing in me.

To my two angels, Sameret Essoy and Mekdes Kebede, thank you for extending a hand when I was new in town, and for being vital stepping stones at the start of my journey.

To the dynamic duo, Angel Li-Jun Yang & Richard Yu, thank you for your warm hospitality and unforgettable dinner parties. They will always be cherished. Angel, thank you for getting me out of my rut, and for making me live a little and laugh a lot. Your endless encouragement and support helped me stay positive, on track, and focused on the goal. Thank you. I'm very grateful for your help.

To Eric Shapiro and Hy Bender, thank you for the editing and constructive criticism. Your feedback was greatly appreciated, and your input helped strengthen and mold my story.

Last but not least, I want to thank the reserved and soft-spoken Blair Patrick Schuyler. In the short period of time I have gotten to know you, I've been able to watch your work on the final edit and polish of my manuscript, which was carried out diligently and completed with finesse.

To all who have contributed to this labor of love, my book would not have been possible without your help and service. From the bottom of my heart, thank you!

ABOUT THE AUTHOR

Zenay Bekele Ben-Yochanan was born in Ethiopia and grew up in Israel, a land rich with holy sites, prophecies and whose every inch is soaked in history and magic.

As a result of being raised by strong, independent women, she always dreamt of powerful female characters, and the ones who stood tallest were the legendary Amazons. Thus began Zenay's whirlwind affair with mythology.

She could never find the fierce, brave, unyielding Amazon warriors precisely as she imagined them in the stories of others. So, she did the only thing she could: she put her vision of the Amazons into books of her own.

Gods & Queens is the first volume that shares Zenay's lifelong passion for the Amazon Nation, and the relentless, sexy, deadly women who battle for its right to survive, and thrive in an ancient world dominated by men.

She hopes that you too will fall in love with these proud, unbreakable heroines.

www.theamazonlegacy.com
https://www.facebook.com/TheAmazonLegacy/
https://twitter.com/TheAmazonLegacy